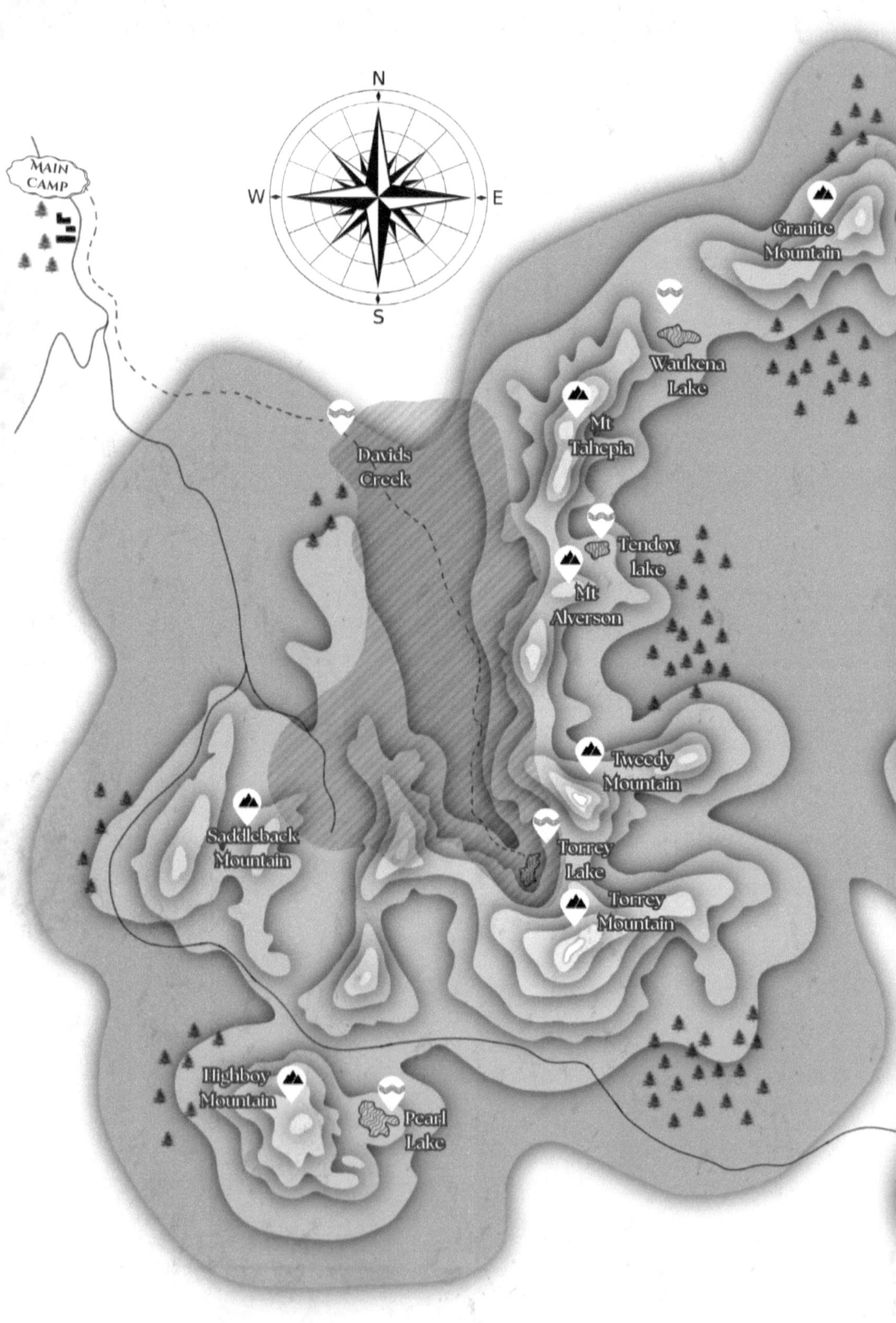

N
W
E
S
MAIN CAMP
Davids Creek
Granite Mountain
Waukena Lake
Mt Tahepia
Tendoy Lake
Mt Alverson
Tweedy Mountain
Torrey Lake
Torrey Mountain
Saddleback Mountain
Highboy Mountain
Pearl Lake

KISSING FIRE

SAMANTHA TREAT

ISBN: 979-8-9912007-0-7

eBook ISBN: 979-8-9912007-1-4

Made in the United States of America

First Edition: September 2024

Cover Design: Nathan and Sunny Stufflebean

Editing: Cameron-Rose Neal ~ crose-editing.co.uk

BEAVERHEAD NATIONAL FOREST
RUBY VALLEY MT
Lakes
Fire Zone
Roads
Rivers
Trees
Elevation Lines
Buildings
Trails
Storm Peak
Storm River
Brownes Lake
Lake Agnes
Call Mountain
Sugarloaf Mountain
Twin Adams Mountain
Thunderhead Mountain
Ruby Valley River
RUBY VALLEY
RVW FIRE STATION
OLE JOE'S PUB

Authors Note

Kissing Fire is a subversive paranormal romance. This book is intended for mature audiences.

Before you dive into this wild ride, let's have a quick chat. Yes, there are religious themes and characters in this book. But let's be clear—the world and story I've created are products of my imagination, and while they may draw inspiration from various mythologies and religious concepts, they are not meant to imitate, represent, or comment on any specific religion. It is important to me that readers understand that this story is not intended to offend or challenge anyone's personal beliefs.

Our main love interest is a demon. He absolutely acts like a demon. And though he may prove that demons make great lovers, he is not an upstanding pillar of good morals. We all know demons are the ultimate bad boys, right? Expect some sizzling tension and a whole lot of trouble!

As it is my wish that all readers are able to experience KF in a safe and fun environment, here is a list of some of the major notes of advisement. PTSD, family death, domestic abuse (not against FMC), religion, Satan/Devil/demons, sexually explicit scenes. For those who like to be extra prepared, there's a full list available on my website.

Once you're ready, grab a snack, get comfy, and enjoy the chaos!

Dedication

To those who find solace in the shadows, courage in the face of doubt, and who wish for a love that defies space, time, fate, and everything else standing in the way.

Kissing Fire Playlist

Wreckage by Nate Smith
Devil in a Dress by Teddy Swims
Black Smoke Rising by Greta Van Fleet
Square Hammer by Ghost
Devil's Backbone by The Civil Wars
Power Over Me by Dermot Kennedy
Sweet and Dark by Miles Hardt
HELL REPLIED by Grey
Always Remember Us This Way by Lady Gaga
Demons Are a Girl's Best Friend by Powerwolf
Far From Home by Sam Tinnesz
23 by Chayce Beckham
If I'm There- Unplugged by Bad Omens
Play with Fire (feat. Yacht Money) by Sam Tinnesz, Yacht Money
hostage by Billie Eilish
Cold by Jessie Murph

Chapter I
Valencia

I'm not gonna make it.

I race through the trees, my head tipped down to stop the smoke from billowing into my face. The soles of my feet pound against the ground; each step deafening. The air is tinged with the sharp, pungent scent of charred material as smoke and ash waft through the air around me.

I can barely see the twins through the amber haze.

"*Fire!*" I scream at the top of my lungs. They don't notice.

The fire's roar is too loud. I'm only 20 yards away but the fire is rapidly approaching. They've got their backs turned, working diligently to clear the edges of the firebreak we dug earlier this week. We didn't expect to make it here so soon; we were fighting a losing battle against high winds. It caught us unprepared.

Another gust of wind blows through the trees, picking up burnt debris and ash. The fire soars through the air, fueled by the extra oxygen, and sweeps closer to where they work.

"Move!" I shriek. I pump my arms as I run, pushing my body to its limit. There's a burning in my legs and my back screams in pain as the heavy weight of my oxygen tank slams against my back with every step. *Almost there.*

Jake must finally notice the heat from the flames because he looks up over his shoulder. The fire is right on top of them. The trench is only a couple feet wide but, we'd managed to make it pretty deep.

Jake's eyes widen as he takes in the flames and turns to his twin, shoving him into the trench. His brother, Jack, flails—arms swinging wildly from the unexpected push. He disappears beyond my view.

I'm only a couple of steps away now. I can see the resolution on Jake's face as he looks up at me. He thinks this is it—that he can go happily because he saved his twin.

Nobody's dying today.

I push my body to limits I've never reached before. Sweat trickles down my face as the heat of the flames lick the exposed skin. I hear the wind roaring through the trees, heading right for us. My fingertips burn inside my gloves, the skin hot and searing from the heat. Jake's eyes widen in shock as I tackle him, my shoulder slamming into his stomach, taking us both down into the trench. I hear a sharp yell, as our bodies collide roughly with the hard ground. I throw my arms over Jake's head, covering his face. Our full-sleeved coats are made with special fire-resistant material. I didn't have time to deploy my fire shelter, so I hope it's enough. I spread my body as far as possible, covering as much of the two bodies beneath me as I can.

The fire blazes over us, rolling along the edge of the trench. Seconds feel like hours as we huddle at the bottom, our limbs and gear a tangled mess. Above, the intense heat surges. It burns me from the inside, boiling my blood as my body heats rapidly. The heavy gear protects me from the worst of the flames, but it compresses my back, making it harder to breathe. There's a flash of heat along my legs before it all disappears just as quickly as it came.

The roaring lowers to a loud, dull hum as the fire begins to break along the edge of the trench. With the wind dying down and all the debris gone, nothing is left for the fire to burn. Smoke fills the trench and I choke, my throat constricting tightly as my lungs beg for clean air.

The bodies under me start to move, jerking as the smoke chokes them, too. I hurriedly untangle myself from their thrashing limbs and stand, pulling Jake up by the straps along his back.

The smoke isn't as thick now but it's still difficult to breathe. We've got to get our masks on or we'll be in trouble.

I rip the mask off Jake's back, reaching it around his body. He grabs it and slips it over his face before opening the oxygen valve. He sucks in a big breath before reaching down to grab Jack. As he lifts his twin, I put on my own mask.

As soon as the steam evaporates, I can see through the hazy plexiglass cover. I realize Jake managed to put a mask on Jack while we were all tangled in the trench.

We look each other over, checking for injuries. The fabric on the back of my pants is badly burned but the skin underneath is untouched. Other than general exhaustion and some pain in my back from the heavy pack, I'm fine.

Jack holds his right arm tightly to his body; he's hunched over a bit but he's still on his own two feet. Jake, seemingly with no issues, nods at Jack before turning to check me over.

"Are you okay?!" He yells, voice muffled by the mask.

"Yeah!" I call back with a nod, pointing to the top of the trench and motioning for us to get out. I grip the edge, bending a leg back for Jake to push on as he helps lift me to the top of the trench.

It's high enough that I can't lift myself out while weighted down with all my gear.

Once out, I turn around and help him lift Jack out. He's still got a tight hold on his arm, so it takes us a moment to do so. When Jack is out, Jake jumps and pulls himself out of the trench.

Topside once more, we all grab our gear and start racing along the trench to the rest of the team. The fire has now mostly burned out, as the trench finally served its purpose in preventing the fire from spreading any further.

When we reach the rest of the team, they're all gathered around the small patch of fire that remains. As soon as they put it out, they turn to us. They've all got their masks on, so Chief Miller hand-motions for us to go east—through the forest and back towards the trail that got us here. We each follow his order without hesitation, heading back the way we came.

My body burns with exhaustion. I can feel my legs shaking with the strain of hiking back, my gear feeling heavier than ever.

We've been clearing a line through the forest for four days straight, trying to prevent the fire from moving through the park. Clearing a fire line is grueling, back-breaking work. Even with firefighters working only a few feet apart, you can spend hours digging breaks to stop the fire and clearing debris to deprive it of fuel. The trenches are just an extra precaution.

The process is physically demanding and mentally taxing, but it gives firefighters a critical advantage. A stark strip of bare earth the last line of defense, protecting what stands behind it.

Beaverhead National Forest sits in the southwest seat of Montana, a true jewel of the West due to the many mountain peaks, miles of scenic byways, and abundant wildlife.

But now, the once beautiful, forested mountain in the large park is marred by a grotesque patch of land reduced to cinders in the fire. Smoke, ash, and despair are all that remain in the ravaged areas; a charred graveyard with no headstones.

My quads burn as we descend the mountainside single file, sweat trickling down my back with each step. My body begs for reprieve but we still have a couple miles to go. One thing we learn as new firefighters is that you're only as strong as how far your legs can carry you. Sometimes, being able to walk for miles and miles can be the difference between life and death, so the majority of our workouts consist of building endurance for long-distance hiking.

And, not just any hiking, but hiking at extreme grades of elevation.

We also do resistance training to ensure we're able to lift anything we may need to. Like tools, debris, or even people. The fire started a week ago during an early fall storm. The first couple of days were managed by some surrounding stations. We nearly had it contained until high winds from the south blew in, ruining all our progress and shifting the fire to the side of the park we hadn't protected yet.

We rely on nothing but hand tools and hard work to keep a fire from burning millions of acres or putting us in early graves.

The fact that Jack, Jake, and I are all walking out of here with minor injuries makes us all extremely lucky.

The trail looms ahead, a seemingly endless path. It's rough, winding terrain and I can feel every stone underfoot—a fresh reminder of the exhaustion that has settled into my body.

Everything hurts. My lungs work overtime, sore from the smoke I inhaled before getting my mask over my head. My head pounds with a steady drumbeat and fatigue causes my mind to waver between the desire to stop and the need to push on.

Even my mind screams for a break as I force myself to push through the emotions that surge to greet me. Only my training and team keep me going, their silent support helping me persevere as we continue to make our way.

***

A small spark flickers in the bottom of the fire pit just behind the station, dancing around despite the direction of the flames. The spark's movements seem indifferent to the fire's natural flow; I stare harder as if the strain on my eyes will correct the spark's actions. It hovers just above a fiery log. In an instant, the spark flies towards the sky so fast that my eyes can barely track it.

I pinch the bridge of my nose and sigh deeply. I had debated finding a random hookup to release some of my frustration and help me forget, but this week has been a living nightmare, so I didn't even try. And, either I'm going crazy or that fifth whiskey was one too many.

I stand up and attempt to stretch the stiffness out of my limbs. The cool October air has left a chill in my bones and there's a soreness that a whole week of sleep won't cure. Nonstop firefighting multiple days in a row isn't for the weak.

A crack sounds in the pit; the small fire sputtering out. My waning energy is finally sapped. After putting the snuffer lid on the fire pit, I turn and head inside the station. The ice in my whiskey glass rattles as I walk.

I had come out here to get away for a second—the rest of the crew having gone inside to watch a football game that we missed while out in the field—but I needed some time to decompress from the events of the week.

My body feels weighed down by invisible chains and I didn't want to weigh down the team too.

The firehouse door swings open with a low groan. Hinges nearly as old as I am struggle loudly, as if the weight they bore over all these years is finally beginning to wear them down. I sigh for probably the thousandth time tonight—I feel like those hinges.

"Well, you look like shit."

Yup, definitely *not getting laid anytime soon.*

I look around the darkened room, searching. "Show yourself, scoundrel," I say with as much warmth as I can bear. It's not much. Memories of the past keep flashing through my mind.

A lamp flickers to life near the back corner of the room, illuminating the area in a soft glow. Next to the lamp, my best friend, Parker, stands with a glass in his hand that's identical to my own. His hand isn't shaking, though. He's probably had fewer of them tonight.

"Seriously, Val, are you okay? You really do look like shit." Parker speaks in a tone an older brother would use. Although we're not related, he treats me like I'm the little sister he never had.

"C'mon, *Parks and Rec.* Flattery never gets you anywhere." He scoffs at my light-hearted jab, a welcome normality between us.

"Oh, I beg to differ—and so would," Parker pauses, bringing his empty hand up to his face. With a snap, he continues. "Ah yes, I think Darcy from last night would also beg to differ."

Parker smirks at me, all glowing white teeth and full lips. I cringe inwardly. I'd have to be blind to deny the fact that Parker Rand is an attractive man. He's a couple inches over six feet tall with dark auburn hair that matches the best color in the fall, and baby blues so clear they could put Lake Tahoe to shame. Not to mention the lean muscular frame that is nearly always on display. The man is allergic to a shirt. But, to me, he'd always just be my best friend. And, picturing him with Darcy from last night was definitely *not* something I wanted to do.

"I'm good, man. Just fire life getting to me this week," I shrug.

"I get that. It's a freaking miracle you guys weren't hurt worse. Jack said his shoulder was jammed, so thankfully no broken bones," he pauses, staring at the wall behind me briefly as he recalls the past week. "That wind was wild, but we did good work. I heard 3,000 acres were burned before containment."

"I feel as if it were a million. Sometimes, I wonder if the wind will be the death of me before the fire ever has a chance." I admit, voice shaky. Behind my eyelids, unshed tears threaten to spill over.

We almost lost two friends out there. Had I been a second slower, Jake would've been swallowed by the fire.

My stomach turns at the thought of what could've happened if I hadn't gotten to the twins when I did. I joined the Ruby Valley Wildland Fire crew here in Montana four years ago. Over the years, we've battled countless fires. From tiny, nature-related fires to human-caused devastation that consumed thousands of acres. Working day after day with little to no rest fighting a fire that does nothing but destroy everything in its path.

Fire is an unforgiving element; it takes and takes. Sure, life returns, sometimes even more bountiful than when it was destroyed but I feel each loss personally, every tree, every animal, every person.

It's why I get so frustrated when a fire is caused by humans. A careless individual can cause a mass burning of thousands of acres. Fire can destroy lives.

It's one thing to not care about destroying your own world. It's a whole different deal when you affect everyone else while you're at it.

Some see the world only through a small lens of their own making. To them, a tiny cigarette butt is meaningless and expendable. Looking at what can be lost due to a single careless act is unforgivable when you know the kind of destruction it causes. I'd even hold the executioner's ax if these people were to be held accountable for the destruction their actions cause.

"Earth. To. Valencia!"

I jump, snapping out of my daze. Parker looks at me with concern, his eyebrows pitched down. I've probably been quiet for too long, lost in thought. I never shared my past with Parker; I didn't have to. He knows me inside and out. I continually fight to forget that night exists, keeping that memory where it belongs; gone like everything else.

"C'mon, Parks, it's late. Let's continue this lovely little chat tomorrow," I say with a heaviness in my chest.

"If you need anything, I'm here for you," he responds sincerely. I turn and catch one last glance at his face; his eyes are cast in shadows.

I open my mouth, on the precipice of saying something I only hope is insightful but then close it. For all he's there for me, I don't know how to help him. I leave the room. Although it's late, I hear the common room is still full of people. Loud, boisterous voices, full of life spill into the hallway. I wonder if the game is still on, or if they're simply enjoying each other's company at this point. I make sure to quickly duck into my room, avoiding the others and their jovial moods.

The quiet and the shadows give me a small amount of peace.

I strip down, not even bothering to put clothes on before I crash face-first on the bed. Exhaustion and too much whiskey prevent me from performing even the most minor tasks. I use the last of my effort to climb under the covers and let sleep take over.

CHAPTER 2
VALENCIA

THE FIRE BLAZES BEFORE my eyes, illuminating the darkness with its glorious doom and heat presses in closer and closer and—

I jerk awake, my legs tangling in the covers. Shiny sun rays sneak past my curtains to give my room a cheery morning glow and a light warmth fills the space they touch. But, despite the calming glow, the shadows of my nightmare darken my mood.

I take a few deep breaths to help calm my racing heart. It'll only last a few minutes before everything is back to normal, as if nothing ever happened.

It's always the same dream.

BANG! BANG! BANG!

"Val Pal, get your ass up! Meeting starts in 20 minutes!" Parker's voice carries through the closed door. The knocking is grandly unnecessary. Parker's voice alone can bring down a mountain. His ability to contain the energy of an entire swat team in one body is astonishing.

Shaking off the last of the dreamy haze from Hell, I look around my room to reorient myself back into reality. My room is barren at best, housing only the essentials. I'm no slouch, but I'm also no housewife. No space in this room would be mistaken for being homely; I've lived here for the last four years. Besides my bed and a small nightstand, the room remains primarily bare. No family photos hang on the wall and nothing distinguishes my room from any other room in the firehouse.

Jumping out of bed, I hurriedly start getting ready. After a quick shower, I take a second to look in the mirror. My hair lays against my body, dripping down my back and onto the floor and my usually bright blue eyes stare back at me with a dull hue. The soot and ash may have been washed clean but, internally, the filth remains.

Living can be backbreaking work when you struggle just to survive. On top of the nightmares that leave me feeling like I haven't slept, firefighting for several days in a row allows no time for proper rest.

With no more time to dwell, I head back into my room to get ready.

I grab the closest shirt, not sparing it a glance before I pull on some pants. I skip a few times around the small space to get them on. Thick thighs aren't made with women's fashion in mind.

Finally ready, I head towards the conference room. I make it there with precisely 25 seconds to spare, which is just enough time to find the open seat next to Parker and settle in before the meeting officially starts.

"So, the Sugarloaf Mountain fire has been confirmed one hundred percent contained. I want to thank you all for putting in the many hours and extensive effort." Chief Miller's voice easily carries around the room. "With the help from the other fire teams, we managed to reach containment at 3000 acres in 7 days."

A soft murmur travels through the room. Although the fire was extensive, it's almost a miracle that we could contain it so soon. Thanks to another local fire team, we contained the fire on the south side in the first couple of hours. Another few fire teams were able to close the path on the east side fairly quickly as well. That left the north and west sides open, but our team worked hard day and night to prevent as much destruction as possible.

"Now, onto our favorite part," Chief Miller continues. The reverberation of groans is much louder this time. "CAFA will be coming today to interview us, so I'll need a representative to go to the fire site for verification. Any volunteers?" Silence meets his question, no one wants to draw attention to themselves. We all sit in silence before he continues with the meeting. Since no one volunteered themselves, I'm sure he'll pick someone once the meeting is over.

CAFA, formally known as the Citizens Against Fire Association, is a group of individuals who respond after wildfires are contained to help assist with the aftermath. They're responsible for determining the long-term effects of wildfires on local wildlife and the surrounding communities. Despite all the benefits they bring to those affected by the fires, it's never fun being the chosen liaison between our organizations.

The rest of the meeting passes in a blur and Chief Miller finishes going through the last of his notes on the fire before releasing us for the day.

"So, who do you think will get the shit end of the stick this time?" Parker says as he matches my steps easily. We follow the other crew members to the kitchen for breakfast.

"All I know is, it better not be me. I worked with them on the last fire," I mumble.

"Everyone knows you're the best choice, Val. It's not like any of the other guys are going to volunteer. Plus, I wouldn't trust some of these guys to not mess up. You remember what happened three years ago?" He mocks, dramatically placing a hand on his chest.

"No one should've even let you out of the truck," I laugh softly under my breath. When Parker had been chosen to work with CAFA on a minor fire, the CAFA representative had swiftly left, running out of the station with tears streaming down her face. To this day, even I'm not sure what was said between the two. Park tended to have people running *towards* him, not away.

"Valencia, a word." Chief Miller stands inside the kitchen, blocking my path to the counter full of food with his 'World's Best Dad' mug steaming in his hand.

"Sure thing, Chief. Your office?"

With a nod, he leaves me standing there. I turn to Parker, who smiles at me smugly. I snatch the muffin out of his outstretched hand and head toward the Chief's office. If this is about CAFA, I swear I will shove this muffin down Parker's throat.

Chief Miller's office is on the other side of the firehouse which gives me just long enough to engulf the muffin. I pull my fingers out of my mouth, cleaning off the last of the pastry as I make it through the office door.

I freeze just inside the room. *Holy Fuck.*

A man sits in one of the chairs across from the chief. In the bright fluorescent light, his features stand out against the plainness of the room. His sandy beige skin is matched perfectly with his golden blonde hair. A light dusting of scruff covers his face, but nothing can hide his striking beauty. Few men can pull off being beautiful, so perfect they lack even minor flaws. I'm not usually one to fall victim to a pretty face, but this man stops me in my tracks.

Just then, the man turns his full attention to me. Eyes the color of steel bore into my own, anchoring me in place. His stare is like blinding headlights—and I'm a deer waiting for my reckoning.

He stands with fluid grace as Chief Miller makes his introductions. "Valencia, this is Dane Moore, he's the Citizen's Against Fire Association representative."

A tight, plain-colored polo showcases Dane's muscular frame. He offers me his hand without breaking eye contact. I grasp it with a modicum of strength, expecting a tight grip in return. Fooled by his lethal frame and movements, I'm shocked that his grip is soft. His fingers curl gently around my hand, skin smooth and unmarred by imperfections.

"Valencia, nice to meet you. I look forward to working with you." Dane's strong voice carries a light accent. It's a melodic, soothing tone that makes the hairs on my arms raise. I silently appreciate the way he spends time on each word as if the English language isn't a good enough vessel for what he has to say.

If I were a betting woman, I'd say this man knows his way around a praise kink.

Despite my initial attraction to him, something about him puts me on edge. However, I shouldn't dwell on that considering I'm about to spend a lot of time with him. Most investigations conducted by CAFA last days, if not a few weeks. As the volun-*told* representative, I'll spend most of that time by his side. It's the firehouse's responsibility to ensure CAFA members can conduct a thorough investigation of the fire for all those affected and for future fires as well. There's nothing like starting your day unwillingly doing extra work.

"Hi, Dane, nice to meet you." I motion towards the chairs and take my seat.

"So, now that we're acquainted, let's go over the details for this investigation." Chief Miller flops a set of identical files on his desk, motioning for us to take them.

"This was a weather-related incident?" Dane doesn't bother to open the file, just directs that steely gaze my way.

"Well," I start, opening to the first page even though I know the details by heart. I look down at the papers to avoid his stare "It's been a dry autumn. A weather front came through last week with lots of lightning and little rain. So, between the high winds, dry ground, and lightning, the fire had the perfect habitat to thrive."

Finally opening his file, Dane explores the information in the packet. "I see. I'll need to see it in person but I'm sure we will determine the right course of action once there." Dane looks over at me as he speaks, his gaze penetrating.

"Well then, Valencia will escort you to the suspected ignition site. Dane, nice to meet you." With a nod to both of us, Chief Miller leaves the room without another word, leaving me alone with Dane. It's technically our day off so I'm sure he's eager to get back to his family. It's not like I had any big plans, but I would've loved to at least take a break before turning around and climbing Sugarloaf Mountain all over again.

"If you don't mind, I can show you to our common room. I just need to change into field clothes before we leave," I stand, intending to lead him out of the room.

"I rather like this outfit." Although his expression gives nothing away, his voice makes butterflies attempt flight in my stomach.

I quickly glance down at my outfit. A large cherub covers my chest with *'Angel Baby'* scrolled across the front. In my haste to avoid being late for the meeting, I grabbed the first thing I could. It just so happened to be the worst possible option in my closet.

"Yeah, not my most professional," a small laugh escapes me as I head towards the common room. "If you'd like, most of the guys are still here. You can ask them about the fire while I get dressed."

"I'm more interested in what you have to say." There's something about how his voice carries in the small space that reaches deep inside me. His tone is soft and calm, no different from how he spoke to Chief Miller.

"I'm just one piece of the puzzle," I respond, a little flustered but still trying to sound casual. I laugh nervously. I can't tell if it's his penetrating eyes or his imposing frame but, either way, this man is commanding more than a few of my thoughts. It's both amusing and nerve-wracking.

Once we make it back to the common room, I point Dane towards the couches where everyone sits and run to change out of my horrible choice of clothing. "I rather like this outfit," I mock quietly as I redress in my room, though my voice is nowhere close to reaching his lyrical tone.

I'd rather like it if he was nowhere near my life because I have no room in my heart for this kind of entanglement. I guard my heart behind layers of irritation and detachment when it comes to expectations and commitments.

I prefer the temporary escape that fleeting connections provide—connections made far away from anyone close to me mean that questions I don't feel like answering aren't asked. The men here may flaunt their random hookups, but it's different for women. It's just not as accepted, no matter what anyone tries to say.

Plus, I've found no evidence that finding a man will actually solve any of my problems. More likely, they would just cause *more* problems, and Dane seems like the kind of man who could ruin you for all others and then leave without a trace.

Yeah, *no thanks*. I have enough abandonment issues to contend with without adding *that* into the mix.

With that in mind, I grab another shirt, sporting a few holes gathered over the years, and throw it on with a pair of trekking pants that have seen better days. A glance in the mirror confirms this is no outfit to entice the opposite sex, the only things I'll be attracting are the bugs out in the wilderness.

I'm gone for no more than five minutes. Yet when I return to the common room, I find Dane lounging on one of the couches. The men in the room lean intently towards him, hanging on his every word. I pause.

Don't get me wrong, he's attractive, but I wasn't drooling over the man.

Parker and Landon sit to Dane's right, fully engaged in the conversation. The youngest in our crew, Tucker, sits with Greg—who's the only one already married—and Bill, our oldest member, sits on a couch at Dane's left. The twins, Jack and Jake, listen from the kitchen bar as they finish their breakfast, each lifting spoons of heaped, sugar-loaded cereal to their mouths simultaneously—their typical creepy twin behavior was in full form today.

"So, you're telling me you've never bagged a cougar?" The snark in Landon's tone instantly has me on edge.

Landon isn't my favorite person in the house, and I tried to avoid him most of the time. Between the sexist jokes that are a little too serious and the drunken fondling, he's quickly made it to the bottom of my list.

"I don't tend to degrade women in any manner. I'd prefer it if you didn't, either," Dane's eyes track my movements as I enter the room and he stands, quickly ending the conversation. I should take notes.

"I see you're making friends," I say with a laugh.

"They're of no concern to me. Shall we?" Dane speaks gently—as if I haven't dealt with this sort of liaison multiple times over the last four years. I nod and wave goodbye to the rest of the crew. We make it through the firehouse and to the parking lot with no more unwanted interactions.

I head towards my 4Runner. It's old, but it's still got a lot of life left. The black paint has faded, with large sun-bleached patches covering more of the SUV than not. Color may fade, but memories are just as much a part of the car as its constant oil leak is.

"I'll drive." I don't give Dane any room to argue but, by his enthusiasm to get into the passenger seat, I doubt he would've fought me that hard in the first place. Not much happens in this small town, but having your own vehicle in the instance that you need to ditch some asshole in bum-fuck Montana is always a plus.

Dane's magnetic presence is almost suffocating in the small space, and sends a jolt through my system; each move tempts me to lean closer. I resist, rebuilding my defenses against his mysterious allure.

This drive is going to test my control. In my experience, distraction is a better tactic than avoidance.

"So, tell me about yourself," I ask, pulling the car out onto the road.

"What would you like to know?" Although he answers me quickly, I can tell there is no enthusiasm in his words.

"Where are you from? How old are you? Favorite Disney princess? Anything you want to tell me to make time go by." The crunch of the gravel under tire surely can't hide the sound of my racing heart as an uncomfortable tension fills the small space.

"Well, I'm from the north. I'm probably older than you'd imagine—and," he pauses, a slight hesitation in his voice, "I don't have a favorite princess, but I'm sure you can enlighten me."

I can feel his eyes boring into the side of my head and swallow down the lump in my throat, his undivided attention fraying the edges of my composure. My hands start to sweat and the fabric of my shirt becomes increasingly attached to the skin on my back.

There's something about how he speaks that has me utterly riveted in place while simultaneously making me want to crawl all over him. I roll my window down to cool my raging hormones.

Don't get me wrong, I *know* he's bad news. The problem is getting my body to understand this as well.

"Doesn't get more north than Montana—unless you're from out of country?" That would explain the light accent, at least.

"You could say that. What about you?" Dane says as he focuses on the scenery out of his window.

"I'm from here. Lived all over the country but somehow ended up back here." I speak just to fill the silence, not really considering what I'm saying.

"And why leave in the first place?" His questions with a note of curiosity.

I hesitate, unsure how to answer without revealing memories I don't want to share.

"Just where I ended up," I murmured back, not bothering to elaborate.

Thankfully, he doesn't press the issue. One thing I can appreciate, above all else, is my secrets being just that. *Secret.* I can't fault the man for not wanting to share his personal life with someone he just met. Especially when I'm not willing to share anything of my own.

I crank the radio up, effectively ending the conversation.

Chapter 3
Valencia

The sound of gravel and rock churning beneath us reverberates through the car as I turn into the trailhead parking lot. The suspected ignition site at the top of Sugarloaf Mountain is just a few miles from this lot. Thankfully, we wouldn't have to walk through the charred remains that lie to the south side of the mountain.

"We've got a few miles to hike till we get to the site. It's rough terrain, and we're not able to take motorized vehicles on the trail, so you good to walk it?" I narrowly avoid taking a slow gander at Dane's body. I think we're both aware the man is extremely fit.

"I think I can manage," he assures.

This trail is no joke; even the fittest can struggle between the steep inclines and the high elevation. It's a winding path leading around Sugarloaf Mountain. Most of it is wooded, with trees providing decent coverage from the elements. Loose gravel and rock cover the trail in some parts but, in others, it's just firmly compacted dirt.

The hike was no problem for me. I've managed to stay physically fit throughout the years. Sure, I work out with the guys at the station, but I'm not a *gym bro,* as Parker puts it. I mostly train for long-distance hiking and occasionally do some yoga.

I've noticed over the years that my abilities far outweigh my peers. Where the others struggle, I excel. I've also avoided serious injury more times than I can count; the memory of tackling the twins into the trench comes to mind.

Despite the harrowing event, I came away amazingly unharmed. I'm not sure an Olympic sprinter could have accomplished the same feat, and that's without the added weight of gear and elevation. I'm not even sure how I managed it. Both of the twins suffered at least some minor burns from the heat exposure alone and Jack was still sore from his shoulder sprain.

"Valencia?" Dane's lyrical accent draws me out of my thoughts.

I quickly grab my travel bag from my 4Runner and sling it over my shoulder. After securing the straps comfortably, I glance at Dane.

The man is undoubtedly a sight to behold. Between the tight-fitted polo shirt and rough khaki pants, focusing on the job at hand was going to be difficult with this type of distraction.

Dane gives me a small smile, clearly catching me checking him out.

"I'm ready if you are!" I sing in cheerily in an attempt to cover my awkwardness despite the clearly false tone.

"After you," he states with a light lilt to his voice.

Before we head down the trail, I direct a pointed look at Dane. He stops short, narrowly avoiding running into me and I take a steadying breath.

"This trail is very steep in parts." I start seriously. "I'm confident we are both more than capable of managing that part but you *must* tell me if anything is bothering you. Keep your eyes on the trail at all times."

"I can manage both." His remark is soft, his voice nor expression giving away his emotion. "If you insist."

I'd meant for this conversation to be brisk and to the point but, instead, he has my insides doing gymnastics in a sauna. The heat from earlier returns to my cheeks. He's somehow managed to liquefy my insides with a few choice words and some well-timed looks.

I cough uncomfortably. This wasn't like me. I'd normally ignore these sorts of emotions, but something about him keeps drawing me in. I'm in a tug-of-war battle with desire and self-preservation—and I think I'm losing.

I lean in a little closer, the hairs on my arms starting to rise.

CAW! CAW! CAW!

The loud sound echoes through the trees, reaching us in waves and I nearly jump out of my skin as I search to find the source.

A group of crows sit in a tree about 20 feet down the path—and they all have their attention directly trained on us. On an average day, I'd barely notice them—there must be thousands all over the park—but I can appreciate this group for so expertly interrupting an inevitably horrible idea I was about to have.

I laugh softly and look back to Dane, intending to mention we should get started on our hike, but rage flashes across his face. It's the first unhindered emotion I've seen from him today but it's gone in an instant. However, I can't miss the disgust that still lingers in his eyes.

"Let's go," he clips. Though the anger is no longer present on his face, it is evidently still in his body; his arms are stiff and his spine rod straight.

I shake my head and turn to head down the path without a word. The crows watch, now silent, as we pass.

I can feel the tension rolling off of Dane in waves.

"Ornithophobia?" I ask, keeping my eyes down on the rocky trail.

"What?" His voice once more holds no emotion.

"It means you have a fear of birds," I say without looking at him.

"Oh," he pauses like he wasn't expecting that despite his odd display just minutes ago. "No, I'm just not a fan of those specific birds."

"Okay," I laugh. "So, you're a racist against crows; good to know. You know, before we *really* got serious," I try to joke. The man could use a laugh or two to loosen him up.

"I wasn't aware getting serious was an option."

"Well, it's not. But who said you couldn't dream?" I say. I hear a cackling overhead and notice the crows watching from the canopy. Dane shoots a barbed scowl at the feathered creatures above.

"Wow, they must enjoy your loathing and disdain," I comment and begin to climb over a fallen tree.

"I'm sure they're aware of my feelings," he replies flatly.

"They're crows—I'm not sure they'd be overly concerned with your feelings even if they were aware of them." Another round of cawing and cackling floats through the trees behind us.

"You and I agree on that, at least," he huffs. I can't help noticing he's expressed more emotion in that one sound than he has nearly the entire day. Peculiar to have a member of the CAFA be against anything animal related. They were usually knights of the crusade for all things nature related.

If I wasn't curious about him before, I definitely am now. Not that I'm distraught that he doesn't like crows or anything—but the way the irritation nearly consumed him was strange. It was like, if he had the opportunity, he would've dealt a death blow to every crow he saw in his path.

I take a breath and remind myself that this is just a job; the sooner he completes his findings, the sooner he'll be out of my life. And I can go back to my blissful man-free boringness.

I face forward and continue along the trail. We're quiet the rest of the way, both too focused on the rocky terrain to speak. As we draw nearer to the site, I mentally prepare myself for the thousands of questions he's sure to ask. I can't hold it against him—it's a pivotal part of his job. So, despite my dislike for the process, I'll help him if I can.

"So, this is the tree." I point up to the charred remains of a tall tree. Though most of the tree remains intact, a large chunk is missing from the bottom. The hole is so large you could see the mountain peaks across the valley. Deadly, charred lines snake up the rest of the tree, giving insight into its tainted past. The scorched veins sinuously wrap around the entirety.

This used to be a beautiful meadow; now, all that remains is a black mess of ash and cinder. Lifeless spikes of blackened pines protrude from the earth like a fossilized spine.

"What brings you to the conclusion that this is the specific ignition site?" Dane questions.

To me, the signs are obvious. I would've generally expected the same instincts for him. The fact that this tree is still mostly intact while the others are burned beyond recognition was enough evidence alone. Coupled with the fact that the grass surrounding the tree for about 10 feet was untouched, it was clear that something had ignited the tree before any burning embers likely floated to the ground, igniting the nearby grass.

Add some wind to the equation, and there you have it: wildfire.

Without giving him a Wildfire101 class right here in the meadow, I decide to just list a few details that stand out to me. He nods in the right places and surveys the area again. Still, I couldn't help but notice he didn't write a single note or even bring a pen and paper with him.

Strange. Most CAFA representatives ask endless questions, transcribing everything into a little journal for later use. The whole reason we were out here was so he could take notes. I'm not one to complain about having less work but he's either distracted or careless.

Maybe he has a superhuman memory or something.

After a few more questions, he says he's ready to go back and I don't argue, it's not my job to monitor him or make sure he does his job. I'd make a statement in my report for the Chief and move on with my life. Better to put one foot in front of the other and hope that today is the last time I have to deal with Dane Moore.

We head back on the trail, the midafternoon sun bringing warmth to the day. Rocky, uneven paths or the steep inclines couldn't deter us from the astounding beauty surrounding us. Mountains on all sides and fall foliage give the valley a calming energy. This is the kind of day you savor, and I wasn't one to waste a good time.

"Let's stop here for lunch." I direct Dane to the sandy shore of Lake Agnes. Pristine waters reflect the surrounding mountains in flawless precision. This isn't a trail I get to travel much but I'll take advantage of the view when I can.

I carelessly throw myself down on the beach. The sand is warm on the surface, but I can feel the chilled temperature beneath as I settle in.

Dane gracefully lowers next to me, poised even in a sitting position. I don't know if the word *relax* is even in his vocabulary.

I toss Dane one of the on-the-go meal packs and open my own. It's not much, a protein bar, some dried fruit, and a bag of my favorite homemade trail mix. It won't sustain someone stout like Dane but it'll make the trip a little less miserable.

"So, how long have you been a firefighter?" Dane's voice carries across the vast open space, undoubtedly scaring a few harmless critters into their dens.

"Four years with this crew. I also spent a few years traveling across the country, joining different crews, but none stuck until I met the guys." It isn't a lie. Nowhere ever felt like home until I found this place. "What about you?"

"This is the only job I've ever known." He intently inspects the snacks, avoiding my gaze.

"Do you enjoy it?" I ask.

"I have known nothing else," he continues, "I cannot determine if I enjoy it or not when it is my only purpose in life." Sometimes, when he speaks, it's like no earthly language suits his words.

"Being a part of CAFA is your one sole purpose?" We're touching dangerously close to personal questions but he started the conversation and I don't see much point in making the day awkward by ignoring him.

"Not CAFA—*this*," he sweeps his arm in front of him, slowly pointing out the beauty surrounding us. There are tall pines that softly sway in the breeze surrounded by the melodic singing of nature. "Keeping a balance between God's creations is my purpose," he finishes quietly.

"You're religious?" I can't hide my confusion. I have no idea where he's going with this.

"I am nothing else." He stares at me, gaze locking me in place. The gray steel of his eyes glows. I may have my doubts about him, but the reverence in his voice was undeniable.

CAW! CAW!

I turn to my left, the noise drawing me out of his prison-like stare. Just down the beach, a crow hops around, head tilted, its gaze directly trained on me.

Wild animals aren't typically this comfortable around humans, but crows are known to be particularly intelligent and often understand how to take advantage of a couple humans eating their lunch. Hopefully, the grizzlies never catch on.

I toss the crow a raisin out of my trail mix. It hops enthusiastically to the raisin and gulps it down in an instant. Two more hops bring it closer as it stares intently at my snacks.

"You're asking for trouble with that one," Dane states.

"He's harmless." I toss a peanut to the crow this time, though I notice it takes it with less enthusiasm. "*Picky*—but harmless."

"Nothing in this world is harmless. He is only benign to you because you are not a worm." The disgust in his voice is unmistakable.

"Why does God create the worm in the first place if its predator is as clever as the crow?" I try to mask the distaste in my voice, though I doubt I'm very successful.

The crow takes two more hops closer—now only ten feet away from me. I toss a couple more pieces of trail mix, not paying attention to Dane.

"You do not believe in God?" He asks quietly.

I hesitate, looking out at the softly rippling water. I don't want to offend him. Especially not on something he so clearly believes in. But I also won't lie about my beliefs. Who am I to judge? He's clearly passionate about his faith and that, in itself, is beautiful. Unfortunately, faith is not something we share.

My faith is drenched in the oily negativity of my past. I don't say that, though. He's a complete stranger and not someone I plan to share my sordid history with.

I look at the crow, its small, beady eyes gazing in my direction. I notice that two raisins and a chocolate chip lie uneaten on the sand. Even the crow is more interested in my answer than the opportunity at a tasty treat.

"It isn't that I don't believe." A bubble of emotion forces its way into my throat, silencing me for a moment. I struggle for a second to withhold my pain. "God has only ever taken from me. I'm the worm, and God is my crow."

He sighs. We make eye contact again and I can tell he wants to speak but doesn't.

"Let's head back, I've got some things to do back at the station." It's a lie. I'm off for the next couple days but he doesn't need to know that.

He nods as if equally happy to avoid any more awkward conversation.

I grab our trash, stash it in my bag, and rise before dusting leftover sand off my legs. Dane stands, gazing at the lake as though in deep thought.

We make our way back to the trail and start the steep journey back to the car. A flutter of black catches my eye and a crow flies over our heads. It perches on a tree further down the trail and follows us, hopping down the path, tree by tree, softly cawing at us if we go too slowly or too fast for its liking.

I breathe a sigh of relief; at least I won't have to suffer the hike back alone with Dane.

Chapter 4
Valencia

To my left, the rocky mountainside descends sharply for hundreds of feet. It's not a straight edge, but the slope is steep enough that it could quickly turn into a slip-and-slide from Hell without proper focus.

Large groups of giant western pines randomly break into empty spaces along the winding path. It's saturated with trees, but just twenty feet from the edge is an open patch of land down the side of Sugarloaf Mountain.

We're quiet as we focus on navigating the dangerous terrain and my eyes drift to my feet, tracking each step carefully. I'm thankful for the lull in conversation because my soul feels raw. Dane found a sore spot and I prefer to not reopen those wounds.

I thought today would be simple and boring. Show Dane the fire site, answer his questions, and send him on his way. With any luck, there'd still be time for me to end up in front of a small fire in the pit behind the firehouse and drink a few too many fingers of the whiskey that I had waiting patiently for my return.

I sigh and draw my focus back to the trail. The canopy above filters most of the October sun through its sharp pine needles, leaving patches of the rocky path illuminated in warm light. The trees on this part of the trail are less dense than in other spots, so I can see the outline of the road ahead with ease.

I feel Dane's presence behind me; his mood quickly darkened after we left Lake Agnes.

His stare bores into the back of my head. I'm not sure how I can tell he's staring at me but it's distracting, nonetheless.

I reminisce on the conversation we had on the beach. It's easy to envy the conviction he has in his faith. Anyone with that much reverence for God is to be admired but it doesn't make him any more right than my lack of faith makes me wrong.

I believe in Heaven and Hell and have surely done plenty to earn a spot in each place. While I'd assume I'm more suited to the latter, there's still plenty of life left to live.

Movement out of my left eye catches my attention. I assume it's the crow attempting to move me on my way but, before I can turn and get a good look behind me, my right ankle shoots to the side and rolls awkwardly on a rock.

"*Agh*!" I bellow as a sharp, blinding pain shoots from the outside of my ankle and up the rest of my leg. I stumble a couple of steps as I regain my balance while I try to keep my weight off my leg.

I suck in deep breaths, centering myself around the pain and assessing what just happened. I take a few seconds to take a mental scan of my injuries. The rocky trail blurs as my eyes fill with tears.

Standing straight again, I ignore my surroundings for a moment and balance my weight on my left foot, lifting my pants to glance down at my ankle.

Ugh, it's worse than I thought—the swelling has already started and putting weight on it sends jabbing pains throughout my entire leg. A frustrated groan escapes me. I'll need Dane's help down the rest of the mountain.

There's a little less than a half mile left to go, but I'm not thrilled by the thought of relying so heavily on him while injured.

Suddenly, I feel Dane coming up behind me and the hairs on my neck rise on instinct. His hand curls around my right bicep and his fingers press painfully into the muscle. An acidic feeling churns in my stomach but my mind struggles to focus on anything other than my injured ankle.

The next second, I'm yanked around by the hand on my arm. The world blurs as I stumble again and through my hazy gaze, I watch as Dane drops his grip on my arm and steps back out of reach. My whole body swings gracelessly. I desperately try to not put any weight on my injured ankle as I reach toward him for balance.

Time slows to a crawling pace—as though someone wants me to live every detail of this moment vividly.

I step to the side for balance but my right knee crumples beneath me, causing my foot to slip over the trail's edge. The world turns as I pitch backward and I look at Dane in panic. I'm still reaching for him but my fingers grasp empty air.

He's motionless as I fall. And, then he's gone.

My arms flail, searching for purchase. Even though I still have one good leg, it's useless on the rocky terrain—like trying to get balance while standing on a bowling ball

I hit the ground a few feet from the trail's edge, the once flat surface of the trail now a steep incline of the mountainside. I start sliding on my back, feet dragging uselessly. Air is forced out of my lungs, leaving me gasping. I try to gain control, but pain ravages most of my body; rocks flay the skin on my back through my thin shirt.

It's agony. My only hope is that I hit something on the way down to stop my rapid descent. Even then, I'm sure it'll hurt like a bitch.

It does.

Then everything goes black.

***

I blink rapidly. My head is spinning, the world whipping around so fast my brain can't keep up. For a second, I fear I'm still falling.

Still falling?

I blink a couple more times, trying to clear my watery vision, and groan in pain. The sky rotates in a whirlwind around me.

I take a deep breath, head heavy. It's like an evil fog has penetrated my mind with its claws, mercilessly ripping through the soft tissue of my brain.

I attempt a small look around me. The world twirls a couple more times before settling again. My stomach rolls. *I think I'm gonna be sick.*

I felt like I was falling because I *did* fall. Nearly twenty fucking feet off the trail!

In my current position, all I can see is the Montana pines standing proudly above me. The tree I'm currently leaning against stands proudly among the rest, its lowest limbs a few feet above my head.

My right shoulder and head rest against the tree, leaving the left side of my upper body hanging haphazardly off the side. My lower body points up the slope, the sharp angle sending all the blood straight to my head.

"Fucking Hell," I curse. My head pounds. Most of my body is throbbing, stinging, or in some other level of discomfort. I can feel something wet falling down the back of my neck and arm.

My left arm hangs loosely off the side of the tree while my right arm lies across the rocks on the ground beside me. I slowly wiggle my fingers and toes and am relieved to learn I can still feel them.

Looking down at my body, I realize I'm fortunate to be alive.

The right side of my body took most of the damage and there's a cut on the outside of my right arm. It's covered in blood that's starting to dry around the edges.

With each breath, stabbing pain radiates along my right-hand side, from my ribs to the center of my chest—meaning I most likely have at least one cracked rib.

And I can't forget my stupid ankle that got me here in the first place. I can feel it burning with a vengeance.

My pants are, thankfully, still intact—only a few small tears that I can see—however, my shirt is a different story. The old, tattered fabric had no chance against the hardened stones and hangs in shreds, leaving most of my torso bare. Bright red splotches stain what material is left, and I can already see bruises gathering on the skin underneath. Everything seems intact, but getting out of this won't be easy.

I look back up to the trail, expecting to see an extremely worried Dane—harrowed and frantic, trying to determine how he's going to save me—but, instead, there's just an empty trail. I listen for a second, hoping that maybe he's just further down the mountainside, getting help. The gravel road isn't far from here.

I'd surely hear if he was down there but it's silent.

I'm alone.

My entire life, I've been surrounded by danger and I always manage to escape with little to no injury. One afternoon with Dane and I nearly slid down a mountainside to my death.

From this position, I can't tell how many more trees I have behind me, but I doubt there's many. I don't dare look, afraid the movement will cause my injured body to shift and topple me further down the mountain.

CAW! CAW! CAW!

"Stupid bird," I grumble. A crow hops around on the edge of the trail frantically. Its head tilts side to side with each hop.

I give a hollow laugh as the gravity of my situation becomes clear to me. Instead of a colleague hanging around, frantic to help, there is a small black crow doing a jig on the trail's edge as if laughing at my misfortune. Like my current situation isn't shitty enough.

CAW!

With another high-pitched screech, the crow flutters on ebony wings over to my tree, landing just a few feet above my head.

"What do you want?" I seethe, directing my fury at the crow. It must not understand because it continues to caw loudly, hopping uselessly around me. Each screech sends shoots of pain through my skull.

I try my hardest not to focus on the fact that Dane is nowhere to be found. Did he push me?

My thoughts are too jumbled to focus on that right now. I've still got to figure out a way to get off this mountain.

I might as well put my big girl pants on and get to work saving my own ass.

Who needs Prince Charming anyway?

Chapter 5
Corvus

This woman is infuriating. If it weren't for the weight of Hell resting on my shoulders, I would portal my ass home. I can feel the interstice between Earth and Hell like a thread hanging off a shirt sleeve. It flutters at the edge of my consciousness, waiting to be pulled.

Instead of relaxing at home, I'm hopping around in my familiar form, squawking at a chick about 10 inches away from making an early trip to Hell.

I flutter my wings; the annoyance of the situation is making my feathers itch. My crow form is hard to maintain for long periods on Earth. In Hell, my familiar form is like a second part of me that's hidden from view—ready to pull on whenever I need. Being in Earth's realm cuts off that part of myself, forcing me to possess the bodies of real crows who definitely do *not* appreciate the intrusion and usually fight me the entire time.

They're never strong enough to kick me out fully, but they certainly know how to annoy me in the process.

Muscles I only have in my crow form strain with exhaustion. Following the pair throughout the day was more time than I cared to spend in this realm.

"Fucking Hell," her voice drags as if the two words take more effort than she has to give. It's the second time today she's muttered that curse.

Hell didn't get you in this mess. I try to huff my irritation but the sound comes out as the rattling click of a crow's squawk.

She's lying flat on her back on the side of the mountain, less than a foot away from falling to her death. That bastard dared to chat her ear off all day and then turned around and watched her fall down the mountain because he disapproved of her opinion. Righteous zealot.

I skitter a little farther down the branch I'm on, hoping to get a better look at her face. I heard 'Dane' mention her name on the beach. The Devil never mentioned it when we met a few days ago, just told me where and how to find her. Now that I'm here though, I feel like he may have left out some other important information—like the fact that the woman was also being pursued by one of the Archangels.

As I get closer, I'm struck once more by her beauty. Her eyes are so blue the ocean would envy their color, framed by long, dark lashes that make the color stand out. Her long, dark hair hangs in a wild tangled mess over one shoulder and the delicate features of her pretty face are marred with signs of pain.

Bare skin peeks out from the tears in her clothes and what was once a beautifully sun-kissed color is now pale and dirty. Dark patches of bruising already starting to cover most of the torso I can see. Her lean muscular limbs lie limp on the rough ground. Blood covers one arm completely, though it's already dry now that the bleeding has slowed.

I imagine her twisted ankle is bruised as well—that limb clearly unusable now thanks to the injury. The cut on her arm has surprisingly stopped bleeding but using it will be painful and likely cause more damage if she tries. She probably has more scrapes—and likely bruises—all over the back of her body from sliding down the mountainside.

She needs help—and fast. I think I prefer her alive, not dead.

I can smell strong hints of blood in the air. My sense of smell in this form isn't as strong as in my other forms but the iron-like tang is unmistakable. That means that every predator in a 5-mile radius can probably smell her blood in the air, too.

In the short time she was unconscious, I flew up and down this trail, searching for anyone who could help her. Once I concluded that there was not a single person on this forsaken mountain besides the two of us, I hurriedly flew back to her.

I arrived by her side just in time to see her waking up.

She curses at me, taking her anger out on the only thing she can. Her speech is slightly slurred, likely due to the blood loss. I understand her frustration; I nearly feel as helpless as she does. Getting her down the mountain safely as a crow seems impossible but I'm not willing to risk shifting into my middle form. The Devil would have my ass in a blender if I shifted on Earth without permission.

That leaves me helping her find her way 20 feet up the mountainside as a crow. I have no arms, no legs, not even fucking thumbs.

CAW! CAW!

Irritation flows out of me, causing my dark feathers to ruffle. I would prefer to berate her verbally but, for now, I'll have to settle on crow body language.

A rock whizzes past, narrowly missing my head by an inch.

"What do you want, you insolent creature?" She glares at me, taking on a screeching tone. She's managed to sit up, her back mostly resting against the tree instead of on the ground. In my distraction, I hadn't noticed her moving. I can't tell if the movement causes her much pain or if there are other injuries I can't see.

What I can tell, however, is that her eyes are glassy and unfocused. She looks around but not directly *at* me—as if her eyes can't focus on my exact position. It probably saved me from being beamed with a rock but it's a bad sign for her health.

I chirp a few times as my nerves start to ramp up. If she dies, the Devil will surely consider this mission a failure and I do not want to find out what happens then.

There's nothing left of the last demon who failed one of the Devils tasks.

"Listen here, you little shit. If you don't leave me alone, I will let Dane end you! Right before I kick him off the fucking mountain top!" The words tumbled out of her mouth, a deep raspy edge after every few syllables. Her cheeks are bright red as if she can hardly contain her anger. Or she's starting to get a fever.

Sweat drips down her forehead, leaving a light-colored trail against her otherwise dirty skin. It's so stark against the dirt stains that it reminds me of a tiger's stripes.

A cool breeze rustles through trees, ruffling my feathers.

Shit. My timeline to help her is running short.

I fly from my branch and land on the ground next to her, but not so close she can smash me with her fist. I tilt my head in her direction and then to the mountainside behind her.

Her bright green backpack lays about 10 feet behind her, further down the mountain. She's been wearing it all day, and it's a miracle the short rocky slope didn't tear it to pieces.

She monitors me with a somewhat sharp eye as I hop past her but doesn't move to watch as I fly down to the bag. I reach my beak inside a large tear in the fabric and, with force, drag a thin, coiled rope from the bag.

The rope's end lies like a rough noodle in my beak as I fly back to her. She jumps, causing a pained moan to fall out of her mouth, as I land softly on her left knee. I can feel the warmth radiating from her body—the fever is now really starting to set in.

I can see sparks of recognition flutter in her eyes. As she was packing this bag at her car in the lot, I saw her pack this rope, some random medical supplies, and a cell phone.

"I'm sorry for calling you stupid," she groans. I know the pain is probably starting to weigh on her, mentally, but the relief in her voice is evident. Bags darken under her watery eyes and more sweat beads dapple across her forehead. She takes the rope from me and grips it tightly in her palm.

"Now what, little bird?" My wings flutter, though this time in pride.

I fly back down the mountain to the bag. It takes me a few tries, but I eventually tie the other end of the rope around the handle. It's difficult when you don't have thumbs—or any other fingers on a hand to help the process along.

I miss my fucking fingers.

When I return to her, her shoulders relax, visibly dropping down a couple of inches.

"Little bird," she snaps her fingers a few inches from my head, shocking me out of my thoughts. "Now what?"

I grab the rope in my beak and hop across a couple of rocks. She looks at me with wide, calculating eyes, still holding her end of the rope tightly. As I drag it with me a couple more inches, it pulls the rope from her grip. Her lips twitch slightly, almost into a smile, but not quite. I can tell she's already caught on to my idea. I'm amazed, considering the state she's in, but I don't think to question it.

"Clever bird," she murmurs and reaches forward with her left arm, her right arm still lying limply across her stomach.

CAW!

I shake my head rapidly a few times. She freezes. The last thing I want is her reaching towards me and hurtling down the mountain because of it.

I fly to her, perching on her knee, with the rope still in my mouth. I drop it in her open hand and tilt my head to the side. She squints at me, so I tilt my head again, pointing my beak towards the rope.

She curls her fingers around the cord and, with a gentle tug, begins dragging the small pack up the hill.

Any time she moves too quickly, I chirp at her. She catches on quickly and we work together over the next 10 minutes to get the bag close enough for her to reach out and grab it. Thankfully, none of the bag's contents fall out as it drags over the rocks.

Once the pack is securely in her fist, she flops the thing across her lap. A stray strap slaps me on the back of the head. I fluff out my feathers but don't miss her smirk as she starts rummaging through the bag.

Glad to see her sense of humor hasn't suffered.

With shaky hands, she pulls out her cell phone and immediately begins to type. I can see from my perch on her knee that the phone wasn't damaged in the fall. Too bad she didn't have the same luck.

She takes a deep breath before lifting the phone to her ear.

I hear a soft ringing from the phone and, a few of seconds later, a deep, muted voice answers and begins to speak incessantly. She doesn't even get a chance to say hello before he rambles about her curfew and something about a woman named Marcy.

"Parker." Her grip on the phone is so tight, I can see the whites of her knuckles. The man continues with his pointless one-sided conversation.

"Parker! Just shut up for a second," she snaps and there's blissful silence on the other end of the phone. "I was in an accident. I slipped down the mountain. I'm about 20 feet off the trail's edge, probably half a mile from the trailhead."

I can hear his sharp inhale through the phone from here, but he's otherwise quiet as she continues. "I need help. I'm banged up pretty bad and the incline is too sharp to safely make it up by myself. I don't know how long I've been here—I passed out at some point. The sun's gonna set in another hour or so, so I'm going to need you to come get me."

Slipped, huh?

"Are you alone? Are you okay? What happened? Where's the guy from CAFA?" The questions fly out of him rapidly, voice sharp as though emotion is stealing half of his words; everything is muted through the phone speaker. He's worried for her. It's good that she has someone coming to help her because I've reached my limit on what I can do.

"Just get your ass here, I'll tell you more about it later." She hangs up on him and sets the phone back in her lap. Her eyes close as her head drops back against the tree. The shaking in her hands hasn't stopped and I assume that the adrenaline is wearing off and the pain is starting to set in.

A low groan escapes her lips. The sound is a mix between a sigh and a growl.

Pain shoots from the top of my head and down my back. I can only stand to be in this form a little longer. My essence is already trying to crawl out of this tiny vessel. Being in my crow form is like trying to fit a demon dog on your lap; it works, but not for long. Despite the pain, I refuse to leave her side. I must see this through, there's no other option for me. Part of me feels bad about it all, that important life choices are being made for her by beings she doesn't even know exist. The other part of me just wants to get this over with.

It doesn't matter that I have no idea why she's important to the Devil—I must ensure that nothing happens to her before she gets off this mountain. I'll need more time to assess why she's so special and figure out a plan for how I'm going to complete this mission after we manage that.

I had no idea what I was getting myself into when the Devil sent me her way.

Seeing her pain brings me an odd sense of discomfort. I don't know this woman, but I can't shake the fact that I feel drawn to her. It's not unusual for me to be drawn to a pretty face but this is somehow more. A protective side me of that I haven't felt in a long time struggles with the side of me that just wants to get back to Hell. There's so much more going on than I'm aware of, and that was *before* 'Dane' pushed her down the mountain.

What a stupid fake name.

If it wasn't for that bastard getting to her first, I would've ensured our first meeting went differently. Preferably with me on two legs, with arms, hands, a body, and most importantly, *thumbs.*

The leg I sit perched on suddenly jerks. Her eyes are still closed, and I can see her pulse flutter beneath the thin skin in the crook of her slender neck.

She passed out earlier, so I worry she has a head injury on top of the many others. I chirp at her a couple of times but receive no response. I lightly jab the top of her thigh with the tip of my beak. She swiftly jerks awake, slightly sending her off the edge of the tree, but she regains her position quickly. The muscles in her jaw feather as she grits her teeth against the pain. "Little bird, don't push your luck with me right now."

CAW! CAW!

"You know, I'm starting to see why Dane didn't like you," she huffs a laugh, looking through the trees off to her right. "It is odd, though. You're just a crow."

Oh, just you wait, Honey.

"Where are all your friends?" She asks me as if she's fully capable of holding a one-sided conversation while we wait for her rescue party to show. At least it keeps her awake.

If I was in my mortal form and could respond, I'd tell her that I am a demon lord, the thousand-eyed crow that watches over Hell, and I do *not* make friends with birds, I control them. However, that would be a complex argument to make right now, as I am currently sitting atop her knee as a bird.

I tilt my head at her in response.

"Are you one of those birds that work for the government? I bet someone is laughing at me right now." I hop back and forth on my tiny feet, laughter coming out of my body physically. "I know for a fact God is laughing right now, 'cause my life is clearly a joke to Him."

At the mention of God, a sharp chill runs down my back again. It doesn't necessarily hurt to hear His name, but the mere mention of the holy higher power is a grating discomfort to Hellspawn. It's a tactic used by the divine to prevent us degenerates from cursing His name in vain.

"There isn't a thought in that little head, is there?" She reaches a curled finger out towards me. This is when I should fly away and watch from a distance. I've already lingered far longer than I should.

As her finger inches closer to the feathers on my chest, I let her touch me. At this point, it doesn't matter. I'm clearly well past acting like an ordinary bird and onto full-blown irrationality at this point. The back of her finger strokes softly down my chest twice. Warmth radiates off her finger and fills my small body with thousands of tiny electrical shocks.

"Shit, you're real," she murmurs like she's surprised despite all I've done in the last fifteen minutes trying to save her ass.

A sense of wonder fills every part of empty space there is in my soul. Technically, it's not even *my* soul; the Devil owns it. I'm surprised it's capable of such feelings.

"Your feathers are very soft, Little Bird." Valencia's shaky finger drags down my chest one more time and then freezes in midair. I hear the crunching of gravel beneath tires below us. In my frantic flying to find her help earlier, I saw the trailhead parking lot down the trail a short way from where we are now.

This is it—my countdown. I have a few minutes left with her. At this moment, my desire to lift her into my arms and carry her down the mountain is more potent than it has been all day. The need to shed this useless skin and rise in my middle form is battering against my resolve.

I hear the people gathering supplies and hurrying up the mountain. The October sun is not far from setting, so their flashlights flicker through the trees as they rush toward us.

"I won't forget this. I promise I'll come back to visit you sometime soon." Her voice shakes, exhaustion taking over.

"Val! Can you hear me? You awake?" A man skids to a stop at the trail's edge and throws down an arm full of gear, his auburn hair burning like fire in the setting sun.

Others gather behind him moments later. It only takes the humans mere minutes to strap gear onto the red-haired man and send him slowly down the mountain toward her.

Who is he to her? I try not to focus on the question as it pings through my mind, but the unknown weighs heavily on me. I know she must feel relieved that her rescuer is here but, for some reason, all I feel is dread. I have no idea how I'm going to complete this mission. I already decided killing her isn't an option and I've been ordered to sway her to Hell's side, no matter the circumstances.

I can't help but feel like she may be already swaying me to her side, instead.

Knowing my time has come, I fly off her lap and land in a nearby tree. I watch from my spot as the man lifts her lightly into a rescue basket and both slowly make it up to the trail. Once at the top, the man and a few others reach to lift the basket with her in it.

"Guys, I have never been happier to see your faces, but if you don't let me out of this basket, you'll be the next to take a trip down the side of Sugarloaf Mountain." Her fingers grip the edges of the basket and her voice wavers weakly.

"Valencia, you're in no position to walk down the mountain, much less kick any of us off of it." The red-haired man tells her softly but sternly while the others prepare the trip back to their vehicles. "So just lay there and be quiet."

I agree with him, but it'd be a lie to say that I don't appreciate her inner strength. Not many could live through this situation and come out of it able to crack jokes. She may be beaten up physically, but her sharp tongue and quick wit are still intact.

I follow the crew as they slowly make it to the parking lot. Valencia is ushered into a waiting ambulance while the others rush around, loading into various emergency vehicles. I notice that the red-haired man jumps into the ambulance with her, shutting the door behind himself.

For a split second, just as the doors begin to close, she manages to look directly at me. The last I see of her face is a giant smile, directly pointed at me.

I sit and watch as the ambulance and other responders pull away in their big vehicles, oblivious to my presence. I stay in this spot until the forest around me becomes quiet and peaceful again. I wish I could linger in this moment, taking in the last signatures of her presence.

Only when I'm sure there are no humans left in the area do I pull on the thread that attaches me to Hell.

The crow flies off with a loud repetitive screech as it regains control of its body.

On a soft breeze, I blip through the fabric of space between the two realms; off to make a deal with the Devil.

CHAPTER 6
CORVUS

I SHAKE OFF THE grimy grip of my astral form as I portal into my living room. Light glows from various lanterns around the open space. Off to the right, two worn black leather chairs sit haphazardly beside a floor-to-ceiling bookshelf. A few feet from that, a forest green couch sits atop a large rug with swirls of dark colors that draw the eye to its mysterious patterns.

The couch faces a small fireplace which offers a comforting blanket of warmth to the open space. On the left of the living room is a small cottage-style kitchen with a table to the side and the kitchen counter is covered in jars full of spices and other ingredients. A few leftover dishes lie dirty in the sink.

I look at the room around me and can't help but bask in its comforting ambience. My home sits just inside a large mountain, the interior flowing into the bluff like an artificial cave. The space is cozy and open but not overly large. Most of the structure consists of rock and natural material, furthering the feeling of being underground.

It's a necessary characteristic of having a home in Hell.

Humans mistake Hell for being a place filled with fire and lava however, despite popular opinion, Hell is much like Earth. As humans evolve and change, so does Hell. Time is different here, though, so it's not a direct correlation.

While Hell looks the same on the surface, what hides in the shadows here is much deadlier. The difference is, there isn't much room for happiness in this realm.

We have cities and technology, but it's not very reliable. We even have modern advancements—if you're clever enough to build them yourself or vicious enough to steal them from someone else. We have a lot of the things humans take for granted.

And most importantly we have something the humans don't have. *Magic.*

The kind that would break a human's mind if they were ever faced with it.

But there are also the deadly creatures that roam this realm who like to prey on the unsuspecting souls that end up here. And if you manage to escape them, there's a demon around every corner, ready to throw you into endless suffering.

There are a few who've managed to rise through the ranks of Hell, but it's rare. This realm is full of vicious beings who are willing to do *anything* to reach the top. To survive.

I've killed thousands to get where I'm at now.

I don't feel bad for what I've done. It was always me or them. Each life I claimed leaves a shadowed mark on my soul and I'm shackled by the chains of my making. Life and death were never a choice for me. I was *made.* And though my soul is weighed down by the sins and atrocities I've committed over the years, redemption is such a fleeting dream that I no longer wish for it.

I am a lord of Hell. Darkness is my legacy. I live in a tapestry of shadows—but being a lord of Hell does have its perks. Having a home to call my own is one of them.

I chose this cave many years ago, and I've fought and killed hundreds to keep it.

A cave-style home is the only way to regulate temperature and ensure my safety in the event of some terrible force of nature. Because, when it comes to the weather, Hell is on a constant rotation of the worst weather imaginable. Either too hot or too cold, there is no in-between.

There were no seasons or climate separation. Just shitty weather followed by, you guessed it, shitty weather.

Caves are also easier to defend. The deadly creatures that roam this realm freely prefer easy prey found in the open ranges. They're much less likely to attack a fortified homestead, but if you're smart, you still take every precaution.

There are no laws in Hell. It's kill or be killed. Hell is a place for sinners to be punished and the sinful to play. It is an unholy playground of debauchery.

Though I find myself on the higher end of Hell's hierarchy, I am not immune to the petty squabbles that arise throughout this dreadful place.

I flop onto the couch, the warmth from the fire relaxing the tension throughout my body. I take a second to watch the fire sprites dance in the open flames. Their bodies are so small, they're easily mistaken for an ember or spark. Despite their size, a horde could intimidate even the strongest of demons. A cold fire could anger even the kindest of fire sprites.

I'd do well to remember to keep the fireplace well-lit.

Closing my eyes, I tilt my head back to rest on the couch's cushion and inhale sharply through my nose.

Thudding steps sound through the open space behind me.

"Not now, Van," I mutter. I know it's him because we're the only two beings in this entire realm that can get through the front door.

"I didn't take you for a quitter. If you give up so easily, I may as well end you now." The cold bite of metal touches the side of my throat. No doubt it's a sword tip. Its chilly touch kisses the delicate skin that barely covers my jugular.

With a growl, I open my eyes and take in the male standing over me. Most Fae are not violent—preferring battles of wit over fists—but Van is a trained warrior and he looks every bit the part. Standing just an inch under 7 feet tall, he's like a great tree hovering over me—lean like a runner, but with strength rarely rivaled.

His long black hair hangs loosely down his body, the dark tips reaching well past his waist. His bronzed skin matches his leather belt's warm reds and browns—a pair of deep green pants hang low on his hips. Thin leather straps hold his pants just below his knees, leaving toned copper calves in view.

As I study his face, bright green eyes stare unwaveringly back at me, like looking into two tiny emeralds. His prominent brow casts a shadow on his high cheekbones and hollow cheeks. His nose flares as his full lips quirk in the slightest of grins.

I swat at his sword, tired of its deadly point resting against my throat. He sheathes the blade and sits down next to me with ease. We both know that despite his height and strength, a battle between us would be anything but easy.

"What makes you think I failed?" I lift from the couch and head to the kitchen.

"Well, here you are. Alone. You've lost your touch, my friend."

"You know full well that I have not lost my touch." I grab a can of beer I had a lesser demon bring me from Earth out of the pocket in the kitchen wall and pop the tab. The fizzing sound of the beer offers a balm to my anxious nerves. "I was stuck in my fucking familiar form the entire time," a deep swig starts to wash away the stress from the day.

"The Devil has still not granted you permission to travel up top in this form?" He questions in disbelief.

"No." I take another long drink, grab a second can, and make my way back to where Van sits. I slide heavily into one of the leather chairs and swivel it around to face him. I lift the can in offering but he shakes his head. I know he doesn't drink human beer, but it feels rude not to offer.

"I fuck one nun, 200 years ago, and I am still being punished for it."

Van laughs, but the laugh doesn't reach his eyes. "As I remember, you were explicitly warned to stay away from God's disciples. Must you go against the Devil at every chance?"

"It was Halloween," I groan. I pretend it's a good enough excuse, but we both know I was fully aware of the sin I was committing. Sometimes the easiest sin to commit is the one we're told to stay away from.

I finish off the first beer and crack the second. Even though I would have to drink an elephant's weight in beer to get drunk, the motion calms a part of me that teeters on the edge of sanity.

"So, what was she like?"

"Hmm," a gruff sound escapes me. Words stick halfway through my throat, blocked by some unseen force. I trust Van with my life; he is my most loyal and trusted friend. Yet I hesitate to tell him about Valencia. He's known about the mission since the Devil called on me a couple of days ago but, now, there's something in me that wants to hold everything I've learned about her to myself.

I shake my head and, with a nod, tell him everything.

"She was nothing like I expected. Annoying—as humans usually are—but, beautiful." I say. "Captivating, really. It was distracting." I think back to the many curses she unknowingly sent my way. "She's tall, athletic. Hair like yours and eyes like the ocean. And a mouth worse than a demon dog's bite." I laugh softly, thinking back on the day.

An image of her leaning against the tree, bloody and bruised, makes my insides sour. "That bastard archangel got to her first. I spent the first half of the day listening to him spew nonsense like it was shit coming out of his ass." Van listens intently, nodding once to acknowledge he was aware of which archangel.

"He pretended to be a part of some organization that she works with. Had a fake name and everything, though he didn't disguise his looks—minus the feathers, of course. I caught up with them in the mountains, followed along in my crow form."

I take a deep breath, forcing myself to continue through the day's events, even though recalling how she looked after falling sends a sharp pain ricocheting through my chest.

"They talked for a while. He brought up the Father, like the ever-dutiful psycho son that he is. He disapproved of her answers so, when she fell down the mountain, he left her there to die. She's lucky to be alive."

As the story rushes from my throat, I'm left with a burning aftertaste.

"Since you are here and not at the Devil's door begging for forgiveness, I assume she is, in fact, alive?"

"Yes, but not without injury. I did what I could." I know he understands my meaning. I feel sickening frustration at being trapped in a form as incapable as a small bird.

"You are wallowing, then?" He asks as he leans against the couch arm, settling in.

"No, Van, I'm not wallowing. When have you ever seen me wallow?"

"Well, there was that time during the la—"

"Don't finish that sentence," I interrupt. "That was *not* wallowing. I lost half of my platoon!"

"I'm afraid I don't think you know what the definition of wallowing is because that was most definitely what you were doing." He responds, cool and unruffled as ever. Somehow, he always manages to push every one of my buttons.

"Remind me why I allow you to enter my home?" I don't acknowledging his last statement. I had a right to be upset after that battle.

I had just won the tournament to become the third lord of Hell. My first mission as a lord was to infiltrate a secret group of angels that were sneaking into

Hell and end them, no matter the circumstance. That battle cost me my entire platoon, half to death and the other half to desertion.

We were ambushed, trapped, with nowhere to go but through a hundred angels eager for a fight. For a kill. It was brutal, and if Van hadn't gotten wind of it sooner and come and saved our asses at the last minute, I very well could've died with the rest of the fallen demons.

"You allow me in here because I am your most trusted friend and the only being in Hell, besides the Devil, who can stand to be in your presence." He tells me curtly and smirks.

From anyone else, it would be an insult. Lesser demons make up most of Hell and they can't stand to be near beings with higher power than them. It drives them crazy. Well, crazier than they normally are.

"Speaking of the Devil, this is such a shit storm of problems and I'm already over it. Why would he not tell me she was being pursued by an Archangel?" I ask him, frustration building in my chest. Dumah knew exactly who I was. He even mentioned to Valencia that I was more than she should expect when he saw my crow form.

I'm lucky he let me follow for so long without retaliating. My only theory was that he knew I would've shifted if I could have, so he took advantage of my issues with the Devil and forced me to watch as he attempted to fuck my life in a single day. Fucking angels.

"I'm not sure. Why would the Devil send *you* for her in the first place?" Van asks.

"The Devil only knows. At least she's alive so I still have time to find out," I mutter.

"You did well then. Tomorrow is left for fighting. Tonight is for rest. We will go to the Devil in the morning and plead your case."

I nod in gratitude but leave my appreciation unspoken. To thank one of the Fae is to create a soul debt; not even death can spare you. Not even our lasting friendship is worth trapping myself into a soul debt with him.

Van leaves silently. The only reason I heard his steps earlier was because he wanted me to. I think back on the years of our friendship, cherishing the many good memories we've had together.

I met Van in battle, our blades even clashing a time or two. Many had died in those days, and it was a miracle we hadn't claimed each other's lives in the process. Once we both realized we were stronger together, we overthrew our leaders and created our own armies, leading side by side. We were an unstoppable force in those days.

Once I'm certain Van is gone, I hop off the couch and head towards my bathroom. I flip the lever to my shower; hot spring water bursts from the nozzle, dowsing the room in a blanket of steam.

I step into the hot water and allow it to soothe the aches in my muscles, left over from the strain of being forced to remain in my crow form for so long. I try to focus on anything other than the raven-haired beauty I met today.

Valencia captivated me, her smart mouth and striking eyes would make her a worthy rival in our future battles, and I was sure there would be battles between us.

After quickly cleaning off the remaining stress of the day, I turn the lever on the wall, shutting off the hot stream of water.

Over the years, I've worked tirelessly to turn this cave into a home that I can retreat to. This space is sacred to me, so I never let another being in Hell know of its location.

Except for Van, of course—but he's poor company most days.

Forgoing a towel, I head out of the bathroom and into my favorite room in the cave. I sweep aside the heavy leather flap, the hide of some random creature serving as a door. It isn't the sturdiest of barriers, but it serves its purpose well.

The room is open, with vaulting ceilings that reach nearly 20 feet high. A large bed, far greater than any bed I'd seen on Earth, fills almost the entire back wall. Dark blankets are piled haphazardly on the bed, while pillows lay scattered everywhere.

I chose this particular room for a bedroom for two distinct reasons. One, it is the only room I can sleep in without feeling as though the entirety of the rocky mountain above is weighing me down in my sleep. Two, the room resembles a midnight sky. Tiny dots glow as if a thousand glow-in-the-dark stars have strewn across the high ceiling, like a million little suns shining down on me each night.

Chapter 7

Corvus

I WAKE WITH A start, the remnants of a dream still clutching me like a lover's embrace. My eyes blink open as the soft light from the glowing stones above focuses in and out. I spent most of the night with my cock making a miniature tent of the sheets, thanks to erotic visions plaguing my dreams. Despite my lack of clothes, I still feel the sticky dampness of sweat coating my skin.

Valencia had ruled my thoughts throughout the entire night. It seems I will only escape her in my waking hours and, even then, it's a struggle not to think of her constantly. I barely know her, only having spent a few hours in her presence, and that didn't even count considering I was stuck as a crow. In the dream, she felt so intimately familiar.

My head pounds as I try to make sense of it. The details of the dream are already beginning to fade, leaving behind only a mixture of desire and bewilderment in their wake.

Why her? Is my mind trying to tell me something about her, or has my body just taken control? It's been a while since I've been with anyone, but not so long that the idea of her phantom touch should get me this hard. Did the Devil know I would feel this way? It wouldn't be entirely out of his realm of ability, to know such a thing. It would also be a great way to fuck with me, which he so enjoys doing.

I take a deep breath, pushing it out of my mind. I have more important things to worry about today.

I throw the covers off and rummage around my room for some pants, finding them stacked in neat piles on a wooden shelf. I grab boxers first and then slip on the dark denim, the coarse material rubbing against my legs.

The cool stone beneath my feet soothes my overheated skin as I pad my way out of my room, grabbing a shirt as I go.

I decide to forgo eating, the thought of a heavy meal sitting in my stomach is nearly as unpleasant as all the groveling I'm sure to do today.

My boots remain untouched by the door since I'll be flying to the Devil's palace. No sense in trying to carry them with me when I can just create new ones when I get there. I make sure to draw a sigil of protection over the door when I leave. Any creature other than myself will only see the bluff's rocky edge, the entrance will remain invisible to any unwanted attention. It's a necessary precaution when your closest neighbors are the dead and deprived.

I quickly shift to my crow form and head directly to the gardens outside the Devil's palace.

"Bright morning to my fearless friend. Did you eat breakfast?" Van's voice carries over the decorative shrubs as I land softly on my feet, shifting effortlessly mid-flight.

"I'm a demon, Van. You know I don't eat breakfast." I snap.

"I implore you to try harder to prevent whoever pissed in your cereal." He responds, arms crossed in front of his chest.

"You just can't resist thinking of cock, can you, dear friend?" I give him a Cheshire smile. "As much as I'd love to fulfill your fantasies, we have serious business to attend to this morning."

"Yes; your failure." Van's words cut deep. Even though he means them as a joke, I feel them down to my marrow.

"The Devil is unlikely to permit me to use this form on Earth without a good reason. Any ideas?" I ask. No matter how badly the Devil wants Valencia, it can never just be easy.

I stride over to where he stands, the grass soft under my bare feet. Large shrubs shaped like various mythical creatures block our view of the palace beyond the garden. A giant, leafy version of Cerberus towers over us.

"You will need to grovel," he states plainly. "You must show remorse over your past transgressions in that realm."

"I know this, Van. Any *new* ideas?" I exhale in exasperation, the hairs at the back of my neck standing to attention.

"I do, but you won't like it."

"Well, I'm not gonna like groveling like some lesser demon panting at his feet. It can't be much worse than that."

"You know the Devil will prefer this mission not to be easy for you and, given your last trip to Earth, he will want to ensure the same mistakes aren't going to happen again. Which means, you—like this—isn't going to work. You agree to go to Earth with a glamor—crippled and ugly so no man or woman will want you. Problem solved." He lifts his hand, waving it in my direction.

I stare back at him in silence. I appreciate his idea—it's a good one that the Devil will most likely agree to. The Devil will enjoy sending me to Earth in the body of a shriveled old man and still expect me to gain the favor of a beautiful young woman.

It isn't the *worst* plan. Being a male of any age would be better than being stuck as a crow, but I can't help the sinking feeling of doubt weighing heavily on my shoulders. I'm not planning on seducing the woman but I don't enjoy the idea of deceiving her as the archangel had.

I glance across the green garden, staring blankly at the many palace windows. "This feels like an ask-for-forgiveness type of situation." Looking back to meet Van's eyes, I see his thoughts starkly etched on his face before he even speaks.

"If you wish to be stupid, why force me to witness?" He arches his eyebrow and sends a brutal, unforgiving stare, which almost seems to penetrate my soul.

"Fine! I will plead my case and hope he believes I deserve a second chance." With a shudder, I start to take on my lesser form, stopping the shift temporarily so I can manage the last word in this imaginary fight, "Anyway, you're about as stupid as it gets, you giant fuck." Loud crow cackles fill the garden as I fly high into the sky, darting towards the palace hall.

I'm sure I will pay for that comment, but Van's look of pure rage is worth it.

The Devil's chamber is ever-changing. One day, it could resemble something from medieval times. The next day, it could be like walking into a modernized boardroom.

Most assume that the ever-changing scenery is random—but I know better. I know that the interior redecorating is actually a deeper insight into the Devil's moods.

Today's a good day. High arching ceilings hold large chandeliers of glowing candles. Brick and stone cover most of the walls and large metal beams give the illusion of there being an exposed structure. It reminds me of what the old Viking halls used to look like.

The Devil has always been one to romanticize various aspects of human history and not one to shy away from the dramatics.

I'm not sure why this design reflects his happiness, but I'm not in the mood to question it. All I can hope is that his good mood will work in my favor today.

"Lord Crow!" A boisterous voice booms through the open space as we enter through the door, our boots thumping against the rock floor.

"Sire," Van and I echo in perfect unison, our slight bows a mark of respect. I can feel the tension radiating off of Van's body but he thankfully remains quiet.

"Corvus and his trusty sidekick. To what do I owe the pleasure?" The Devil beseeches from a large chair that sits in front of a burning fire pit.

The small glow of the fire illuminates his relaxed form. He's reclined in the chair with a leg hiked up over one armrest, as if he hasn't a care in the world. A dark, scruffy beard covers his face but it doesn't distract from his piercing amber eyes. They're an odd color by human standards; gold and completely unnatural, seeming to gaze directly into the parts of you that are covered in shadows.

A hog slowly rotates on a spit above the fire but the lack of smell suggests that it's just a part of the illusions. If humans knew that the Devil—and even some powerful demons—were capable of this kind of magic, they'd be trying to figure out how to monetize Hell at the first opportunity.

"A favor, Sire," I state plainly.

"A favor?" The Devil's eyes gleam. "Now, this is interesting! Greta dear, bring the wine."

A couple of snaps of the Devil's finger later and we could hear the muffled clanking of glass. A moment later, an older woman strides into the room, carrying a tray of wine-filled chalices. She appears to be slightly older, with salt and pepper hair and a gentle yet wrinkled face. It could be another illusion, as aging in this realm is wildly inconsistent. Her hair barely reaches her shoulders and her black dress shuffles across the floor as she makes her way to us.

Her grip on the tray is steady as she hands each of us a glass. I notice that she serves Van first, then me, and then finally the Devil. He doesn't seem to mind and sips the wine without comment.

I bring the wine to my lips and let the liquid glide across my tongue and down my throat. The rich flavor hits my senses and I close my eyes in appreciation of its decadence. A good wine for breakfast—now this is more my style.

When I open my eyes, the entire chamber has changed. Long gone is the large, open space. I look around the new room, and notice that it resembles a small office. Shelves of books line two of the walls; on the other two, artistic depictions of the Devil are showcased in brilliant color. Some seem to be done by an expert hand but others are so terrible they appear to have been done by a child.

I realize then, that most of them look as though they've been drawn by humans, showcasing a large red body, dark black horns and a spiked tail. Nearly every painting also has some form of pitchfork, too.

I decide then that he must hang them as a joke; only a few accurately portray him. His tall, lean body, scruffy brown hair, and bright amber eyes. They're encroaching even in painted form.

"Sit," he commands, tone leaving no room for argument. Van and I struggle to fit our large bodies into the unnecessarily small wooden chairs provided. On the other hand, the Devil flops gracelessly into an oversized round chair, a few pillows dropping onto the floor. He brushes a hand through his hair, making an even bigger mess of the dark strands.

"So, a favor you ask of me? Do tell," he practically purrs and a shiver runs down my spine. "I hope it's not because you changed your mind about this little mission I have you on?"

"No, Sire, the mission is still on," I begin, but the words catch in my throat. How or where do I even start?

Deciding that honesty is my best route, I take a deep breath and tell the Devil almost everything. I tell him my thoughts on Valencia, how the angel beat me to the punch, and about his deceitful actions. I tell him of Valencia's injuries and how I helped her when she lay helpless on the mountain.

I don't, however, tell him about the feelings she sparked inside me. Not how beautiful she is, nor how her smart mouth made me want to feel her sharp bite. I absolutely don't tell him how visions of her naked body underneath mine kept me up all night with my cock in my hand and a moan on my lips. I keep those details to myself because the last person you entrust your innermost feelings to is the Devil, himself.

With a subtle shake of my head, I attempt to dismiss the thoughts that sneak up on me. My mind must enjoy playing tricks on me at the worst time, blending reality with fantasy.

"I see." The Devil's deep voice is soft and muffled by the hand he drags over his face, and he keeps me waiting a moment longer.

In the silence, I wonder if being honest was the right decision. I'm an expert at lying but I couldn't bring myself lie about what happened on that mountain.

While I'm not on my knees right now, I'm no less vulnerable than if I were. The last demon who failed one of the Devil's missions went into the Erebus River and never came out.

"I commend you for your honesty, Corvus," The Devil says and directs his intense stare at me. "But I cannot so easily forget your past transgressions. On the one hand, I recognize your loyalty and how you've stood by me without fail all these years since then...but, on the other," he shifts his eyes to Van before quickly trapping me back in his endless stare. "I do not know whether you are ready for *favors*."

I take a breath. "Sire, with respect, the incident you speak of occurred 200 years ago. I have not failed you since, and I will not do so now." I knew it would come up, but it irks me all the same.

This is why I can't fail this mission. One mistake cost me a 200-year punishment; I can't imagine what the Devil will do if I piss him off now.

"And you," The Devil shifts his soulless gaze to Van. "What are your thoughts?"

Van's turns his gaze on me, refusing to meet the Devil's stare. I can practically see his tension—like a visible aura, rolling from him in waves.

I initially asked him to accompany me because I appreciated his expertise, but now I realize it was selfish of me to bring him here.

Van despises the Devil—possibly even more than I do. Van isn't like the other Fae. He has a dark side the Devil has taken advantage of one too many times. The Devil's no stranger to using Van for his particular skill set or for using his weaknesses against him. It's widely known that Van cannot lie, nor is he one to mislead or deceive. It seems to be the Devil's tactic now.

"I believe he is ready for such a task. He has proven his worth and is a formidable ally and warrior. You could do much worse." Van's voice is near monotonous. "But he has a weakness for beautiful women. This should be easy for him, so long as he keeps his personal desires in check."

I inwardly cringe, Van's honesty isn't misplaced, yet it stings all the same. I'm grateful that Van was able to not include the thoughts I shared with him—how Valencia captivated me. The Devil may want her to join his side but that doesn't mean I need to hand her to him on a silver platter.

"Ah, Van, who doesn't have that weakness? Beauty is my favorite sin," the wicked smile on the Devil's face twists my stomach into a tight knot.

"I have heard your case, Lord Crow. And I'm still struggling with the decision. If there were only something that could sway me to your cause."

And here is where I yet again sell my soul to the Devil.

"In exchange for your gracious permission to allow me to go to Earth in this form," I begin, "I will bargain with you."

The Devil leans forward, eyes gleaming.

"I will complete this mission; the woman will join our side. And, I will refrain from any indulgences with random females while topside. If I fail, I will pledge 100 years to the Death Pit."

Van's sharp intake of breath further proves the insanity of my offer. It isn't the plan we talked about outside. It's risky, but I refuse to deceive Valencia further.

And, I admit, a tiny part of me wants her to see me as I am.

"Hmm, very interesting indeed." The Devil leans back in his oversized chair once again, and contemplates my bargain. He would be crazy to refuse the offer, but there isn't a soul in this universe that would question his sanity.

The Death Pit is nearly a perfect replica of the Roman Colosseum, but the sands in Hell remain stained in the blood of thousands. Failing this mission would now mean a one-way ticket to the Death Pit as a gladiator slave. Sure, losing a lord of Hell would cause the Devil some issues, but the profit would be worth it. Simply setting foot in the dreaded sand would send the Hellspawn into a frenzy, and nothing bolsters the Devil's coffers like fights to the death.

Though Van's face is near expressionless, I know him well enough to see his shock clearly. Thankfully, he remains quiet and doesn't demand that I take the deal back. He and I are both aware of the consequences Valencia will face if she attracts even more of the Devil's attention, so I can only hope he turns his gaze to me, instead. Who better to deal with the Devil than a lord of Hell?

"A most agreeable bargain!" The Devil finally chirps. "But. one condition. You have proven your worth to me over the years, Corvus—for that, I am willing to reward you."

I nearly slump in my chair, the relief washing through me even while I'm filled with a sense of trepidation at his reward. A gift from the Devil is sure to be as painful as it is beneficial.

"I will allow you any indulgence you desire. You can fuck your way through the entire human population on Earth for all I care; have your fill." He says with a mischievous smirk and I suck in a breath. "But Corvus? The woman, Valencia, is off-limits to you. You get pleasure from her before you complete the mission, and your 100 years will start before the cum can finish shooting out of your cock. *That* is the bargain for this favor you ask of me. Now, leave me."

Pain sears through my back as the evidence of our bargain burns itself into my skin and I force myself to grit my teeth through the pain.

Van and I both stand and bow briefly, then wordlessly leave the room.

My insides tremble with a mixture of rage and remorse. I wasn't planning on seducing Valencia to our side, but what creature doesn't crave something more when they're told they cannot have it? Regardless, no woman is worth 100 years of grueling servitude.

As we exit the palace and enter the gardens once more, I sigh, feeling a weight settle on my shoulders once again. I got what I wanted, yet I can't make myself feel happy about it.

Beside me, Van shifts his body in my direction, no doubt wanting to scold me for making such a foolish deal.

Not wanting to hear the worry in his voice, I swiftly shift to my crow form and glide into the threads of shadows that separate Hell and Earth.

As I make my way to the humans' realm, I contemplate my next steps. I try not to think of the Devil, his shitty rules, or Van—and the apparent concern etched into his entire being—and I try to avoid the sinking feeling in my gut.

I try my hardest not to think about the fact that all three of us know that my biggest battle to come will be keeping the head in my pants from ruining the mission before it even begins.

Chapter 8
Valencia

With a swish, the hospital doors slide open and the cool morning air rushes in through the open gap, sending a shiver down my back. The parking lot is mostly empty, with only a few cars parked close to the entryway. I spot my beat-up 4Runner a few spaces back and suck in a breath at the surrounding scenery.

A giant red fire truck sits just to the left of my car and nearly everyone on our fire team stands next to it, waving and smiling obnoxiously.

"I'm going to kill him," I say quietly.

"Now, now, is that any way to thank a friend?" Parker says as he sidles up beside me.

"Because I'm *so* thankful you made me spend the night in the fucking hospital," I mutter angrily beneath my breath.

I give him a warning look as we make our way over to the small crowd and force my eyebrows down in an attempt to look angry, but the boyish grin on Parker's face prevents me from accomplishing the look. Instead, I roll my eyes at him and switch my attention to the friends before me.

Despite recent events bringing my mood to an all-time low, I can't help but appreciate everyone showing up. They say the best family to have is the one you get to choose.

"Valencia, so happy to see you up and well," Chief Miller says with a smile. He has light circles under his eyes, which is strange to see on his usually cheerful face. Still, his smile lines are ever-present as he greets me.

"And up and walking!" Greg calls out, his wife clutched to his side.

I smile, making my way around the group, passing out hugs and gratitude like they're gifts from Oprah.

I take a few more minutes to chat with everyone, catching up on the details of my rescue that I missed. Once I've made it around to everyone, I approach Parker, my hand out in front of me.

"Keys." I know he has them, along with the hospital bag that contains my other belongings

"No way, girl," he says. "I'm driving you home. You're in no position to drive."

"Parker, I swear to God—if you don't give me my keys right now, you'll be the one spending the night in the hospital." I pinch the bridge of my nose and take a deep breath, trying to steel myself against the rising tide of fear that all of this has brought to the surface. It's terrifying—the lack of control I had while stranded on the side of Sugarloaf Mountain. Nagging thoughts taunt me with reveries of seeing Dane's angry face, feeling pain consuming my entire being, and once again seeming trapped in my own body.

Parker laughs at the indignant look on my face, not taking my snarky comment personally. I know he means well, and I genuinely attempt to not take my anger out on him, but the events of the last 24 hours have weighed heavily on my patience.

"Listen, Val, you didn't see yourself. You don't know how awful it was to see you all bloody and bruised." He takes a deep breath and lays a large hand on my right shoulder, avoiding the newly stitched gash. "I just. . ." Parker takes a deep breath in, and then starts again, "I just want to take care of my best friend. Please let me."

I sigh and concede, nod once, and wave goodbye to the crew as I make my way to the passenger side of my 4Runner.

I can't blame him. If the roles were reversed and I had to rescue him from a near-death experience, I would be no less of a mother hen.

"Not to add more to your plate, but I looked into Dane," Parker says plainly as I close my door.

"Why?" I ask, brows furrowed.

The events of the accident sit in my mind, replaying over and over again on a loop. I remember twisting my ankle. I remember Dane grabbing my arm and then losing my balance and falling off the side of the trail. I know hitting the tree knocked me out for a bit, though I'm not sure how long. There's a dark spot in my memory during that time. I had woken up thinking I'd find Dane frantically searching for a way to save me but, instead, I was met with a nosy crow that seemed far too intelligent.

"Because we show up—and you're alone, hanging off the side of a tree ready to fall the rest of the way down the mountain. And no Dane in sight." Parker deadpans. "Of course I looked into him. I'm pretty sure the Chief has already sent in a report to CAFA as well as the police department."

"Oh great." I mumble, my head pounding with too many unanswered questions. "We don't know that he was involved,"

"We don't know that he wasn't, either," Parker responds, his blue eyes piercing mine before looking back at the road in front of us.

I don't speak, unsure if there's anything I could say that would make this situation less of a mind fuck.

The drive back to the firehouse is slow and uneventful. I spend the hour recalling every detail of the day with Dane, using Parker as a sounding board to speculate on what the hell even happened. Parker listens intently, asking a few questions—but mainly allows me to work through the events, myself.

Despite the effort, I'm no closer to understanding what caused Dane to behave so irrationally.

It takes some effort to recall every moment of the event. My head is still pounding from the minor concussion. I ache. Bruises, cuts, and muscle soreness litter my entire body from head to toe. Thankfully, my right ankle is not broken, though the sprain is severe and will likely bother me for weeks. The gash on my right arm only needed a butterfly stitch. I could feel the strain on my skin as the bandage pulled the two edges back together.

Thankfully, the doctor cleared me this morning to head home, though he urged me to take a couple of days off to rest and recover. I heal fast, so I'm sure that's all I'll need.

Once back in the comforts of my own room, I crash face-first into my small bed. It's not the most luxurious piece of furniture, but anything beats the hospital bed I spent the previous night in.

I kick off my boots and shimmy out of my sweats. Parker was kind enough to bring me a change of clothes to the hospital, so I didn't have to leave in a back-tied gown this morning. Due to the absolute wreckage of my clothes from the fall, they now live inside a random hospital trash can.

I feel exhaustion creeping through my body and mind; sleep is not far off. Thankfully, I have plenty of time off, so I plan to sleep for the next few days. I snuggle my way under the covers and drift off quickly.

By the time I wake up next, the sun has set low in the sky, and I've slept most of the day away. I grab my phone off the nightstand and check the few notifications I have.

Today 10:52 AM
Chief Miller

> Glad to have you back in house! Take whatever time you need to recover. Ruby Valley PD has been unable to locate Dane Moore. CAFA is unaware of the situation. We'll get to the bottom of it. Let's meet when you're ready.

"Oh gee, thanks boss—a meeting. Just what I wanted." I grumble softly to myself.

Today at 11:01 AM
Parker Rand

> Glad you're home! I called CAFA to check into the Dane guy, and the lady I talked to has never heard of him. Big surprise.

> We'll keep digging, figure out who this asshole really is.

Today at 4:05 PM
Parker Rand

> So how about some rock climbing?

> Too soon?

"Jesus, Parker." I quickly go through the rest of my notifications. There are a few more 'get well' texts from the crew and a couple more random emails that I don't bother looking into.

I toss the phone back onto the side table and lay back on my pillow. My head is still pounding and, judging by the loud gurgling coming from my stomach, it's well past time for some food.

I get out of bed with an audible groan and head to my dresser, throwing on an oversized band shirt and a pair of flannel shorts.

Although all the guys who live here full time have seen me in much less, and this outfit is far more modest than my typical swimsuit, I still prefer not to push the fact that I'm the only girl. Being the only woman in a house full of men has many perks, but being able to walk around naked wasn't one of them.

Not everyone in the crew lived at the firehouse full time; Greg stayed home with his wife most of the time. But, for the rest of us, with no families and nowhere else to go, the Ruby Valley Wildland Fire Station was our home.

I count my stars as I find the station to be blissfully quiet as I make my way to the kitchen. It's early evening; the clock on the stove reads 7:32 PM. Looking through the window above the sink, deep shades of purple and blue linger in the sky as the sun makes its final descent.

Where would I be right now if that crow hadn't been there to help me? Perhaps it makes me crazy to admit it, but I most likely wouldn't be here if it weren't for that small bird, but I still can't wrap my mind around its behavior without feeling like I'm going insane.

What happened yesterday was beyond the laws of nature and, if I focused hard enough on it, I would have to question everything I know.

Because having an existential crisis on top of my injuries is not on my agenda for today, I stop dwelling on the unknowns, throw a quick sandwich together, toss some chips on a plate, and return to my room. I shut my bedroom door softly behind me, not wanting to disturb the unusual peace, and flick the deadbolt to its locked position.

I'm sitting on my bed, already digging into my meal, when I hear a small sound.

Click Click

I look to the window on my left, but don't see anything unusual. The sun has finally set, so the dim light from my lamp glares across the glass. I decide it was most likely my imagination and turn back to my food.

I bite into the sandwich and savor its flavor; it's the perfect meal to erase the bland aftertaste of my breakfast this morning in the hospital.

Click Click Click

Irritated by the interruption, I set my plate down and limp to the window. I try to convince myself that it is just a branch on the window or something equally trivial, but my heart begins to race all the same.

"Oh!" I lurch away from the window as movement outside catches me off guard. I feel pain shoot through my leg as I forget myself and put a little too much weight on my right ankle.

At first, it's impossible to understand what I'm looking at, so I step closer to the window and squint at the perched object on my windowsill.

A small, black crow stares back at me, its head tilted to one side as though it can't understand my jumpiness.

"You've got to be kidding me," I mutter to myself and reach to unlock the window. "What am I, Snow White?" As I slide the window up, the crow remains seated, not leaving the windowsill as I lean closer.

"There's no way you're the same bird," I say, yet reach out slowly to stroke the back of my knuckle down its belly. When it doesn't hop away, I attempt another stroke, smiling at the wonder of the situation.

Each time I pet the bird, its wings ruffle—the feathers flicking in and out again and again.

I've heard that crows are intelligent and can even recognize friendly humans versus bad ones but this takes it to a whole new level. For this to be the same crow from on the mountain, it would've had to follow me to the hospital last night and again to the firehouse this morning.

I think I'd be more willing to believe I actually *was* Snow White.

The crow clacks its beak twice, then proceeds to tap its beak against the plastic windowsill.

Click Click

"So, it *was* you making that noise."

Dark black wings spread wide before tucking back close to its small body.

"I don't have any trail mix for you, Little Bird, but I may have something even better." I turn my back on the window and reach to grab the plate off my nightstand. Only a few potato chips have been left uneaten.

Grabbing a chip, I carry it back to the window and smile as the crow continues to sit, near motionless on the window ledge despite having easy access into my room.

"Here you go, as promised." I reach out and hover the chip close to its small black beak.

The crow snatches the chip from me and quickly gobbles down the salty snack. Once finished, it hops back towards me and tilts its head in what I can only assume is impatience.

I spend the next 10 minutes slowly feeding the bird the rest of my food, speaking absentmindedly as I do; the memories rush out of me in a shaky rambled mess.

"Can you even believe that? I mean, if you're the same crow, then you were there."

I lay the now empty plate on my side table and reach out, stroking my knuckles down the bird's belly for a final time, enjoying the feel of the soft feathers against my skin.

"It's time for bed, Little Bird," I say with a soft laugh. "Maybe one day you'll bring me a prize instead of stealing all my snacks."

With a smile, I slowly shut the window, lock it, and—like a weirdo—offer an awkward wave to my new friend.

"It's official; I'm going crazy," I mumble to myself.

I head to my bathroom, intentionally avoiding any reflective surfaces to avoid seeing what a wreck my face is, and grab a bottle of ibuprofen from one of the drawers. I take a few and hope that they're enough to soothe all the aches and pains.

In bed once again, I grab my phone and shoot a text to Parker.

Today 8:10 PM

Me

> Hey, thanks again for everything. You're the best.

I take a few minutes to contemplate what I want to say next.

Today 8:13 PM

Me

> Let's get together tomorrow. There's something weird going on here. Dane played his part well, went through all the right channels, or else Chief wouldn't have had him here. Gonna crash for the night. Cya tomorrow!

A beeping sound fills the quiet room a couple minutes later, and I look to see Parker's response.

Today at 8:15 PM
Parker Rand

> Any time for my BESTFRIEND4EVA. But really, you owe me. So you can pay for dinner this week

> Let's bring this asshole down *skull emoji*

> Nighty Night, Val *sheep emoji*

I can't help but laugh out loud at the messages as they come through. Parker is my best friend for this exact reason—despite all the shit that's happened recently, he still manages to bring a smile to my face.

***

"How was the meeting with the Chief?" Parker asks as I slide into a chair. The conference room is quiet. Everyone else is outside enjoying the weather or relaxing in their rooms, leaving just Parker and I behind.

"Fine," I say. "Basically, all he said is that Ruby Valley PD is looking for Dane as *a person of interest.* He also wanted to check and make sure that I'm mentally fit to return to work—offered me an early release from the fire season if I want. I know it's October already and fire season is just about over, but I reminded him that it's not like I'd leave the station, and I'm mentally okay, so I don't see a reason *not* to jump back into work," I continue. "Everything is sore but I'll have a couple more days to recover and that's all I'll need."

I fiddle with a few of the papers lying scattered on the table. I am okay mentally, so at least that's not a lie, but I'm so confused—my mind hasn't had a chance to be upset over it all yet.

"Basically, you're skipping out on a month-long vacation because you have nothing better to do with your life?" Parker asks as he continues to organize the papers, though I can't tell what he's planning to do with them yet.

"Ouch, Parks," I roll my eyes. "It's not like you'd be any different."

"Touché sister. Touché," he says with a laugh. "Okay, so here is what I've gathered so far," Parker throws a large stack of papers onto the table before me.

We've not yet formulated a plan, but the first three Parker offered each broke at least a few laws.

I've been quickly learning that revenge is rarely dealt with legally.

I pick my way through a few of the different pages, but nothing sticks out as familiar or recognizable. Most of the files are just random publications that Parker has copied from some online platform.

"Don't take this the wrong way—because I am grateful for your help—but how does any of this pertain to my situation?" I lift a piece of paper—a copy of a front-page news article titled, *Grand Promotion for Dubois City Mayor.* "And how did you even find all of this stuff?"

"Well, when you were taking a nap in the hospital, I was doing some research. I was able to trace this guy all over the country while simultaneously not being able to find anything about him in the process." Parker huffs a frustrated grunt, snagging the paper from my hand and skimming through the article.

"For instance, this article was posted online three months ago and, at first glance, it just seems like a normal small-town publication. A woman was elected mayor and won by a large margin. What threw me off, is why this article would be triggered by my search for Dane, so I looked into the woman a little more."

Parker grabs a different sheet and sets it in front of me. On the page is a headshot of a beautiful woman staring back at me. The image is printed in black and white, but I can still tell she has a natural beauty. She looks older—I'd imagine nearing her 50's—yet her face has remained youthful. Under the photo, there's a text box with some general information.

"Okay, so how do I know. . . Sandra Polanski?" I look up from the woman to Parker's smiling face.

He slaps down another picture, a triumphant look on his face.

"*You* don't."

A bubble of air gets stuck in my throat painfully as I look at the new image. I was skeptical that Parker could find anything out, so I didn't bother mentally preparing for this moment.

I slowly drag a finger over the printed image. Even though it's a little blurry, I can still clearly make out that it's Dane Moore staring back at me. His handsome face smiles at the camera; one happy-looking Sandra Polanski stood under his arm. Behind them, a pretty church shines brightly in the sun.

"Okay..." I pause. I can't help but wonder, *what now?* So, we've found evidence that Dane is, in fact, a real person and not just a fucked-up figment of my imagination. I can't pretend the cuts and bruises aren't real. Still, it's hard to believe the events actually took place.

Now that I am staring at the face of the man that left me stranded on that mountain, I find myself even more exhausted by the situation.

I take a deep breath and try to inject some confidence into my voice that I don't really feel. "So, all this tells us is that this Dane guy knows some random woman who is the Mayor of a tiny town in nowhere Idaho. I still don't understand how that ties back to me."

I slam the picture onto the table and pinch the bridge of my nose. No amount of ibuprofen has touched the blasting pain in my head that has been constant since I woke up in the hospital.

"This specific situation doesn't connect to you. Actually, none of this stuff does," Parker goes on, undisturbed by my lack of enthusiasm. "I was finding all sorts of things—this dude has been all over the freaking country—yet, every trail I followed had a similar end. A couple hits, then dead. According to this research, he has managed to be all over the country simultaneously. He's either Santa's Little Helper, or this information has been planted online to cover his true identity."

I listen in mute silence as the information washes over me and, as Parker rambles on, pieces start to click into place. Dane *was* different from the typical representative I'd encounter through the organization.

He was too interested in my personal life and not near interested enough in the fire. He seemed to only want to know 'my opinion' on the fire. He didn't even talk to anyone else at the station and any one of us could have provided some great insights into the cause of the fire. We all worked it. At the time, it seemed like a funny comment but, now—with everything that's happened—I feel there may be a more sinister reason he was so interested in me that day.

I absently glance over a few of the other random articles and see that Parker is right. Most were published around the same time, from random dates over the last four months, but they're from all over the country. Dane would have to have a superpower to manage that kind of travel. Not even a little black credit card could surpass the limitations of time zones.

"This is so overwhelming," I murmur and rub my temple. "I don't even know what we would do if we could find him. Maybe we should just leave it."

"No." Parker nearly growls the single word at me and I look up, startled. His face is flat as he looks me directly in the eye. "Absolutely not. This psycho almost *killed* you, an—"

"*Technically*, the fall down the mountain almost killed me," I offer.

"Right, because you're one to talk about technicalities," he teases, then quickly returns to his ranting. "Here's the deal, Val; we're going to need help finding this guy. We need someone who is good at this kind of thing. A private investigator, the police, the Mafia—I don't care. Someone who does this all the time and knows which leads to follow. Otherwise, we will run ourselves in circles—but that doesn't mean we shouldn't try."

I sigh, my heart heavy. I take a few deep breaths, close my eyes and inhale the clean scent of the room.

"I know Parks," I begin. "It's not like I want this guy just out and walking free, able to do this to anyone, but I also don't know whether I want to go on some Wild West quest to find the bad guy. If he ever shows up, we'll be ready—but I don't feel like hunting him down. We wouldn't know what to do if we found him."

He frowns at me. "I get that. I hate that you got hurt and I wasn't there to protect you. I couldn't help you then—but I *can* help you now, and that makes me feel better. I know it's selfish, but I need to do this." Parker's voice cracks as he speaks and something tears through my heart at the sound.

I know that I would feel equally guilty if I were in his shoes, so I can't punish him for it.

"How about this," Parker continues, gathering the splayed papers as he speaks. "You just relax and worry about getting better. I'll continue researching and try to find out more that could help us."

I nod and am silent for a moment before asking; "and CAFA has really never heard of him?" I grab one of the papers lying in front of me, quickly skimming through the article.

"That's what's crazy, the person I talked to stated they never even sent a representative."

I pause and throw my hands up. "That doesn't make any sense! That just leaves us with more questions. The Chief would never send any of us out with someone unless they had proper credentials. Dane couldn't even know who the Chief would pick to work on the case! It was completely random that I was the one out there with him."

My heart is racing as I shove my chair back and start pacing around the room.

I stalk over to the room's only window and glare at the Montana sky. Big wisps of clouds fill the sky, concealing most of the bright blue that Montana is known for, but not even the beautiful view can bring me the peace I desperately need right now. I feel like I'm one awful thing away from having a mental breakdown.

I turn back and take my seat across from Parker. "Parker, what if it wasn't even about me? What if Dane is just some asshole and I was in the wrong place at the wrong time?"

His face is a picture of frustration and remorse. His bright blue eyes hold so much depth; there are no walls or barriers between us. I'm reminded of how lucky I am to have him in my life.

His friendship means the world to me, and I hate seeing the defeat on his face.

"Val, I refuse to not at least *try* and understand what happened to you. You'd do the same—if not worse. We both remember what happened with Jennifer."

Ah, yes. Jennifer. Parker's crazy-ass ex who had a taste for domestic abuse.

Two years ago, I found Parker sporting a broken nose and busted lip, sitting by the fire pit. He had a beer in one hand and an ice pack in the other. We had spoken a few times about Jennifer taking things a little too far—but he always assured me he had things under control.

I remember staring at his beaten face for less than a second. The next moment, a red haze overtook my body and I turned away, not even checking to see whether he was okay. Instead, I went directly to my car. It was a 30-minute drive of listening to all the fucked up shit the devil on my shoulder could come up with.

When I arrived at her apartment, I was so consumed by anger that I kicked her door in—using years of practice to ensure I kicked the spot where I knew the door was weakest, sending the shattered remains bouncing against the wall.

Jennifer had come running at the sound—I'm sure with the intent to lay back into Parker if it were him standing there.

She didn't see the right hook coming. Nor the knee to her stomach—or the elbow to the jaw. She didn't have time to block or defend herself. I attacked without remorse. It didn't matter whether she was at fault for his most recent injuries or not. She was guilty of months' worth of abuse and pain.

I made sure she paid for every single minute of it.

Looking back, I'm able to at least appreciate that I didn't get shot. Or worse.

I chuckle beneath my breath. "Jennifer had it coming."

"You're lucky Chief's lawyer friend got that assault charge off your record!" He laughs softly, shaking his head at me, a slight tilt up of his lips. "But yea, she had it coming."

I had been lucky the Chief not only had his lawyer friend help me out of the assault charge but that I was also allowed to keep my job. This crew was family. All of us hated seeing the pain Parker went through for months.

Snapping back to the present, I glance at the window behind Parker's head. The sky is still full of clouds, the big white puffs floating by ever so slowly.

My mind feels like those clouds, full of air.

"Parker, I love you and appreciate everything you do. Just—" I pause, trying to make the jumbled thoughts in my mind form into words. "Just give me some time to rest and then we can look harder into this."

"Fair enough," he says, "go get some rest. You look like shit."

I flip him the bird as I walk out of the room and make a beeline for my bedroom.

CHAPTER 9
VALENCIA

I JOLT AWAKE. THE fire alarm blares in my room and echoes down the hallway outside my closed door. Between the loud beeping of the alarm and the flashing lights, not even the dead could sleep through dispatch calls.

BEEP! BEEP! BEEP!
"Dispatch. Station 20. Dispatch."
BEEP! BEEP! BEEP!
"Station 20. Fire in Progress. Station 20. Code 17. Fire in Progress."

I scramble from my tiny bed and run to the closet, throwing on a uniform in record time. Plain carbon, fire-resistant pants and top to cover my body from wrist to ankle; a must when fighting blazing wildfires.

I can hear the others begin to noisily gear up in their rooms—the majority also having been woken from sleep. A glance at the clock on the stove as I run through the common room to the garage has me huffing a grunt at the time; it's just past 3 AM. Nothing like a rush of adrenaline to start your morning. I'm thankfully feeling much better after a couple of days off, otherwise getting up and moving would be a problem.

Heading directly for my locker, I yank my fire gear out of the cubby—muscle memory from years of practice taking over. I zone out, the habit of donning my fire gear now second nature. In my periphery, I'm vaguely aware of the others rushing to their designated lockers and gearing up, too.

I'm the first to make it into my gear, and rush to check over my truck and ensure that all of the necessary equipment is stocked and ready to go.

The automated alert blares the message again.

There is an extensive code system—one for any kind of disaster—but, this particular code has my stomach twisting. Code 17. Structure fire. And, not just any structure fire—no, Code 17 is reserved for the very worst.

"What's a Code 17 again?" Tucker asks and I look over, finding him in front of the locker next to me, struggling to attach his bib strap correctly.

A chorus of groans reverberates through the garage. Even though we've all been the new guy at one point in our career, we can't help but harp at their lack of knowledge.

It's never fun being the new guy.

"Structure Fire!" The twins respond in tandem across the garage as they run the checks on their own engine. The twins have the largest tanker in our fleet; it holds the most water and the most equipment. It's the pride and joy of our firehouse—we've dubbed it Engine 1.

My engine, 'Rogue', is far smaller by comparison—it can only hold around a third of the water and a limited selection of medical supplies. What makes it special, however, is its off-road ability. Out here in the mountains, the large tankers aren't always capable of making it to the fire site. That leaves me and my small engine team traipsing throughout the mountains to reach the fires.

"Not just *any* structure fire. A matchbox fire!" Parker explains in a rush as he throws the last of the equipment on Engine 1 and hops in behind the twins, Greg, and Landon.

"What's a—" Tucker starts, but the Chief rushes through the garage towards his Tahoe before he can finish.

"No time, rookie, get in the truck and figure it out on the way! Team, Load up! We're out in 30 seconds!" Chief Miller yells.

His Tahoe holds minimal equipment, and he usually travels alone. As the Chief, he's expected to be first on the scene. Chief Miller is the best of the best, his punctuality and expertise have saved many lives, including members of our very own crew.

Once all the equipment is loaded, everyone piles into their designated truck, and we're off.

"So, Val—what's a matchbox fire?" Tucker asks from across the cab of the truck.

I handle the tanker on the mountain roads easily. We're the only two crew members in this engine, as water or equipment takes up the rest of the space. The location of the fire is a 15-minute drive from the station, which leaves plenty of time for questions.

"Trailer Park fire. One starts, and they just all catch on one by one—kind of like a matchbox." I watch the road closely, following behind the Chief as efficiently as possible. We're headed to Richland Mount Mobile Park, a well-known mobile home neighborhood near town.

"Oh. That actually makes a lot of sense." He laughs softly to himself. "Why didn't I think of that."

"A lot of the stuff you learn early on in fire life barely makes any sense. Don't give up, just keep trying to learn." I say.

I remember what it was like to be young and new to this game. He took a considerable life risk by choosing this profession. The least I can do is try and help him be the best firefighter he can be.

Fire life isn't easy. The numerous dispatch codes, the constant fluctuation of rules and regulations, and the unpredictability of the fires, themselves—Tucker may not have the hang of it yet, but he's determined to learn. That's half of the battle.

Sometimes, you get kids out here, seeking fame and fortune, yet all they find is disappointment and a kick in the ass. This isn't a leisurely profession. Nearly anything can start a fire out here; weather strikes, car accidents, and even poorly planned 'gender reveal' parties can turn into a thousand-acre inferno in a matter of hours.

"What would cause a trailer fire this early?" Tucker asks, thumbing through the procedure book he has sitting open on his lap.

I glance at the time on the dash. 3:27 AM. The witching hour. There are only ever two reasons a fire would start at this time—a storm with hot strikes of lightning can easily cause a fire, but the sky is crystal clear and the stars are shining as brightly as ever, so I rule that option out.

"Well, we can easily rule out the weather," I respond, Tucker nodding eagerly. "That leaves human intervention. My guess? A party probably got out of hand and, instead of calling us in when the fire started to creep out of the pit, they waited until the first house caught fire. By then, it's too late. I'll be surprised if any of the trailers are left standing before the night is over. If we do our job correctly, we will be lucky if there is no loss of life. In situations like this, that's our main priority."

"People. Pets. Possessions." Tucker ticks off his fingers as he speaks, reciting our firehouse motto. It's something every firefighter who walks through our doors learns from day one.

"You got it," I commend, proud of his eagerness to make sure he has the protocol memorized. "You've really impressed everyone this year, not many can make it in this field, but you've always been a great addition to the team, Tucker."

"Thanks, that means a lot. I'm trying—I really am," he says and looks out the window but I can hear the appreciation in his tone.

"What made you want to be a firefighter, anyway?" I ask him to help fill the time. When I ask the question, though, I realize that I really do want to know the answer.

"Well, it's kind of a long story," Tucker smiles over at me but, for the first time, there seems to be a dimness to his eyes. "It's kind of the family business."

"What's the story?" I ask. "We've got a little time." I hate sharing, myself, but if I've learned anything about Tucker in the year he's been with us, it's that he'd rather get something off his chest than hold it in. I envy him for that.

My head holds too many bad memories, and I often find them rivaling each other for attention while driving me closer to madness.

Unlike me, Tucker releases all his bad thoughts and feelings into the world and simply lives his life. His smile can brighten a room and his eyes never withhold the happiness he feels. It truly is contagious, and is one of the reasons he's one of my favorite members of the crew.

"My dad died when I was younger," he starts, continuing to look out of the windshield as we race through the countryside, our emergency trucks the only vehicles on the road in the early morning hour.

I open my mouth to start offering my condolences, but he continues speaking before I can. "I was too young to know him but...old enough to miss him when he was gone. I was troubled. Constantly getting into fights, arguing with my mom at every chance—just being a menace, really. I bottled everything inside until it would explode, hurting everyone around me."

He pauses, as if caught in memories of his past and we sit in silence for a couple of minutes before he starts again. "My mom, bless her, was not able to handle me by herself while constantly battling her own grief. In an attempt to give me an outlet for my anger, she signed me up for a summer youth baseball league," he says and laughs softly to himself. "I hated it. I hated baseball, I hated my teammates, and I especially hated my coach. He was arrogant, strict, and just a downright asshole."

I laugh too, though I don't really understand the humor in the story. Either way, he already seems less tense than he did before, so I don't interrupt.

"I had to spend extra time with Coach Jones because I was so bad. I spent most of the time on the bench, and that only made me angrier. Over time, I started to like the game, though. The game was my way of taking my mind off of everything. It gave me something to do that wasn't destructive or hurtful—my relationship with my Mom got better, too. Everything was going really well; I found a way to cope in baseball and found a friend in Coach Jones. I played for Coach Jones for four years straight and somehow, in that time, he became the father figure I needed in my life. He was an asshole but—only when you deserved it. He was strict, but fair. He was strong enough to parent me when my mom couldn't.

"Once I got into high school, I started playing for the school team. I wanted to get a scholarship for a college team, or even play for the majors. I didn't want to stop seeing Coach Jones, though, so I invited him over to my house to practice one-on-one. I even helped him with his teams over the years while I played in high school. First, it was practices, then it was dinners and then—all of a sudden—my mom and Coach Jones are getting married."

"Oh shit," I mutter, eyes widening as I accidentally interrupt him.

"I know right, I never saw it coming." Tucker shakes his head and smiles tightly. "I should've, though. He was good at that—sneaking into your life, and then—*boom*; you love the guy and can't get rid of him. I was shocked at first, and a little upset. But my mom was happy—happier than she'd been in ten years—and it was Coach Jones. I already loved him as a mentor and friend, so, it wasn't that hard to love him as a stepdad. He's been great to my mom, they've been married three years now."

I nod slowly. "So how does that tie into firefighting?" I ask, not understanding what got him into this field if he was hoping to be a baseball star. "You're only twenty-two, shouldn't you still be in college?"

"I never went. I had an injury playing my senior year and the scouts didn't want to take the risk." Tucker coughs slightly before continuing with a shake of his head. "When my stepdad wasn't coaching youth baseball, he was a volunteer firefighter. His dad and his grandpa were both firefighters, too. When I got injured, I felt lost. I didn't have any other skills—baseball had taken up so many years of my life by that point. One night, at dinner—while I was moping around—my stepdad told me to join the volunteer fire station that he worked with. I would get a free room and board and the chance to try something new. They'd teach me everything and, most importantly, give me a way to move out of a pair of newlywed's house.

"I volunteered the next day." We both laugh this time. "After two years with the volunteer station, I decided I wanted something a little more permanent, so I applied for this position. I'm still somewhat shocked I got the job, but I've loved it since I started. Fighting fires sure isn't playing in the majors, but it's a hell of a lot more exciting."

"Wow," I say, smiling along with him. "I never knew all of that,"

"Yeah, it's not exactly public knowledge—but, not many of us talk about our families here."

It's just an offhanded comment, but it hits me straight in the gut. I blink for a moment, realizing just how many of us on this crew are here because this is all we have. Tucker, at least, has a happy family that he could go back to at any point; they probably miss him when he's gone and worry while he's away. I want to say something—break the awkward silence—but I can't bring myself to share anything about myself with him.

"So, I notice you share a last name with your stepdad?" I ask instead of sharing something of my own.

"Yeah, he asked to adopt me the same time he asked me if he could marry my mom. I was turning 18 in just a few months, so he didn't need to, but he said it was because he wanted me to know I was family to him, too—not just my mom." Tucker grins. "No lie, I cried."

"Shit, I think I'm gonna cry, too" I mutter, jokingly adding the sound of tears in my voice. It is sweet, though, and it does explain why Tucker turned out to be the man he is.

"Like I said, long story. Anyway, what got you into firefighting?" He asks. I can feel his eyes burn into the side of my head.

"It's, uh—a long story, too," is about all I manage to force out. At least my voice doesn't crack—but it drops an octave and I feel like the cabin's gotten ten degrees cooler as the blood in my veins turns to ice.

Tucker starts to ask another question but is cut off by the Chief's voice coming through the radio.

"Chief to House 20. All be aware fire is currently in progress. Engine 1, get started on the fire. Current estimation: 1 building burned, 4 buildings with fire in progress, 7 buildings remaining. Rouge, work on evacuation and setting up water routes if needed. Everyone, be safe out there."

Chief Miller cuts out, and the static of the radio the last thing we hear from his call.

Chapter 10

Valencia

There's no time to contemplate the information as Richland Mount Mobile Park comes into view. Smoke billows over the road and surrounding houses as we round the corner into the parking lot. Cars and people are scattered everywhere and, despite the obnoxious lights and sirens on our vehicles, pedestrians still stand in the way.

The last engine to arrive, I park Rouge in the center of the lot, leaving room for other stations to park their trucks if needed. A few different trucks are here already but I imagine with the nature of the fire, more are bound to show up.

"Tucker, get all the people in the lot to one area and tell them to wait there!" I yell at the rookie, throwing my door open and hopping out. I run to the back of the truck and yank out the two water hoses we store on this truck. After attaching the first to the water tank, I rush to the other and run it towards the nearest hydrant.

Grabbing both hoses, I race them across the lot and strategically place them near the two mobile homes closest to the traveling fire. As the crew works the fire, the hoses will be ready for when they reach this side of the park.

Once I'm happy with the placement, I return to the truck and grab a crowbar and oxygen tank. Our motto is 'people first' and, as there are currently four structures actively on fire, I'll likely need the tank sooner rather than later.

My chest heaves, my breaths heavy as I run toward the Engine 1 crew where I can see three members of the crew battling the fire with two different hoses. From this distance, I can't make out exactly who is who—but that doesn't really matter.

I trust all of the Engine 1 crew with my life, so it gives me a sense of comfort as I near the first building that's actively on fire.

"My *babies!*" A loud screech fills the night air and I turn and startle. An older woman dressed in a long flannel nightgown clutches her face in horror, watching as the building in front of us burns brightly.

"Ma'am! Who's in the house? *Ma'am!*?" I yell as I approach.

I check the woman over, scanning her from head to toe and looking for any sign of injury. I find nothing physical, yet it's clear she's in a panic. I'm unsure she heard me the first time, so I grab her shoulder and try calling out again.

"My babies are in there!" She grips my sleeves tightly—a firm hold for someone her age. "You *must* get them!"

"Are there people in there?" I demand, not wanting to run headfirst into the fire for something material when there could be a person on the edge of life or death in the next house over.

The woman is no help as she continues to yell and ramble the same thing. I glance around us, searching for any sign of someone who can give me more information on this building but it appears it's just us two in the vicinity. I suck in a breath and decide to check the house anyway, since there is no way to confirm what is or isn't still there.

"Rouge entering structure 4, possible victims. Mask on," I yell into the radio on my shoulder, alerting the other crew members of my plan to enter the house.

Thankfully, the fire is currently segregated to the farthest end of the trailer but, as these structures are typically made of the most flammable material known to man, I don't hold out hope that it will stay that way for long.

I kick open the front door and am greeted by clouds of smoke. I look around the first room—what I assume is the living room—and don't notice anything out of the ordinary and no signs of life. I work my way through the house, going from room to room as the fire begins to encroach upon me. My thighs burn as I rush quickly through the small space.

Upon reaching the last room, I spot flames and smoke rolling out from the door's frame to engulf the entire ceiling. The heat forces me to crouch as I come to the final room—what's inside is reserved for nightmares.

I grit my teeth as understanding hits me. This woman was wailing—near hysteria—over a room full of *dolls*. They're everywhere, on every surface, in all shapes and sizes. Most of them are a melted mess but a few are still able to glare at me with a deadly stillness. It's terrifying. And, risking my life for someone else's obsession is *not* how I planned to go.

I crawl back into the hallway, moving as fast as possible, toward the central part of the trailer where there are two exits. A loud bang fills the living room and, to my dismay, a large piece of the ceiling crumples. The next instant, it blocks the end of the hallway and my route out.

The fire roars from floor to ceiling, leaving me trapped in the hall. The tops of the walls curl with the heat, and the remaining ceiling seems to warp in spots.

"Fuck!" I race back the way I came, veering into a small bathroom. I slam the door behind me, hoping it'll offer me a few more minutes to escape.

I remove the crowbar from my belt and begin to rain heavy blows on the window. The glass breaks easily but a loud bang echoes out, making my ears ring. My shoulder wrenches back as the crowbar slams against something solid and my stomach drops.

A large, crisscrossed slab of wrought iron covers the only exit I have left.

A large piece of wood secures the iron bars to the side of the trailer, and no amount of damage I inflict manages to move them by even an inch.

What psychopath has a room full of dolls *and* bars on their windows?

A deep, frustrated growl escapes my lips, and I try to force a calming breath down my throat. I know from experience that the best thing you can do in situations like this is remain calm. Calm thinkers are problem solvers. Panic and stress can get even the most experienced into a lot of trouble.

I'm about to call over the radio for help when I see a dark form rush towards me through the window but, between the darkness outside and the smoke surrounding my mask, I can't determine what it is.

The dark figure stops before the window—and a loud groaning follows.

I mutter a few blessings as I realize that this is likely one of my fire crew here to rescue me. I throw my *full* weight against the bars and the two of us work to quickly tear down the crisscrossing iron bar.

Once it's gone, I prepare myself to jump out the window—my gear preventing me from being as nimble as usual. However, before I can even attempt an exit, two large hands reach in through the window and grab me by my coat. One hand grips the fabric covering my right shoulder and the other reaches over to grasp the material on my back, beside the oxygen tank.

With one swift yank, I'm sailing through the window. I expect a hard landing but am met with strong arms instead. They carry me through the window, dragging my limp body across the yard and a strangled sigh of relief bursts through my lips as the heat recedes.

Then, I stiffen.

In the rush, I assumed another firefighter had come to my rescue—but, with one glance between the arms holding me up and the legs carrying me, I know this is not a firefighter.

My rescuer is in all black—not a stitch of fire-resistant clothing on their large body. Black combat boots eat up space as they stride away from the burning building. I'm still airborne, practically cradled against what feels like the enormous chest of a man.

This thought sends a jolt of electricity thrumming through my body, and my brain is kickstarted back to normal function.

"Put me down!" I holler at him—to no avail. I shift my legs under me and attempt to regain control of my body, but the man seems extremely determined to carry me off to who knows where.

"I said: put, me, *down!*"

Rolling my body around in his arms is difficult, but I eventually get an arm free. Though he has most of my weight held in his arms, I use my now free hand to reach up to forcefully grip his side. I know it's much worse than a simple pinch—and I hear him grunt his response to the pain in seconds.

All of a sudden, the ground is rushing towards my face. I land unceremoniously, my ribs and shoulder taking most of the fall. The sudden impact on the ground sends a harsh bolt of pain throughout my body, reminding me of my recent trip down the side of Sugarloaf Mountain.

"What the fuck!" Each word wheezes out of my body, my lungs struggling for the tiniest bit of air.

I can hear the man muttering to himself, but I can't make out what he says over my own pain-filled groans.

A few days off was *not* long enough to recover fully from my many injuries.

Rolling onto my back, I yank off my mask and get my first real look at my rescuer.

Holy Hell.

This is not a man. This is a monster.

A very *handsome* monster.

If someone had told me this morning that I would be pulled through a window, out of a burning trailer, by the hottest man I've ever seen in my life—I would have set the fire myself.

I'm convinced that this man is the reason the fire started in the first place. Someone this attractive can't walk around without setting the ground on fire as they go.

His hair is so dark it appears black as it lies in a shaggy mess over his forehead. I can tell from here that the sides are shorter than the top, but it's so unruly that it's hard to tell what the style really is. Molten brown eyes stare down at me, his gaze fixed on my face as I lie on the ground at his feet. A scruffy beard covers most of his face, but I can still see the sharp angles that lie beneath.

He towers over me—gripping his side and glaring at me. From this angle, he looks as tall as a skyscraper.

Broad shoulders, thick with muscle, are barely restrained by a black long-sleeve Henley. Black denim pants encase thick legs, and I can only imagine what kind of power he wields with them. The guy is a muscle factory, the bulk of him straining against the clothes he's wearing.

I look him over from eyes to boots once more, internalizing every detail I can manage in such a short amount of time. Even though he most likely just saved my life, I can't help but be extremely irritated that he dropped me.

"Do your muscles have an expiration date or something? Because I'm pretty sure I asked you to 'put me down' not drop me!" I huff in annoyance, the last part coming out in a near growl.

"Do your hands turn into claws? Because I'm pretty sure ladies aren't supposed to scratch like angry little kittens," he rasps without missing a beat. There's a gruffness to his voice like he just spent even more time in the smoky house than I did.

A small laugh escapes me before I can force it down. I'm both shocked at the hilarity of the situation yet still irritated about being manhandled by this barbarian. He reaches a large hand out towards me, clearly reading my intent to stand.

Though I am tempted to smack his hand away, I take the help he offers. It's better to be on even ground than down at his feet.

A flash of arousal flares through me at the thought of being on my knees for a very different reason.

Jeez, I need to get laid. This is twice this week that my mind has gone dirty at just the mere sight of an attractive man. Although, this time, I'm not certain I wouldn't jump off a mountain on purpose for just a *chance* with this particular man. Even in the brief moment of checking him out, I can already tell this is the type of man to ruin you. Mind, body, and soul.

Shaking the strange, lustful thoughts from my mind, I use his hand as leverage to pull myself up. Once stood on my own two feet, I'm reminded that this Neanderthal of a man might have saved my ass just now—but he sure had an issue turning on his listening ears.

"Thanks for the help, Barb." His eyes squint at the name, yet he doesn't question it and I don't explain.

It's not like I'm going to explain that I've nicknamed him Barb because he's acting like a barbarian. I turn to leave, but his alluring voice makes me pause.

"They cleared the other houses and the fire's mostly put out. Just small stuff now. Everyone made it out okay."

He reaches his hand out in the space between us. His knuckles each adorned by a different tattooed symbol, none of which I know. The symbols all bleed down onto the back of his hand before blurring to a mass of intricate black designs that disappear beneath the sleeve at his wrist.

I grasp his hand, my glove providing a protective layer between our skin. Giving it a firm shake, I meet his molten stare once more. He's looking at me with such intensity, that I can feel shivers beginning to crawl up my back.

He lightly squeezes my hand and rasps, "I'm Corvus."

CHAPTER II
VALENCIA

CORVUS STANDS BEFORE ME—HIS hand still gripping mine and eyes roving up and down my body. I stare at him in kind, mentally taking note of every detail that I can.

The fire burns through the remaining debris, its orange glow illuminating part of his face with a radiant glare. Crisp snaps and crackles continue to pop behind me as the trailer dwindles to little more than ashes. The sound shocks me out of my dazed stupor, and I drag my hand out of his grasp.

"Hi," I say. "I'm Valencia. Like I said, thanks for that." I wave my hand at the rubble behind me. "I would've been pissed if I died over some freakin' dolls."

"I imagine there are a few more interesting ways to go." The rasp of his voice is slightly more even now.

Corvus looks at the building over my shoulder, releasing me from his intense gaze. The world finally comes back to me and I realize that, while I've been chatting, the team has most likely been scrambling to finish getting everything cleared up.

I can't quite understand why his presence distracts me so easily. We've just met—there's no logical reason I'm experiencing such an intense reaction. It's not his looks—though he is undeniably handsome—but something else. There's a strange darkness to him that calls to me—gets under my skin. It makes him impossible to ignore.

I shake it off, reminding myself it's just a simple distraction.

"Well, thanks again." I take a step back. "I've gotta help finish up."

"Wait," he snags my wrist before I can turn away completely. "Can I help with anything?"

Anxiety consumes me. The last random man that came into my life sent me down a mountain, nearly to my death. Granted, Corvus pulled me from a burning building, so I guess he should get a point in his favor for that, but I'm scraping the bottom of the barrel if the standard is a man saving me instead of trying to kill me.

In any other situation, I would dismiss the help; even the most honest intentions can cause undue distractions. And this man? His picture is in the dictionary next to the word distraction.

Against my better judgment, I refuse to have this brief moment be our only interaction, no matter how reckless it may be. "Sure. Follow me; we can see what's left of the cleanup."

I head towards the flashing lights of the emergency vehicles. By now, a few of the other fire teams have arrived—I recognize trucks from at least two different local units.

The sound of raised voices grows louder the closer I get. I can't hear Corvus following along, which is odd for a man of his size, but his strong presence raises the hair on the back of my neck so I know he's still there.

"I told you to clamp off that fucking hose! You idiot!"

Twenty yards ahead, a large group of firefighters stand huddled together. Only bits of the conversation can be heard from this distance, but the tension is unmistakable.

"Don't call me an idiot, man. We're a team!" Tucker's voice rings through the early morning with a high note of stress present. I can't see who he's talking to, but I'm already irritated he's talking to my rookie that way.

"Ha! And you're the team MVP. Can't even keep track of a couple hoses!" The man facing Tucker growls.

"I swear I clamped it and moved on to the next truck! You were the last—"

Before Tucker can finish, the man swings for him. Tucker ducks out of the way and barely has time to defend himself from the next swing.

I'm already nearing the group but as soon as I see that first swing I'm kicked into action. The angry dude has swung a fist at Tucker at least twice and, though

Tucker hasn't retaliated, I can see the anger starting to shine on his face, too. Thankfully, their heavy equipment prevents either of them from being a prized fighter.

Fuck, just what we need—a fight between local departments. I can see the headlines now, 'Local Fire Department Defunded: Man With Small Penis To Blame.'

We hadn't seen a fight between firefighters in Ruby Valley but, just a couple of weeks ago, I read that a firefighter in Detroit went to jail for assaulting a fellow firefighter.

I make it to them in a few short steps. The man's entire attention remains on Tucker, so I grab him by the straps of his oxygen tank and yank him back towards me. As he shifts his weight around to counter the pull, I put my left foot behind his and continue to pull him hard. He loses balance in an instant and topples over my leg, landing with a dull thud on his back.

"You," I growl at the man on the ground. It's not some random man from a different department attacking one of my team members; it's Landon.

I feel an all-consuming rage overtake me and anger starts to burn in a fever rush. All I know is that my hatred towards this man is taking over. A crimson trail of blood rushing from a broken nose would look perfect on his stupid face right now.

Has anyone ever told you not to kick a dead horse while it's down? Well, I want to set a fucking grenade off on this stupid jackass.

Any thought beyond attacking leaves me. I clench my fists as another growl escapes before I lunge for him.

"Not so fast, Kitty Cat." Strong arms encircle me and twirl me through the air for the second time tonight.

I fight as hard as I can against Corvus' firm grasp. He's so strong I can barely move beyond kicking my legs wildly. With my arms trapped against my sides, my feet uselessly bounce off his shins.

"Stop fighting me," his gruff voice echoes out, his mouth so close to my ear I can feel his hot breath against the heated skin of my neck.

"No," I snap as I wiggle to get out of his tight grip.

Corvus turns, walking us away from the small crowd. I can still hear raised voices behind me, but they blur together the farther away we get.

"Hey, take me back!" My heart pounds in my chest. I need to get back there and protect Tucker. My instincts beg me to break free. To push through the arms that chain me and get back to where I'm needed. I twist and pull against his tight grip, muscles straining from the force. The grip wrapped around me tightens and I feel the frustration building inside me, turning desperation into rage.

"You can't help him if you're hurt or arrested for assault," he says sharply, but the words barely register. Logic and reason have no place in my might right now.

He continues walking us further away from the group. Lights flash behind us and I can still hear voices but they're too quiet to understand now. We've nearly made it to a dark corner of the trailer park.

"*You're* what's stopping me from helping," I snarl. I know I'm fighting on principle because I'll be damned if I let this heathen manhandle me for fun.

With a final surge, I thrash against his strength. My heels hit his large shins and an arm slips free for just a moment. His grip returns stronger, and I'm hauled further into the dark.

"Stop!" He growls in my ear once more. He drops me to my feet and releases his arms from around me. Before I have a chance to move away, he spins me around to face him once more.

"Stop. Just breathe." The cool timber of Corvus' voice slowly lowers my blood pressure back to normal, and I feel the rage slowly release from my body.

I focus on his face for a brief moment, letting the gravitational pull I feel towards him drag my attention away from everything else. He carries himself so confidently without arrogance. I become hyperaware of his every move, using it as a tool to center me back to the moment, and begin to lose the intensity of the fight.

"I understand you're angry, but ladies should remember to not be feisty little kittens all of the time." There's a humorous note to his voice though I don't see a smile on his face.

The anger surges back through my body with blinding speed.

He watches me intently, and I can see his apprehension clear as day. Different emotions cross his face so fast that I can barely keep track of them, but I notice the doubt easily.

He doesn't trust me, which is smart. He may command attention with the unspoken authority that emanates from him, but I'm determined to match his posture and intensity.

Stepping back, I cross my arms and relax as much of my body as possible. I carefully inspect the back of one of my gloves, not paying a second of attention to Corvus.

"You didn't have to," I state. There's a slight tremor in my hands that I disguise by crossing my arms. I know it puts me in a defensive position, but it helps me remain composed.

His brows pitch down. He knows I'm up to something, yet his curiosity overrides his hesitation. Confusion clouds his tone. "Didn't have to what?"

"Didn't have to stop me; I had it handled," I respond. Still closely inspecting my gloves, I see Corvus start to turn away from me. I hold still as best I can, maintaining a relaxed and carefree posture and ignoring the heat that gathers at the tips of my fingers or the way my heart starts to race.

The devil on my shoulder is trying to take over. It whispers sweet words of demise in my ear, urging me to make a move. It begs for retaliation and the opportunity to burn away some of the vapid energy that's been building since he pulled me from the burning trailer. I don't know what it wants or why it begs for retribution at every slight.

I tamp down the urge to express my frustration physically. Corvus has already saved me from one assault charge, no need to risk another.

I know how to use my words just as easily, even if it isn't as satisfying.

"Is that what you call handled, Kitten?"

I can feel heat rising in my face, my cheeks flushing despite my efforts to stay calm. "I didn't ask for your help," I reply, choosing to ignore his keen observation.

I attempt to step out of his range, but his arms are nearly as long as his legs and he grabs me quickly, making any escape futile. His grip tightens as I try to twist away, and a single spark of fear ignites in my gut. I realize there's a thousand scenarios where he could've hurt me in this dark corner of the park. His commanding presence does nothing to soothe the growing sense of danger I feel. Before the incident with Dane, I would've never worried about being alone with him, but now every moment is drenched in doubt.

My muscles tense, and I prepare for an even bigger fight. He doesn't seem mad, but that doesn't mean he won't retaliate. His anger could be lurking just at the edge—how mine so often does. Why did I even think it was a good idea to argue with him? No matter that there's something that draws me to him, he's just as capable of being dangerous.

Maybe more capable if you consider his size.

I swallow hard, forcing down a lump in my throat. Corvus instantly loosens his grip and, to my utter amazement, a boisterous laugh explodes out of his chest. "Damn you're something else."

I finally step away from him. I can see the laughter shine through his eyes as a small smile takes over his face. Bright white teeth gleam behind full lips. The sound of his laughter somehow softens my worry, making me wonder if I ever really needed to be worried in the first place.

The fever that was coursing through my blood in anger turns into a million little electrical shocks throughout my entire body. It isn't fair for someone to be this attractive, and I'd like to file an official complaint with whoever was in charge of his *Build a Dude* workshop.

Fuck me sideways. I can feel a dull burn starting to grow in my stomach and my clit aches as it pulses. I attempt to squeeze my thighs together for relief, but there are too many thick layers preventing it from helping.

I can't wrap my head around the reaction in the first place. One minute, he makes me so angry I can feel rage burning at my fingertips, the next I'm unsure and worried—then again it jumps to extreme arousal? My thoughts are a jumbled mess of uncertainty and rated-R visions. The way his smile lingers in my thoughts, the sound of his voice echoing in my ears, it all seems so irrational. The magnetism I can't deny—a pull that's as frustrating as it is intoxicating.

I'm supposed to be working, and instead, I'm currently thinking of every old person I know to prevent accidentally ruining the panties I'm wearing by the flood my pussy is attempting to create at the sight of this man in front of me.

His eyes rake up and down my body, leaving an inferno in their wake. I'm unsure if it's my imagination, wishful thinking, or reality, but I swear his pupils dilate as he focuses on my center. I know a heaping pile of protective gear hides the shape of my body, yet his burning gaze feels like the softest caress across every curved line I have.

No matter how bad it ends up being for me, I want his hands, lips, and teeth to discover every inch of my body. I've never been turned on by a man's smile or laugh, but this man paints a sexy picture.

My panties are doomed. *That is it.* I have to walk away before I combust into a walking, talking nymphomaniac.

"You'll do well to remember that this kitten bites." I show him my teeth in a vicious smile as I walk by.

I head back towards the group still gathered around. I swear I hear Corvus mutter something about his dreams behind me, but I pay him no mind.

Despite my ire at his method, his tactic of disarming my anger was oddly effective. The burning rage from moments ago is all but gone and all that remains is a lightness I haven't felt in a long time.

See, we women aren't that hard to please, after all. Give us a nice smile and get our panties wet—and *poof*, problem solved.

"I'm not sure, Chief. Landon was the last to be at the truck, but it's unlike him to make such a simple mistake. And Tucker is young and green, but he's also the best rookie we've seen come through here in years. It's hard to say what really happened." Parker's voice is strong and sure, and I feel a flash of comfort that he's remained unharmed through the craziness of the morning.

"Well, I expect reports by noon sharp. We'll get to the bottom of it either way." Chief Miller turns to leave but stops as he catches my eye. "Valencia, I heard on the radio you went into a structure. All clear?"

His clear blue eyes gaze into me with an assured calmness, which is why he's the Chief. No matter the event, the stress, or the circumstances, he can stay calm and lead our team efficiently. I hate to see him put in this situation. Fighting within a unit usually never has a good outcome.

"A woman was distraught outside one of the buildings. She made a statement that she had babies inside but was too hysterical to clarify. I went in to investigate. Almost got stuck but, thanks to a bystander, managed to get out."

Chief Miller's eyes drift over my shoulder and focus on something behind me. It's unsettling and exhilarating all at once to feel the pull of the man behind me—how I'm able to tell he's there just by the way the hairs on the back of my neck rise.

"You?" He asks my newest shadow.

"Yes, him," I respond before Corvus has the chance. Not that I think he will lie or disagree, I just want one more moment of pretending I wear the pants in this situationship.

"Well, thank you. Val's one of our best, and we appreciate the help." The Chief reaches around me to shake Corvus' hand. "You know, if you're interested, I could get you the contact information for our hiring team. We could use men like you."

I suck in a sharp breath. There is no single spot in this universe where my dignity and this man could survive living in the same space. Although it's selfish of me to hope he declines, I do.

"I appreciate it, but I'm stuck with my current job. I don't think I'd look as good in the uniform, anyway." Corvus responds to Chief Miller, but I can't help feeling like that last statement was directed at me.

Before I can respond, Parker finally pipes up, "Not as good? Dude, I'm pretty sure we could make a whole calendar of you in the uniform."

An awkward silence fills the space as we all pause. Then, all four of us laugh simultaneously.

Leave it to Parker's big mouth to break the tension.

"Folks, good night. Val, Parker, reports from you and the team. Noon, today." Chief Miller pats Parker on the back as he leaves. I do love a man who gets straight to the point.

"Yes, Sir." We both echo in unison as the Chief turns and heads towards his cruiser. He's usually the first to leave the scene, so it's up to Parker and me to finish directing the cleanup crew.

"What in the actual fuck, Val!" Parker turns a disbelieving scowl on me. Before I can get a word out, he continues, "You go into a burning trailer alone? Have you turned into a clown overnight—out here making jokes?"

"I like this guy," I hear Corvus murmur behind me.

"Shut up," I snap at Corvus without looking over my shoulder. He's remained behind me the whole time, completely void of my peripheral vision. "And *me*? What the fuck happened with Landon and Tucker?" I hiss at Parker.

"Nothing new. Landon is the leading idiot of a village of crazy people, and Tucker is a princess in the next Disney movie. You couldn't *create* a freaking fire with those two working together, much less put one out."

"Ugh, we need to get rid of him," I mutter to myself.

"As wonderful as that would be, the team can't really lose anyone. And since the terminator here won't join, I guess we're stuck with the village idiot for now." Parker motions toward Corvus, the laughter clear in his voice.

"Yay," I mutter back. The adrenaline is starting to wear off, and all I'm left with is a sense of exhaustion that I can feel starting to creep in. A couple of days off wasn't nearly long enough to fully recover. "Guess I can live with Landon for now. Might as well make sure everything's all cleaned up so we can head home."

"What about him?"

I want to avoid turning around and looking at what Parker is pointing at. Corvus hasn't moved more than five feet from me in the last 30 minutes.

Despite my earlier apprehension of the man, I know he isn't a harm to me. At least not in the way that would concern Parker.

"I'll take care of him, you go. I'll catch up." Parker doesn't ask. He sends one last look over my shoulder and then turns around and heads back towards the group of firefighters finishing the last of the cleanup.

"You'll take care of me?" Corvus finally comes into view, one eyebrow cocked and his large hands resting on his hips.

I think I become possessed by that crazy nymphomaniac version of myself because I respond, "Like it's hard?"

I mimic his expression and stance, hoping to convey the same confidence level as he does.

His top lip ticks up the slightest bit, as if he's holding back a smile, but he doesn't respond in any way. I stare at him a little longer.

A small part of me wishes I met him under different circumstances but, the arguably more intelligent part of me, knows that it would be for the best if this is where our story ended.

"I've got to go help clean up. Thanks again for the help tonight, you saved my ass. See you around." I wave awkwardly as I turn and leave him behind. He responds quietly, but my brain has already moved on to the various tasks we need to complete before we go, so I don't catch it.

For the first time since I've met him, I no longer feel his cloying presence following me.

I make it to the trucks and help the crew finish up. It isn't until I'm alone in the quiet cab of the truck that my brain finally registers what Corvus said.

See you soon.

Chapter 12
Valencia

I set the envelope holding my debrief of the mobile home fire down on the cluttered desk. Blank manila folders cover almost the entirety of its surface, only a small space for the Chiefs computer, keyboard, and favorite coffee mug is clear.

Chief Miller has his work cut out for him. Not only does he have to read at least 8 different accounts of the same fire but he has to deal with the drama of the fight.

It wouldn't have been an issue if they had just exchanged words; it's a tough job, and everyone experiences high emotions and tense tempers at some point in their career. For some, it's a consistent issue. Keeping a level head is pivotal, but once the adrenaline wears off, it isn't uncommon for the rush of emotions to affect you.

But, it is a big deal that Landon actually took a swing at Tucker, in plain view of multiple agencies and citizens. There is no chance this isn't turning into a whole investigation. Jobs are in jeopardy; even the entire station could be at risk. I put my hands on Landon so, even though it was in defense of Tucker, I could still get in trouble. I guess I have Corvus to thank that my involvement wasn't more severe.

Left to my own devices, I would have likely landed a vicious punch to Landon's nose and then been up for investigation, myself.

"Val, c'mere!" A voice calls out loudly through the station.

I leave the Chief at his desk with a nod and head toward the common room. I'm not even sure the Chief noticed I was there—his aggressive typing clearly consuming his attention. Again, I do not envy his position.

I find Parker, the twins, and Bill huddled around the fireplace on the various couches we had thrown together. None of them match; the fabrics are different, but we all love them immensely. Nothing beats a comfortable couch after spending days in the backwoods fighting fires and coming home to a comfy couch and a good glass of wine.

I flop unceremoniously on the couch next to Bill. Parker sits alone on the couch across from us, but he will undoubtedly start picking on me as soon as I get within his vicinity, and I'm not in the mood to play his brand of games.

The twins sit on opposite ends of the loveseat between our two couches. They look like a flipped mirror of each other—both men have their arms resting on the arm of the sofa, their outside legs hiked up, and their ankles resting atop their knees.

In the beginning, it was nearly impossible to tell the two apart. They both have the same haircut—a mess of chocolatey brown locks—and two sets of mossy green eyes that border on brown but show emerald in the sun. Their boyish faces have a mysterious, unexplainable edge and they regularly wear the same clothes to throw people off—I'd bet my entire salary that they switch places often. Jake and Jack are good men; they're hardworking and cause little drama, mostly sticking to themselves.

"I swear!" Parker loudly exclaims, drawing me from my thoughts. "She said it was as big as a truck!"

Bill scoffs and Jake laughs, but neither says anything.

"Park, that woman was high as a fucking blimp. There's no way anything she said is credible." Jack says, snatching his beer off the coffee table. They're all drinking domestic beer of some sort. I've never been a big beer fan, as it always makes my stomach revolt almost instantly, and the grainy taste never makes up for the pain.

"I'm telling you, boys, Betty Sue saw Big Foot, and I believe her." Parker raises his beer as if saluting Betty Sue and then tosses back the remaining drops, pitching the can in the trash when he's done.

"Val, you wanna beer?" Bill's gruff voice draws my attention to him.

"No thanks. I'd kill for a Dark and Stormy, though." My mouth waters at the thought of my favorite drink—not that it's popular here. Not many know how delicious the ginger beer and Irish whiskey combo can be.

"I know just the woman to help supply your cravings!" Parker jumps up with a clap and skips off towards his room. He rushes back a moment later, phone in hand, typing away. "Okay, we're set! A table is reserved for us at 7. Go shower, you nasty fucks—it's date night!"

"You say that like Ole Joe's has a Michelin Star," Jack grumbles, but unravels himself from the couch, anyway.

Ole Joe's is our local bar. It is one of the only places in a 100-mile radius where you can find food, music, and drinks all in the same place. As a unit, we've all spent plenty of time there. Since Greg married JeanAnne two years ago, no one else has even hinted at settling down, leaving the rest of us a lonely bunch with nothing but each other. Thus, date night was born.

"Well shit, guess you better get your good shirt on then, Bill." I pat Bill's knee as I get up and head to my room to change.

An hour later, we pull into Ole Joe's parking lot. The bar is exactly what you'd expect of a small-town tavern. It's nestled in the heart of Ruby Valley, directly in the center of the town square. The wooden exterior gives off a worn and western charm that instantly puts you at ease. Many take advantage of the rocking chairs on the front porch and the large outdoor patio out back. The railing to the porch even has a hitching post for horses; I've seen a few of the ranch cowboys using it over the years. Two years ago, one of the cowboys passed out in a rocking chair and his horse, Martini, somehow unhooked herself from the hitching post and made it back to the ranch before he ever woke up. No one in this town has let him live it down ever since.

We waltz into the bar, all fresh-faced and clothed in our finest. Ole Joe's is packed tonight—the ambience no longer conducive to a calming night of chatting with friends. Shoulders bump as patrons wait by the bar for drinks. Crowds of people, primarily women, dance on a tiny dance floor shoved into the corner of the large room. Tables are covered in plates of food, filled glasses, and boisterous conversation.

There's wood everywhere, the furniture, the walls, and—hell, even the ceiling is made of it. Peanut shells lay scattered across the concrete floor, masking the stickiness from spilled drinks. Between the small bowls filled with uneaten peanuts on the tables, and the broken shells on the floors, there's a warm nutty aroma to the room. The bar is a magnificent solid slab of oak that Irma swears Joe cut down himself. Its worn surface shines from years of use, thousands of cold drinks, and countless tales told over it. Shelves of stocked bottles stand proudly behind it, lit by a warm amber glow.

The crowd tonight is a mix of locals, like us, a few of the ranch hands that live nearby, and some tourists who seem to be trying to catch some of the wonders the area has to offer before the winter weather rolls in.

We make our way to the back patio area. It's a chilly October evening, but the roaring fire in the pit will make up for the cool fall breeze. It crackles into the night, mixing in with the conversation that fills the air. The smell of smoky wood mixes with those of hearty food and bodies.

We find some open seats that circle the fire pit, and the men light cigars, passing them around the group. I don't partake, choosing to just settle into my chair and bask in the moment. I grab a few peanuts from the small table beside me and, as I snack, I toss the shells onto the concrete patio. Irma urges us to do so, stating the broken shells help shine the concrete and keep away the smell of stale beer that gets spilled accidentally.

Parker graciously bought my first round, which he hands me as he takes the seat at my side. The small table sits between our chairs, putting just a small bit of space between us. He's got a beer bottle in one hand and a ranch-dipped steak fry in the other. The plate of fries now sits on the table next to the peanuts. The smell of them wafts into the air, overpowering the scent of burned wood, and my stomach growls.

I consider stealing a fry, but he's usually pretty protective of his food, so I don't try. Instead, I sip my Dark and Stormy, watching Irma flit around the patio, conversing with patrons and cleaning as she goes. I smile softly as I watch her. She's the epitome of *'don't need no man.'*

Irma's a stout woman—a German immigrant who came to America when she was young. When she made it to this small town, she could barely speak a word of English, but she was a striking beauty. The language barrier didn't deter her suitors, so it wasn't long before she married Joe Thornsone. I only knew Joe for a couple of months before he died but, even in that brief time, I could tell he wasn't a nice man.

Irma was still young enough to maintain her late husband's bar, much to the surrounding area's delight. There wasn't a meal Irma couldn't perfect and a drink she couldn't turn into the best sip you'd ever tasted.

When Joe died, the station helped Irma remodel the bar. We had come around often as a group but, over the years, I tended to make trips here on my own. What started as just a task to help a fellow citizen turned into one of my most cherished friendships.

Metal rattles softly beside me and I turn to look at the small table to my right before gasping in surprise. Sitting perched next to my bowl of peanuts is my buddy, the crow. Dark onyx feathers gleam in the moonlight, the wind slightly ruffling them in the breeze. I'm not sure how, but I know this is my crow.

Bottomless, beady eyes stare deeply into mine. The crow clacks its beak a few times in expectation, never taking its eyes off of mine as the group around us quiets. It hops on the table, twisting its head back and forth a few times before jumping onto my forearm.

I practically feel the crew's shock. I'm still not convinced that this is real and not a figment of my concussed brain's imagination. Writing off the crow's actions when I was alone was easy, but its behavior is glaringly unavoidable with so many witnesses.

"What the...fuck?" Parker murmurs. His mouth hangs open as he stares wide-eyed at the crow.

"Val, don't move. I'm pretty sure it thinks your eyes are edible," Jack mutters from across the pit, his shoulders tense, as though he's afraid to make any sudden moves.

"Got a new pet there, Snow White?" Bill chuckles, he still shoots a couple of unsure glances towards my crow.

I have two options right now; shoo my feathered friend away and mark it up as a freak coincidence or lean into the crazy.

One ticket, please, headed for crazy town.

"Hi, Little Bird," I slowly reach out a hand and stroke my knuckle down the crow's chest. Loud inhales echo around me but I tune them all out, focusing solely on the crow. Its feathers are soft and its tiny heart races beneath my finger.

I steal a large steak fry from Parker's plate and he gives a soft grunt which I ignore. Tearing the fry in half, I take care to check the temperature in the center. We just got our food, but the crisp Montana air worked fast to cool the fry down. Content with the temperature, I hold it out to my friend and the crow clacks its beak twice, snatches the fry from my fingers, and gobbles it whole. The crow tilts its head a few times and puffs it feathers out with a flutter of wings.

"I know, fries are my favorite, too," I chuckle. I reach out again to stroke its belly.

Landon makes his presence known with a loud belch delivered directly over my left shoulder. He flops down into an open chair across the fire pit, effectively ruining the calm moment. In an instant, the crow takes off with a caw and perches above our table on a long branch from a nearby tree. Although I despised Landon's presence, he offers a nice distraction to the *Disney* show Little Bird and I just put on.

"I'm telling you, man, the ladies in there are feeling me! Better get your earmuffs out tonight, boys!" Landon laughs loudly. It's so loud, in fact, that he fails to notice that no one else laughs with him.

Jack is much like me and usually tends to pretend that Landon doesn't exist, so it doesn't come as a shock when he blatantly ignores Landon and speaks to Bill.

"So, do we have everything for next week's open house?" Jack speaks to Bill as if there isn't a whole human sitting between them. I smirk behind my glass, enjoying the scene far too much.

"Oh, I imagine something will come up, but for now, we're good." Bill also doesn't attempt to acknowledge Landon's presence. I wonder if Landon is oblivious or doesn't care what people think of him.

"Something always comes up. Remember the year Greg forgot shredded cheese?" Jake chimes in.

We all burst out laughing. The open house that the Fire Station is putting on next week is a yearly tradition. Each October, our little town holds a town-wide event; Ruby Valley Fall Days. Shops and organizations have open houses for locals and newcomers to meet their town officials and business owners. A few big caterers always come in to feed the town for the event, and some locals pitch in here and there with random dishes. It isn't a Ruby Valley event without Irma's famous giant pretzels and beer cheese.

The station hosts an open house every year during the event and we are all expected to attend. Though it's always nice to get to know the community, this event is pivotal for the station's longevity. A large portion of our yearly budget comes in as donations during the open house.

We had a station full of residents from a local retirement home two years ago. Chief Miller had the grand idea of offering tacos to anyone who came in; everything was running smoothly until we realized there was no shredded cheese. Greg had been in charge of the food that year and he forgot the sacred shredded cheese. The residents were *not* happy. Who knew retired people had such a hard-on for cheese?

"I'm pretty sure Greg keeps spare cheese in his duffle just in case, now," I laugh again, my drink nearly sloshing onto my hand.

"No wonder he smells so bad in the summer," Jack says as he finishes the last of his beer. He unfolds his tall body from his chair and heads to the bar.

"Parker, I expect you to be ready by 10," I give my friend a sharp look.

"I thought it started at noon?" He mutters, scratching his temple.

"Oh, that's for normal people, Honey—and you certainly don't fit in that category."

"Whatever, Val, like I'd let anything keep me from the very important people of our town!" He scowls at me, but I can see humor shining in his eyes.

"AKA, Cougars," Landon whispers but we all clearly hear what he says.

"Hey, I take animal welfare seriously, too!" Parker scoffs and takes off after Jack, clearly hunting for a drink and maybe some nicer company. Most of the guys follow them inside. Thankfully, Landon goes with them. Bill is the only one who remains out by the fire with me.

A cackle sounds above me, serving as my only warning as Little Bird swoops back down to the table beside me. "Hello again, friend. I don't have anything else to offer you."

The crow hops closer to me, and I finally realize there's something in his beak. I can't tell what the object it is beyond the fact that it's shiny. I doubt the bird will give up its possession, but I lay my hand out anyway.

The crow hops closer, stopping when it's nearly standing in my hand, and drops the small trinket in the center of my palm. I expect it to fly away when I pull my hand closer to my face to inspect my new gift, but the crow stays rooted to the table, watching me closely.

I examine the small bauble—a piece of wire bent crookedly, almost like a 'V'. Three tiny beads have been threaded through the wire. One bead is pearly white, and I marvel at its luster. Another bead is as black as the crow's eyes. The last bead looks like a lava rock. Its rough red and black surface is strikingly similar to the stones in the fire pit beside us. The lava bead sits beneath the black bead, with the white one on the opposite side. The tops of the wire curl under, which I imagine helps to prevent the beads from falling off.

I'm shocked. Speechless, really. I turn to Bill, to see if he's seeing what I'm seeing, but his attention is focused on something else, across the patio. The hair on my arms raise and my mouth opens and closes, words escaping me.

I look at the crow who is still perched next to me, patiently watching with its dark gaze.

"Thank you, Little Bird." The crow nods at me in what seems to be a strangely human fashion, then hops closer. He nuzzles his head against my forearm, then flies away without further interaction.

I watch as he goes, quickly disappearing into the darkness of the night, and hold the small gift the rest of the night. Occasionally, I catch myself rubbing my thumb against the rough texture of the lava rock. I eventually put the trinket safely in my pocket.

CHAPTER 13
CORVUS

I SIT ON THE perch of the branch and watch the fire crew from above. Even from outside of the group, you can tell how close they are by how they gravitate towards each other. Perhaps excluding the annoying guy with too much ego, but since everyone else ignored his presence, so did I.

Most of the men have gone back inside to refill their drinks and get away from the cold. It's downright chilly now, enough that even I feel it. I ruffle my feathers, trying to chase as much of the cold away as I can.

I've been watching Valencia since she left the fire at the trailer park earlier this morning. They haven't done much besides fill out some reports for their boss and chill at the Fire Station. I couldn't see much from outside, but it seems as though the day was blissfully boring for them, too.

I wonder if coming here was a good idea. My first meeting with her didn't really go to plan. I had hoped for a more cordial, low-stakes setting considering I came back in the middle of the night but, instead, I get back to Earth to find them racing through the station, a message blaring through their loud PA system. Realizing I wasn't going to get anywhere with her while she was working, I decided to follow and simply observe. I had hoped I'd be able to find something about her that could give me an in—I didn't expect to save her from a burning fire.

Tempers were high and our adrenaline was pumping, so our first interaction feels like a wash to me. I overheard them talking of an open house next week, but I feel like crashing it won't be the best idea, either, considering it's technically a work event.

Right now, she's sitting in a chair—clearly cold—sipping the last watery drops of a drink she finished a while ago. I take a breath and fly to the ground, shifting to my middle form when I'm a couple of feet above its surface and my human feet hit the earth with a soft thud. The crow flies away with a loud caw.

I pause as I realize it didn't fight me so hard this time. Crows on Earth are never usually happy being possessed but this one tolerated it. It felt more like a connection—a companionship. The crow seemed happy to share space with me if it meant being in her proximity.

I make my way around the tall fence and into the bar. It's still crowded—as busy as it was when they first got here over an hour ago. Bodies dance in a dark corner to one side of the room while others pile around a long bar on the other. A few workers race around, filling orders and taking empty glasses and a particularly older woman seems to eye me suspiciously, her dark gaze penetrating. Uncomfortable with the way she's looking at me—as if she knows more than she should—I do my best to avoid her.

She reminds me of the Devil's butler. Old, knows too much, and gives me *that* look when I come into a room.

I sneak through the bodies surrounding the many tables and make my way outside. I recognize a few of Valencia's team but, thankfully, none of them notice me. I find her in the exact same place that I left her but she's curled up in the chair, wrapped in blanket with a steaming cup in her hand.

"You know, the beauty of modern technology offers this thing called electric heat. It's inside, if you're interested," I say and slide into the chair that her friend, Parker, was in earlier. I remembered him from the fire this morning but I didn't recognize the others, besides the idiot who was caught in the fight. I still haven't learned his name, but I don't care enough to ask for it. Her eyes track my movements before widening briefly in recognition.

"I like it out here," she responds softly, taking another sip of her drink. "The fire is warm enough." The sharp tang of whiskey and lemon permeates the air and makes my mouth water.

"Don't you get enough fire at work?" I ask as I think about my time in Hell. Surrounded by death and despair, I definitely don't crave more of it.

"In a way, yes," she chuckles. "But, that kind of fire just takes and takes. All I see is destruction—damage. On the other hand, all that this fire offers is warmth. It's not taking anything from me or anyone else, and I appreciate that. I can happily bask in its nothingness, knowing exactly how much it's capable of." She stares, almost dazedly, into the flames and the orange glow is reflected in her eyes.

I turn and glimpse the flames, both stunned and at a loss for words. My next breath catches in my throat. I still and allow the crackling of the fire be the only thing that breaks the silence between us.

Something about her words made me think she spoke of more than just the fire she faced tonight, and that bothered me. The shadows of her past—and her strength against them—drew me in. It's not like I need a reason to like her. If anything, I probably need to find fewer reasons.

I've seen and experienced so much in my many years alive. Beauty was always easy to find; it could be created, illusioned, or you could simply ignore something when it lacked in it. Strength, on the other hand, couldn't be bought and it cannot be faked.

This woman, with all the shadows that hide behind her eyes, showed more strength in that one comment than I'd seen from some of the scariest demons in Hell. The willingness to face your fears was something to be admired.

"What are you doing here, Corvus?" She asks, snapping me out of my thoughts.

I appreciate the distraction.

It's a good question. A really good question, considering I don't even know the answer, myself. I still haven't figured out why the Devil specifically chose me for this mission over everyone else. The other lords are most likely doing other things for the Devil and, as far as I'm aware, the severity of this mission didn't need one of them to complete it—or else they would've been sent in the first place.

The question rolls around my head constantly, taunting me. I like to consider myself far too important for a mission of simply keeping a human alive. Usually, I'm supposed to kill them. Or possess them—but that makes me feel unstable afterwards, so I tend to avoid those missions.

How do I answer a question I don't know the answer to? With caution, I decide to err as close to the truth as I can. "Well... I was in the right place, at the right time, to save you," *twice*, "and our conversation didn't really go as I planned for it to, so, when I saw you in the bar, I thought I'd remedy that."

She looks at me over the top of her cup, the steam slowly drifting up past her face. "How did you plan for the conversation to go?"

"Maybe with less boxing and more gratitude?" I try to joke but it comes out stiffly. She was so angry with me the last time I saw her; I worry I may be doing more harm than good by speaking with her now.

She's silent for a second before her sparkling laughter fills the otherwise quiet space. A smile lights up her face, chasing away the shadows that hide in the depths of her eyes. The change to her expression made her even more gorgeous, which only managed to spark a sense of frustration in me. A bitter taste fills my mouth as a tormenting blend of desire and exasperation at our predicament burns in my chest.

My attraction to her isn't the only problem, anymore. Feeling this way—knowing I can't have her, that she's off limits—makes everything worse. Something dark inside me becomes restless with a hunger and I know it will never be sated.

The best thing I can do, for the both of us, is find some random human in this bar and curb the desire that threatens to consume me. She's a tantalizing glimpse of a brightness I could never have. And, maybe that's why I want her so badly. I've been attracted to her from the beginning but everything feels amplified now. Maybe, all along, I've only wanted her this badly because I can't have her.

I refuse to believe it's anything else.

"Corvus?" Valencia's voice once again drags me out of my tumultuous thoughts. I've missed what she's said—was too caught up in her laughter.

"Yeah?"

She smirks at me. "You party too hard last night?" she asks over the top of her cup.

My brows pinch in confusion. "Uhm, no?"

She just shrugs her shoulders, my puzzlement at her question unacknowledged. "I just figured there was a party last night that caused the trailer park fire. I figured, since you were there, you either lived there or were at the party."

Oh. That actually makes a lot of sense but, considering I didn't get there until she did, I feel caught in a corner.

"Nah, no party for me—though I'm sure they had a fun one last night." The words bounce across my tongue with a slight burn, but I maintain eye contact the whole time.

"Hmm. So, you live there?" She asks, watching me with her bright blue eyes that seem to miss nothing. My muscles tense as I refrain from squirming under the pressure.

"Uh, yeah. Sort of." Devil take me, that was the worst lie I've ever tried to tell. She doesn't question me further—just nods her head slowly before taking a sip of her drink. I notice the steam no longer drifts from the top of the cup, so I imagine she'll be ready to head inside soon. As little as I want to be around other people, I'll be grateful to get out of the cold. The fire has died down and almost everyone else has gone inside to escape the cold but, curled up in her fuzzy blanket, she doesn't seem too concerned by it.

"So, how is your teammate that got in the fight?" I attempt to direct the conversation away from myself.

Her eyes light up briefly but I can't tell if it's in anger or something else. "He's fine, a couple scrapes—but otherwise, fine. They both had a talk with the Chief. It was determined a *heat of the moment* incident, and didn't deem any need for further action. Bullshit, if you ask me, but—they didn't."

She sets the cup down beside her on the small metal table. It's still got a plate with a few leftover fries and the same bowl of peanuts. They don't look as enticing as they did to me earlier, when I was the crow. Now, it just looks like bar leftovers that I wouldn't touch if I was starving.

Familiars are weird.

"Yeah, I'd imagine I'd be frustrated in that situation, too."

"Thanks for asking, it means a lot. This team is all I have left and I can get a little protective over them. Thanks for pulling me away when you did, I know I took my anger out on you, but I appreciate it—you saved my ass."

More times than you can count, I think to myself.

"It's no problem, I can understand wanting to protect someone you care about." My voice drifts off as memories of protecting Van in a battle many years ago springs to mind. Unwilling to get lost in thought again, I force the thoughts from my head, and try to focus on the woman before me.

What is it about her that draws these feelings out of me, that I've not felt in such a long time?

Is she really so important to the fate of Hell that the Devil had to send one of his lords after her? If she's meaningful enough to warrant his attention, there must be more to her than meets the eye. I guess it's up to me to figure out what that is.

However, as I think, one thing does come to mind. I recall how, when she was on the mountain after Dumah left her, her badly cut arm had healed too fast—for human standards, at least. While she didn't heal as fast as I would have, it was definitely faster than a normal human. Also, she left the mountain with what seemed to be a broken ankle but, she's now walking around as if nothing's wrong. Well, almost, anyway—I noticed she favored it slightly early this morning after the fire incident, but she wasn't treating it as though she'd broken a bone less than a week ago. Surely I would know if she were a demon—unless she were powerful enough to hide it from me, which would take an immense amount of power.

"Have you ever had to protect someone you care about?" She stares into my eyes as she asks, not letting me avoid the question, and I shake myself from my thoughts.

"Too many times to count. My best friend is pretty much a walking hazard where we're from. Not good at making friends, that one." I laugh as I think of all the shit Van has gotten himself into simply by being Fae in the realm of the damned.

He's like a coveted jewel to the demons, his powers outmatching nearly every being in Hell, but his inability to lie making him weak against deceit. The demons love to fuck with him every chance they get. It doesn't help that he's simply *different*, which is never as fun nor easy as everyone makes it out to be. Thankfully, Van doesn't let it get to him, and is unapologetically himself.

I admire him for it.

"God, don't I know how that feels. My best friend, Parker—you met him this morning—he's a walking billboard for chaos. Although, he's great at making friends. Probably *too* great. It gets him into more trouble than good most of the time."

My ears burn with a vengeance as she calls out the Father's name, but I ignore it as best I can, and try to focus on what she's said about her friend, instead.

"Let's hope they never meet, then, as they'll surely cause too much damage when they're together," I say in response, a laugh in my throat.

"*Or*, I say we do let them meet—and they can take care of each other. Then, we're free from being their babysitters." She laughs as well, surely envisioning the trouble our best friends would get into if they were together.

"What would we do with all our free time, then?" I mean it as an innocent question—I swear I do. As soon as the words leave my mouth, so does the innocence of the statement. Her gaze is rooted to mine, the shadows finding my center.

With that magnetic pull of hers, all thoughts leave my mind. *I'm Fucked.*

It was somewhat easy to ignore the emotions she stirred in me before, when I barely knew her, but the more I learn, the more her brightness dashes away the shadows inside me, pulling me towards her despite all logic and reason.

We stare at each other in silence a little while longer, neither of us willing to speak what we're both surely thinking. I may have grown accustomed to darkness, but the light she offers is addicting. Just as I start to say something—anything—to drive us closer together, the shrill sound of her ringing phone pierces the moment.

"Sorry, hold on." She answers the phone, speaking briefly to Parker on the other end about leaving. They're ready to go and are waiting for her inside the bar. He mentions that he saw her with me and didn't want to interrupt.

"Well, I've got to go, but it was good talking with you, Corvus. Thanks again for everything," she says as she stands and begins to fold the blanket.

"Wait," I rush out, though I'm not sure what I want to say. We both freeze, the moment extending into what feels like an eternity. As irritated as I am, I feel saved—in a way. There's nothing more dangerous than pursuing a woman that the Devil strictly told me to stay away from. I just hope I can stay strong until this mission is over. "What if I want to see you again?"

She looks at me closely—I'm sure silently weighing everything she knows about me. I'm not certain what meeting again would even accomplish, but it at least gives me another opportunity to see her and figure out what all of this is about.

It's definitely *not* because I just want to see her again.

"Next week, the station is hosting an open house during the festival. It's on the itinerary; stop by anytime." She nods her head at me and leaves.

As I contemplate my next move, I start to wonder if we're actually playing chess with all this back and forth. What move am I on now?

How many moves do I have left before it all crumbles in my face?

CHAPTER 14
CORVUS

PEOPLE MILL AROUND THE station in random groupings; there's no order to the event, many things happening simultaneously. Who knew sneaking into a fire station would be so easy? Though I guess it's not really sneaking if I was sort of invited.

A young boy runs past as I head to the open bay area of the station's garage.

I've been here a few times as a crow, but seeing this place with human eyes brings so much more gravity to the situation. This does little to ease my anxiety about the importance of what I'm about to do.

I'm trying my best to remain hopeful, but convincing Valencia to join Hell in a war she knows nothing about seems pretty fucking far-fetched. I'm gambling my freedom on this task, and I've had two conversations with the woman so far, neither of which got me anywhere other than frustrated and more confused than ever.

I want to rub a hand down my face, but people tend to be wary of lone men. My large frame and tattoos are unlikely to help me in that regard, either. My best bet is to look like I belong here before I find Valencia and come to the next step of the plan.

Hopefully, I'll have thought of a plan before I find her.

"And, over here, we have what we call a—"

"FIRETRUCK!" a chorus of young voices respond with gusto. Their shrill yells pierce my ear, and I hurry to the door leading into the station.

As I look around, I notice that it's mostly just people inside, whereas this garage was filled with various emergency vehicles before. I stand off to the side for a second, taking everything in and trying to formulate what I should do next.

"So, how was the honeymoon, man?" I hear a man standing near me ask someone in his group. I don't turn, though, not wanting to draw attention to myself or alert them that I'm listening.

"Amazing," another man gushes, "you've got to check out the Keys. It was beautiful. I swear, all we did was snorkel all week."

"And fuck," someone else coughs, laughing under their breath.

"Hey! That's my brother," a man snaps, irritated.

"I'm sorry Will, but have you *seen* Finn? Harrison, you really outdid yourself."

"Thanks, Finn *is* very handsome. I'm the muscle in our relationship." Who I assume must be Harrison responds with a laugh, his voice deeper.

"Guys, I'm standing right here." There's a light thumping sound behind me, followed by an exaggerated '*ow*'.

"That's it, I'm switching departments," the irritated man groans, his footsteps echoing as he stomps away. The rest of his group just laughs, continuing their conversation. I dial my focus back into the room, scanning through the faces, searching for one I recognize.

A large group of people are standing near the door, but it doesn't appear they're trying to get anywhere. Drawn to the crowd, I step up next to a man standing in the back and look towards the door. The crowd forms a half circle, bodies stacked shoulder to shoulder, starting from the door frame and wrapping in a large arc. In the center of the group, there is a gap of about twenty feet between the wall and the first row of bystanders. Even though I'm behind at least six different people, I can easily see what's happening.

In the middle of the half-circle are two figures, racing. Both people rush to quickly don the protective gear I saw Valencia wearing just a few nights ago. Their movements are so smooth that they appear unnaturally fast—it's clear that they've done this a hundred times—maybe more—before.

It's her. I can tell without seeing even one signifying feature. It could be the way she moves or the confidence in each motion. My chest expands with a large breath, and my nostrils flare. My heart starts to race, and I can feel the skin on my back prickle with anticipation.

"Time! Val wins again!" A middle-aged man says off to the side. I recognize him as one of the firefighters that rescued her off the mountain but don't know his name.

Valencia turns to the person next to her and gives them a thumbs up. Or what seems to be a thumbs up since it's hard to tell with the bulk of her glove-covered hands. The other person rips their helmet off. I don't know his name, either, but I recognize him as a member of their team.

Anger radiates through his body as he shakes Valencia's hand with a jerky stiffness and storms off. Some of the crowd seem to take note of his odd behavior but most are so focused on the stunning woman standing in the middle of the crowd that they don't even register he left. She's so consumed by the people around her that she doesn't notice his dark glare as he walks away. But I do.

Turning back to Valencia, I realize she's removed more of her gear. Her long dark hair sits haphazardly on her shoulder, an absolute mess from the helmet she holds at her side. Her eyes shine brightly, resembling a pair of blue beryl stones. Laugh lines crease the edges of her eyes as she smiles brightly at the people in the crowd, surrounded by curious onlookers—many of which are children.

She hands a young boy her gloves while answering a rapid-fire, myriad of questions that a young girl sends her way.

As the group starts to dwindle, I attempt to mentally prepare myself for what the fuck I am even going to say to this woman. My heart starts racing again, the gravity of the situation weighing heavily.

As Hellspawn, I'm not typically unnerved by the fairer species. Females in Hell are usually out to use you just as much as you want to use them, and long-lasting relationships aren't really a concern for anyone there. So, I have yet to spend much time practicing being charming or even approachable.

The last time I flirted with a woman on Earth was *the nun*. I'd be lying if I didn't admit to feeling excitement when I realized I was defiling His congregation.

The six months that I spent running around Hell being chased by the Devil's Hellbeasts, however, expunged me of any further desire to mess with His children again.

So, it's safe to say my flirting skills are a little rusty. I shake the nervous energy away and step towards her.

A hand grabs my shoulder, stopping me from moving any closer.

I can tell by the firm grip that, whoever this is, they mean to redirect me. Fingers pinch my shoulder tightly and while it's uncomfortable, it irritates me more than moves me in the direction they want. I turn to face the person behind me, but I know who it is before I even see their face. The pungent smell of misogyny leaks out of his pores and douses his aura in a slimy texture.

"Hey man, I remember you," he says. "You pulled that she-devil away from the, uh, altercation the other day."

I can't sense any hostility directed at me and I don't want to take any chances with his poor attitude, but he could be a good starting point for working my way into the station. I need to keep a tight leash on my temper—the last thing I need is to be kicked out of here for finishing what Valencia tried to start at that fire a few mornings ago.

"That's me," I answered, unsure of what else to say.

"She's lucky you saved her ass," he mutters. "I can't stand her."

"She's," I pause, thinking of the best way to describe her without sounding too interested, "something. That's for sure."

I watch Valencia as she shows a young teen how to attach the helmet properly. The way her entire focus is on the kids surrounding her is admirable, and part of me wishes for some of that laser focus, myself, but I refuse to be jealous of a bunch of children.

I draw my attention back to the man and realize he's been speaking the entire time I was looking at Valencia. Thankfully, he's busy taking off his extra gear and isn't aware that I haven't heard a single thing he's said.

As he finally pulls off the last piece of his uniform, he looks at me expectantly. I have no idea what he wants. To prevent myself from looking like an idiot, I stare back at him. I easily tower over him by over a few inches and, though his thin frame has plenty of muscle where needed, he's still a third of my size. I'm demon-fed, and this poor boy has been living off corn.

My gaze has no malice, yet his shoulders stiffen, and the area around us dampens with the scent of his fear. He's now realizing that having my attention may not be the best thing for him.

It takes a brave soul to face me without fear; I still don't understand how my presence didn't affect Valencia. Excitement thrums through my blood as this weak shell of skin and bones that calls itself a man shudders under my full attention.

I'm one of the three lords of Hell—a demon. This human's fear is the smartest thing he has done since being in my presence. The bunny knows when to fear the fox.

A small laugh escapes me, my lips curving in the slightest smile. He flinches, and it takes a lot of control to not laugh in his face. That will not help my quest to get closer to these people.

I quickly breathe through my teeth and look at the door over his shoulder. It leads into the station and, though it's farther away from the real reason I'm here, it will be good to scope the place out.

He relaxes as soon as my gaze is no longer on him, yet his fear only lessens a small amount.

"T—there's food and drinks inside. Uh, can I get you a beer?" His voice is shaky, but he gathers himself by the end of it.

A genuine smile takes over my face. "A beer sounds perfect, friend." We are not friends. But I will gladly use him for intel and an ice-cold beer any day.

At my smile and endearment, he relaxes, most likely mentally excusing any reasons for being afraid of me. I follow him as he heads for the door that leads into the station but, before going inside, I pause and glance at Valencia one last time. She still hasn't noticed my presence—so engrossed in the kids around her.

The crowd has thinned down, giving me a clearer view of her. She's mostly facing away from me, but I glimpse her full lips moving as she explains something to those who remain. My movement must finally catch her eye, because she starts to turn my way. Not ready to face that conversation, I walk the rest of the way into the station, blocking her view of me.

Soon, Kitten. Better sharpen your claws.

I may be ignorant of many things about modern women, but I know anything to do with *this* woman will undoubtedly sting.

The man in front of me is utterly oblivious to my lack of attention, walking and talking as if he's a tour guide. The kitchen and living room are both full of people talking. I notice a few familiar faces, but none pay attention to us as we walk through them.

The kitchen counter is covered in a variety of food. I recognize some, like cookies and raw vegetables, but others are strange to me—which isn't necessarily surprising as the food in Hell is not nearly as appealing or creative. Unfortunately, not many world-class chefs cook for the masses in Hell.

One plate in particular draws my attention. Round balls, that appear to be made of bacon with sticks, cover the dish. I've seen many around the room with sticks on their plates but no bacon balls. I'm tempted to grab one for myself, as the smell makes my mouth water.

"Here," A brown, glass bottle is shoved before my face and I grab it, the cold instantly biting into the skin of my palm. Thankfully, the top is already popped, so I lift the drink to my lips and swallow deeply. I don't even bother to look at the brand; there are so many nowadays and, as soon as the cool liquid hits my tongue, I nearly moan in delight.

There isn't much an ice-cold beer can't fix, and it helps to relieve some of the tension in my neck from dealing with this walking headache.

"Thanks," I tell him, lifting the bottle in a slight salute.

He nods his head as he takes his own sip and quickly scans the room. He's not sure about being alone in my presence, and I bet he's hoping to find some comfort in numbers.

To his delight and my demise, a tall figure approaches us. I sigh internally. I don't think this person is any safer to be around than Valencia, herself.

"Well, hello, boys. What are we cheerzing?" The man standing next to me pierces me with his bright blue gaze. His eyes that are full of suspicion and doubt.

"Parker." He reaches out his hand. I shake it firmly but briefly.

"Corvus," I say back. I know he remembers me from the fire. From his first reaction to me that morning, I'd almost wondered if he was attracted to me. However, based on the feminine scent coming from him, I imagine I'm not really his type.

Parker stares at me, not even acknowledging the man beside us. He's more relaxed, but I can see his fingers tense slightly around his own glass. Though I mostly smell the mix of his scent and whatever woman he's recently had, I can also detect the slightest tinge of fear on him.

I don't tower over Parker as much, and he's got more bulk on him than the other man does but, still, he's no match for my large frame. He smiles at me, but it's not entirely genuine. It's not the smile I've seen him give Valencia. I might even feel a little jealous of him for those smiles, but I refuse to acknowledge the feeling.

"You come for the calendar photoshoot after all?" He says to me as he takes a drink from his glass. I don't miss the way he narrows his eyes, squinting. He tilts his head, as if weighing the evidence of what he sees in me.

It takes me a second to catch on and, once I do, I laugh quietly and shake my head at him. "Nah, I forgot to do my hair and makeup."

He looks at my hair; the dark, messy locks have no pattern and my scruff is bordering on being a full beard. He smiles at me, shaking his head, then lifts his other hand, sweeping his fingers through his own hair. It messes up the longer strands on the top of his head but somehow, he makes it look intentional.

"You know, the ladies really love the scruffy look. Landon here still firmly believes in the clean-cut look, though." He points to the man's clean face and over-styled hair.

So, his name is Landon. *Typical.*

"I have no problems with the ladies. Just ask the twins, their rooms are right next to mine." Landon drinks his beer, a slight smirk on his face. His overconfidence is very telling—no one who brags this much is actually successful with women.

I take a second to look between the two men. I appreciate Landon's ability to give me a reason to get inside the station without suspicion but, I swear, if I have to hear him attempt to brag about anything else, I might accidentally show him my sadistic tendencies.

By the sour look on Parker's face, I imagine he feels the same way. Unfortunately, neither of us can shoo him away without it appearing as blatant disrespect. The last thing I want to do is waste my time while he does nothing but erode good air.

"Ah, there's my girls! I'll see y'all sorry asses later." Landon slams his beer, tossing the empty bottle in the trash. He stalks towards a small group of women, patting a tall blonde on the shoulder as he makes it to them. She turns to him, stepping away slightly so his hand drops from her shoulder.

I imagine they're now in the same boat Parker and I were just in. The women squirm under Landon's attention. The blonde woman slyly shoots glances at Parker, but neither of us makes a move.

"He doesn't have a lick of chance with any of them, and I have it on good authority that the blonde has a thing for redheads."

Parker grins at me, his hair seeming redder now that it's not the middle of the night and he's not wearing a protective helmet.

I can smell a fruity perfume emanating from his skin—it's muted under what I imagine is his natural smell.

"I assume that's what has you smelling like a strawberry?" I ask him, finishing off my own beer.

"Plead the fifth and all that." He holds his hands up in mock surrender. "So, what brings you here? If it's not a chance to start your budding career as a fireman or be a calendar model, surely there's not much else here for you."

"About that," I start but pause.

What do I even say? *Hey, I need to talk to your friend because if she doesn't join Hell in a celestial war, I will have to fight as a gladiator in a vicious arena in Hell for the next 100 years.* No, the truth is not the best tactic. Maybe not the whole truth, at least.

He looks at me in suspicion but waits patiently for me to explain. I hoped he might make it easy and start the conversation, himself. We both know why I'm here—or, he at least suspects what my reasoning is. "I'm here for Valencia."

"No shit," he sneers but doesn't offer anything else.

Okay, the hard way it is.

"I need to talk to her." At this point, we're in an awkward standoff, seeing who can say the least while still getting the point across.

"Need? Sounds important." He snatches a bacon ball off the dish and shoves the whole thing in his mouth. The smell of bacon bursts in the space around us and I swear my stomach audibly growls. I eye the dish briefly but refocus my attention back on him.

"I'd really like to talk with her—get to know her better. That's all," I say. I can tell he doesn't believe me by the slight tensing of his shoulders and the way his lips tip into a small frown.

"You see, I think there's more to it." His bright blue eyes don't leave mine as he reaches for another ball.

"And, if there is, are you her secretary? She's an adult. She can make her own assessment of me." I spin the empty glass bottle in my hand to try and burn some of this nervous energy. His opinion of me doesn't matter but he's important to Valencia, so I tread somewhat carefully. I don't know why I'm even arguing with him, she invited me here so it's not like I couldn't just say that.

Parker eyes me, his brow creasing briefly, but he doesn't respond. Instead, he picks up a third bacon ball and promptly puts it in his mouth. I want to growl in frustration but remain silent, pointedly fixing him in my stare.

Parker shocks me by saying, "You should really try one. They're Val's." He points to the dish with the small stick he pulled out of the ball he just ate.

The conversation change throws me off for a second, but I'm grateful for it. I'm tired of pointlessly going around with him, anyway.

I give in and reach for the plate, grabbing one of the larger balls and pulling out the small stick. Upon closer inspection, it appears to be a ball made entirely of bacon. I bite it in half, not wanting to shove the entire thing in my mouth, and audibly groan as the flavors hit my tongue.

Parker never takes his eyes off me and watches as I shove the second half of the ball in my mouth, licking the tip of my thumb in the process.

What I thought was just a small ball of bacon all crumpled together is actually some savory-flavored filling wrapped in bacon, in the shape of a ball. All of the flavors complement each other, and I'm no longer surprised at how Parker was just inhaling them. I want to finish off the dish, myself, now.

"Addicting, right?" He says as I toss the stick into my empty bottle. I nod, already eying which one I plan to grab next. I reach for it, but Parker's words stop me before I can. "Seriously, man, I can't believe you don't like them! I think *tastes like shit* is a little extra, but okay."

I eye Parker incredulously, my eyebrows pinched in confusion. I start to say something, but I realize the devilish grin is back on his face. That's when it hits. The smell of the bacon is immediately overpowered by her smoky, citrus scent as it engulfs my senses.

"What the fuck? What assholes are you licking that makes you think my bacon-wrapped stuffing balls taste like shit?"

When I shake off my nerves, I turn to face her. She's stood directly to my side, both hands on her hips, as if preparing to go into a serious debate over her little snack. I'm not sure how I even missed her approach.

Her words finally register, and I can't help that some of the blood from my brain starts making its way south. She's asking me what assholes I've been licking. I shamefully imagine laying her out naked on top of this counter, my head between her legs.

I shake the sinful thoughts from my mind. Any other time, I would devour her without hesitation but there's too much confusion and mystery surrounding this situation. The best thing I can do is try to stay away from her until I know more.

"Parker must be confused. I love them," I say and roll my eyes.

"Oh, my bad." He looks at me smugly. I'd love to punch that look off his face, but I just ignore him. Somehow, he manages to irk me just as much as Van does.

"Parker, you're an asshole. And you smell like you got fucked by a rotten strawberry." She jabs him in the stomach as she walks past to grab some bottles from the fridge.

I'm pleasantly surprised when she hands me one, the top already popped off. We each take a sip, eying each other over the tops of our bottles.

"Hey, where's mi—" Parker huffs from the side.

"Get lost, Parks. You," she points to me, "follow me." She doesn't wait to make sure I'm behind her and leaves Parker and I standing there as we watch her turn and walk away.

Parker laughs as she leaves and grabs a beer for himself. He pops the top and takes a quick drink. "My boss will see you now, Sir." He points to where Valencia is still walking away with the most genuine smile he's directed toward me yet.

Clearly, he remembers me asking if he was her secretary.

I follow the feisty woman without wasting time on goodbyes. I'm about to be used as a kitten scratch pad, and I can't wait for the burn.

I follow Valencia out a large, creaking door to what appears to be a private parking lot behind the station where the vehicles are parked.

She walks to the fire truck and sits down on the edge of the front tire. "So, you made it."

I take the briefest moment to let my nerves wash away, swirling the beer in my hand before taking a drink. It's cold—but it's cold outside, as well. The cold October weather really seems to be settling in. I can feel the bitter bite of it in the air through my jacket and hope it doesn't snow soon but, considering we're in Montana, I don't know if I'll get so lucky.

"You did invite me." I retort. "Plus, I needed to talk to you." I roll my shoulders in an attempt to relieve the stiffness.

"Needed? Sounds important." Her response echoes Parker's statement from earlier. They may not be involved romantically, but it's clear that they're close if they think the same way.

"Your life holds a certain significance to me," I say, taking another drink of my beer in hopes of masking my anxiety. I'd love to tell her the truth, but I don't need to send her running for the mountains in fear. I can't risk losing her.

"Meaning, you wouldn't have saved someone else because they're not as *significant*?" She asks, a hint of sarcasm in her tone and glances at me, curiously.

"I wouldn't have," I reply gravely, my expression serious. I try to match her lightheartedness, but the severity of the situation weighs too heavily on my shoulders. I don't know if it's her severe tone or the humorless expression on my face, but her smile falters as she takes me in with a wary scrutiny that has my heart racing.

"There was no way you could've known who was in that building. So, how did you know it was me—if that's the only reason you intervened?" She eyes me suspiciously, the question hanging heavy in the air between us.

Fuck. How am I not even three minutes into this conversation and already failing miserably? I've never been so bad at lying as I am when I'm around her.

"You misunderstand me. I would've helped anyone. It just wouldn't have made them important to me," I explain, my voice coming out with a breathy pitch in my haste to curb her suspicion. I'm not sure it's enough to appease her, but I beg the Devil that it is.

"Hmmm." Valencia takes a long sip of her drink, watching me silently.

I take it as a sign to hurry up and move this conversation along a different route. "I just want to get to know you. You said to come to the open house and thought it would be a good opportunity to introduce myself when you weren't attempting to get yourself killed in a fire or entering a boxing match. Though, the second one I wasn't so sure about."

Her laugh is a glorious sound. It's a different laugh from the one I heard the other night. This one isn't as open, but it draws me in all the same. Her eyes light up and her whole face transforms when she laughs. Normally, she's got a blank expression on her face, as if to hide what emotion she's feeling, but—when she laughs—tiny lines pop up around her eyes and her face takes on a look of joy with a hint of mischief.

It reminds me that, despite everything, she's just a human with no idea about her place in the world.

"We're never too far from a boxing match around here," she laughs, looking towards the door to the station. "We're a rowdy bunch."

"Seems that some are closer than others?" I ask, finishing off my beer. I toss the empty bottle in the can next to me and shove my hands into the front pockets of my pants. It's an awkward fit, but I need to do something with them other than what I really want to do, which is grab a handful of her hair.

She places her bottle on the ground and stands, stepping closer to me without answering my question.

Heat radiates from her and my nostrils flare as her smell invades my senses. She reaches up and plays with the button at my chest. She's focused on what her fingers are doing, and I'm thankful for it because I'm sure I'd get lost in her bright blue gaze.

I feel a sharp breeze flow down my chest as the button on my shirt pops open. The back of her knuckle brushes my skin, sending tiny shocks throughout my chest. I don't move my hands from my pockets but I desperately want to grab her and close the small gap between us.

The chilly Montana air has nothing against the heat of her skin on mine. She softly rubs a small circle on my chest, the contact sending burning heat through my body that just so happens to head straight to my dick.

She's off limits for so many reasons. I know this. The voice inside my head screams it constantly. The Devil strictly forbade me from being with her, it's too messy. I can't be this attracted to her—it's too complicated, too dangerous, too *everything I don't need in my life*. Yet, here I am—caught in her trap.

My brain is so scrambled from this simple touch that it takes me a couple of seconds to realize that she's now staring up at me. There's a longing in her eyes, the blue swallowed by her dilated pupils. Her scent is even more profound than it was before. The citrusy scent is smokier, somehow.

She continues to stroke my chest as she did when I was a crow—only it's skin she's petting, not feathers.

I'm struck mute, words caught in my mouth as I stare down at her with fire, electricity, and need coursing through my body.

Goddamn, but I want this woman. And it will doom me if I ever do have her.

CHAPTER 15

VALENCIA

CORVUS TOWERS OVER ME and I'm reminded of his monstrous size as his expansive chest nearly fills my entire field of vision. I feel his gaze like a burning touch, but I'm not brave enough to meet it yet.

My eyelashes flutter, my chest rising rapidly as my lungs work hard to get oxygen into my body. The air is doused in his dark scent—it's like being surrounded by a damp forest with trees overhead and moss and dirt underfoot.

Every inhale of his essence flows throughout me, a tangible thing that I can feel glide down my throat and make a home in all the empty spaces inside me. My mouth waters and I have to lick my lips to make sure I'm not drooling. This consuming desire for him is probably not very healthy for my future, but I struggle to care.

I feel him freeze; his body is like an immobile slab of ice—not even his chest moves to breathe. The deep brown of his eyes has been swallowed whole and are just endless wells of black.

I continue to play with the smooth skin of his chest that I've exposed. Dark black lines and detailed shading peeks out of his open shirt, completely covering one side of his chest. The tattoo's edges appear full of whimsical clouds and other small details that I can't place from this angle. I fight the urge to rip his shirt open so I can see the rest of him.

My fingertip lightly traces the dark lines, his skin warm to the touch. His sharp inhale is a balm to my aching soul. He's equally as affected by my presence as I am by his. My desire for him feels like being shackled to an evil twin whose type is *'men who are terrible for my mental health'*.

Last week, I was shocked when he walked up to me at the bar. Irma had just brought me a hot, spiked tea to help chase away the cold. I hadn't wanted to go inside. I didn't mind the cold, anyway, and the fire felt nice, especially after Irma brought me the blanket. When he appeared, creeping out of the shadows, I couldn't help how my heart started racing. We somehow have this uncanny ability to be in the same place at the same time and I'm starting to wonder if it really is just a coincidence.

Once I had settled down, and the nerves went away, we had a nice conversation—but some of his answers just weren't adding up. When I asked if he lived at the trailer park, he said 'sort of.' He also said he hadn't been there to attend a party, which I later confirmed *was* the reason for the fire that night. So *why was he there?* A friend's house? An errand? Not as likely at 3 AM, but I guess he could've been there for an errand of the physical kind.

I wipe the thought away, not wanting to think of him in that sense—too dangerous considering the confusing emotions I feel every time he's near.

I take another deep breath, trying to remember what got me into this position in the first place. I want answers that I feel only Corvus can give. When we first met, he was pulling me from a burning building. Then, later that night, he's saving me from yet another disaster. I feel as if that whole night is just a blur of one shit show after another. I remember the feel of his arms around me, how their tight hold seemed frustrating at first but, by the end of the night, I was appreciative of his strength.

Too many incidents have happened for him to not know *something* about the strange misfortunes that have found me as of late. Manipulating answers out of him with sexual energy doesn't seem like the best tactic, but here we are.

Finally finding the courage, I lean back and meet his stare. Doubt and insecurity attempt to take over but I hide them behind a thick wall. With everything going on in my life, the last thing I need to be worried about is if he likes me or not. I just need answers. Why was I left on the mountain to die? How did Corvus appear at the perfect moment to save me from yet another near-fatal event? How did he know I was at the bar that night?

Why am I so attracted to him when no other has appealed to me in this way?

"So," I begin, trying to get my voice steady despite a rollercoaster of emotions. "You wanted to talk to me?" I say with a seductive purr.

Corvus flinches as if in pain. A large hand reaches up and grips my wrist tightly, his fingers curling around the delicate bones and squeezing slightly. It's not too tight, but is enough that I imagine I will sport an imprint of his fingers if he holds on for too long.

"Let's not forget, you invited me," he starts.

"Did I?" I question. *Yes, I did.* I did invite him, and I don't know why I'm being an asshole about it, but something's got me on edge and I feel like I need to hear him explain himself and can't just enjoy that he's here.

"You did." Corvus still has a tight grip on my wrist, but I ignore it.

"You sure you didn't come here for something else?"

"I'm attracted to you, that's undeniable. But I know what you're doing." He squeezes my wrist tightly, causing a gasp to escape my lips. "That's not why I'm here."

My eyes flare in anger. "What am I doing, then? Besides giving you what you want?" The question comes out roughly.

He drags my hand away from his chest but doesn't release my wrist from his grasp. I take a split second to miss the feel of his heated skin under my touch before I refocus on the present.

"You're trying to distract me," he says. "I just want to talk to you, Valencia. I don't know what's happened between the bar and now, but at least give me the chance to talk to you." It sounds like he's nearly pleading, which isn't something I'd ever expect to hear from him.

"Well, please get to the point then," I respond with an edge to my voice, not wanting to give away how much the feeling of his skin under my fingers affects me. Still, it doesn't stop my frustration from building. How many times must I ask him what he wants before he finally gives me some answers?

"Like I said before, I needed to talk to you."

"And I need a vacation in Tahiti. What do you want? Because if it isn't to ask for tips on how to put out a fire or to offer me a mind-blowing orgasm, then I don't think I need to talk to you." I'm tired of this back and forth and, if I don't get away from him soon, I'm bound to make some bad decisions.

I attempt to pull my wrist away from his grip, but he squeezes sharply. I growl in frustration when I'm unable to get my wrist free.

"Maybe if you used your brain to listen instead of using it to run your mouth like a feral coyote, we might have gotten straight to the point." His dark eyes bore into mine.

"Asshole," I growl and suck in a breath. "You're a waste of good oxygen."

"Naughty words, yet still you fail to shut your mouth." His deep brown eyes fixate on my lips. "Do you ever stop? If not, I know of something you can choke on that'll keep your mouth so busy you won't be able to talk," Corvus says cuttingly.

There's an edge to his voice now, but I have a sneaking suspicion that he's enjoying this.

Or maybe that's just wishful thinking, you hussy.

His large hand releases my wrist to clench the back of my neck instead. His grip is firm and unyielding. I feel the heat of lust and anger combine, burning through my cheeks and down my chest. It frustrates me how easily he assumes control of my body and how quickly my anger burns into salaciousness.

What I also cannot stand is how the rising heat has also traveled all the way to my clit, causing the traitorous little muscle to pulse. It feels deplorable to be attracted to someone so infuriating.

"I would never cease talking—if only to annoy the hell out of you," I snap.

"Ah, Hell is in my blood, Kitten. There's no getting it out." His grip tightens almost to the point of pain. He draws me in close, our bodies just barely touching. Our heat combines to stave off the cool Montana air and my eyes drift closed for a brief moment.

Corvus leans his head close, his nose just barely brushing mine. "Now, shut up, or I'll do it for you."

Corvus leans back, his eyes briefly flashing to my lips before jerking back to my eyes. A burst of desire flares through my body, forcing me to tense in restraint. There is a very thin line between hate and desire, and I feel as if I'm dancing along its brink.

Defiance and desire course through me in equal parts. One side of me—the side currently controlled by my clit—thrums with the imagination of what it would be like to be controlled and pleasured by this monster of a man. The other, more logical side, wishes for nothing more than to hear his choking gasps of air after I throat-punch him as hard as I can.

The air crackles with tension—a confusing mix of conflicting emotions from both sides.

"You listen here, you great-value barbarian," I snap, my fingers wrapping around the large wrist currently manhandling my neck as if I were a doll. "Let go of me before your family jewels pay the price."

"I love it when women don't listen. You want to know why?" His fingers flex around my neck but don't release.

"Because you have mommy issues?" I spit.

Corvus laughs softly, then murmurs. "No. So I can do this."

The hand around my neck loosens and, for a second, I'm freed from his scorching touch. Not for long, however, as his palm rests on my cheek, his touch surprisingly gentle. His eyes flash back and forth between my own before focusing on my lips.

I stifle a moan. My heartrate skyrockets while my chest inflates with a gasping inhale. My thighs flex and I desperately wish to rub them together for relief but don't want to make any sudden moves.

An unspoken acknowledgement passes between us, and I see the instant his control finally snaps.

Corvus' lips crash down on mine. The kiss is not overtly passionate nor sweetly tender. It is a mesh of heated disdain and unspoken longing.

I hesitate for the briefest of moments before returning his kiss in kind. A low groan escapes his lips and slides into my mouth, sending electric shocks through my center. I gasp as his hot tongue slides into my mouth.

His giant hand slides across my cheek, burying in the thickness of my hair at the back of my head. He grabs a handful and directs me where he wants me, taking complete control of my body as he continues his savage caress.

I know I should pull away and stop this insanity before it goes any further, but the horny evil twin is now in control of my body—and she'd rather jump off a cliff than stop.

Caught in the moment, I press forward, smashing the front of my body to his. Corvus grips my hair tighter and leans his large body over me, consuming all my senses. It's like kissing fire and loving the burn.

Our size difference is glaringly obvious in this intimate position. I can feel the evidence of his desire against my stomach, which causes a pool of wetness to gather between my legs. Any longer in his arms and my panties are bound to be soaked through.

A moan escapes me as his lips draw a searing path down my neck.

In a sudden burst of motion, Corvus grabs my hips with both hands and lifts me up. Instinctively, my legs wrap around his waist, drawing us even closer.

I can no longer feel the bulge of his erection. Instead, my jean-covered pussy rubs against his toned torso. Our layers of clothing dampen the sensation, so I'm forced to ground my heels into his back to press myself against him as hard as I can.

Corvus recaptures my lips, his desire so potent I can smell it rolling off him in waves.

I wheeze out a shocked huff as my back is firmly pressed against the side of the firetruck and he leans back, breaking our kiss. Our eyes lock in a blend of uncertainty and longing. The air is charged with the residue of our passion.

We both remain clasped in a standoff of wills, trying not to break the spell of false peace as we internally grapple with what just happened.

I open my mouth to speak, but he interrupts me before I can.

"I'm sorry." Corvus promptly sets me down on my feet, taking an obscenely large step away as if my proximity is now poisonous.

Embarrassment rumbles through my chest, burning away most of the lingering passion. Hearing his apology shatters the post-kiss high, leaving only a fog of distress.

A venomous grin covers my face. "Sorry that you're such a bad kisser?" I sneer, tasting the anger and shame on my tongue.

His eyebrows rise in disbelief. "You moaned an awful lot for it to be bad."

I shake my head in irritation, praying the anger can wash away the remaining tingles of desire. "Good seeing you, Corvus, but I've grown tired of your company."

I attempt to leave, walking around his large body. Quicker than I can see, he grabs me by the wrist once more. My first reaction is to yank my hand away, but the feel of his touch on my skin stops me.

"Please, I just want to talk. I'm sorry I kissed you. I was out of line, but we really need to talk." He's pleading, but shame still burns in my mouth so I try to pull my arm away. He doesn't budge.

"Don't mistake my brief lapse in judgment as a right to any more of my time." I grasp the wrist that's holding me, digging my nails into the tender flesh there. "I don't want to hear what you have to say."

Corvus sucks in a breath, the pain from my nails a dull bite, but doesn't let go. "Don't be stubborn for no reason; this is important, Valencia."

"I swear, if you don't—"

"Val!" As my name is called, a slamming door echoes through the parking lot. It jolts my focus away from Corvus. I look towards the door as Parker rushes toward me, phone up to his ear.

"Val, we've got to go. Right now. Irma thinks," he pauses, glancing at Corvus before looking back at me.

"Spit it out, Parks!" I snap, urgency in my voice.

"*Irma-saw-Dane-Moore-in-town!*" He rumbles so fast I can barely catch what he says.

My body freezes as the words finally piece themselves into a coherent sentence. The shock is immediate and chilling. Ice floods through my veins, finally erasing all the remaining traces of salacious heat. All that remains is anger and, frustratingly, fear.

"Let's go talk to him!" Parker rushes. He takes off across the lot towards his Tahoe.

Feeling rushes through my body like the tingles after waking up a previously numb muscle. It's an uncomfortable awareness but kicks my body back into gear.

Parker has already taken off towards his truck, and I turn to follow.

"Wait, I need to tell you some—" Corvus cuts out before I can fully take off.

"Corvus I can't do this right now," I snap. There is no more time for his odd mind games.

"I'm coming with," he says.

Corvus keeps a hold of my wrist as he starts to drag me with him towards Parker's truck. I try to pull away, but it only manages to get me dragged across the lot behind his long strides.

"This is nothing, you don't need to come," I try to command, though my words come out breathy from trying to pull away from him. He's so *strong*.

"It doesn't seem like nothing," he barks. His grip is tight—borderline uncomfortable—but not painful. I'm sure I could save myself a lot of trouble if I quit fighting and actually started walking, like a mature adult would, but my irritation over the kiss has the reins right now, and I can't help but pull against him.

"*Ugh*, you're infuriating!" Rock crunches under my feet as the soles of my boots drag across the ground. His large body blocks everything else from view, so all I can do is watch as the muscles in his back ripple from use.

"I'm coming with you." He repeats.

Words flow out of me before I can stop them, "This isn't your problem, Corvus. Let me handle it."

He pauses, his grip loosening slightly. Without the force of him pulling me, I stumble a bit before I stand up. "You don't have to handle it alone. I'm already here, might as well let me help you."

I want to argue with him and question why he thinks he has a right to join us, but his words hit me like a shot to the chest. His eyes burn with a mixture of anger and concern, and I'm not sure which is directed at me.

The sound of crunching gravel catches my attention. Parker leans out of his window, looking between the two of us.

No time for doubts, I guess.

I look to Corvus, who simply nods his head. Not wanting to waste any more time, I head to the passenger side of the Tahoe.

As we load up into the truck, I take a moment to let the anxiety of the situation consume me. There's no turning back now and, whatever happens next, we're all in this together. Part of me is riddled with nerves that I could get either of them hurt, but the other part is thankful for their presence—even if I didn't have much of a choice in it.

It isn't every day you attempt to run down the person who came close to nearly killing you.

Chapter 16
Valencia

"Okay, explain exactly what Irma said," I demand.

"I asked Irma to keep an eye out for him last time we were at Ole Joe's—showed her the picture of him with the Mayor. You know she's got the memory of a damn elephant. She just called and said she thinks she saw him walk by."

I shake my head, tension building steadily behind my eyes, "If Irma thinks she saw him, she could probably tell us exactly what he was wearing and the color of his eyes."

"Blue."

"What?"

"She said he was wearing a blue Polo," Parker responds with a laugh.

"Of course she did." I want to laugh, but my anxiety at the situation overrides the humor.

"Who is Irma? And who is *him*?" A deep voice rumbles behind me.

All my irritation from earlier has dissipated, leaving me with an empty, hollow feeling. Heat creeps up my cheeks at the memory of our heated kiss, but I shove that down.

Focus with your brain, not your vagina. I internally reprimand.

"Irma owns Ole Joe's bar, and she's a close friend of Val's. *'Him'* is—*ouch!"* Parker hisses at me in pain. "What was that for?"

"Quit telling my business, Parker." I pat the spot on his thigh that I just pinched.

"She's got vicious little claws, huh?" Corvus prattles and I turn to glare at him. Then, I freeze.

His arms rest atop the seat, hands nearly touching each door. Dark clothes are stretched tight across bulky muscles. Large hulking thighs splay out wide, giving me a direct view of his crotch. His hips shift slightly, but it's enough to shock me out of my daze. A blush covers my face.

I quickly looked back to the front of the car, mortified that I had not only spent more than a few seconds staring at his crotch but that he caught me doing it. Though I only looked for a few seconds, even a blind person would struggle to miss the intimidatingly sexy expanse of body.

"Earth to Val!" Parker snaps his fingers in my face, and I realize he's been attempting to get my attention. "I mean, seriously, how do you expect to not tell him what's going on when you're the one who invited him?"

"I did not!" I argue, a childish pitch to my voice.

"Well, I sure didn't invite the walking sex on legs to join us! How am I supposed to pick up women when you've got every woman's wet dream following you around like a lost puppy?"

"Parker, we're not in town so you can pick up women, we're looking for Dane."

Parker glances at the rearview mirror with a big smile on his face.

"Don't stop there; you were just getting to the good part," Corvus' velvety voice rolls from the back.

"*Ugh*, fine!" I throw my hands up in exasperation. "I'm only telling you this because you've somehow wormed your way into my business and it doesn't seem like I'm going to be able to get rid of you anytime soon."

"Fat chance," Parker says at the same time that Corvus mumbles something like *not likely* in the back. I choose to ignore them both and proceed to tell Corvus about the fire, CAFA, my accident on Sugarloaf Mountain—and how Dane Moore connects to it all.

It's a risk telling him my story while there's still an investigation going on, but the police haven't done anything useful as of yet. Plus, I don't actually know that Dane Moore is guilty of anything other than being a coward. Even though Montana has a Good Samaritan Law, if Dane got a good enough lawyer he would most likely be absolved of any criminal chargers. It's the reason Parker and I decided to try and find him ourselves—so I could talk to him myself and figure out why he left me on the side of a mountain to die.

I'm just not sure what I'd do if I found out he's the reason I ended up there in the first place.

Corvus listens patiently, not interrupting or interjecting once. For a second, I think he's sleeping he's so quiet, but a deep *'mhmm'* lets me know he's still paying close attention.

After I finish, a thick silence fills the cab. Anger practically radiates from Parker, his previously jovial attitude washed away as I tell my story.

I don't look back at Corvus, but I feel his gaze on my neck like a physical touch.

A murky feeling fills my veins, and my palms start to sweat. Parker's anger may radiate off of him but Corvus' suffocates, stealing all the oxygen from the cab. It's like breathing through a chloroform-covered rag.

My chest heaves as I draw in large gulps of air, but it does nothing to stifle the suppressing mood. I finally dare to look back at Corvus; he's sitting in the same position, but I focus on his face this time.

His once deep brown eyes appear entirely black, and his eyebrows dip into a deep scowl. The depths of his onyx eyes seem endless and I can't tell if he's looking at me or somehow through me.

"Corvus," I bark. Although I don't fear him, an airborne poison has filled the space, forcing me to feel dread when I usually wouldn't.

He doesn't move or speak—just stares straight at me. I reach out a hand, patting the knee closest to me to get his attention. His leg jerks under my touch, so I start to pull away but a large, tattooed hand smacks the top of mine, holding my hand to his knee.

My heart almost stops beating. There's a flicker of intensity rolling from him in waves. He looks through me, caught in thoughts I can't see. His gaze is predatory, assessing, calculating, and *dangerous*. The truck cabin suddenly feels too small—the air too thick with emotions that aren't my own. A strange fear bubbles in my veins and my mind races. The arousal I normally feel when I look at him is still there but now it's taken a back seat to this strange dread. He may be more than he seems—and I can't afford to make any more mistakes when it comes to judging a man's character.

Corvus blinks once, and then warm brown eyes stare at me once more. His nostrils flare several times, but his eyebrows are no longer forced into a scowl.

The toxic atmosphere disappears so fast that I wonder if I made it all up in the first place. My mind races as the painful weight of whatever that was releases me, taking all my doubts with it.

"I'm happy to help you hunt him down," Corvus squeezes my fingers once, then returns to his previously relaxed position.

"I think *'hunt'* is a little harsh, Rambo, but I appreciate the help," I admit, even though it feels like sandpaper leaving my mouth. I've always been uncomfortable asking for help.

After spending so much of my youth alone, I learned it was best to count on myself. Although I struggled to ask for help, it wasn't beyond me to appreciate having a grizzly of a man on my side.

As I turn back to face the windshield, I take a few deep breaths and attempt to regain control of my emotions.

"So, what's the plan Val?" Parker asks, taking his eyes off the road for a second to look over at me. There's still the normal lightness to his features, as if he completely missed the strange vibe that filled the cab.

"Well, all of us cornering him is probably a bad idea. I'll approach him alone and ask him why he left that day."

"Nope," Park says forcefully with a shake of his head.

A deep *No* comes from the back seat, though it's not as pointed.

"Just because I think he might've had something to do with my accident doesn't mean he actually did. And he'd be stupid to do anything to me in such a public place."

"I said no, Val, he's dangerous." Parker shakes his head as if that will make me more likely to listen.

"You don't know that, Parker! Maybe he's just a chicken-shit and ran 'cause he was scared of being blamed."

"Or maybe he's both," Corvus states.

"Definitely both," Parker agrees.

"I'll be fine. You guys can wait right around the corner so you can do the whole hero act if necessary."

"Valencia, it's not safe to be around him alone." Corvus' deep voice moves closer. Out of the corner of my eye, I notice him leaning towards me, his elbows resting atop his knees, staring intently at me. The emotions he was drawing out of me just moments ago are gone now, leaving room for the arousal to sneak back in.

"I agree," Parker nods, smiling in the rearview mirror as he listens to Corvus.

"Since when are you two all buddy-buddy?" I grumble in agitation.

"Oh, you didn't know? Corvus and I are basically besties now. Right?" He glances back at Corvus.

"I'm not into redheads, sorry." Corvus rolls his eyes, but his lips tip up into a slight smirk.

"Ouch, man, that hurts." Parker mimes stabbing himself in the chest.

I pinch the bridge of my nose and struggle to prevent a loud laugh from escaping. "Just so long as you two don't blow a gasket or anything before we can at least hear the guy out."

"Whatever you say, Oh Mighty Leader. Oh, Corvus, did you know that this one time, Val completely lost it on one of my exes? She literally—" Parker starts, but I cut him off by cranking the music up as high as possible.

I just need a couple of moments to compose myself and gather all my thoughts and ensure the darker, more deprived ones are all locked away in a secure place.

The rest of the ride to town goes smoothly. The only hiccup is Coruvs' growling, "Is he serious?" when Parker proceeds to turn on his Disney playlist and belt out every song. I can barely hear him over the loud radio and Parker's unholy singing, so I ignore him.

We all exit the vehicle together and make our way inside Ole Joe's.

Irma stands behind the bar, vigorously wiping down the bar top. It shines with a sparkling luster—which puts into question why she was even wiping it down in the first place.

Irma isn't one for idle time, though, so I imagine she just enjoys the physical activity.

"Ah, mein kleinen Feuer. You get here quick," Irma says, throwing the rag over her shoulder as she stares at us. Her silvery hair shines in the light when she rounds the bar top.

"Irma, thanks so much for calling," Parker responds as he leans against the bar.

The stout old woman comes up to me and places her small palm against my cheek. "My sweet *Flamme*, what have you gotten yourself into?"

Cold fingers cradle my face gingerly. I jerk at the contact, somehow unused to it even though she does it nearly every time she sees me. The icy bite of her touch doesn't detract from the warmth that spreads throughout my chest at the endearment.

"You know me, just living life on the edge," my voice cracks at the end, and it takes immense willpower to not break down in her arms. My heart is made of a thousand tiny cracks, just waiting to break completely. If it ever does break, I'll be eviscerated.

"You maybe try to live life in the middle," with a pat on my cheek, Irma makes her way back around the bar.

As she bends down to grab something, she finally acknowledges my two companions. "You boys help *mein Flamme*?"

"You know I couldn't miss out on the fun, Irma!" Parker replies excitedly. He remains leaning against the bar, a beer bottle resting beside his arm. I have no idea where he got it, but I wouldn't be surprised if he just reached over the counter and grabbed one out of the cooler.

"You are trouble—like a little child," Irma says, slapping a familiar newspaper on the bar top and then focusing her attention on the third member of our group.

"*Du bist eine Gefahr für meine Flamme*," she rattles so quickly that I miss half of what she says.

"*Das möchte ich nicht sein.*" Corvus' deep voice articulates the complex language with ease.

The sudden shock takes over me as I realize he fully understands Irma and is fluent enough in German to respond. He is relaxed and doesn't appear worried about whatever she says to him.

I only have seconds to try and process yet another strange piece of information about this man before their conversation continues.

"It no matter what we want, matters what we do," Irma snaps at Corvus. "You help *mein Flamme*, and we will see, *Krähe*."

"Okay dude—are you an alien and, like, got implanted into our world? 'Cause you're strange as fuck," Parker jokes, taking a swig of his beer, but I can see new tension in his frame.

Neither Parker nor I have been able to communicate with her fluently. Despite spending the last few years around Irma and studying randomly, we continue to struggle understanding her when she speaks her native language.

I could only catch *'you are a'* and *'my flame.'*

She's clearly talking about me, as the woman has referred to me as her flame almost the entire time I've known her.

"Listen, we're getting distracted. Irma, you think you saw Dane? The man he showed you the picture of?" I attempt to get us back on track.

Though I fully plan on circling back to whatever clusterfuck of a conversation that was, I want to steer us back to what's most important. I can only deal with one shit show at a time.

"Yes, yes—I see him. He stand outside, speaking on phone. Very angry man, stomping around. He looked crazy—stand there a while, then he walk toward back of bar. Maybe still there."

"Let's go," Parker pushes off the bar and starts heading for the back door that leads to the patio, leaving his half full beer behind.

Corvus, who has oddly remained quiet since interacting with Irma, silently follows Parker.

"Thank you so much, Irma. Just stay in here while we deal with him." I step up to her and grip her two small hands. Her fingers are still deathly cold, but I ignore it.

"Don't worry about me, *mein Flamme*," Irma squeezes my fingers back, "you be safe. These men, they're bad for you."

"Aren't they all," I laugh without humor and go to pull my hands away, but her once gentle embrace turns into a sharp pinch.

"You must listen. Crazy man; bad for here," Irma taps a finger to my temple. "*Krähe*, bad for here," she now taps the same finger to my chest, right over my heart. "One is in your future—be careful which."

She finally releases my hand and steps away. Irma grabs the discarded newspaper and crumples it between her fingers. Her grip is tight, and I can see her knuckles whiten from the strain for a second, but it's hard to tell with her pale skin.

"I will be fine, Irma, I promise. I appreciate you looking out for me, but I've gotta get out there and see what's going on."

"You go. And don't let them put out your fire, my sweet *Flamme*." With that, she walks off, disappearing into the kitchen.

I finally make my way to the patio, thoughts of German words I don't understand, dangerous men, and confusing feelings plaguing my mind.

I shake all thoughts besides finding the guys as I push through Ole Joe's patio door.

Parker and Corvus stand shoulder to shoulder, facing the back of the patio. I only see a little beyond their large frames so, when I finally come around beside Corvus, I see what has them frozen in place.

There, in a patio chair, lounging like a lizard out in the sun, is Dane Moore.

Chapter 17
Valencia

"Angel Baby, you're just in time," Dane's smooth, melodic voice flutters on the wind. How I ever thought his voice was attractive amazes me. All I hear now is pretentious, self-righteousness.

I berate myself mentally. I came here to give him the benefit of telling his side of the story before accusing him of anything but just seeing his face draws up all kinds of nasty emotions.

He doesn't really seem like that great of a guy now that I'm meeting him for the second time. Or, maybe I'm biased since he left me to die on the side of a mountain.

"Just in time for your groveling apology, I hope," Parker sneers at Dane.

Dane just smirks, as if amused by Parker's snappy tone.

My muscles refuse to do anything other than shiver in restraint. Sharp pricks of pain shoot through my palms as my fingernails dig into the soft skin.

I'm consumed by rage so quickly that I barely register it's happening. My jaw throbs from gritted teeth, and a strange heat burns at my fingertips.

Don't kill him. Don't kill him. Don't kill him.

"Do tell, for what should I apologize?" Dane's focus remains on Parker.

"He's joking, right? Is this guy for real?" Parker scoffs.

Parker moves to face me and Corvus, but I can't look away from Dane. He still lounges in the patio chair, his lean body relaxed as if we were chatting vacation plans.

"Du—Dane. You've gone too far." Corvus says calmly, although I don't miss the break in his voice.

Apparently, neither does Dane.

Dane taunts, "He speaks. Though you may need some extra lessons, stuttering is most unbecoming."

"You almost killed my best friend, asshole! I'd say that's *'most unbecoming,'*" Parker mocks back at Dane, mimicking his lyrical tone with a nagging edge.

Any other time, I think I'd laugh.

As the rage starts to build inside me, it burns away everything else. All my thoughts and desires outside of Dane, and what he's done, are irrelevant.

Don't kill him. Don't kill him. Don't kill him.

I beg myself, pleading against the rage—but it is too hungry for vengeance. This was a bad idea.

"You keep company with the most dangerous creature to walk Earth, yet you're worried about me?" Dane laughs openly, the sound as beautiful as it is unsettling. It does nothing to ease my nerves or calm my rage.

"Worried about you? You pushed her off the trail and then left her there to die! I'd say that makes you pretty fucking dangerous." Parker argues expertly. His emotions are high but he's still able to communicate. At least that makes one of us.

"Does it?" Dane asks, a mischievous smile on his face. "I think, with a good enough lawyer, it can all be explained away."

For some reason, I tried to give this guy a chance and not blame him for something he didn't do but, with every sarcastic answer he gives, he falls further and further from innocence in my eyes.

"Just tell us why you left her on the mountain—that's all we want. We won't involve the police any further but you *will* tell us what happened," Parker demands.

"I don't think I will," Dane laughs again, smirking at the anger on Parker's face. Even though it's a sickeningly beautiful sound, it flips the switch on the last bit of my resolve and the rage finally takes over.

Kill him.

With a growled, "You motherfucker," I charge at Dane.

He stands from his chair, my running lunge startling him into action, but he's not fast enough to fully rise to his feet before I'm upon him.

His eyes widen and he attempts to grab me but I duck beneath his swinging arms and ram into him from the front. My arms wrap around his middle and the rounded curve of my shoulder hits him squarely in the stomach.

He grunts loudly, the air escaping his lungs, as we topple over his chair and onto the ground.

We land hard on the rock patio and blinding pain shoots through my right knee down to the ankle I twisted a couple of weeks ago. It's been pain-free for a while, but the jarring slam against the rough patio reminds me of the fact it wasn't long ago that I was walking out of a hospital with some serious injuries.

Something jams into my center, causing my stomach to roil—but it distracts me from the pain in my leg. I instantly feel nauseated, and the muscles in my lower back spasm from the impact.

Scorching agony tears through my fingers as I grip Dane's sides. He grunts as though in pain, face contorting into an angry snarl. A vicious smile overtakes my face at the sound of his suffering.

I hear curses ring out around me, but adrenalin has clouded my brain. The only thing I can focus on is the rage consuming my body and urging me to maim the man below me and hurt him beyond repair.

I know I'm not a killer but, at this moment, I'd be happy for him to be my first.

The heat flares up my arms and courses along my body, leaving my fingertips aching. Then—I'm ripped away.

Strong arms encircle my body, trapping mine at my sides. I thrash against the hold, wildly kicking my legs out and, as I'm dragged away, my left foot catches Dane on the inside of his thigh. I grin when I hear him grunt in pain again.

He scrambles to his feet, a hand held against his side. Large holes mar his shirt over his ribs and a few large spots begin to darken to a deep brown color.

Parker lunges for Dane as I'm pulled further back.

"Parker, no!" I yell for him to stop but I'm too late.

Park swings a solid hook, but Dane dodges easily. He strikes Parker's chest with a single punch and Parker falls to his knees. He folds in on himself, forehead resting on the ground and eyes scrunched tightly closed as he attempts to suck in ragged gasps.

Dane steps over him, as if he's simply an obstacle in the way. I fight against the arms that contain me with renewed vigor.

"Be calm, Parker's going to be fine; it's us who are in danger now," Corvus mutters in my ear, grunting as one of my heels connects with his shin.

All I can manage in response is a rage-filled growl.

I have to get to Parker. I *have to* hurt Dane for hurting Parker.

"And then there were two. Let's even the odds." Dane reaches behind his back and I instantly realize our mistake; we've brought fists to a gunfight.

I gasp in shock, fear seizing the air from my lungs but, instead of a gun, Dane pulls out a vicious-looking sword. At least—I think it's a sword. It's long and thin, with a slight curve at its end.

Burning, writhing flames sizzle and sparks fly as Dane drags the tip of the sword across the ground.

What. The. Fuck.

"*Why*?" I scream.

He glances at me. "Your death is better than another soul joining the damned."

Dane lunges forward—the sharp, deadly tip point aimed straight at my heart. Corvus turns, dragging me along with him.

His deep grunt of pain fills my ears and something warm and wet soaks my shirt, causing the fabric to stick to my skin in places. Pain pinches my arm, but I'm shoved hard before it gets any worse.

I stumble a couple of steps before regaining my balance and turning around. I mentally check myself over for any other signs of injury. A thin red slash runs across my right arm, nearly overlapping my still-healing cut from the fall. The new cut is seeping, and a small drop of blood runs down my arm. The surrounding skin is slightly red but, otherwise, looks normal.

Corvus looks up at me, eyebrows scrunched deeply through the pain. His eyes widen as he surveys my arms. My fingers are covered in blood—as though I've dipped them in a bucket full of it. Tiny specks of the dried residue cover my wrists as red drops continue to drip from my fingertips.

He kneels as he holds a hand to his side. Blood drips through his fingers at an alarming pace, already pooling on the ground beneath him. His shirt is singed around the edges and what visible skin I can see looks marred by severe burns.

I want to rush to his side to treat him, but the look of doubt he sends me makes me pause.

I peer at him for a moment, hoping for a sign, something to help me understand but nothing comes. Then the realization slams into me.

Whereas I only suffered a tiny cut, Corvus looks like he's suffered a third degree burn. The skin over his ribs is charred black and he's still bleeding slowly.

That could've been me.

If he hadn't turned so fast—it would be me suffering from a violent injury.

I look at Dane to find that he's frozen in place, staring at me with such intensity. His eyes frantically track the cut on my arm, his sword hanging limp in his hand. Bright flames lick against his hand and leg, but he seems impervious to the burning heat.

Somewhere beyond, Parker still wheezes on the ground, unable to stand. I consider trying to take Dane on again, but I don't want to risk it with Corvus and Parker both badly hurt.

"No," Dane mutters, stepping back from me as if in fear. He flicks his wrist and the sword disappears. He makes for the woods behind the patio and, with a graceful jump, he's over the back fence and blending into the shadowed forest.

I furrow my brow, contemplating the pros and cons of following him for a split second—but, instead, turn to Corvus and run my hands across his shoulders and arms with a soft touch, so as not to cause him anymore pain.

"What can I do?" I murmur frantically.

"I'll be fine. Check on Parker," Corvus mutters, his words straining through gritted teeth.

I glance over to where I last saw Parker and find him still kneeling, curled around himself—groaning. I holler over to him to check and ensure he's still conscious and get a shaky thumbs up in response.

I'm torn between checking on his vitals to make sure he's actually okay and staying with Corvus but, considering Parker was suffering from a hard hit to the solar plexus and Corvus was struck by a flaming sword, I remain where I am.

"He's fine, he's alive." I focus my attention back on Corvus. "You, on the other hand, are not fine. Stay still so I can take a look."

"Just need to rest for a second," he hangs his head low so that his chin nearly touches his chest.

"Let me look, I can help." Gravel digs into my knees as I rest my full weight on them. His eyes are closed and he still grips his side as though in severe pain.

"Why?" He asks so quietly that if I wasn't right next to him, I don't think I would've heard it.

"Well, for starters, it's my job," I ignore the way his shoulders slump as if in defeat, "and secondly, because I don't want you to die."

Corvus jerks his head up and instantly winces and sucks in a breath through gritted teeth. He searches my eyes frantically, pupils rapidly moving back and forth like he's a human polygraph.

"What—you're growing on me," I murmur as I break eye contact. It's not that I don't enjoy staring into his beautiful dark eyes; it's that I enjoy it too much.

Air rushes out of his nose in silent laughter, leading to a pained groan. I take the opportunity to look more closely at the damage to his side, where his large hand is firmly pressed. The skin is charred, but the bleeding has thankfully stopped. The edges of the cut must have been cauterized by the heat of the flaming sword. He'll have a nasty scar—and the cut will definitely need stitches if the amount of blood he lost is anything to go by.

When my fingers wrap around his wrist, Corvus jerks, but he doesn't pull away from my touch. "I just need to see what we're working with."

I slowly pull his hand away from his side.

It's impossible to contain my gasping shock.

Years of being a first responder couldn't prepare me for the onslaught of his damage. A gash runs across his entire side, the wound lies open with an almost two-inch gap at the beginning of the injury, tapering along his rib cage. The milky white of his lower ribs shines through the vicious red of his exposed muscle.

The skin surrounding the wound is so burned that the edges have cracked like cooled lava. Never in my life have I witnessed a burn so severe—at least not on someone still living. He's clearly in immense amounts of pain but, with an injury of this magnitude, he should be dead. I have no idea how he's still conscious.

This is beyond my capabilities—beyond anyone's, besides what an ER surgeon could do to help him.

"Corvus, I don't know how the fuck you're alive, but we need to get you to a hospital. Right. Now." With panicky breaths, I start to stand but he stops me—placing a large, blood-covered hand on top of my thigh.

"No hospital," he snaps.

"Are you fucking with me right now?" I ask incredulously.

"Valencia, I know this sounds crazy, but *I'll be fine*," Corvus states, the pain still evident in his voice. He squeezes my leg as if in reassurance.

"Crazy? *Crazy* is you getting nearly severed in half by a psychopath with a sword. Oh, and did I mention the sword was on *fire*? Crazy is you even being *alive* right now." With each word, my panicked breathing turns into downright terror. "What the *fuck*, Corvus?"

"Take a deep breath. Go check on your friend," he urges, kneeling a little straighter, but still holding a hand to his side.

"Seriously, modern medicine is the *only* thing than can save someone from this kind of injury. If it's the cost of—" I try to convince him, but he interrupts me.

"Money is the least of my worries, I just need time." He explains. Once again arguing against the only logical solution at this point.

"Corvus, I swear to G—"

"Don't you *dare*." With blinding speed, he reaches out and pinches both of my cheeks with his thumb and pointer finger, stopping me mid-sentence. "Listen to me—I need you to trust me. I don't know if he will come back. I need you to get your friend off his ass and then both of you need to help me get up so we can all get out of the fucking open. We are sitting ducks, ripe for hungry vultures out here. I know you don't understand—but I can't explain everything right now."

Unfortunately, that makes sense—but it doesn't stop the anger from coursing through me at the disrespect. Nor does it stop the blossom of hurt that chills my blood. I've seen people die from less severe injuries and, despite knowing I shouldn't, I care about him. He's acting as though I've reacted like an ignorant child.

I pull my face away from his tight grip and snarl, "Don't grab my face like that."

"Then don't be such a fucking brat."

"Fine! But if you die, I am *not* writing your eulogy!" I stand up, done with his confusing split personality and storm off to check on Parker.

I don't bother mentioning that I absolutely do plan on taking him to a hospital, regardless of what he wants. Any minute, and an injury like that could kill him and I refuse to have it happen when I'm around. I won't be responsible for another needless death.

I find Parker still knelt on the ground where he landed after Dane punched him in the chest. He's no longer wheezing but I can tell by the labored rise and fall of his back that he's still feeling the remnants of the strike.

"Parks, you good? We gotta get outta here. Corvus is badly hurt and we don't know if Dane will come back."

He groans and, with my help, rolls his lanky body into a standing position. "Fuck," he mutters more to himself than me. "What a fucking asshole."

"You're tellin' me. Now let's go," I gently grab him around the arm above his elbow and lead him to Corvus.

"Fuck man, he got you, too?" Parker huffs at Corvus.

"Something like that." Corvus curls around his injury, holding his arm tightly to his side as if that will help—effectively blocking Parker from seeing the worst of the damage.

Two sides of me war against each other. One side demands that Corvus explain what is happening while we head to the nearest hospital—the other just wants to get in the car and drive as far away as possible.

Parker puts Corvus' free arm over his shoulder so they lean heavily on each other and we clamber to the truck, where Corvus and Parker promptly fall into the back seat.

I hop into the driver's seat and we're off. As we make our way through town, I'm stunned to see people milling throughout the sidewalks and stores, enjoying the nice fall weather and festivities when we've just gone through what we have.

"Val, where are you going? The station's back the other way," Parker says, somewhat leaning through the gap between the two front seats.

"The hospital," I mutter quietly. It's not quite enough, though—because, when I look in the review mirror, Corvus' dark eyes are narrowed in on me.

"Why do we need the hospital? Are you hurt?" Parker leans forward further in his seat to get a closer look at me.

"Not me," I state, again looking at the two men in the rearview.

"I'm good—my chest fucking hurts, but I'm good. Corvus, you good ma—oh, *fuck*! Dude, I can see your insides." Parker gags in the back as he finally gets a look at Corvus' injuries. "Val, go to the hospital right now!"

"No hospital," Corvus mutters simultaneously as I snap, '*already tried that.*'

Corvus opens his eyes to pin my friend with his dark glare. The fact that he is still awake amazes me. Between the walk to the car and the bumpy road, I'm sure anyone else would be passed out from pain alone.

I try to shove down the worry like I do with everything else—but his wound needs to be treated soon.

"Why the fuck not? How did this even happen?" Parker exclaims frantically. I bask in a brief moment of gratitude that he missed the flaming sword spectacle because I really don't think I could handle a hysteric Parker and a dying Corvus at the same time.

"Dane, who is also currently MIA. And, hospitals ask too many questions," Corvus grunts.

"Hospitals are where people usually go to stay alive." Parker snaps, rummaging around in the back.

"I need you guys to trust me. I know you're both confused—and, honestly, I don't really know what the fuck is going on, either, but until we know more, the hospital is more dangerous than not right now. We were just in a fight in the middle of the day, in a very public place." There's a strain to Corvus' voice but he pushes through. "What are the chances that no one saw that?" Corvus asks sardonically.

Fuck. I never thought about witnesses. I also notice he doesn't mention the fiery sword Dane pulled

"What do you think is going to happen when you two show up with me having a giant wound on my side? I can tell you right now, they're going to ask you two way too many questions that you're not going to be able to answer. Then, they'll lock your asses up under suspicion. Let's say they don't question you—you'll be locked up, anyway. Or, maybe they keep me there and send you two home. Then what? You'll be forced to leave me defenseless while you go back to the station—potentially even taking the danger back to your teammates?" He pauses.

"Do you see where I'm going with this?" Corvus finishes, a little breathless and croaky, but otherwise strong and to the point.

I suck a breath through my teeth, trying to find a hole in his argument, but come out struggling.

He's right—and it burns me from the inside out to admit it. I have no idea what we're up against and the last thing I want to do is take that danger back to the station.

"Corvus, this goes against everything I—no, *we* believe in. It's against everything we've been trained to do in this very situation," Parker says.

Corvus glares at me through the rear-view mirror. "I understand that," he says. "But—realistically—you can't force me to go to the hospital if I don't want to. So, you're stuck with me."

"You understand fully that if you refuse medical care by professionals, i.e., *refusing to go to the hospital*, you could die or be seriously injured for the rest of your life?" I ask, the question coming out with a mix of monotone anger. I've made the statement many times before to people injured during fires, but I've never been as emotional during it as I am now. I try to glare back at him through the mirror, but I have to focus on the road too much for it to be effective.

"I understand that, too," Corvus urges seriously.

"You're asking a lot of us, man," Parker sighs.

"I know—I'm sorry." He truly sounds remorseful but, at this point, I'm struggling to determine what's real and what's fake.

Real or fake, truth or lie, win or lose—it's all starting to blur into nothing and everything at once.

"Okay, so you'd rather just die in the back seat of my truck, cool," Parker says to Corvus. He huffs and leans in to take a closer look at the wound. "If you fucking die in my truck, man, I will seriously kill you."

Through the mirror, I see Corvus nod and chuckle softly before closing his eyes again.

"At least let me field dress it. You're somehow not bleeding, which is either a bad sign or a *really* bad sign. I don't have much in here that can help but we've got to do something."

"Have at it," Corvus grumbles, as if he doesn't care what Parker does.

"Val, toss me the water bottle in the cup holder."

I grab the half-full bottle and hand it back. Parker takes it, and a tapping sound fills the truck.

"Why are you doing that?" Corvus asks Parker.

"I'm putting a small hole in the top of the cap so I can have a nice stream of water that I can use to clean the inside of your wound without touching the burned area of skin. All your nerves are most likely gone in that area, but we don't want to mess with anything too much until we can take a closer look at what we're dealing with and get you a shit load of antibiotics." Parker explains, then grumbles, "Which is going to be hard without a fucking hospital."

I don't turn around, but I can feel Parker glaring at the back of my head. From the front of the truck, I hear a soft grunt of pain followed by the low, hissing sound of the water being squeezed out of the bottle.

It's a trick Chief Miller showed us on one of our survivalist weekend trips.

"Here's the deal. The cut seems fairly clean but it's wide and absolutely needs to be stitched. *Surgically.* There's not much I can do for your burned skin. It's so bad. I—I don't know what to do about that, man, you *really* need a hospital," Parker explains, voice shaky. Although we deal with injuries all the time, it's always harder when it's someone you know.

"I'll be fine—just need to lie down for a second." Corvus pants.

"Val, you have the worst taste in men." Parker briefly squeezes my arm, so I know he's just joking. Mostly. I think.

"Parker, any idea where we should go? I've just been driving around but we'll have to stop at some point. I don't like being out in the open like this." I frantically scan the streets, afraid Dane will hop out at every corner. My hands clamp around on the steering wheel, palms damp with sweat. "We can't go back to the station, and since the hospital is also off limits," I shoot Corvus a dirty look in the rearview mirror but his eyes are closed, "does anyone else have any bright ideas?"

"Go to the Heath Cabin. It's secluded enough and few people know about it. No one will be out there with the city in full swing like this," Parker responds, already handing me his phone with the directions pulled up.

With winter coming, no one will likely be there till spring. That's the best-case scenario. Showing up with a dead man walking wouldn't look too good, I'd say.

CHAPTER 18
VALENCIA

I PULL PARKER'S TAHOE into the drive at the Heath Cabin, parking in front of the closed garage door. The cabin sits off the drive just a little way into the woods. The wooden exterior can barely be seen through the trees and the autumn-colored leaves rattle in the wind.

It's a small studio cabin, tucked back in the woods on the edge of the Beaver-head National Forest. It was owned by the founder of the RVW Fire Crew, Michael Heath, who then gifted it to the station upon his passing.

Many of the others have used it for weekend getaways and secluded trips, but I haven't gotten the chance to make it out here yet.

I hop out of the truck and hurry to help Corvus, who groans as he rises to his feet but somehow manages to lock his knees and stay standing.

Parker is already heading for the cabin, most likely to turn everything on and start a fire. It has electricity, which means air conditioning in the summer. In the cooler months, like now, the fireplace is the only option for heat.

I gently grab Corvus' wrist and direct his arm over my shoulders. Due to our size difference, I can't take all his weight. He looks down at me, and a flash of something crosses his face. I break our eye contact to lead us to the cabin, thankful that Corvus can walk the whole way with minimal help.

As we approach the cabin, its glorious details come into view.

The small A-frame building is nestled among surrounding trees, with a large wooden deck surrounding it on three sides. In the front there's a small retaining wall made of natural rock and a variety of plants that have already succumbed to the fall's frost. Green-painted, wooden siding runs vertically along the front of the A-frame with a beautiful hand-carved door, that's home to intricate designs that swirl along its pane—a unique piece of the cabin. A large triangular window sits atop the door, and mirrored lanterns sit either side.

A big plant holder sits beside the door and a cute, mountain-themed doormat rests on the decking. Not a lot else fills the space out front, but I know from pictures that there is a huge seating area on the deck out back alongside a hot tub, an adorable picnic table, and an outdoor kitchen on the back patio.

Corvus and I finally make it through the front door and he wastes no time gingerly lying down on the bed that's only a couple feet away. It's covered in a patchwork quilt and what looks like about a hundred pillows. Well, maybe not that many—but there's a lot. The bed is small, so he takes up nearly the entire surface as he carefully lies on his back. His long legs hang off the edge—one foot planted on the floor and the other hitched, so the tip of his boot sits a couple of inches up. He has one arm flung over his eyes while the other arm still tightly holds his side.

Exhaustion weighs on my bones from the fight but I step past the bed and move further into the room. I don't think my nerves will let me rest for the next 20 years.

Parker kneels by the fireplace, fiddling with the logs in attempt to start it. Thankfully, it's not too cold right now but the afternoon sun is quickly fading to evening, and it won't be long before the temperature drops.

The kitchen is across from the bed, on the other side of the front door and tucked into the corner. Bright white cabinets shine with the sun that beams through the front window and the butcher block countertops seem to radiate homely warmth. Various tools and spices lie out on the counter.

Since the cabin is used often by firefighters and their families, there should be plenty of food in the pantry, but the fridge is likely hit or miss. I open the fridge to see some condiments, a few bottles of water, and in the door are two beers and a bottle of wine. As much as I'd love to indulge, there's still too much to do. I grab a couple bottles of water before shutting the door since I don't find anything else in there that will help us.

"Hey," I tap the elbow across Corvus' face. "I got something for you."

He shifts his arm just enough for one dark eye to peek at me. I expect a thank you or even just a grunt in response. What I'm not expecting is the absolutely sinful sound that escapes him.

It's a mix between a pain-filled groan and a sound men get paid to make. I can't help the heat that gathers in my lower stomach nor the butterflies that come to life in my chest.

I shift, trying to squeeze my thighs together for relief, but it's no use. Our heated kiss spirals through my mind and my pussy nearly weeps at the memory. I feel like I'm constantly getting edged by just being in his presence.

Corvus sits up slowly and gently grabs the water from my outstretched hand, his large fingers brushing against mine. Fire burns along my arm, rushing straight to my clit and I'm forced to bite back a moan of my own. He takes a deep, drink purring in the back of his throat.

A drop gets left on his bottom lip but he licks it away.

I abruptly turn away, heading back to Parker.

"Okay, the fire's finally going. Now, let's talk about what to do with our patient—hopefully, he's not dead," Parker mumbles as he gets up from the fireplace.

"Not yet," I squeak, prompting Parker to narrow his eyes at me. I don't acknowledge the look.

"Okay... So, does someone want to start explaining what the fuck is going on or should I keep asking questions that you're probably not going to answer?" Parker turns to me, then Corvus.

I spin and lean against the back of the couch, facing the bed. Corvus is still sitting up, but his shoulders are hunched over, and the water bottle rests in his large hand on top of a bent knee. Parker walks into the kitchen and leans against the kitchen counter.

"Parker, you seem like a good guy, but I'd prefer to have this conversation with Valencia. Alone." Corvus' normally gravely tone sounds even raspier than usual.

"Yeah, and you look like a dead man, so who cares if I know your secrets?" Parker snaps.

"Parker!" I hiss.

"What? We both know there's no way he should be alive right now. Maybe he could survive the cut with immediate intervention, but between the burn damage and the shock he should be unconscious at the very least." Parker focuses his attention on Corvus. "Don't play games with me."

"No games, I promise. I want to keep her safe; for now, the fewer people who know, the better. When it's safe for you to know, I'll personally tell you everything."

"See, that's not gonna work for me. Unless you plan to try and make me leave?" Parker sneers at him and pointedly looks at his side.

Sitting up a little straighter, Corvus growls. "You'd be a fool to underestimate me, no matter the state I'm in."

"For fucks sake, guys, why don't you just get a ruler? It'd be faster!" I holler at both of them.

"You wanna see how I measure up, Kitten?" Corvus' purrs at me. Heat climbs in my cheeks but I refuse to make eye contact with him. Instead, I keep my gaze on Parker, which thoroughly douses any budding desire.

"Unless you've got a magic anaconda in your pants, I think you'll be found wanting." Parker taunts, with evident agitation in his voice.

How dare I assume I was dealing with adults.

"Okay, that's enough. Parker: outside," he opens his mouth as if to argue, but I cut him off. "Now!"

He tosses Corvus one last look and stomps outside where he flops down on the front step.

"I like it when you get all bossy, Kitten." Corvus smirks at me, sucking his bottom lip into his mouth. Thankfully, my anger at the situation overrides the lust brewing in my body.

"I'm going to go out there and convince my best friend that it's a good idea for him to leave. The least you could do is be respectful of the position we're putting him in." I can't keep the scathing tone from my voice.

Corvus hesitates, blinking a few times but otherwise remaining quiet. He takes a deep breath, wincing slightly in pain, and nods his head as if in agreement with some silent conversation he's had internally. In a serious tone, he says, "You're right. And, I'm sorry—I'll make sure I tell him the next time I see him. Perhaps he could wait outside till we're finished talking?"

I appreciate the apology, though I wasn't expecting to get one so easily. "You're right, he deserves your apology more than I do. But, it's October in Montana—there's no way he can sit out there while we talk. I'm going to tell him to go home—but, trust me, if you try anything after he leaves, I'll make sure Dane's attempt on your life is successful."

I don't really mean that but it feels right to say, at least. I don't wait for Corvus to respond, heading outside without another word from either of us.

Parker hears the door shut and stands to face me. "You're going to ask me to leave, aren't you?"

"I'm sorry; I have to. I need to know what's going on. Please, go home and get some rest. You got hurt tonight, too and I can't stand the thought of something happening to you. You're the only family I have left. And Corvus won't hurt me—I promised him death if he tried." We've spent the past four years practically inseparable and he's the closest thing I have to a family. I don't want to make him leave, but I have to know what's really going on and, for some reason, Corvus doesn't want him here.

"I don't care what he wants or thinks—and even though he seems decent, we don't know anything about the guy—he could be as shady as Dane." He implores.

"I know Parks, I do. I trust him, though."

"Why?" he shrugs, confusion and uncertainty flaring in equal parts across his face. "What has he done to earn your trust?"

"He saved me. Twice!" I push. I have to get him to believe me. "Twice, my life has been in his hands and he's been the only reason I lived. I have to believe that means something. I have to believe that he can help me understand what the fuck is going on in my life right now—because, otherwise, I think I might just lose my shit." By the end, tears are watering at the corners of my eyes and my words are half-garbled, but I use all of my willpower to hold them in.

Parker watches me in silence. It's not long before his usual devilish smirk is on his face.

"Oh... Okay, I get it now; I expect a check in every hour," he states. With a nod he stands to draw me into a tight hug.

"Of course." I squeeze him a little harder, tucking my chin into his chest and basking in the safety of his arms.

"Wait, what do you get?" I ask in confusion.

"Be safe, girl. Condoms are in the nightstand drawer." He murmurs quietly in my ear.

"Parker!" I lean back and lightly slap his chest. "The dude is basically half dead. I just want him to stay alive."

"But, what a way to go, right?" Parker smirks, though I can see his eyes are just as watery as mine. "I'm honestly just honored to have finally gotten to see how you act when you have a lady crush."

"Jeez, get out of here, I'll see you later."

Parker makes his way down the path, heading back toward his Tahoe.

"Bye, Kitten." Parker mocks Corvus' deep voice and silly nickname and I promptly flip him a double bird. He laughs and turns, disappearing into the trees.

The sun is finally settling into the evening, and forest shadows surround the cabin. The thump of the truck door shutting echoes through the trees and, the next moment, I hear him take off back towards the station. He leaves with a whistle and a smile on his face while all I feel is doubt.

I hate lying, or at least not telling the whole truth. He'll be pissed if he ever figures out I wasn't trying to convince him to leave so Corvus and I could have sex. At least for now, it's a lie I'll have to live with.

A second of panic flares through my chest as I realize that I'm now completely alone with Corvus—and, as far as we know, Parker is the only one who knows where we are. Parker will be back in the morning to pick us up since we don't have a vehicle but plenty can happen in one night.

My biggest concern? Parker shows up in the morning and I've spent the night with a dead body. But, against all my knowledge and training given he suffered a fatal injury, I have a strong feeling that Corvus won't be leaving this world anytime soon.

Time to face the music, Val.

I turn and face the beautifully carved door.

With a final fortifying inhale, I step inside to hear the fat lady sing.

CHAPTER 19
CORVUS

Sharp voices carry through the building and while I try not to focus on the words, it's impossible not to listen to what they're saying.

I'm the reason Valencia has to try and convince her friend to leave her here alone with me and I hate the position it puts us all in. I have tried my hardest to stay genuine and honest with her—both of them—since we met.

Although—what good does that do me when I haven't told the whole truth? There's been so little time since all this started, yet it feels like an eternity with all the shit that's happened. It's starting to feel like a losing battle.

It's not common knowledge, but not every demon is a liar and a cheat. And, not every angel is as holier-than-thou as many would believe.

We all can make our own choices and govern our morals as we see fit. Am I denying that it's easier to follow a particular path? No. If it walks like a vampire and bites like a vampire—let's just say it's probably not an angel. But humans don't usually care for the particulars.

The different scenarios of how this could all blow up in my face flash before my eyes. I take a second to wallow, letting the events of the last few weeks press against my brain. I dread the thought of what the Devil will do if I fail, but I'll try my hardest to avoid that fate at all costs.

Starting with taking care of the little problem that's currently making me feel like I've been ripped in half.

Dumah's blade was made of angelic fire, which just so happens to be capable of causing fatal harm to the damned—like me—even ones of high degree. It's ironic, if you ask me. All Hellspawn are impervious to fire in any state, so the angels get a kick out of the fact that their biggest weapon against us is just that—fire.

Any blade made of angelic fire is known to be able to cut through even the toughest of Hellspawn hides. Had I been in my higher form, I may not have suffered such a deep cut or severe burn, but it would still have hurt like a bitch. Being in my human form put me at a significant disadvantage, which Dumah took great joy in monopolizing.

So, not only can their blades cut you in half, but they can burn you to death at the same time. They really love their little *fuck you* moments.

As if living in Hell isn't enough.

The fact that Valencia isn't severely hurt has nothing to do with the fact that I took the brunt of the attack. I pride myself on my quick reaction to save her, but not even I could've saved her from the onslaught of the burn she should've suffered.

My entire rib cage was burnt to a crisp and the woman didn't even have a welt on her. I've been so consumed by the pain of the cut that I haven't thought about that snippet yet. Humans and demons are all susceptible to angelic fire.

I hear their conversation winding down, so I heave myself out of the bed and stand tall on wobbly knees. I slam the rest of the water she gave me and toss the empty bottle in the small trash can that's sitting in the corner. Being the third lord of Hell does have its perks, but I still suffer the pains of wounds inflicted by holy weapons. Had I been awarded the opportunity to fix it before now, I wouldn't have had to suffer the pain as long. But, since neither Valencia nor Parker knew anything about the supernatural world, I wasn't able to. When Valencia followed Parker outside, I breathed my first breath of relief.

Quickly ensuring that neither of them is looking inside, I take the second I've been given and shift. To the untrained eye, it would appear as if I just disappeared entirely for a few seconds and reappeared instantaneously. Time occurs differently between the realms.

I only need the few seconds it takes to portal into Hell and, then—with a quick step—I'm back in the Earth's reality as though nothing changed.

Instantaneous healing powers are not common in demons. Everything between the realms is about balance. While most beings in Hell are able to conduct powers of death and destruction, beings of Heaven are more suited to healing. Having a familiar form definitely helps, but nothing beats the power that comes with being able to travel through the realms. By shifting between the realms, I'm able to regenerate the damaged cells rapidly. No one knows this is a power I have. Or more likely, a loophole I've found in the system. At first I kept it a secret to ensure I wasn't sabotaged in the trial to become the third lord. Then, I was too fearful on the consequences if I confessed. Now, I simply don't care the reason—it's *my* secret. The only downfall of never telling a soul of this secret power I have is never having the chance to understand it fully.

The gash on my side is now reduced to a bright white scar and what skin had been burned to a crisp is now beautifully healed—it appears just a shade lighter than the surrounding area. I can heal from almost anything without even a speck of the injury remaining, but holy weapons will always leave a lasting mark.

My clothes remain as they were, unfortunately. A giant hole where the sword burned through the thin fabric exposes my new scar at my side. I could've fixed my clothes, but that would have taken more time than what few spare seconds I had. I couldn't risk remaining in Hell long enough to change my clothes to simply come back to an entirely different decade.

I plan on telling Valencia everything, so a hole in my shirt is the least of my worries.

I glance back out the window and see the pair hugging, their heads tucked low and eyes closed, as if to block out anything other than each other.

Jealousy and longing flares through me like icy fingers constricting around my heart. I shove the feeling down—I don't have the time to focus on such things. It would be a disservice to myself and to Valencia; I can't guarantee a future for us.

What the fuck? *A future for us?* I remind myself that there is no *us*. There's me, and there's her. Oh—and there's that little thing called *the deal I made with the fucking Devil*.

I hear Valencia and Parker say their final goodbyes, so I head to the fridge and peek inside. Unfortunately, I'm not so lucky, as the only things left are a couple bottles of mustard, a tub of edible cookie dough, and some alcohol that sits in the fridge door. It's tempting to steal one of the beers but I'd prefer to have both of my hands free. I shut the fridge door just as she enters the cabin. Her eyes land on the empty bed first and her shoulders jerk as she realizes I'm no longer lying there. She quickly scans the small room till her gaze lands on me, standing near the fridge.

"How are you up?" She snaps, her shoulders rising with tension.

"Why don't we sit on the couch and I'll tell you everything." I don't wait to see if she follows and make my way over to the couch and sit down.

The soft tapping of her boots against the floor sounds behind me, and I see her come around the couch. She stubbornly stands over me, arms crossed and eyebrows pinched into a scowl.

I pat the small space on the couch at my side for her to sit down, but she responds with a silent glare. It's a cute look on her—and I begrudgingly admit to myself that I like her fire; her willfully stubborn attitude that unfortunately turns me on. I lean back and rest a forearm on top of the zipper of my jeans in the hope I can force some release on my growing erection.

"Start talking," she demands.

Show instead of tell it is.

I lift the edge of my shirt and flash my healed side to her.

With a gasping breath, she stumbles back, tripping over one of the dining table chairs. I jump up and wrap an arm around her waist as she begins to fall. I pull her against me as I stand back up.

"I told you to sit down," I huff as I set her on her feet.

"And I'm not some bitch in heat who's panting for your next command!" She backs away from me, putting extra space between our bodies. The color drains from her face, lips slightly parted as if she's trying to speak but is unable to force the words out.

She traps me in her glare once again, murder in her eyes. The vein in her neck flutters so fiercely, I can see her pulse. She does well to mask her fear with the anger she's directing at me, but I can practically smell it on her anyway. I can almost taste her fear; it's a peppery aroma that shouldn't be attractive but somehow is.

With a raspy edge, she growls my name, "Corvus."

I hold my hands up in a surrendering move and reclaim my seat on the couch.

"There's no better way to explain this than with brutal honesty. What I'm about to say will seem impossible. All I can ask is that you listen with an open mind."

She cocks an eyebrow but says nothing.

Here goes everything.

"I'm not human."

A thick fog of silence descends over the room. Valencia is a frozen statue of doubt and confusion, the emotions playing so clearly across her face that I can practically watch them like a dance. The glare is now long gone, instead replaced with a large-eyed expression. Her lashes bounce up and down in frog-like blinks.

"Then what are you? Besides a cryptic asshole."

"I am the third Lord of Hell or the King of Crows, to some. But, in a more generalized sense, I'm a demon."

"A demon... Lord of Hell. The third one." The cogs in her brain work hard to piece together the life-altering statement.

"Don't forget a King."

"Of course, your Highness, how could I have forgotten." She bows at her waist but doesn't take her heated eyes off of me. The glare is back.

"Bowing is nice, but I usually prefer my subjects to kneel." I return her glare with a blank expression but can't keep the smirk out of my voice.

The room is engulfed in the tangy scent of her anger. She stands back up and snaps, "Go fuck yourself."

"Well, that's not quite as fun—but if you insist. Care to watch?" At this point, I'm toying with her and I can't really even explain why. I crave her spicy attitude and snarky mouth. Pushing her doesn't necessarily help me achieve my goal, but I'm a victim to her alluring presence and can't help but press every button she exposes to me.

"Is this a fucking game to you?" Her nostrils flare in anger as her fists clench tightly. Tension consumes her from head to toe. I wonder how many more buttons she has left before all-consuming rage takes over her like what I saw at the bar earlier tonight. She did manage to take Dumah by surprise, which would've been impossible for an average human.

Average, she is not. But angry—she's definitely angry—and I'm dancing the fine line of her fury. Typically, I'd lean into that anger just to see how far her wrath will actually go. I'm a demon; we love chaos and destruction. Despite my desire to push her further, I'll have to feel the kiss of her outrage another time.

"No games. That's the truth, as impossible as it seems." I lean forward and rest my elbows on my knees, interlacing my fingers.

"Okay, let's say I believe you—which I don't—but let's pretend I do. That leaves me with more questions than answers! How did your wound heal? How did you not fucking *die* from that? How does Dane play into this? How do I play into this? What the fuck is going on?" She starts counting the questions on her fingers, animatedly speaking with her hands. The last one is spoken so softly I know I wasn't meant to hear it.

"I shifted; it takes a lot more to kill me than that. Dane isn't human and, I suspect, neither are you," I answer at once.

Frog blink. Frog Blink. Frog blink.

"I'm not—what? Human?"

I nod.

"Yes, I'm not human, or yes, I am human?" she asks shakily.

"Valencia, there's no way you're entirely human." I can see she wants to interrupt me, but I lift a hand to stop her, "How long have you been cheating Death?"

She remains quiet, but shadows cloud her eyes. I can see the wheels turning in her head. She wants to argue my point but knows I'm right. In the week I've known her, she's survived three near-death situations.

One week. If Death has had this close an eye on her up to now, I can't imagine what she's survived in the past.

"Humans don't cheat Death. They always pay their due. You, Kitten, are a feisty little cat with your claws dug so deep into your life force that not even Death seems able to defeat you."

"So—what, I'm a demon like you?" She mumbles, the confusion starting to rise above her panic.

"You saw what that sword did to me—saw the severity of the aftermath. Yet, you were left unscathed. You were touched by the infernal blade and left with barely a *scratch*," I breathe. "You'd have been burned if you were even *part* demon."

"Okay, so if I'm not human and not a demon, then what?" she scoffs, shaking her head as if I'm completely deluded.

"I'd say you and Dane have much more in common than you expect." Bright blue eyes flare with irritation when I say his name.

"What the fuck do me and that piece of shit have in common?" Her lips twist with a sour expression.

"His real name is Dumah, and he's an Archangel of Heaven. He is most definitely a self-righteous bastard. He wasn't always that way but—that's a story for another time."

"So, you're saying I'm an angel? Have you met me? I'm pretty sure God would Sparta-kick me out of Heaven if I ever showed up to his pearly gates."

"That's where things get tricky."

"Oh, because everything else makes so much sense," she snarks.

"Just listen. Humans have it wrong—as they normally do. Humans think that Hell is some fiery realm full of endless suffering. And, there is some of that, but not all of it is as they would assume. Hell is a mirror of Earth. As humans and Earth have progressed over the years, so, too, has Hell. Technology, civilizations—anything you can imagine, there's a mirror image in Hell. That means all the bad things on Earth show up in Hell but, sometimes, there's good as well."

She interrupts me, "And how does this geography lesson on Hell help me to understand how I'm not the worst choice for an angel in history?"

"Because not only did humans get it wrong about the realms, but they also got it wrong about the beings. Heaven and Hell have been opposing parties since the start of time, yes—but angels and demons have not."

She pauses. "That doesn't make any sense."

She finally pulls out a chair from the dining table and sits, though she perches on the edge—like she wants to remain ready for anything.

I can tell she's far from believing me but she's not running, screaming, or outright denying me so I continue my explanation. "In the beginning, angels were from Heaven and demons were from Hell. In a remarkable turn of fate, humans were created—and so was free will. Humans think free will is all about them, but it's about every being in this universe.

"Angels fell from the sky and demons rose from the ashes. Some angels warred against the decisions of their higher power. Some demons no longer enjoyed living a life surrounded by death and despair. Demons who were originally from Hell were given grace and redemption. Angels who fell from Heaven were seen to be leading wicked crusades. At this point, a being's fate was not determined by their species but by the accumulation of their choices.

"That all leads us to now. Being of one realm or the other doesn't inherently mean you are meant to reside in that realm. It's a choice. Or, more accurately, a long list of choices made over an infinite amount of time." I look at her. "So, even though you are an angel, you still get to decide. Your soul is so young that the option of all three realms is still open to you. Fate is a guide but we are not required to follow it. Every choice we make could change our destiny forever."

We sit in silence for a moment, the only sounds the popping crackles of the fire.

"Okay." She scrunches her face and taps two fingers against her forehead. "So you're Lord King Demon. Dane—I mean Dumah—is an Archangel Bastard, and I'm his little angel choir girl. Does that sound about right?"

"I mean—"

"Angel Baby," she scoffs quietly to herself, interrupting me.

"What?" I question, completely confused.

"Dane—*Dumah*—called me Angel Baby at the bar. I didn't catch it, then, but it makes sense now if your unbelievable story is true."

"I don't think he knew what you were until after he attacked us. I didn't suspect anything until then, either."

"Oh," she looks off to the fire, silent for a few seconds. I start to brush it off, but the recognition brightens her eyes before she looks back at me. "When I first met him, I was wearing an old shirt from high school. We were the Kewpies, so our mascot was literally a baby doll. I was in this girl's group after school and we had shirts made. It says 'Angel Baby' across the front. He made a comment about me not changing that day—that he liked my shirt—and I just thought he was flirting or had social anxiety."

"Dumah isn't known for his sense of humor but you unknowingly walked right into that one," I laugh bitterly, tension setting in my jaw.

She leans heavily into her chair. "I almost died that day because of him. He asked me all these weird questions about God and life and I just thought he was, like, really religious. I never saw it coming. Does that make me stupid?" Those bright blue eyes bore into me.

"You're not stupid. You didn't know what he was capable of. I'm the fool here. I didn't think he'd go that far; I should've stopped him sooner. I'm sorry, I truly am."

"What do you mean, 'you should've stopped him?' I didn't meet you until after the accident."

"I was there."

"No, you weren't," she argues.

"Yes, I was. I've been with you nearly every day since that first on the mountain."

Slowly, her anger returns, and I realize it may be a defense mechanism. Any time I see her fearful or unsure, the anger comes creeping in, replacing those fears—protecting her from them.

"So, you demons have super healing *and* invisibility powers? Cut the shit, I'm tired of the mind games. Just tell me the truth, Corvus." She demands, smacking her hand down on the table.

"I am!" I snap. "I told you before, I healed because I shifted between the realms. I don't really have time to explain how right now but—I have what you would call a familiar form. I can shift into a crow," I tell her pointedly.

"A crow." A single eyebrow arches as if my ability to shift is the most absurd thing she's heard today. "You want me to believe, on top of everything else, that you can literally shapeshift?"

"Really? You'll believe that I'm a Lord of Hell—that you were nearly killed by an Archangel, and that you, yourself, aren't entirely human—but *shapeshifting* is where you draw the line?" I ask, incredulity creeping into my tone despite myself.

"Well, when you put it that way," her voice trails off quietly at the end but I don't believe she'll so easily give up. "Okay, so shift then."

"It's not safe for me to shift. I shifted earlier so I could heal but I won't risk more than that while we're still not sure of Dumah's whereabouts. And—before you ask why it matters—each shift leaves a trace of my essence behind. Too many powerful beings, one of which is Dumah, can be led directly to our location if they know what to look for. The shift earlier was seconds, which leaves a marker so small it's like finding a needle in a haystack. Any longer, and the search becomes much, much easier. I won't risk it." I don't mention that I portaled to Hell in order to shift—not wanting to drop too much at once, or she *really* won't believe me.

"Okay, Bird-Man, and how else do you propose proving it?" She crosses her arms and stubbornly looks at me as if my unwillingness to shift proves that I've been lying this whole time.

I stand up from my seat on the couch and reach into my pocket. Valencia narrows her eyes at me but doesn't comment.

Better toughen your skin cause you're about to meet kitten claws.

Out of my pocket, I pull a replica of the trinket I gave her that night at the bar. The beads are all in their exact place, the wire shaped into 'V' just so. I walk over and place it on the table next to her.

She stares at the item as if it's about to jump off the table and bite her.

I murmur to her quietly. "You once asked me for a prize. It was the best I could come up with."

CHAPTER 20

VALENCIA

I STARE AT THE token. Whatever I thought would happen, this wasn't even on my top 10 list of options. Corvus' unbelievable story kept getting crazier and crazier—and I decided to listen if only to hear his sexy voice ramble on.

When I asked for proof, I didn't think he'd actually be able to provide any.

I gingerly grab my token in my jacket pocket. For some reason, I'd taken to carrying it around with me. I often catch myself toying with the beads, spinning them around the wire like a small fidget tool. If I didn't know—with clear assurance—that *my* token was still in my pocket, then I could easily accuse him of stealing mine and pretending it was a copy.

The contrast between the smooth beads and the textured lava rock sends alarming signals through my nervous system. Tingles in my spine fizzle through my back and the hairs on my arms start to stand on end.

Without taking my eyes off the token still resting on the table, I pull my own out of my pocket and lay it next to the other. They're strikingly similar, down to the smallest details. I ignore Corvus and continue to run through all the possibilities of him having the same item.

Both are far too similar to be made by the same bird. Sure, it could've been taught to create such an item but, without thumbs, it would surely be impossible for the crow to craft identical items.

The second option is that Corvus could've made the items himself and trained the crow to bring one to me that night at the bar. This one seemed far more likely—and I wish, so badly, that it's true. But one thing held me back from demanding Corvus tell the truth, again.

You once asked me for a prize...

So many flashes of moments from the last few weeks blur through my mind at blinding speed. All the times the crow was there—behaving so weirdly. I just thought I was living my own Disney princess moment.

Being a secret Disney princess would've been so much better.

Instead, I find out I'm actually part angel. I'm being hunted by an Archangel who definitely has it out for me. And I've been hanging out with a demon who is also a lord of Hell.

What the fuck has my life come to?

"You're not what I expected a demon to be. I expected more. . . horns?" I say, finally acknowledging Corvus for the first time since he placed his twin token on the table. He's resumed his position on the couch, his thick forearms resting atop his knees.

"I have them, just not in this form," he responds coolly.

"How many forms do you have?"

Instead of answering, he looks at me with a pointed gaze. The tiny muscles beneath his eyes contract slightly. I haven't spent much time around the man, the. . . demon—but I can already tell he's trying to see inside my mind with this look.

"You're not reacting to this how I thought you would. I expected more. . . claws?" The even timber of his voice glides over my body and stirs up an untimely heat in my gut. I ignore the sensation as best I can.

"Oh, don't worry, I'm freaking the fuck out." I fiddle with the tokens, rolling the beads around. It's an oddly soothing motion but it doesn't do much to dampen the all-consuming sense of fear that's begun to settle over me. Thankfully, my many years as a first responder on the front lines of disaster have taught me how to work through even the most consuming of emotions. Still, I'm not ignorant that, at some point—most likely sooner than later—the emotions will boil over.

"Well, then—to answer your question—I have three forms. This one is my main form, or what I generally present as. It's the easiest to use. Like I said earlier, the crow is my familiar form. The third is my true, demon form—horns and all."

"That seems like a wildly vague explanation." I return his stare, the deep amber in his eyes drawing me in. He truly is a beautiful man. Between the short beard, tattoos, and muscular frame he paints a ruggedly sexy picture. He's larger than most men and—with a start—I wonder whether that's because he's not really a man at all.

Is it rude to call him a man? I think about what the etiquette for demons could be. The only experience I have with demons is stories of Catholic priests performing exorcisms.

I'm pretty sure demons aren't supposed to be sexy packages of sin that looked more suited for a good fuck than a scary possession. Or maybe they are? He said humans got it wrong before and, now that I think about it, hot demons make way more sense.

"Valencia?" Corvus' blurts, knocking me out of my daze.

He looks at me with a cocked brow, expectation lining his face. I realize I've been spaced out in my thoughts long enough that I missed what he had to say.

I hesitate. "Sorry, I was lost in thought. What did you say?"

"What were you thinking about? This will go much more smoothly if you think out loud so I can help fill in the blanks." Corvus leans against the couch, seemingly relaxed, and I have to actively prevent my eyes from hungrily eating up the view. I don't look away from his face as he reclines, so I don't miss it as the corners of his mouth slightly rise; like he's trying to suppress a smirk. Damn him for his ability to see right through my avoidance.

Determined to change the direction of my thoughts, I blurt out the first thing that comes to mind, "So, is it rude to call you a man?"

He laughs now. He doesn't suppress the deep, rolling sound. It just isn't fair for anyone to be this attractive in everything they do.

It's starting to make a lot of sense why Eve gave in to temptation.

"No, it's not rude at all. At least, not to me." He softly scratches his bearded jawline, and my attention is drawn there. I can barely hear the audible scrape of his nails through the coarse hair.

The thought of his beard scraping against the delicate skin of my inner thigh is mind-numbing. Thankfully, he continues—unaware of my dirty thoughts.

"Some do dislike it, though; they take their demon heritage very seriously. But, most could care less, and wear their human form predominantly or per-manently—depending on the species—so, getting called a human term isn't of consequence."

"*Okay*," I draw out the last syllable. I have so many more questions, I don't know where to begin. I think back on the previous few weeks and what I've learned in the last hour. All of that combined leaves one thing circling unanswered in my head.

"So, why me?" I ask.

"Why you—*what*?"

I huff as I stand abruptly and start pacing around the small space. "Let's start with this; why is Dumah after me?"

"Without giving you another history lesson, which I'm sure you don't want to hear, it's hard to explain." I don't stop my pacing, but I shoot him a look that screams *'get on with it'*. He continues, "Heaven and Hell are at war. It's less about winning and more about who can amass the bigger army. Dumah is like...a recruiter, for that army, and he originally sought you out to test whether you'd be a good fit. For Heaven—that is. The problem with angels is, when you insult their higher power they have a tendency to grow vicious. Nothing you said to him that day was insulting, but he must've decided it wasn't worth the trouble of changing your opinion."

"But what drew him to me in the first place? He infiltrated a large organization and presented all the proper credentials. This was a well-thought-out plan, not some random happenstance." If the floor was made of something other than sturdy wooden planks, I'd be concerned about pacing a hole straight through it.

"Your angel heritage, however small, places you in a higher tier than normal humans. Whatever side you join will gain whatever power you have—Dumah would be looking to ascertain that power for himself and Heaven. Angels are more power-hungry than you'd expect."

"I don't have any powers."

"Yet."

I stop my pacing to stare at him. He's still leaning back on the couch, taking up the majority of it in that way men tend to do. Despite witnessing his ability to heal with my own eyes, I can't imagine what kind of powers he could be talking about.

Super healing and a flaming sword are the only mystical things I've witnessed with my own eyes and I'm a firm believer that *seeing is believing* and all that. To conserve as much of my sanity as possible, I decide to put aside this conversation for a later date. Preferably much, much later.

"When someone joins either side of the war, their power transfers to that side, too?" I ask, making sure I understand. "Do they lose it when this happens?" I restart my pacing.

"No, it doesn't affect the amount of power the individual has—it boosts the entity as a whole. Every being gets a little sip of that power, all the way to the top." Corvus states matter-of-factly.

I glance at him from the corner of my eye and find that his eyes are focused on the couch cushion where his large fingers fiddle with a pulled thread. "You're joking, right?" I pause, placing both hands on my hips as I face him.

"No?" There's no hesitation in his answer but I can hear the question in his voice.

"You're telling me that the celestial war between Heaven and Hell is basically just an MLM?"

"Emellem?" His dark brows pinch down and I realize he thinks I've said a word, not an acronym.

"M - L - M," I sound out each letter slowly so he can distinguish the letters outside of the sound. "It's called multilevel marketing. It's basically a seedy way for salespeople to sell shit without doing any of the work themselves—like a gang but for housewives. Those at top make money from every individual below them. Sound familiar?" With a shake of my head, I laugh at the insanity of it all.

"That sounds. . . oddly similar," he murmurs, a grimace on his face.

"No shit," I huff and turn and face the fire. My thoughts race. "You said that this war wasn't really about winning but that it's about the armies. What does that mean?"

He considers his words for a moment. "Heaven and Hell have been at odds since the start of time. The Scale was created to ensure that one side didn't overpower the other—or, at least, not for long. Based on the amassed power, the scales are tipped to one side or the other. The Scale demands balance and it will do anything to achieve it. The scales tip back and forth as humanity grows and new souls are added. Humans have always managed to throw a coin to one side or the other throughout history."

"But you said that each side has good and bad? So, who determines which side you go to? The Scale?"

"Generally, the individual decides. Humans don't always get the choice, as they don't have any power, so the decision is purely based on the accumulation of their deeds. They go to Heaven or Hell, or maybe stay right here on Earth as ghosts. Ghosts are probably the one thing humans have gotten right throughout the years, actually. For the other species, if given the opportunity, they can decide. If they cannot—then, yes, the Scale decides."

"So, it matters where the soul goes because that's where the power goes? And humans don't matter because they're not really that powerful?" I ask, trying to put together the invisible puzzle pieces that currently make up my current reality.

"Yes—more or less. What's important is that Heaven and Hell both are willing to do *anything* to get a hold of more power. To take it for themselves—and keep it from each other. Most times, they send recruiters like Dumah to acquire the power and, usually, they accomplish this through death, since it's the easiest way to harvest a being's power without a fight. Whether it be death or decision, though, it doesn't really matter about the *how*—just the outcome."

"Dumah told me *'death is better than another for the damned.'* If he'd have killed me, would that mean I go to Heaven?" The questions and answers have knotted together so much that I can barely tell the truth from fiction.

"Not necessarily. He would've claimed your power at that moment, therefore gaining more power for Heaven, but at the cost of your mortal life."

"For every answer you give me, I have more questions," I murmur toward the fire, my eyes closed. We've been talking long enough that the logs are thoroughly engulfed—we'll have to add more soon to keep the cabin warm.

Clothes rustle together but I don't open my eyes to look, so I startle when I feel large hands grip my shoulders. Before I can pull away, he begins to slowly knead the back of my neck with his thumbs.

It feels too good to push him away or ask him to stop. A low moan escapes my lips. Corvus' fingers tense briefly but quickly resume their soft massage.

Drowning in the comfort his slow ministrations provide, the weight of everything happening finally starts to lift from my shoulders. His fingers work magic on my tense muscles, and I begin to imagine what else he is good at.

The thought of him using one hand to grip me by the hair while the other fucks me to oblivion is an intoxicating daydream. I can practically imagine the feel of his thick fingers as they stretch me, preparing me for more. Though he seems to get off on my snarky attitude, Corvus strikes me as the kind of man who demands control in the bedroom. How I would love to test his patience in that area.

A sharp sting of pain flares down my right arm as he rubs a particularly sore spot. My headache has eased but the pain from the knot he still works is enough to wake me up from my needy trance.

Jumping into bed with a man when my life is falling apart isn't the best idea. Jumping into bed with a demon seems like an even worse one.

I slowly pull away from his grasp, glad he releases me easily. It's not that I think he'd hold me against my will, but his resistance to let me go certainly wouldn't help my willpower to step away.

"I know it's a lot, and I'm sorry I'm the one to have to explain this to you," Corvus says soothingly, his apologetic tone clear. He truly is sorry but, unfortunately, sorry doesn't get us out of this mess.

"Who else would've explained all of this to me?" I ask.

"Well, the most likely scenario is that it would be whichever parent your angelic lineage comes from."

The thought of my parents sends a blinding pain through my chest and I struggle to keep from audibly gasping. It's an innocent comment, and there's no way he could know the severity of his statement, yet it hurts all the same.

A thought occurs to me, then. Corvus once asked how many times I've cheated death. In the last week, death has sure seemed hungry for me—but it wasn't the first time I'd faced an untimely demise and unexpectedly survived.

"You said a powerful being could steal another's power through death?" I look over my shoulder at him. A nod is his only response.

I grimace and look back at the fire, allowing my thoughts to roil together like the flames of the fire. "All the times I almost died, something was trying to steal my power?"

"I'd say most, if not all, were a result of something like that, yes."

"My, my family—" I choke on the words, a sob clawing its way up my throat.

I pinch the bridge of my nose and close my eyes, squeezing them as tightly as I can to lock the tears inside. Flashes of fire appear behind my closed lids—though it's more of a blur of bright colors than a clear image.

I'm thankful that Corvus remains at my back, so the despair on my face is hidden from him. An aching pain has started to grow behind my eyes and at the back of my neck. If I spend any more time with my past, a migraine won't be too far away.

With a deep breath, I push through the pain and try again. "My family died in a fire when I was eleven. My parents and my younger brother. Do you think—" another sob works its way up my throat and I have to take a second to tamp the emotion back down. "Do you think someone was after me that night?"

"I think that it was an extremely unfortunate accident, and I'm so sorry that happened to you." He responds gently, as if his voice alone could soothe my aching soul.

"I should've died that night." My hands start to shake and my lungs struggle to draw in enough air.

"Valencia, it wasn't your fault," he speaks softly, like any loud noises might tip me over the edge.

"They're all gone and it was supposed to be me who died." I shake my head sharply, squeezing my eyes closed. No matter how hard I press them together, the images still consume my vision.

My chest begins to heave hard and fast, barely offering me enough time between them to draw my next breath. My throat constricts with the effort and something damp pools in the corner of my eye. I choke. My lungs feel like they're about to burst and like they'll never get enough air all at once.

I double over as creeping darkness echoes at the edges of my vision.

The fire's so bright, I have to hold my hand against my eyes as I try to get a good look at what's happening. The flames engulf the roof, licking higher and higher into the sky. The roaring fills my ears. Heat lashes against my skin, an invisible force that begs me to step closer. Its touch is like death and despair combined—a chaos greater than any I have ever experienced.

Panic takes hold of my limbs, rooting me in place as the house burns down.

Where's my family? Are they in there?

My heart races, body shaking uncontrollably. What have I done?

What have I done? What have I done? What have I done? What have I—

"Valencia!" A loud voice snaps me out of the past and I blink, black circles clouding my eyes.

Strong hands wrap around my arms and turn me. I no longer try to force the tears to remain inside—there's no stopping them now.

My breaths are ragged, and I inhale deeply through my nose as the nausea that churns my stomach is riled once again.

Corvus uses the pad of his thumb to swipe at the tracks of tears running down my cheeks. Warmth seeps from his palms into the sides of my neck and the strength of his grip offers me a sense of comfort. His controlling hold would usually piss me off but, in this moment, I'm grateful for it. I'm thankful for the ability to let loose these catastrophic emotions and know that he'll be there to hold me through it.

"Just breathe, I'm right here."

"I can't," my throat constricts and the tears fall even harder. I lost my entire family, and I spent my whole life believing that it was just a random act of shitty fate that took them from me.

But, now I'm supposed to just go along with the knowledge that it wasn't random and that whoever was responsible for killing my entire family is still coming after me? They may as well have killed me that night—taking my whole family. Why must they continue to hunt for a heart that's already severely broken?

I couldn't save them then—and I'm not sure I can save me, now. Once again, I'm at the mercy of fate as my world is derailed around me. How many more people must I lose before they finally win?

Who else am I willing to sacrifice to live a little longer?

The final straw is the thought of Parker—burning—along with my family.

My airways constrict so tight and I'm again robbed of the ability to breathe. I'm trapped in a body that won't listen to my commands.

A hundred sharp stings of pain flicker across the back of my head, startling me from the horrors of my past and into the deep depths of warm brown eyes. Corvus looks down at me, pupils so blown that they take up almost his entire iris. It's like he's forced them into black holes that can swallow me whole.

"Stay with me," he growls, the sound cutting through the sound of burning wood. His deep timber reaches my soul and grabs on tightly, ripping me back to the present. Though I'm here now, no longer a victim trapped in my past, I still can't breathe. White dots dance in my vision.

"Breathe!" he commands.

The stings of pain returns and I realize his hand has grasped a fistful of my hair, directing my attention back to him.

A gasping breath fills my lungs. It's nearly as painful to take as it was to have it ripped away in the first place. Shaky inhales flutter through me but barely touch the well of panic I'm drowning in.

"What do you need? Just tell me what you need," he begs, his own fears clearly evident in his concerned expression.

I try to think about what I need, but nothing comes to mind. I need to force the memories back into their tiny box in the dark corner of my mind. I need to escape the grief of the past so I can focus on what to do with my life in the present. I need to ensure that nothing terrible happens to the people I care about again.

I don't want to do any of that, though. I want to forget about it all. Usually, that would require a bottle of whiskey but there's not enough alcohol in this cabin to even cause a mild hangover.

Corvus lightly squeezes my neck to draw out a reaction.

I may not have any alcohol but there is something else that could take my mind off everything. I don't break eye contact as I dip one hand to grip his side. He doesn't outwardly react to my touch, so I continue.

My hand easily slips under the hem of his shirt and the heat of his skin against my fingertips elicits in me a new type of burning.

"What are you doing?" he asks, concern and confusion battling their way across his expression—but he doesn't pull away.

I slip my other hand under his shirt and slowly glide it across his stomach and sides. There are so many dips and valleys—my mouth waters at the thought of running my tongue across each one.

My hands travel higher, brushing across the expanse of his chest. I know his shirt is riding up but, with the tight grip he still has on my hair, I can't look down to see what a delicious view I'm exposing. I gently bring my hands back down, scraping a nail across his left pectoral in the process.

"Valencia," he warns.

I continued to ignore him, afraid that tears will escape if I say a single word. What I'm doing is pretty obvious, so I don't know why he keeps pretending as though he doesn't understand.

For a brief moment, I wonder if he's not into me—and that's why he's questioning this. Then, I remember all the flirting and naughty looks he's given me since I met him, so I continue.

My fingers finally make it down his tall body, and I fumble with his belt clasp.

With a groan, he releases the hand on my neck to catch my fingers in one hand, somehow managing to snag enough fingers on each hand that I can no longer move them.

He growls, "We're not doing this."

I blink. "Why not? You said that you wanted to know what I needed. Well, this is it. I want you to make me forget everything. I want you to fuck me so hard I forget life outside of this moment." The words rush out of me in a sharp, panicked ramble.

The whites of his eyes gleam brightly and his nostrils flare as the dirty words leave my mouth. Desire surges through me and I struggle to pull my fingers from his grasp so I can resume my exploration of his delicious body. He just stands, still as a statue, staring down at me. His eyes seem incapable of looking anywhere other than my lips—but he's extremely tense, as if rooted in place.

"If you don't want me, just say so," I mutter, self-doubt finally creeping in and replacing all of my lust-filled bravado with uncertainty.

"I didn't say that," he states. Even though the words sound harsh, I swear I feel his body sway towards me. The lump in his throat moves as he swallows hard, holding himself back for reasons I don't understand.

"Then what is it?" I ask

"I'm not doing this with you right now. You're emotionally vulnerable. I don't want you to ever regret me touching you, nor do I want to take advantage of you. Is that so wrong?" he argues, as if I'm crazy for even asking about it.

He's not entirely wrong. I *am* emotionally vulnerable—but I've not once thought him capable of taking advantage of me. I appreciate what he's trying to do, but I'd rather have the reward of at least one mind-blowing orgasm I know he would give me.

Anything is better than the despair that sits on the edge of my mind, waiting for its opportunity to drown me.

"I know what I'm asking for. I know that I want you. Is that so wrong?" I counter.

"It's not a good idea." He shakes his head, refusing to make eye contact.

"*Ugh*—" I snarl, frustration nearly erasing my desire. I'm not really angry with him, though. I'm more terrified of what he saw.

What will he think of me now that he's seen me lose it so entirely? My anger is just a grand mask for my pain but I'd rather him think I'm a raging bitch than weak.

"If you're not going to give me what I want," I say, "then fuck off so I can find someone else who will."

His eyes flash as he surveys me for a moment. He leans forward and drags me towards him, using the large handful of my hair to direct me where he wants. He has my head tipped back at an angle, his dark gaze intently trained on me. Our hearts pound so loudly, I swear I can hear them.

A battle has raged inside him, and it seems he's finally lost.

"Over my dead body," he snarls back. "You're *mine*."

Chapter 21

Corvus

This is a horrible idea—but I've never been one to back down from a challenge, and that's exactly what she's done. She's challenged my resistance, control, and sanity. And I've loved every second of it.

What I don't love is the thought of her with another man. I don't have any right to claim her as mine but I'm doing it anyway. I'll be damned twice over before I allow her bratty attitude to go unpunished.

I'm playing a perilous game but I guess that's part of the fun.

My hand grips her hair so tightly that she's forced to look up at me. Bright blue eyes widen at my claim. I could drown in the oceanic depths of her eyes. Maybe her secret power is being able to bring me to my knees, drowning me above water.

There's no room for any more words in this heated moment. I know telling her she's mine shocked her; her gasp when I said so was easy enough to read. I don't want to take advantage of her but my ability to resist her flew out the window when she threw down the challenge. If this is what she needs, I need to respect that. She's a grown woman who knows her own mind.

Who am I to deny her pleasure when she wants it?

Without breaking either hold, I drag her to me, so our bodies are completely flush. Because of our considerable height difference, my cock is pressed against her stomach and the tight denim constricts against my swelling erection, causing tingles to rush down the shaft with each movement.

Finally, I lean down and devour her mouth.

I fuck her mouth with my tongue as if I were fucking her elsewhere.

A groan rumbles up my throat, and she swallows the sound with a moan of her own. Our tongues battle briefly before I feel the sharp sting of her teeth bite down on my lip. It's not enough to break the skin but the tingle of pain rushes straight to my already straining dick.

The cotton fabric of my boxers is not nearly as soft as her skin would be—nor as warm—but, with the amount of precum leaking out, I imagine they'll be just as wet if we continue this much longer. I kiss her deeply again as I rub myself against her stomach. The drag of the denim across the tip sends shudders down my legs and another moan creeps out of my mouth.

Valencia then sucks my sore lip into her mouth, which drives me even crazier. What I wouldn't give to feel her hot mouth wrap around my cock and suck me so far down she chokes. I'd fuck her mouth so hard she wouldn't need lipstick for her lips to be red.

I lean back slightly, breaking our kiss, the thought of her swollen mouth too good to ignore. She groans softly at the space between us. I look down at her and can't help the growl that escapes me at the sight.

Just as I hoped, they're red-tinted and slightly damp. She opens her eyes briefly and our gazes connect. There's so much need in that one look, I'm sure it's close to mirroring my own. I lower my head down again and her lashes flutter at the movement.

Instead of retaking her mouth, I nip just under her ear before gliding my mouth down the side of her neck. Her skin is warm to the touch and slightly salty—probably a tiny bit of sweat from the stress of the conversation earlier. To taste her like this is close to torture. I want to lick the stress from her entire body and engulf myself in the tang of her fear and anger.

My demon side rages at the cage of this body as it gorges on her soured emotions. It's not often that I notice the true demon sitting this close to the surface. In my demon form, a bestial side comes out. I can control it—but it's closer to beast than man. Strong emotions can draw it closer to the surface, whether mine or someone else's. The mix of my own uncontrollable arousal and the smell and taste of her emotions is like offering a bone to a demon dog. Thankfully, I've been alive long enough that I don't need to fear the demon escaping when I don't want it to.

I pull the edge of her shirt and jacket to the side and suck deeply at the crook of her neck. A guttural moan rolls through her—so deep that I feel the vibrations of it in my mouth.

I start to feel her dip on shaky legs. "Corvus, please," she begs, tugging her hands in an attempt to escape the grip I still have on her fingers. Instantly, I release her hair and fingers and catch her before she drops entirely to the floor. The movement breaks my hold on her neck with a suctioning pop.

I grip two handfuls of her ass and bend down slightly so I can drag her up my body. She quickly wraps her legs around my waist, locking her ankles behind my back. My hands squeeze so tightly I wonder if she'll have fingerprint bruises. The thought sends burning heat through my body and my cock begs for relief.

She wraps nimble arms around my neck as she holds onto me. I glance at the side of her neck I just released and am pleased to see the darkening bruise of a hickey at the base. Seeing the evidence of my marks on her fuels the primal urges of my bestial side. The desire to mark her all over floods me till I'm nearly blinded by it.

I've had sex many times with different beings, but nothing has ever been so consuming. Never have I been so out of control. She commands me like a siren, drawing me into her dark depths. If I didn't have proof of her angelic nature, I'd wonder if she was part succubus, instead.

Valencia's little growl snaps me out of my daze, drawing my attention away from her neck and back to her eyes. Pricks of pain erupt across the back of my head and I realize in my haze that she's dug her little claws into my hair, pulling it tightly at the roots.

"Kiss me," she demands, trying to force my mouth back to hers.

It's adorable how she thinks she's in charge. Instead of doing what she wants, I ignore the sharp pain as she tugs my hair harder and shift her weight into one bent arm, which brings her a couple of inches higher up my body. With my other hand, I grip the fabric at her back and start to pull. With a growled, "Off," I tug her shirt and jacket over her head. The move forces her to release my hair.

As her top flies over her head, I'm greeted with the grand view of her bra-covered chest right in my face. Before I've managed to pull her clothes completely from her body, I start sucking and nipping my way across her chest. She wears a simple black cotton bra that's exceptionally soft but doesn't hold a candle to the feel of her skin against my lips.

I toss her clothes to the side and use my free hand to drag her bra down so far that it rests beneath her breasts. Between the bunched fabric and the tight straps, her nipples point straight to the ceiling. I kiss my way to one nipple then I suck the entire tip into my mouth. The tight little bud is so hard it begs to be bitten. I may be a demon, but I'm happy to be the one to answer its little prayers.

As soon as I capture her nipple in my teeth, she moans my name so sweetly that, for a second, I wonder if the sound alone could make me finish.

Valencia resumes her grip on my hair while smashing my face against her chest. The movement causes her nipple to pop out of my mouth, so I move to the other side. Instead of biting this one, I suck and lick at it till the bud is equally as engorged as the other.

She finally manages to yank my head back far enough that she can lean down and kiss me. I snarl at the pain but let her do it. Not because she's in control, but because I want her lips bad enough to let her.

This time, she attacks my mouth like it's her turn to devour me, nipping and sucking before dragging her mouth away to kiss down the side of my neck like I did hers. She doesn't spend long enough in one spot to mark me, but it still sends shreds of electricity through my body every time my skin and her lips connect. As she continues to kiss my neck, I tighten my grip on her body and walk us towards the bed.

A shocked gasp escapes her as I toss her onto the bed on her back. She looks up at me with this wide-eyed expression and the same big frog blinks from before. Her breasts bounce briefly before she covers them with her hands.

For a moment, I think about smacking her hands away but let her leave them there since that makes her comfortable.

I take a second to enjoy the view. Her skin is touched by the barest amount of light but I can see the red rash from my beard across her chest. Her nipples are a dusky red and the ring around them a rosy pink in the dim lighting. The sun set during our conversation earlier and the dying fire is now the only source of light in the room, shedding a soft amber glow.

I quickly undo the laces of her boots and rip them off, tossing them towards the door. I reach up, wrap my fingers around the waistband of her pants, and pause—looking into her eyes.

I silently question if she's truly ready for this next step or if the heated kiss will be enough to take her mind off our earlier conversation but she quickly nods, so I peel her pants down her legs, purposely leaving her underwear where they are. There's nothing like delayed gratification.

Tossing her pants in the same direction as I did her shoes, I lean over her to reclaim her lips in another heated kiss. This one is slower, more sensual and passionate than hungry.

The edge from earlier has been whittled down to an aching lust that consumes me. My dick hasn't been this hard without relief in a very long time. Still, I ignore the straining appendage and focus on her instead.

I'm standing at the edge of the bed, my weight braced on my hands, as I lean over her to kiss her. She tastes so good.

I leave the haven of her lips to drag my mouth down her neck, then the center of her chest, all the way to her panties. I slowly lower myself to my knees as I go, dragging my hands down the sides of her body in the process. I finally reach her center and lean back to take in the view.

There's nothing overtly sensual about her underwear; it's made of plain black cotton that matches her bra. She definitely chose this set with comfort over looks in mind. Regardless, the thin cotton is no match for her damp arousal. I slowly lower my face, my eyes locked on her as I go. She's now perched up on her elbows, pupils blown wide—probably a mix of arousal and the dark room—but she focuses on me and I know she can see enough to want to watch.

I drag my nose along the inside of her thigh, breathing in her sweet scent. It's so delicious—like she's begging to be eaten. "You smell like sex, Kitten. Are you wet for me?"

She answers in a moan, not responding with words. Her thighs contract as if she were going to block me from getting any closer. I wrap one arm around a thigh and drag it to the side, opening her up wide. The scent of her arousal bursts out and I can see a damp spot has darkened her panties at the center.

I dive in, placing my mouth right over the top of the darkened fabric, and suck. The cotton fills my mouth, full of her taste, and I'm instantly harder than a brick. Not sure how it's possible to get harder, but it's like every new thing about her sends every drop of blood I have straight to my cock.

With a growled moan, I suck her in deeper, dragging her essence throughout my entire body. She drops back to the bed, her arms flying out to grip the sheets tightly, and thrashes—as if to pull away—but my firm grip on her thigh prevents her from doing so. Maybe she'll get fingerprint bruises here, too. I don't focus on how much the thought pleases me.

I drag my mouth up to the apex of her center and press my tongue down hard on what I hope is her clit. Then, I shake my head back and forth vigorously, humming in pleasure as she bows off the bed. The vibrations from my moan and movements cause her knees to start shaking uncontrollably. I begin to pull away from her clit—but she presses down on the back of my head.

"No, please don't stop," she begs.

"Don't worry, I won't leave you in pain like this," I murmur against her clit. The shifting of my lips against her now sensitive clit causes more shudders to flow through her body.

With the hand that's holding down her thigh, I pull her panties to the side. The first look at her pretty pink pussy is like a gift from Heaven that I surely don't deserve.

"Ugh, look how pretty you are," I can't help but moan. I don't look away from the glistening pink of her sex—instead, I lower my mouth right onto the center of her and shove my tongue inside as far as it will go.

I swirl it around, savoring the taste of her. It's like drinking down a bottle full of her scent mixed with the taste of tangy sex. A pussy isn't supposed to taste like flowers or fruits; it's supposed to taste like sex, and desperation, and *need*. Everything my sweet little Kitten tastes like—and it's all for me.

I spend a long time fucking her little hole with my tongue before I go back to her clit to suck the swollen bud into my mouth. She continues to whip back and forth, pulling away and pressing herself harder against my face. Her moans and whimpers are like the most beautiful song to my ears.

Valencia thrashes on the bed as if her mind is no longer in control of her body. I know she's close. Between the way her pussy keeps contracting around my tongue and the uncontrollable shaking, it's easy to tell she's right on the edge. I'd love nothing more than to spend the entire night dragging her along that line between pain and oblivion, but I can't wait any longer for the satisfaction of bringing her to an earth-shattering orgasm.

Her moans have filled my needy soul to the brim and I know that if I'm not careful, I could risk it all by pushing us both over the edge. This is supposed to be all about her, anyway. *It has to be.*

Done playing around, I release the grip I have on her thigh and instead grab two handfuls of her ass. I lean back to my full height at a kneel and drag her up with me as I go. She gasps as her back is dragged across the bed, but she doesn't struggle from my hold.

I make eye contact with her through the valley of her breasts, her shoulders and head now the only thing touching the bed. I hold her up to my mouth. The strain in my muscles from the weight of her body is nothing compared to the need coursing through my veins.

"Please," she pleads in a moan-filled whisper. Her legs are hitched over my shoulders, hooked at the knee—trapping her to me. No matter how much she moves around, I've got her under complete control.

With a vicious smile, I drag her pussy to my mouth and devour her once again. Her rolling moans spur me on, dragging a groan out of me in return.

I press my cock against the side of the bed as I fuck her with my tongue. The pressure offers as much pain as it does relief but, no matter how badly I want to, I can't come. At least not while she's anywhere near me. That would result in a one-way ticket back to Hell. The bargain I made with the Devil plays on a loop in the back of my mind.

Valencia is off-limits to you. You get pleasure from her before you complete the mission, and your 100 years will start before the cum can finish shooting out of your cock

I shake the sound of the Devil's voice from my head. I'll have to get myself off later, after she falls asleep, when I'm very far away from the temptation of her body. For now, I settle with continuing to press my erection into the side of the bed.

"Yes, please. I'm—I—" Valencia moans so loudly I swear it echoes off the walls. I yank myself away from the bed and suck her clit into my mouth with a ravenous fervor. "Oh, fuck," she moans sweetly as she comes all over my face. I drown in the flood of her arousal as it covers my face and her thighs and slowly lower her back to the bed, placing light little kisses across her stomach.

She whimpers quietly, still shaking—though not as rapidly as before. Now, it's transitioned into more of a soft tremor. "That was, just. . . wow," she whispers.

I smile softly at the content look on her face. She notices, and a small smile graces her own. I lick some of her arousal off my lips before wiping the rest off my face with the bottom of my shirt. Her bright blue eyes track the swipe of my tongue, heating briefly before dropping to take in the view of the stomach that becomes visible as I do so. I'd love to demand she clean up the mess that she left all over my face but, unfortunately, I'm a dumbass who makes deals with the Devil.

I drop my shirt quickly, though I don't miss the disappointment in her eyes. Pushing off the mattress, I fold up into a standing position. Valencia finally sits up but remains seated on the edge of the bed. This, unfortunately, puts her face right at zipper level.

She could be on the other side of the room and it would be hard to miss the bulge of my erection in my pants. She reaches up a hand, I presume to touch me, but I catch her wrist before she can.

Heat-filled eyes flash to mine, but I can also see the doubt and confusion there as well. She doesn't know what would happen if I indulge in her. I haven't told her about the deal with the Devil yet, so as much as I dream for her to touch me—especially after what just happened between us—I can't allow it.

The doubt takes over the lust in her eyes and she attempts to pull her hand away, stung by the rejection.

"It's not that I don't want you," I state before the doubt consumes her. Her blue eyes connect with mine in a flash, bratty attitude shining in their depths. "I told you before I didn't want to take advantage of you. You needed relief and it brings me great pleasure to give that to you, but I want the first time you touch me to be because you want to touch *me*, not because you need a distraction."

She watches me for a moment longer before giving a slow nod of acceptance and I mentally breath a sigh of relief.

"Okay," she says back. She readjusts her bra to rest comfortably on her body again. It may hide her nipples but the evidence of my touch is still there across the rest of her exposed skin.

I don't think she fully understands my reasoning, but it seems it's enough for now.

Wanting to take advantage of her compliant behavior, I lightly grip her chin and tip her face up so she's looking straight at me. "If you ever threaten me with another man again, I will strip your ass bare and spank you till it's raw."

She growls angrily, slapping my hand away from her chin, which I expected. "It'll be a cold day in Hell when I let you spank me, asshole."

The sweet after-sex glow is gone, and her innocent doe eyes have once again been replaced by those of her bratty side.

"Whatever you say, Kitten," I smirk at her.

Flashes of the night cross my mind as I savor the taste of her on my tongue. For a moment, I wonder if she actually is a sex demon sent to test my will.

Why else would the Devil have told me I can't have her?

CHAPTER 22

VALENCIA

THE AUDACITY OF THIS man. How dare he give me the best orgasm I've ever had and then ruin it. Well, sort of. I'd be lying if I said it wasn't hot how possessive he became when I mentioned another man.

Still, that didn't take away from the fact that he irritated the fuck out of me with that comment. Yeah, right, I'd just let him spank me like that. It was one thing to be a little rough; it was an entirely different thing to think I'd let him spank me like I was some petulant child. *As if.*

Irritation sizzles away most of the remaining lust until I'm able to think straight and I snatch my discarded panties from the bed and drag them up my legs. Standing to pull them the rest of the way up, I'm thankful my knees don't wobble. The feeling of the wet fabric resting against my sensitive skin is unpleasant but, seeing as I have no other clothes, it's either a little bit of discomfort or nudity.

Corvus steps back slightly. If I were to take one step forward, our bodies would be flush. I resist the urge, though it's hard despite the irritation. I enjoyed what we did, but it wouldn't be fair for us to start anything else again. At least not before we had the time to think about it.

It's probably a good idea to take some time to think about the fact that I used sex as a way to cope with PTSD. Not that I was ever officially diagnosed, but I've searched my symptoms enough and they all point to the same thing.

Plus, Corvus deserves more than someone who only wants to use him. Just as he didn't like to take advantage of me, I don't want to take advantage of him.

I almost wonder if he knew that, and his snarky comment about spanking me was just a way to quickly move on from the heated moment without having to focus on it too much. Either way, I'll take what I can get.

Placing a hand on his chest, I lightly push him away. He easily gives to the pressure of my hand and takes a few more steps back without comment. I step around the bed and quickly search the room for the rest of my discarded clothes. Since it's so tiny, I spot them easily.

It's not that I mind being in just my bra and panties around him but it's chilly in here and I'm also irritated, so I don't feel particularly willing to reward him with a view of my body. I'm not sure covering up my body is much of a punishment but I know, for the most part, naked boobs are much nicer than covered ones.

I'm not really that angry with him, though, if I think about it. Everything has been so overwhelming, that I don't have the mental capacity to juggle it all at once. I was just eaten out by a man who claims to be a demon sent from Hell. A demon Lord, to be exact. Not only did I let him go down on me, but I *enjoyed* it. It's practically sinful how much I enjoyed what he did to me. Actually—I'm pretty sure it's the worst sin I've ever committed.

This will surely give the holy higher power yet another reason to send his little troops after me.

Spotting my shirt lying on the floor near the couch, I walk over and pick it up, sliding it over my head in one smooth motion. It's not a tight-fitting shirt, but it's also not overly large. The hem falls just past the apex of my thighs, as if it were the world's shortest dress. I don't care to put my pants back on, but the shirt offers me a small dose of comfort.

I turn to face Corvus, "You have a ruinous mouth."

He cocks an eyebrow at me but still doesn't respond, just watching me. I start ticking off my fingers, "First, you ruin my day with that ridiculous story of yours. Then, you ruin my panties—though I'm not so upset about that one. Then, you dare to ruin my blissful afterglow. What do you have to say for yourself?"

He laughs at me, shaking his head as he steps towards the door that leads outside.

"I'll ruin your pussy anytime," he says as he steps out the door. It clicks softly behind him.

"That's not what I said!" I yell at him. The only indication I get that he's heard me is the sound of his laughter carrying through the walls.

Ugh. Men.

I briefly contemplate what he's doing out there but decide I'd rather shower than investigate it. The prominent bulge in his pants hadn't gone away as he stepped outside.

Not that I was looking at it. I swear, I wasn't. Call it a peripheral hazard. That thing was so big I could see it from the front yard.

I roll my eyes as I head to the bathroom to clean up. It's at the back of the cabin; bright white and modernly decorated. It has a luxurious spa feeling to it, filled with white accents and leafy plants.

I undress and crank the shower up to almost scorching hot. While I wait for the water to heat, I look into the small mirror over the sink and see that Corvus left quite a few love marks on my chest and neck. I trace one of the reddish-purple marks on my neck with a finger and a shiver rushes through my body. The marks all show a connection so intense and raw, that it left visible evidence on my skin. There was something oddly satisfying about the constant presence of his touch, even after he was gone—a physical representation of his ability to bring something out of me that I didn't know I possessed. A wild and chaotic side that felt comfortable and safe in the presence of extreme danger.

Confusion, and other feelings I can't quite name, stare back at me as I glimpse my reflection. Despite how complicated this made everything, I can't stop the growing realization that I liked it. I liked the way he made me feel. I liked the way he left his mark on me, a reminder of his touch and control. I liked that he wasn't human—that he was something *more*.

Unsure how to find comfort in my new reality, I tear my eyes away from the mirror and step into the shower as the steam begins to blur my reflection.

Can't wait to deny the hell out of the marks to Parker, tomorrow. Thankfully, my clothes and long hair should cover most of it.

I suck in a gasp as my fingertips brush over my still-sensitive clit, and I think back to Corvus leaving the cabin. The bulge of his still-hardened erection was unmistakable. I wonder if he's out there, right now, taking care of it.

Whatever. If he'd rather go out and fuck his hand with the bears in the woods, then he could go right ahead. I understood why he refused my touch, but it still stung. Rejection was never fun, even when you were expecting it.

I quickly finish my shower, letting the too-hot water wash away my frustrations. I have so much more to worry about than where and how he got off.

I step out of the shower and towel dry my hair and body but look at my panties in disgust. I don't want to put them back on after my shower. Taking a few moments to search around inside the cabinet hanging above the toilet, I am blessed with not only a hairdryer but also a cup full of disposable toothbrushes and a tube of toothpaste.

I wash my underwear in the sink and, after thoroughly rinsing them out, dry them with the hair dryer. When I slide on my now clean panties, it's almost as good as taking off my bra after a long day. I throw on my shirt but don't bother to put my bra back on—we're stuck here for the night and he's seen me naked already, so I might as well be comfortable.

I quickly brush my teeth and walk out into the main room. Corvus is kneeling in front of the fireplace, adding more wood so the cabin remains warm throughout the rest of the night.

"Hey," I say as I walk up behind him. "There's a spare toothbrush in the bathroom for you. I laid it on the counter if you want to use it." I think of making some snarky comment about his trip outside being *fast*, but I barely hold it in, too tired to be a smartass.

He continued to fiddle with the fire a little longer before standing up and facing me.

"The fire's taken care of and everything's locked up, why don't you go lay down," he murmurs, cupping one of my cheeks in his large hand. I fight the urge to lean into his touch.

Normally, I might rebel against being told what to do, but he speaks so softly and looks at me so sweetly that I don't mind listening to him. Just this once. His suggestion softens the emotions churning in my chest until a calm neutrality remains.

"You'll come to bed," I state in an equally soft tone. It's more a statement than a question.

"If that's where you want me."

I just nod, allowing the action to speak for me. He gives me another soft smirk, and I start to melt for him all over again. Corvus leans slowly—slow enough that I could avoid it if I wanted—and kisses my lips lightly. I bask in the moment, not wanting to take this any farther than he wants to.

He leans back, places another light kiss against my forehead, and steps around me. The bathroom door clicks lightly as he shuts it behind him.

I glance at the fire and smile softly to myself. He's a generous lover, I'll give him that. I'm pretty sure he tried to suck my soul right out of my body through my pussy. If he had waited any longer to make me come, I might've just let him.

Chills of cool tingles cover my body as I crawl under the covers. I lay on the side of the bed closest to the fire in the hopes that if anything goes wrong with it during the night, I'll be able to get to it quickly.

I'm focused on that thought as sleep finally takes me.

CHAPTER 23
VALENCIA

"Corvus?"

My words echo in the surrounding woods, reverberating back to me off the trunks of trees. Leaves crunch against my bare feet as the chilly air blows my shirt around my body. I'm still in the clothes I laid down in, which consists of my shirt, underwear, and nothing else.

How did I get out here? It's still dark outside, so I can barely see anything beyond what's 10 feet in front of me. I don't remember leaving the cabin and I've never been one to sleepwalk or randomly lose periods of memory. Panic boils my blood, constricting my lungs.

"Hello!" I yell a little louder, but the midnight bugs' quiet song is all that answers. I usually love the peaceful stillness of the forest at night, but this doesn't offer any of its usual comforts.

I touch a hand to my throat as it narrows. It's like cotton has filled my mouth and my jaw's been wired shut.

Suddenly, even the bugs are quiet; all that remains is deafening silence. My heart starts to pound so hard in my chest that I can hear my pulse each time it flickers in my neck.

A crackling pop rings through the trees. *I know that sound.*

Spinning, I search the woods around me. A small flicker of amber gold shines through the trees in the distance. I recognize that color—I've seen it in dreams a thousand times before and have spent hundreds of days fighting against it.

Fire.

I race forward, following the direction of the light. This can't happen again. When I went to sleep, the fire was contained in the fireplace as expected—there was nothing flammable nearby.

I checked. I know I did.

I push a little harder, the slaps of my bare feet echoing through the silence. The debris stabs into my feet as I sprint across the forest floor. I barely register anything beyond the pounding of my heart and the burning in my lungs.

Please, not again.

Why would I leave the cabin? I purposely slept on the side of the bed closest to the fire in case something happened. Why would I leave?

I push my body to its limit, until there is no more pain at the soles of my feet and I can barely feel the midnight cold, but the small amber light remains as small as it was no matter how far I run. I'm racing as fast as I can through creeks and over logs, swerving around tall Montana pines standing in my way.

I run for what feels like hours. The forest blurs by until I'm both confused and nauseated. It's like I'm flying through the trees instead of running—and, no matter how fast they soar by, I don't manage to get anywhere.

Abruptly, I come upon a clearing in the woods. I manage to break through the trees, hurrying to the cabin in an instant.

It's on fire. No, it's *engulfed* in fire.

It burns so brightly that I can see through the framework to the inside. Flames billow from the front window in a roil of hot air and hissing pops. The once beautifully carved front door is now little more than a giant hole of infernal heat.

A glance inside tells me more fire awaits. The flames roar so forcefully that the sound resounds through the small clearing. It's so loud, I wonder how I hadn't heard it before. Echoes of it crash off the trees until my ears are full of nothing but the sickening sound.

I make for the cabin. I won't stand frozen while another person I care for is trapped inside. How have I escaped this fate once again?

Surely, Corvus escaped as well. Maybe he's lost somewhere in the woods, just like I was. I try to convince myself he's safe but I'm unable to soothe the panic rising within me.

"Corvus!" I yell into the night but the sound is drowned in a blast of fire that erupts from where the front door used to be.

I see movement inside the cabin and, though my brain swears it's not him, I walk closer anyway. Then I see it. A tall silhouette falls to the floor like a tree falling to the earth.

I start running once again but, before I reach the porch, my feet root themselves to the ground. I can't move any further.

He's in there, and I'm frozen out here.

I want to move but I can't. The only feeling I have is a burning sensation at the tips of my fingers that feels like I've stuck my hands inside the flames. The tips burn like they did when I faced the same fire at eleven-years-old.

Over the crackling inferno, a maniac laugh echoes around me, overpowering the sound of the burning fire.

The laugh is coming from *inside*.

CHAPTER 24
VALENCIA

I JERK AWAKE WITH a gasp. The nightmare tries to drag me back under but I force my eyes to stay open, so I don't fall back asleep.

I can see the edge of the fireplace past the couch, and all that remains are the cooled embers of a nearly burnt-out fire. A deep sigh of relief escapes me. *I'm safe. The fire is exactly where it's meant to be.*

The feeling of a very large and very hot body presses against my back. We've somehow ended up cuddled together in the night. Heat rolls off his body in waves, reminding me of the roaring fire in my dream.

I lightly roll over and try to peek at his sleeping form but jump at the sight of Corvus' deep brown eyes staring back at me. He's lying on his side, facing me. A pillow is shoved under his head and an arm is outstretched in front of him. I realize that I'm probably lying on that arm but I don't move, nor does he. He's close enough that I can feel the rise and fall of his chest with each breath.

The air in the cabin is icy as it licks at the skin on my face but everywhere else is scorching hot. His skin burns against mine as if feverish from injury—but, he completely healed himself, so that must just be his normal temperature. Was having a warm body temperature a demon thing? I'd have to remember to ask him about it later.

I glance out the window behind him and notice the sun barely starting to turn the midnight-black sky to a dusky blue.

"Sorry if I woke you," I whisper, not yet wanting to disturb the peace of the morning.

"You didn't," he murmurs as quietly. "Nightmare?"

I nod my head but don't offer anything else. He doesn't press me and, for that, I'm grateful. I finally roll over to face him fully, lying on my side just as he is. I take in his large frame. He's still wearing his shirt, but I can't see what's beyond the blanket's cover.

Arousal heats my blood once again as I remember what he can do with his wicked mouth. I'm sucked into the memory of last night and my toes curl as his tongue sneaks out to drag across his bottom lip.

"As much as I would enjoy indulging every thought that's running through that pretty head, I'm sure Parker will be here soon and I doubt you want him to catch us with my head buried between your legs."

At the sound of Parker's name, all thoughts of possibly trading sexual favors escape me. He's right; I do *not* want Parker to find us that way. Despite that, I still can't let Corvus off that easily.

"Ugh, you're always ruining things with that mouth of yours," I grumble as I start to get out of bed.

"I'll let it go this time, Valencia, but the next time you say something about my mouth, I will ruin your pussy as promised. And I won't care where it's at or who's around to see it."

Like I said. Panties? Ruined.

I march to the bathroom, grab my pants and socks, and flip him the bird. His light chuckle follows me, and I can still hear it after I shut the door.

I take my time getting ready for the day and, by the time I step out of the bathroom, I'm refreshed and ready to face whatever shitstorm is due. Corvus is up as well. He's made the bed and the fire is going again, quickly warming the small space.

He's got his clothes back on, boots and all, and I'm disappointed that I didn't get to catch even a glimpse of his body. Between last night and this morning, the most I've seen of him is his hands, neck, head, and the slightest flash of his stomach. Not nearly enough to appease the sex monster that seems to take over my body any time he's near.

Unfortunately, he's right, I imagine Parker is already on his way, which leaves no time for a quickie—though that doesn't stop me from warning, "You can't hide your body from me forever, Corvus."

"I wouldn't dare, Kitten," he purrs in response.

I nod my head—I'm pretty sure if I say anything aloud, it will be something along the lines of *'fuck me'*, which is definitely not on the agenda for today.

Nor should it be on any other agenda for any other day, ever. For some reason, this demon has found his way under my skin and I'm not sure how I'll ever get him out.

I walk over to the window and watch as the sun slowly greets the new day; the purple of dawn is already bleeding into the blue of early morning. I check the time on my phone—just after 6:30 AM—and see I have a few texts from Parker.

Saturday at 10:45 PM
Parker Rand

> Did he die?? *skull emoji*

> Can I come back? I'm kidding lol. Mostly. Landon won't stop talking about anal. Anal is fun. Hearing Landon talk about anal is not fun.

Today at 6:05 AM
Parker Rand

> Just got up. I'll be there in 45. Fingers crossed he's not dead

I mentally do the calculations and see that he'll be here in about 20 minutes. I briefly debate whether that's enough time to bust out a quickie but decide against it. Corvus was pretty adamant about not doing more until I was sure I was ready—sure I needed *him* and not just the intimacy. It made me want him even more.

"Parker will be here soon. He'll know something is up with you being completely healed. What do we tell him?" I turn from the window to find Corvus leaning against the counter in the kitchen. He's staring at the coffee maker.

"The more we tell him, the more danger we put him in," he states as his eyes drift back to me. "But, Dumah's already seen his face—the danger has already been presented."

"So, I could tell him the truth, everything you've told me, and there would be no consequence? Even though he's human?" I ask, surprised.

"Technically, yes. You have to understand humans are so low on the scale of significance that it rarely matters what humans do or don't know. The humans want to create crazy religions or follow false leaders? Fine. They want to commit some awful crime, or do some extraordinary deed? Great, who cares—it's not like we're getting much power from them, anyway, so they don't really matter all that much. Not only that, but humans are considered to be so. . . simple, that even if they did know, what could they ever do about it?"

I think about that for a second. I don't want to put my friend in any more danger than necessary but, like Corvus said, he's already in danger—keeping things from him might do more harm than good. They say ignorance is bliss and all, but I'd rather my friend have the power of knowledge. No matter how much it might burden him.

"Let's just see what he says when he gets here and go from there," I mumble to Corvus.

He nods and smiles at me, happy to follow my lead. I walk into his space, my chest brushing against his. Since he's leaning against the counter, he's a couple of inches shorter than usual, allowing me to grasp the back of his neck and drag his face down for a kiss.

This kiss is slow and comforting—a shared intimate moment between two people who just crave each other's presence. There's none of the fire from last night's heated passion but it's no less hot. I should be alarmed, or at least indifferent, but his touch affects me so much. I try to remind myself that there's no guarantee for tomorrow, especially now, so I might as well take comfort where I can.

He groans so quietly I almost don't hear, then he deepens the kiss. Large hands drag my hips further into the heat of his body. I steal a few more minutes in his arms before pulling away and he kisses me even as I do, but doesn't force me to stay. "I'm going to go outside and wait for Parker," I tell him. "He'll be here soon."

He nods. "Okay, I'll be here when you're ready," he responds, looking deeply into my eyes. His focus is so intense, I can feel it throughout my entire body.

I smile, then step from his embrace. I grab my jacket from the floor and slip it on. Once my boots are on, I silently step through the front door and into the cool morning air. I suck in a lungful of the cold air, using it to cool my heated body. The last thing I want to do is greet Parker while arousal courses through me.

I stare at the leaves on the trees as they flow softly in the breeze. Brief flashes of sun burst through the gaps, causing little light shows to dance across the ground before me. Birds sing a hundred different morning melodies.

For years, I've used this demanding job as a way to stay busy, so the thoughts of my past couldn't creep into my present. It left no time for intimate relationships—which suited me fine considering I was never able to fully open up to any of my past partners. How could they love me for who I am, when all I did was hide everything about myself from them? Hookups were easier. They didn't interrupt my routines or way of doing things, and they didn't require vulnerability. The thought of letting someone in—of altering my life to include a partner—terrifies me. My adventures with the team, my time alone—it's my sanctuary and, never before had I given a second thought to changing it. I'd lost too much, I couldn't introduce something else I'd likely eventually lose.

Until him.

The sound of gravel rolling below Parker's tires snaps me out of my poisonous thoughts. I wait patiently on the porch as he walks over, trying to regain some sense of emotional control so he can't see the inner turmoil I'm going through.

His arms full of bags and a blessed drink container full of coffee cups. "Okay, so you're either waiting out here because you missed me or there's a dead body in there, and you couldn't stand the smell."

I snatch a coffee from the container when he gets close enough. "No dead body."

"So, you missed me—I knew you loved me," he chirps. Only Parker could make chirping sound manly and somehow un-annoying.

"Let's go inside and I'll tell you all about last night," I turn, heading for the door. I take another sip of the deliciously hot coffee. It's almost too hot to drink, but it warms me up perfectly after a few minutes in the cold morning air.

As I open the door and step inside, I hear Parker mumble, "Maybe not *all* the details."

I almost spit out my mouthful of coffee.

"So, he really didn't die." Parker eye's Corvus as he walks to the dining table and sets down the drink container and bags. He pulls out two containers of muffins and starts opening them. "Should I even ask how he's standing right now?"

"I'm sorry for yesterday, I was out of line. Thank you for trusting me with someone you care about," Corvus says to Parker.

I see Parker tense briefly; he's not the biggest fan of confrontation but, when he realizes Corvus just means to apologize, he relaxes.

"She yelled at you, didn't she?" Parker chuckles.

"She did. But, I deserved it. I *am* sorry," Corvus responds.

They maintain eye contact, staring each other down. Is this another one of those dick-measuring contests I'm going to have to stop?

Parker smiles, laughing under his breath. "You're good, man. Here's a coffee."

I don't miss the way Corvus seems to perk up as he grabs the small cup out of Parker's hands. I step up to the table and grab one of the muffins, and can't help the soft moan that comes out when I take the first bite. Irma's famous lemon and poppy seed muffins are, by far, a guilty pleasure of mine—one Parker is very aware of.

Out of the corner of my eye, I see Corvus jerk his head in my direction but I resist meeting his stare, sure that I'd melt into a puddle of need with one look at him. The last thing I need is for Parker to know how I feel about Corvus now. If he saw, I'd never hear the end of it.

Corvus said that what we decided to tell Parker was up to me. I hated taking the risk of bringing Parker closer to the danger but, at this point, standing at the edge of it all was looking just as deadly as being at the center.

"Parker, do you trust me?" I ask him.

"Yes." No hesitation.

"I'm going to tell you a little story. It will seem unbelievable, but I need you to trust that I wouldn't lie to you—not about this."

"If you're about to tell me Santa isn't real, sadly, I already know," he jokes, but sits in one of the dining chairs and gives me all his attention.

Parker's default is humor and jokes—but he can be serious when needed. I live vicariously through him, sometimes—wishing I could be that way, too.

To conserve time, I jump right to the heart of it all. Most of it comes out in a rambling mess, and I can see Parker's eyebrows doing a very expressive, high-to-pinched dance on his face as I talk, but he thankfully doesn't interrupt me.

When I finish, he simply stares at me for a moment. He doesn't blink—and I can't tell if he's even breathing. I expected more laughter and a least some denial, but he just sits there, quietly looking at me.

Eventually, the staring shifts from me to Corvus, who leans one hip against the back of the couch. He doesn't flinch at Parker's penetrative gaze or look away.

"That is. . . quite the story," he says after his long, drawn-out silence.

Parker turns back to where I'm sitting across the table from him, slowly munching on a muffin. As soon as I stopped talking, I shoved a big bite in my mouth to prevent any more word-vomit from coming out.

Parker opens his mouth like he's about to say something, but two echoing dings start ringing. Out of habit, Parker and I jump to our feet as we check our phones. That sound only comes from one thing—station-wide communication. Most times, it's used to notify us of a dispatched call if we're outside the station, but it can occasionally be used to send out other notifications. This seems to be one of those rare situations.

RVW Fireteam Group Chat
Today at 7:00
Chief Miller

Hello all. I am excited to announce we will be conducting a department survival exercise. In light of recent events, I hope this will be a way for us to all come together for a common goal, so we can work through any personal grievances. We are a team. A family. Hopefully this event will remind us all of that. Event will take place on October 23rd and 24th. Please arrive at the Agnes Lake Trailhead by 8AM the 23rd. Attendance is mandatory.

I pinch the bridge of my nose. Mandatory. *Great.* That means someone must be dying or already dead to even attempt getting out of it.

I usually enjoyed these events. I loved being outdoors and camping in the BNF was one of my favorite pastimes. I just can't imagine how I'm going to be able to enjoy such a weekend with everything else going on.

How am I supposed to process everything I've learned as though nothing is going on, while trying to save my job by hiking with my team?

How can anything outside of what I've learned matter anymore? Why should I care about my job when angels and demons are after me? When now, more than ever, I want to learn what happened to my family?

I stand there for a moment, phone still out as I try to force myself to remember why I went into this field in the first place. I *like* the chaos of wildfires. I can create plans, be in control, and accomplish important goals.

Although—thinking I have any semblance of control feels like a cruel joke. This kind of chaos seems obscured by a thick cloud of smoke, and I'm terrified of what I might find in its midst.

Regardless, this is still my life. I can't burden everyone else with my problems. The crew depends on me as much as I do them. It doesn't matter that my life has turned into a shit show from Hell—I want to be there for them. Whatever happens next, I'll deal with—just like I have every other bad day in my life.

I've survived them all so far, I have to believe that I can do the same with anymore that are sent my way.

"How the fuck are we supposed to concentrate on team building when we're currently dealing with a sword-wielding madman," I mutter to no one in particular. The 23rd is only two days away—not a lot of time to prepare for a two-day backpacking trip in Beaverhead National Forest. Nor to deal with all the other shit that's going on.

Plus, the last time I hiked to Lake Agnus, I took a small trip down the side of Sugarloaf Mountain.

"Uh, what?" Parker snaps.

"Oh yeah, I forgot you missed that. That night at the bar, Dumah had a sword—a *big-ass* sword. And it was on fire. Or made of fire. I'm not entirely sure about that part—but that's how Corvus got hurt." His eyes grow wider as I speak and I sit, putting my phone back in my pocket.

"I would literally rather go against 10 angels with flaming swords than spend a couple of days in Landon Michaelson's presence," Parker mumbles, also not acknowledging some of the crazier details.

Corvus, who has been quietly listening to our conversation, finally speaks up. "I think one angel was enough. Why are we worried about being in Landon's presence?"

Before I can explain, Parker answers for me. "Because no one likes him. He's a misogynistic, racist, homophobic asshole—arrogant but with literally zero skill to back it up. Need I continue?"

"*Hmm*," Corvus responds with a soft hum, though I see the muscles in his jaw feathering slightly.

"Landon is also the guy you saved from getting a broken nose that night we met." I supply.

He nods, crossing his arms. "And I'm guessing this has something to do with team building?"

I realized then that neither Parker nor I had explained the message, so used to everyone around me being a part of the fire team that I forget that he's on the outside of all of that.

"I guess, with all the issues going on with the team, the Chief hopes to bring us all together with a team-building event. We've done them in the past, but they were more family-based events than just the fire team. We're to meet at the Lake Agnes trailhead in two days to participate in a survival-themed event."

He runs his jaw for a moment. "I don't think that's safe," Corvus finally says.

"I'm inclined to believe you but this is our career. I know all this crazy shit is going on, but our lives outside of it haven't stopped. We're just going to have to figure out a way to get through the next few days safely—then we can go back to hunting down bad guys," I say.

"Or hiding from them," Parker mutters.

"What?" I ask.

"Hiding from them," he repeats. "From Dane. Or... Dumah? Whatever his name is. I mean, isn't that what we're doing now?"

I tilt my head. "I guess you have a point." I think about everything that Corvus has told me in the last 24 hours and turn to him. "So, if you don't shift, he has no idea where you are. And you never said that he knew how to track me. This event won't be advertised, so there's no way he'll know where I am. You can stay here, no one is scheduled to come here anytime soon, and we can just meet you back here after the trip."

He's already shaking his head. "Not happening." Corvus still leans against the couch, posture relaxed, but his tone broaches no room for argument.

But, I've never been one to back down from a debate.

"Why not?" I question. *Seems like a solid plan to me.*

"I'm not letting you go out there alone. You think Dumah is the only one with a reason to come after you?" Corvus acts as if that's common knowledge—but, nothing about my life has felt anywhere close to normal as of late.

"So, why are you here?" Parker asks, and for the first time in a while, I hear a tension-filled sense of suspicion in his tone.

I never asked Corvus why he came into my life. Or I did, but it got lost in the cloud of everything else. There was an overload of information. Too many questions to keep track of, and so many unfulfilling answers.

I never really questioned his personal reasoning for coming to Earth—because, despite all the craziness and the fact that he's a total stranger, he's saved my life multiple times. That had to mean *something*.

At least, I hoped it did.

Deal with battle-hungry angels first, worry about boyfriends later.

"I'm here for Valencia," Corvus reiterates, seeming uninclined to speak any further.

Though he doesn't say a lot, it's enough considering our short history.

"If you have a better plan, speak up," I say to Corvus, taking care to ignore Parker's scoff.

"I don't think Dumah can track you physically, but that does not mean he's not a threat and I can't protect you from here. I won't shift near you, but my familiar form is the only way to stay with you covertly without drawing attention to myself. I know your job is important to you, and I'm not trying to take that away, but I won't allow you to go alone."

"Familiar form? Like, as in *Sabrina the Witch's* cat?" Parker butts in.

"Sort of," I answer, not giving Corvus time to respond. "He can shapeshift—it's a demon thing."

"Demons can shapeshift?" Parker asks looking between Corvus and I. "Into what?"

"A crow," I say at the same time Corvus rolls his eyes and mutters *anything*.

Parker continues to look between us both, then blurts, "The night at the bar, the crow that was being all weird and kept stealing your food. That was *him*?"

"Yeah. He gave me this that night," I pick up one of the matching tokens and hold it up so Parker can see.

"Holy shit, I remember that." Parker grabs one to investigate and then picks up the other to compare them. "How long have you been following her, man?" Parker side eyes Corvus before looking back to the tokens.

"Well, he was there at the bar. Once at my window a few nights after the accident. And he was there on Sugarloaf—holy shit. You saved me!" I launch to my feet so fast that the chair I'm sitting on topples with a loud bang.

Parker jumps at the noise, dropping one of the tokens on the table. There's a loud crack as the tiny pearl busts against the hardwood surface.

"You *saved* me," I repeat, pointing a finger at Corvus.

In response, I receive a blink.

"You said that he's saved you multiple times—no need to give us a heart attack over it," Parker mumbles.

"No, you don't understand, he saved my life when I was on Sugarloaf Mountain. A fucking crow's call is what woke me up! It was weirdly jumping around and cawing loudly. I remember being so frustrated cause my head *really hurt*—but it woke me up. Then it tied a fucking rope to my bag and handed me the other end. My bag was lying *10 feet away*. There's no way I could've gotten it on my own. That's how I used my phone to call you for help. I vaguely remember something weird happening but I was concussed," I finish. "I didn't even remember that till just now."

"He just had to be a superhero," Parker grunts with an eye roll. "He does kind of look like a rugged Henry Cavill."

"Who is Henry Cavill?" Corvus asks.

"No he doesn't," I say at the same time.

Parker just responds, "Superman."

I walk around the dining table and stop right in front of Corvus. His arms are uncrossed and at his sides, but he doesn't make a move towards me.

"You saved me," I say once more, still too dumfounded to say anything else.

"Always," is his simple response.

Without any thought, I reach up, grab his face, and pull him down to me. He doesn't hesitate to bring his lips to mine in a soft and sensual kiss. He leans into me, causing me to lean back farther than natural, but a large hand pressed into the dip in my back prevents me from tipping over backward.

"Well, that answers that question," Parker says from the table beside us.

I let the kiss end with a final, gentle peck to his lips and step back. He leans back against the couch but doesn't move his hand from my back. "Thank you."

"*Always*," he repeats, but with more adulation than I've heard from him yet.

"Okay, lovebirds—*oh my God*, he's literally a love*bird*," Parker chuckles then shakes his head. "Anyway, let's get this show on the road! So, Corvus comes with us. It's not like anyone will question a random crow flying around the BNF. But, don't think I won't have a fuckton more questions for you two later."

"Parker's right, you can come with us," I say to Corvus.

"I'm going to go to Hell first and try to locate where Dumah is hiding, then see if some of my allies know anything about what's going on. Don't worry too much, I'll have eyes on you the whole time."

"You'll be watching me? You can do that from Hell?" I ask.

He nods, still gripping me tightly. "They call me the King of Crows because I am the only demon in existence who can see through a familiar across realms. If anything happens, I'll know," he responds assuredly.

"This is all too weird," Parker mumbles from my side.

"I guess that's good news, then. Do you need a ride somewhere before we head back to the station? You don't have a car here or anything," I ask. It's not like I can give him a ride to Hell, but a lift seems like the polite thing to offer.

"That's what the wings are for," he winks at me.

"Val, your boyfriend is really weird but also kind of hot. I see why you like him," Parker tosses over his shoulder as he throws away our trash.

"Shut up, Parks. He's not my boy—we're not *dating*. This is not a—just, go to the car, Parker." I can't help but stumble tragically through the sentence.

"Yeah, yeah, I'm going. I'll see you at the truck. See ya later, Corvus."

"Bye, Parker," Corvus responds, but he doesn't take his eyes off me the whole time. "You'll be okay," he tells me once he's gone. "I'll be right there if anything happens."

"And *you*? Will you be okay?" I can't help but think that Dumah nearly managed to cut him in half with one swipe. A sharp stab of panic shoots through me at the thought of something happening to him and memories of my nightmare from last night plague my mind, causing my breath to stutter in and out of my lungs.

Large hands grip my face. "I'll be okay, I promise. Now, let's go before I bend you over that bed and take your mind off everything that's going on."

"*Ugh*, you're evil for that," I laugh as I pull away. I look around to find that the cabin is mostly put back together from our short stay and there isn't anything more that we need to do other than lock the door and take our trash to the outside bin.

Corvus and I follow the path toward Parker's parked truck, but he stops me halfway, pulling me into his warm body and kissing me deeply. He kisses me so thoroughly that I wonder if he's trying to imprint the feeling of my mouth into his brain. I sigh as we separate.

I step back, breaking our contact as I look into his deep brown eyes. The fear of what may happen when we aren't together climbs up my throat but, before anything can escape my lips, he disappears into thin air.

If I wasn't entirely convinced of everything, I am now.

I head towards Parker's truck with a quiet laugh. Thank God he left before I could say what I wanted to; I nearly asked him to never leave my side again.

I shake the crazy thoughts from my mind.

CHAPTER 25
CORVUS

When I appear in my living room in Hell, Van is already waiting for me on the couch, reading a book.

"What are you doing here?" I ask.

"Waiting for you," he responds without bothering to look away from the large book in his hand. He must be pretending to read—I know he has no interest in '*Why Humans Romanticize Everything*'. He hates humans, which I think might be a Fae thing. I've never asked him why he personally feels that way.

"Bit of light reading?"

"Humans are deplorable," is all he says in response, focusing on the page. His long, black hair has been scraped away from his face by two braids but the rest hangs freely down his chest. The book—a rather large tome—rests against one of his buckskin-clothed knees as he methodically turns each page.

"How did you know I was going to need you?" I don't wait for his reply as I start readying what supplies I'll need, grabbing the truthstone first. Its blue surface shines with swirls of white. It won't prevent a demon from lying but will encourage them to speak the truth without knowing what's going on. It's an extremely rare stone, and over the years, I've fought many to keep it.

Only four were ever created—I got lucky when I found it in the pocket of a lesser demon who thought to overpower me. Fool. Too bad he didn't have the '*don't be a dumbass*' stone instead.

"You think your best friend doesn't know you well enough to be here?" he asks, instead of giving me a straight answer. Van's tricky like that, always skirting around the truth since he's unable to lie.

I ignore his question, not wanting to waste time in Hell when I need to be on Earth watching Valencia's back. All I can hope is that Dumah doesn't catch on to the fact that I'm not there. It's likely only a matter of time before we see him again—I just hope we're more prepared this time.

"I have Lamium," Van softly shuts the book and stands, stretching briefly before putting it back on the shelf. His gentle care of the book on humans shows no sign of the contempt he feels for the species.

"What's that?" I ask absentmindedly as I also grab a dagger made of the very stone this mountain is made of, deep red with black veins running throughout—its long blade is sharp enough to slice to the bone.

"For pest control," Van's tall body sends a dark shadow through the room as he moves before the fireplace. The fire sprites don't give him as much issue—or, not nearly as much as they do me when I stand that close.

Once I've got everything I need, we head outside. It's night here and the sky is a deep red, a dark contrast to the blood moon that hangs in the sky every night. I don't know if it's real, or what the sky is like in this realm compared to others, but it's beautiful in its own, morbid way. I'm again thankful that the darkness of the night doesn't bother me, since my vision makes everything clear as day.

"So, whose party are we crashing tonight?" Van watches as I secure the cave with sigils, ensuring everything is safeguarded.

"Tornil's. He's the most likely to know something."

"He's the least likely to care that we're there, as well."

Van's not wrong, Tornil and I have a decent working relationship. That's to say, at least we haven't tried to kill each other at any point in the past. Though being an incubus puts Tornil at a disadvantage to many demon species, his ability to manipulate the emotions of even the strongest demons makes him a worthy adversary and not someone to underestimate. Considering he could drain my essence dry and make me love every second of it, I've always maintained a level of respect for him. Not all incubuses are capable of such charm and, thankfully, Tornil doesn't abuse the ability.

The same can't be said for many of the other highly-powered demons of Hell.

"Well, let's hope you're right," I say as I grab Van's arm once we're far enough away. As I envision the front of the Infernal Circus' tent, I drag Van and I through the cold in-between. Darkness not even I can see through engulfs us for the briefest of moments before the bright red and white stripes of the tent's flaps come into view.

I suck in a quick breath of relief before releasing Van and shaking off the shadowy grip of my astral form. I step into the back of my mind for a second and call on the crows of Earth, who I've had watching Valencia while I'm gone. I've only been in Hell a short while but a day has already passed on Earth. The crows send me snapshots here and there, and the sun changes with each one. Nothing too crazy has happened yet, thankfully.

"Your female is fine I presume?" Van asks, standing stoically beside me.

"She's not my anything, she's a job." I snap.

Van *hmms*, not once looking at me.

I roll my eyes and make my way towards the tent. Demons loiter around the outside of the tent, some converse in groups while others sit around the multitude of fire pits that are spread around. I imagine most of them were denied entrance because, if they were able to go inside, they definitely wouldn't be out here. Tornil has a strict no-fighting rule, and any who break it are barred from entering ever again.

As we make our way inside the tent, a large room expands before us. Bright lights bounce off the tent's walls and the deep, rhythmic thumping of bass fills the room. More demons are gathered on the dance floor, writhing against each other with the beat of the music. It's dark and sensual, and very tempting for any looking for a release. I've been out there, myself, a few times over the years, but I've got too much to do to partake right now.

I'm just walking past the dancefloor to a makeshift bar when a slender hand reaches out, catching me by the shirt sleeve. Clawed fingertips track slowly down my arm before attempting to slide between my fingers and my chest instantly swells with need as arousal that isn't mine courses through my body.

"My Lord, I haven't seen you here in a while, I've missed you," the soft, feminine voice purrs in my ear. The melodic tune cuts through the thumping music to crawl down the back of my neck, making the hairs that are there stand tall as a shiver shoots down my back. My cock starts to harden in my jeans and my knees weaken.

A growl escapes me as I snatch away the hand that's touching me. The bones in her wrist crunch under my tight grip as I yank her closer. Her white eyes widen in fear as she shrinks away from me as far as she can go.

"Don't touch me."

I fling her arm away and my emotions instantly go back to normal, the sudden arousal no longer present. The succubus whimpers before scurrying off, her wrist held tightly against her chest. Her long, blood red hair billows out as though caught by an invisible wind as she disappears into the crowd.

I look back to check that Van is still behind me and catch a very pointed look on his face. "What, she was manipulating me," I mutter.

He scoffs and strides past me without a word. Visions of those clear white eyes and blood red hair flash in my mind for a brief second. I've been with her before. A few times over the years, actually, and I specifically remember enjoying the way her red hair contrasted so beautifully with her pale skin and white eyes. Now the thought of her touch only serves to irritate me. Not just because she used her succubus powers to manipulate my emotions, but because as soon as my cock started to harden, the face I wanted to see wasn't hers.

I push the thoughts away and meet Van at the bar. The bartender, a human-looking man besides the small set of horns that jut from his bright blue hair, approaches with a dark bottle in one hand and a wine glass in the other.

"Lord, it's been a while." He hands me the bottle and Van the wine glass, knowing our preferences despite the fact it's been a long time since either of us have been here.

"We're here for Tornil," I state, taking a long drink from the bottle. Hot cinnamon burns my throat as I drink the Hell Spice beer. It's a specialty in Hell, though I won't drink anymore, considering this one bottle could put me on my ass. It's not like human beer which couldn't get me drunk if I drowned in it.

"He's not here tonight, but Danti is here." The bartender points to the door just to the side of the bar and moves to serve another patron.

Having been here before, I know that door leads into another room that is far larger and livelier. Anything from exotic circus shows to burlesque nights are performed. That part of the tent is where most of the debauchery in the Infernal Circus happens, and I also know its Danti's favorite room.

A slight sense of worry rolls through me as I realize that speaking with Danti could be a blessing or a curse. With the ability to reveal secrets, she's the perfect demon to ask about Valencia and what the Devil's plans with her may be. Danti is as much demon as the rest of us though, and she's just as likely to reveal my own secrets than she is to offer me some.

"It's a risk, speaking with her," Van states as we make our way through the darkened door and into the next room. It's just as large as the first though considerably less bright. There's no lights in here at the moment, just a bunch of torches surrounding a dirt arena. It's not something I've seen before, so I wonder what show must be on tonight. Considering the stands are full, I imagine it's popular.

Ignoring all the looks we get as we make our way through the crowd, I spot Danti sitting perched in a large chair on a small, secluded stage that separates her from the rest of the crowd.

"Danti," I call out to her, my voice carrying over the light conversations as the other patrons wait for the show to start. Her dark skin glows with the light from the torches. White lines swirl around her neck and cheeks, causing her face to appear even more striking with her sharp cheekbones and slender neck.

"Ah, Lord Corvus, please join me," she motions to one of the demons standing behind her to allow us up. He nods nervously and steps aside, reptilian eyes down cast as we pass. A lesser demon, though he must have some strength if he's been chosen as a guard.

Despite being powerful, Danti is no match for either of us, so her silence doesn't surprise me. To most demons in Hell, a lord is damn near royalty and, though it took me a while to grow used to it, many treat us as such.

"We came for Tornil but was told he wasn't here. I think you could still help me, anyway." I tell her, watching her face go from blank to frustrated and back to blank within seconds.

"Yes, I'm happy to help however you need," her calm voice comes out tight, and her shoulders tense slightly.

I exchange a look with Van. I've never had a bad interaction with Danti before so her reaction confuses me. I expected irritation but not the fear I can practically smell coming off her in waves. Showing fear like this is the most dangerous thing she could do in a room full of demons.

"Danti, I'm not here to hurt you," I say softly, not wanting to draw attention to her reaction to me but needing to offer her some sense of comfort so I can ask her my questions.

"I'm so-sorry. I just... Well, I'm—okay," she finally murmurs, relaxing ever so slightly.

"Okay," I release a breath and slump down into my chair to try and seem less threatening. "I'm in need of a secret. The Devil sent me on a mission on Earth, regarding a woman, but wouldn't tell me why he chose me or why this woman is important—and she is important, somehow, because the angels are after her, too. Have you heard of such a thing?" I ask quietly, not wanting the details to travel to wandering ears.

She hesitates, not taking her eyes off the arena in front of her.

"I hear you're having an issue with a demon who refuses to leave?" Van interrupts the awkward silence.

"Yes, I am," Danti murmurs and looks at Van with fresh eyes. "He was kicked out of here weeks ago for trapping lesser demons in secret webs and consuming them. Right here in the tent. *Arachnids*," she spits, "can't stand them. He grew angry when I told him he was barred, so he followed me home. I've had to start walking around with a guard nonstop. How did you know that?" The queen of secrets asks my friend and I wonder, not for the first time, where he gets *his* secrets.

"This is called Lamium," Van says, pointedly ignoring her question, procuring a dark green bag and handing it to her in an instant. "The humans know of it as mint, though this is a special breed grown only here in Hell. Lure the demon into a small space and then blow this on him; you will find him very displeased. You can also leave a trail of it around your home to keep him out. It's quite effective."

She opens the bag, lip curling upwards as the scent grows stronger, overtaking the small area before Van pinches the bag closed.

"Fucking pest control," I mutter under my breath.

"Why are you giving this to me?" Danti asks Van, looking between the two of us before settling on him.

"I help you with your secret, you help him with his," Van states, pointing at me. Her cheeks darken slightly, but Van doesn't seem to notice. She stuffs the bag of mint in her pocket before turning back to me. The light blush is already gone, and her dark eyes appear to harden as she looks at me now.

"You play in a dangerous game and you don't realize it, my Lord. So many secrets float in the ash in the winds, and many seldom make sense. But, one has been floating on the breeze since you went to Earth," she pauses, her pupils growing even larger as she looks into my eyes and a chill brushes my skin. The white lines on her face brighten, appearing almost neon as she softly relays the secret to me. *"The woman you seek on Earth has more ties to Hell than you can ever imagine. The Devil grieved the death of her family. You're not the only Lord invested. It's sad, really, when she was the target all along. How strange that she cheats Death when none ever has before."*

Danti's eyes return to normal, and the white lines lose their brilliant glow. Without a word, she turns back to the arena.

Van and I share a look over her head. I'm not sure what to do with that information. It seems to make things harder, not easier. The suggestion that the Devil had some kind of relationship with Valencia's family seems unrealistic. A cascade of questions begin bubbling inside me. She never mentioned anything about the angels being after Valencia, only the Devil and possibly another lord.

Just as I'm about to demand that Danti tell me more, one of the crows on Earth sends me flashes of images of Valencia and her crew in a heated discussion, arguing back and forth. The crows each focus on a different person, giving me a full 360° view of what's happening, but it takes my focus completely out of Hell.

Landon clearly seems agitated and takes a step towards one of the twins. The crows send me images of how they wish to handle the situation. Not willing to let them pick Landon apart, I decide it's time I head back to Earth. I got as much as I could out of Danti, and I feel she was more generous thanks to Van's little gift. Meddling Fae. I'm thankful for it this time, though.

Danti and Van both sit quietly, not acknowledging one another or my silence.

"Van?" I ask as I stand to get ready to leave.

"I think I'll stay here and watch the show. I'll see you when you return." He offers me a small nod before focusing back on the arena, effectively ending the conversation.

As I make my way outside of the tent so I can portal back to Earth, images of the Devil and Valencia as a young girl bombard my mind.

If the Devil grieved the death of her family, why is he after her now?

CHAPTER 26
VALENCIA

"So when will Corvus be back?" Parker asks as we get out of his truck. Thankfully, the couple of days we had to prepare ourselves for the exercise were uneventful. Corvus has been gone the whole time, but I expected that.

"I'm not really sure." I look around the trailhead parking lot, scanning the surrounding trees. I can hear a few bird calls, but I don't know enough about birds to tell the difference between them. Is that black dot on that tree Corvus in his crow form, or is it just a leaf blowing in the wind?

At this point, I could spend all day hunting down any suspicious bird activity in the vicinity, and still not know which one was him. Maybe they all are, for all I know.

I have enough to focus on. Worrying about which bird might magically turn into a sinfully attractive demon should be at the bottom of the list.

"Well, we might as well get started. I'm sure he'll figure it out. He can just fly to us, after all." Parker pauses at the back of the truck, looking at me over the bed. "If we're actually believing that?"

I laugh at his questioning tone, "Unfortunately, I think I do."

Buckles clink against the truck as I pull my backpacking bag from the bed. It's one of my favorite possessions. I spent way too much on it, but quality matters when you're spending weeks at a time in the backcountry. Backpacking was an escape from the relentless pace of fire life. This pack is more than just a bag to carry my supplies; it's a symbol of freedom and independence, a reminder of my resilience through every grueling ascent, freezing night, and hard-won mile.

The large belly of the bag holds most of my supplies. I could've fit more if I'd needed, but since it was such a short trip, I only packed a few changes of clothes, dehydrated meals, and a water pack. I also remembered to grab my water filter but doubted I'd need it.

My emergency gear is in the pocket at the top. It was just a small medical kit—the same one everyone else had in their own packs—a headlamp, flashlight, and my 50-foot rope. It was a bittersweet moment packing that rope, knowing it had saved my life not too long ago.

My tent and other sleeping gear fit nicely inside the smaller pocket at the bottom, and I strapped my rolled sleeping pad to the bottom near the hip belt.

Over the past two days, I've spent most of my free time getting everything ready, even helping some of the others with their gear.

'You pack for every situation because any of them could happen,' I told Tucker, who had questioned whether we really needed everything we were packing. The question reminded me of his youth and the fact he's only been with the team for a year. He still has much to learn. His eyes had widened as I said to him what the Chief had told me many years before. I was as thankful for his expertise then as I am now. It felt good to pass that information on.

I love teaching Tucker what I know and guiding him through the difficult times. And, it was a certain way he tilts his head that made it click for me; his dark hair and youthful spirit remind me of my little brother. Elijah would have even been the same age, had he not died in the fire.

I checked everything one more time before putting my pack on, clipping all the straps, and adjusting them so the weight was in the most comfortable position, using the familiarity of the action to keep me in the present.

Parker and I join the small group next to the trailhead sign. Most are present, with only a few still near their vehicles getting the last of their things together. Everyone on the team should be here except for Greg, who had gotten the flu from his wife.

Since our whole team is here for the exercise—leaving our station unmanned on such short notice—the surrounding fire stations have been tasked with taking on any fire calls that may come our way during our event, but the fire season is gearing down as the cool weather comes in, so I don't expect there to be many issues for them.

"Okay everyone, listen up. Double-check your packs if you haven't already because once we start the hike, there's no pause button for you to try and get your shit together." The anger in Chief Miller's voice is evident. In the years I've worked with the man, I didn't think I'd ever see him be anything other than calm and collected. This whole team-fighting-thing must really be weighing on him.

Everyone takes time to check their gear and ensure they have everything. Once the twins and Bill finally join the group, Chief Miller starts the event.

"Fireteam, on me. Somewhere around Lake Agnes is a dummy that's been hidden. I had a park ranger hide it for us, so even I don't know where it is. Clues have been provided, but we must find the dummy. We're on a time limit, so if we don't find the dummy and rescue it by 5 PM tomorrow, we've failed the exercise. You do not want to know what happens if we fail."

He pauses, looking down at his boots before scanning his eyes over the group, pausing briefly on each person's face. "I have so much faith in this team. It's important that we have each other's backs because it really could mean life or death one day. This exercise may seem annoying or pointless, but I don't know what will happen to the station if we can't get through this together. We're an augment group; they could easily split us all up if they wanted. Let's not give them a reason to do so."

With that, he turns and starts heading up the trail.

He was right. If we didn't work out our differences, the board of directors can easily disband our whole station and send us to any other station across the state. Every person here would do anything to prevent that from happening. Well, I'm not sure Landon would, as he's been the one causing all of our problems lately. Regardless, I'd put aside my distaste for the man to keep the team together.

Foggy puffs of air float in front of each person as we hike up to the lake. I packed all my warmest gear since the temperature has plummeted recently and would remain cold all day long.

Everyone hikes in silence, lost in their thoughts as we work through the most challenging part of the trail. I lean into the exertion of the hike to prevent my mind from focusing on the edge as my mind is plagued with thoughts from the day I fell down this very mountain.

I constantly think back to that day, on what I could've done to avoid such a disastrous end. I still don't think Dumah pushed me, since I didn't feel him touch me until after I rolled my ankle. It is obvious that he left me badly injured, though. Maybe he felt it would be easier that way. *How comforting.*

Parker would've known something was wrong eventually, so I doubt I would've spent the entire night out there. But, still, temperatures in October were known to drop drastically and I had dressed for a warm fall afternoon.

That doesn't even take into account the wildlife or any of the injuries that I had sustained from the fall. So, he definitely thought he was leaving me for dead. What I don't understand, is why.

If he were truly after my power like Corvus suggested he was, then why didn't he finish the job? Sure, while he could assume that I wasn't making it off the mountain, he couldn't have *known*. If it's my power he's after, surely I would've made the acquaintance of his flaming sword far sooner than I did.

This train of thought only leaves me with more questions. I appreciate Corvus answering everything I asked of him, I just wish the answers helped me understand more of what's actually going on. What did all of this have to do with God, anyway? If Dumah is really an Archangel of Heaven, does that mean God wants me dead, too? Is God the villain in my story?

"Val," Parker says softly beside me.

Hearing his voice startles me from my thoughts. We've made it to Lake Agnes.

The trail emerges onto a sandy beach, extending wide on either side. The lake stretches before us and, at its opposite end, the tall, rounded peak of Call Mountain surges up to the sky. There are no other lakes in the great state of Montana with sandy beaches like this one. For that very reason, it's a popular hot spot for visitors throughout the summer months.

High-elevation snow must have drifted in overnight, because the peaks and pines are covered in a dusting of white, making the small valley glisten in the morning sun. The tall, spindly pines stretch towards the sky with their prickly green fingers. All the other plants have taken on the warm amber tones of autumn and the fall colors mixed in with the pearly white snow make for a breathtaking view.

I take a quick second to appreciate it all. Not long ago, I sat on this beach and thought the view was a great example of God's touch here on Earth and how it could heal even the shakiest of faiths. Now, all I can think about is how its beauty has been tainted by one of His minions and how I wish a demon were here with me instead.

I feel a light knock against my arm and realize Parker is nudging me with his elbow. He doesn't say anything, however; just tips his head toward the group where the Chief already stands, reviewing more event details.

"We made good time—so good job, everyone. Because we made it here in under two hours, we've earned our first clue. Before I read it, however, I will hand out a detailed flier explaining the exercise. Please take a couple of minutes to read this over."

I look around the group, wondering if anyone else knows what he's talking about. We've never had clues for these things before. A small sheet of paper is passed around the group. I look down at the one Parker hands me and read it carefully.

Hello Ruby Valley Wildland Fire!

This is your Survival Team Building Exercise Information Sheet.

As you know, the whole point of this event is to rebuild team comradery and work on individual skills and team efforts.

A dummy has been strategically placed somewhere around Lake Agnes and it's your job to ensure its rescue. We've called the dummy Janice.

Janice is a hiker who has been injured and is trapped on the mountain. She is hidden within a 5-mile range of the lake, starting at its center. It's your job to strategize, plan, and execute this rescue as a team!

Better hurry! You only have until 5 PM tomorrow to complete this event. There will be clues provided if your team can find them.

Good luck RVW Fire!

"Okay, now that everyone is on the same page, I just want to reiterate that I am as much a part of this team as everyone else, and will be working alongside you to complete this event as quickly and safely as possible. So—our first clue!" Chief Miller pulls a small notepad out of a pocket on his belt strap and flips to the first page, which he reads aloud.

"RVW Fireteam, congrats on making it to Lake Agnes in good time. Under four hours is quite fast. Good behavior deserves a reward. If you want to find more clues at this time, look for that one special pine."

"Special pine? There's, like, a fuck ton of them—how are we going to find a special one?" Landon blurts when Chief Miller finishes reading.

I suppress an eye roll—barely.

"Well, the flier said we were to strategize and plan, which is how we would conduct a normal rescue, so I say we pick a place to camp so we can all set our bags down and have a quick snack. Then we can start planning," Parker states, directing the group's attention back to the task. Because Parker and I are at the back of the group, everyone turns to face us.

"I agree. It's important everyone stays fueled and hydrated," Chief Miller responds. I notice he doesn't acknowledge Landon's comment or offer other ideas. I imagine he's really only here to study our group tactics and get an idea of our interpersonal relationships when it comes to problem-solving.

Maybe, just maybe, Landon will dig his own grave over the next two days.

Every person here has hiked around this lake and most of the surrounding mountains many times before but none more than Parker and I have, so we led the way to our preferred camping spot. It's about a third of a mile around the lake along the southern shore.

This side of the lake is generally warmer, as the winds from the south are mostly blocked by Sugarloaf Mountain. Instead, the winds drift over the cold water, chilling the northern shore.

"We'll camp here," I state, setting my pack on the sand. I sit down next to my bag and grab a protein bar to munch on. The sand feels cool against my butt and legs. My cargo pants are made for all-terrain hiking and are blissfully waterproof, so I don't worry about getting wet as I sit.

Everyone gathers around and mills about, finding a spot to rest and refuel before the planning begins. We haven't unpacked our bags yet, as it's not really a good idea to set up camp if we're going to be out hiking around the lake all day. We'll leave a few signs of our presence but, for the most part, we'll keep our belongings with us. This prevents unruly humans from stealing our stuff and discourages wildlife from roaming too close to here.

You'd be amazed at what mechanisms a hungry bear can figure out.

Once our camp is set up, the fire's started, and our overall human presence has been established, we won't have too many issues with any four-legged locals. Still, it's always good practice to be prepared.

"Now that we're all settled, does anyone have any ideas on how to get started on our rescue?" The Chief asks the group. No one answers right away, and I see several looks of shock. I guess they haven't caught onto his game, yet.

Since Parker already stepped into the leadership role before, a few heads turn his way, but he remains silent. Ah, my sweet little golden retriever of a best friend preened in the spotlight when he wanted to—but he wouldn't be forced into it, that's for sure.

Every fiber of my being wants to stay in the background. The weight of responsibility is a constant pressure and I'd rather be a reliable supporter than a voice of command. Leading means making decisions that could ultimately hurt someone—or worse. But, even though no one's said it out loud, this whole event is about bringing us back together. If no one steps up, we may end up in a worse position than we started with.

I let a few more seconds pass, leaving just a little more time for someone else to step up. When no one does, I swallow the knot in my throat and start going over the details to help us get started. "Let's go over what we know," I begin. "Janice is located somewhere within a 5-mile radius of the lake. That's a lot of ground to cover without any other hint of a location. If it were a dispatched call, we'd have GPS locators, markers, and possibly other civilians to help aid in locating our stranded hiker. Since we don't have any of that, I think we should focus most of today on getting as many clues as possible; that way, our energy is saved for when we actually need to rescue her," I state bluntly from my spot in the sand.

"Right, because spending our time finding a specific pine tree in a *national forest* is the best use of our time," Landon calls back. Though he doesn't necessarily say it with a condescending tone, his irritation is plain to see.

"No, I think Val is right. A 5-mile radius covers nearly every peak you see surrounding us. Typically, we would have a larger team to cover that much ground—and usually more information." Bill has always been one of my biggest supporters, so it's no surprise when he comments in my defense.

I see a flare of anger spike through Landon. He opens his mouth like he's going to respond, but I beat him to it. "We'll compromise, then. Let's spend a few hours trying to find the clues. From there, we'll spend the remaining daylight hours in active search."

Most nod in agreement as they listen to my plan, though Landon stares me down with that icy hatred of his. I don't know when or how our dislike of each other started, but I've noticed lately that it's gotten much worse.

"And, just curious, but who put you in charge?" Landon sneers.

Hole, meet shovel. *Just keep digging, buddy.*

"Unless you have a better idea, please be quiet so we can continue," Jack snaps at Landon. He's the chattier of the twins, making his *'be quiet'* that much funnier. Thankfully, I'm able to refrain from laughing out loud.

"So, the first clue states we'll find another clue at a special pine. Any ideas?" I ask the group.

"Well, it would have to be something that separates it from the rest. I think we're supposed to look for either a marker or a pine that would have some significance to the park," says Bill. He's also sitting in the sand while he snacks on what looks like a protein bar. He leans against a long, felled log that lies along the beach. Both of the twins beside him atop of it.

"I think a marker is likely, but there's still a lot of ground to cover. We gotta narrow it down even further." Parker paces as he talks. He's the type of man who has to be moving at all times, even when resting. "What kind of tree would be special to the park?"

"Sunset Tree?" Tucker murmurs. He says it so quietly that I almost miss it.

No one else acknowledges his statement—I don't think anyone else heard. He's onto something, though. "What did you say, Tucker?" I ask loudly, drawing everyone's attention to us.

His cheeks take on a soft pink tinge as all eyes land on him. "I said, uh, maybe Sunset Tree?"

"Yes!" Parker claps his hands and points at Tucker. "Perfect thinking."

Tucker smiles shyly.

"What's a sunset tree?" Bill asks, looking between the three of us.

I can't keep the laugh contained. I love Bill but he never gets out of the station to just enjoy the forest, nor does he spend much time on social media.

"Sunset Tree is a geo-hotspot on social media. Basically, somebody on Instagram posted a really nice photo there with a beautiful sunset in the background and tagged the location. Once people saw the post, more showed up to take pictures in that exact area. It's a pine tree just a little further down the beach here." I explain.

"Well, let's go." Landon marches off down the beach towards the sunset tree. He never set his pack down and didn't snack on anything. Everyone ambles around, grabbing their packs and cleaning up any trash to save it from being left behind. As the rest of us leave as a group, Landon's far enough ahead that he's disappeared around the lake bend.

His eagerness to hunt down the next clue after being so against them in the first place has me suspicious of his intentions. Maybe he felt like if he found it first, he'd get brownie points with the Chief or something. We all witnessed his behavior and his generally shitty attitude, so I doubt his being first is going to earn him any gold stars for this exercise.

By the time the rest of us make it to where he is, Landon is leaning against a tree with his hands in his pockets. His left hand twitches as he pulls it from a front pocket and I'd bet my left tit that he's already found the clue and has it in his pocket right now. I don't voice my suspicion and wait to see how it all plays out.

"I don't see anything—" Bill starts to say but Landon quickly interrupts him.

"There's nothing here; I already looked," he snaps, the words jumbling together. Nervous tick or just irritated?

"That's strange—I really thought we were onto something," Parker says. "Why don't we all just take a quick look, just in case you missed something?" Parker's statement seems to be directed at the group, but he stares Landon down with a sharp gaze. Parker may come across as a sweet puppy dog but, get on his bad side, and you'll see how quickly Cujo comes out.

"I said there's nothing here," Landon repeats. "It's a waste of time to keep looking. I say we head to the south end."

"I'm sure you do," Parker says as he stares Landon down. I can see the battle playing in his mind—the same one I'm currently fighting. Do we out Landon, who clearly has the clue but is unwilling to share the details with the group? Or, do we go along with his charade and hope we're not the only ones who can see through it?

The others were already looking around the tree and the surrounding area. It's as clear as the Montana Big Sky that Landon is not the group's choice in leadership and we don't trust his word; there lies our problem. How can we trust him to have our backs when facing a deadly fire if we can't even trust him to be honest about a team-building exercise?

Landon narrows his eyes at Parker, then looks around at the others as they look for the clue. He fidgets with a buckle on his bag before rolling his eyes. "Fine, you guys look for a clue that isn't here. I'm going to go to the south bend."

He turns to leave but is stopped short by Chief Miller. "Landon, this is a group exercise so we will stay together."

Landon freezes but remains facing away from the group and Chief, so I can't see his reaction. I notice his hands briefly clench into fists, but he relaxes them almost instantly and turns around with a massive smile on his face that looks more manic than anything. He nods at the Chief and starts searching with the others.

I look at Parker briefly, who rolls his eyes and joins the group. I glance at the Chief next; he gives me a small smile and nods. There's no way he doesn't know what Landon is doing. In the years I've worked for the man, he's never been one to miss anything.

I return his smile and search for the *'missing'* clue like everyone else.

After about 15 minutes, we've thoroughly checked the entire tree and sur-rounding area—Jake even nearly climbed all the way to the top like a damn monkey. About 5 minutes into the search, I saw Landon turn away from the group and mess with his bag, so I assumed he was about to *'find'* the clue, but he continued searching without a word.

Just as when I'm about to call the man out and demand he give up the clue, a loud "I found it!" rings out around us. We all start walking toward Landon, who's crouched next to a tree a few paces to the right of sunset tree.

Big surprise, Landon finds the clue. Good thing I didn't actually bet my left tit, or it would be gone. Or, actually. . . since I was right, I guess I'd have three tits—which somehow seems even worse.

I suppress the urge to roll my eyes.

No one comments on the fact that he's clearly lying, and we all know it, but I see more than one irritated look directed his way. We just have to make it through this exercise.

I'll consider it a win if I can keep my anger reigned in until the end of the exercise.

"Wow, good eye, Landon," Chief Miller states and he walks up to him.

We all surround Landon, who stands and faces the group with a small slip in his hand. He clears his voice and reads aloud.

"Three geese walk on four feet, but this isn't a wild goose chase—go to the place where you can see your face."

Parker *hmms* and crosses his arms over his chest. "Interesting," he says. He's clearly irritated at the situation but, like me, would rather see how this plays out.

"There's a mirror out here?" Tucker asks.

I watch as an expression of glee begins to consume Landon's face from top to bottom. He must think he knows where the next clue is, which is too bad—because so do I.

"No," I begin, "but the pools in the flats on the south bend are usually so still that you can see your reflection in them." I say, and oh, how sweetly does that glee die.

"You don't say," Jake mutters with an irritated eye roll. Makes sense—he did spend about 10 minutes climbing to the top of sunset tree for no reason.

"You're so fucking smart, yet I didn't see you finding the clue," Landon bites out with a huff, invisible smoke practically blowing from his ears and nostrils. I usually pretend he looks like that angry little character from the Disney movie about emotions. It helps me deal with his ridiculous behavior.

"Don't talk to me that way," Jake snaps.

Landon steps towards Jake, who happens to be standing beside me. Before he can get close, a dark black blob blurs past me, heading directly for Landon's face.

Corvus is here, and he's *pissed*.

CHAPTER 27

VALENCIA

THE SMALL BLACK BIRD dives around Landon a few times who, in turn, starts dodging as best as he can, but it looks more like a bad attempt at dancing than anything else. I notice that the bird never actually touches Landon, but you'd never know that based on the way he squeals in panic.

I so badly want to laugh at the scene, but I don't. Somehow—whether it's actually Corvus or one of his minions—I know this is Corvus' doing. Though, now that I think of it, we never did cover how I would be able to tell whether a crow is him or not. Either way, there was no doubt in my mind that Corvus was behind this particular scene. The crow conveniently attacked as soon as Landon showed signs of aggression.

Parker turns to me with wide, shocked eyes. Before I knew about Corvus, this would've shocked me, too, but with all the information I've learned over the weekend, I'm having a hard time feeling anything beyond gratitude.

It doesn't escape my notice that no one steps in to help. I understood why I didn't. Parker, too—since he knows what Corvus is capable of. But the others? I assumed that someone would step up—the Chief, at least—but they all stand off to the side, watching the action unfold.

Hopefully, this means that the rusted link in our chain is finally being exposed.

"Well, don't just stand there!" Landon yells to no one in particular as he continues to dodge the angry crow.

In response, it caws loudly in his face.

"Don't show fear. They can smell it!" I call back to him. It's mostly a facetious joke but he's so focused, he doesn't catch it.

The crow does, though. As swiftly as it arrived, the bird proceeds to fly away from Landon, swooping over my shoulder and disappearing somewhere into the trees.

"What the fuck, guys?" Landon huffs heavily with exertion.

Bill walks over and pats Landon on the shoulder. "You looked like you had it handled."

"I didn't want it to go for my eyes next," says Jack as he looks after the direction the crow disappeared before glancing at me. It's like I can see the wheels turning in his head. Jack was there that night at the bar when the crow hopped onto my arm. He was just as apprehensive of the crow then and I swear, it's like I can see him wondering whether it's the same crow from that night but can't decide how that would be possible.

Same Jack, same.

"That was something else. Landon, glad you're okay. Let's head to the south bend for the next clue." Chief Miller takes off down the trail, heading toward the far end of the lake.

"Was that the same crow from the bar?" Jake quietly asks as we head down the trail. He's so quiet, only I'm able to hear him clearly over the crunching footsteps on the sandy beach. He must've been thinking the same thing as his twin. I swear their minds are connected.

"Yeah, it was, I think," I stutter. I'm not sure why, but my gut instinct was to not sound too confident that it was the same bird. Not that I don't trust Jake, because I do. I trust every person out here with my life with the exception of one person, who is currently trudging down the beach directly behind us. He remains quiet for most of the walk, but I can feel the animosity in his gaze boring into the back of my head.

"No way, dude," Jake laughs softly under his breath and looks at me with a smile on his face that drops when he catches a glimpse of my expression.

My brows are pitched down in deep thought as I try to figure out how to navigate this conversation. I don't want to lie to my friends, but I also don't want to bring unnecessary issues to them.

"My vote; a Disney princess," Jake states, bumping my arm with his elbow, laughing to bring up the mood.

"Nah, I think she's a witch!" Jack exclaims, jumping around to face us while wiggling his fingers in my direction.

They're tactics work to take my mind off the issue and I smile. I'm trying to not let everything I learn affect me, but I'm having a much harder time as each new thing pops up.

"Witch *does* rhyme with bitch," Landon mutters behind us. No one pays him any mind, though—least of all me.

Jack and Jake start arguing about the differences between the different styles of witchcraft, which drowns out Landon's shitty mumbling. They're so animated and passionate in their debate that I wonder where they learned so much about it all. The last thing I expected was to find out that the twins are secretly witchy nerds. It somehow makes them even more attractive.

Though, nothing scorches like a 6'5 demon with a dirty mouth.

The rest of the hike passes quietly. I can hear a few soft conversations but don't try to get involved. We should've used this time to continue strategizing, but everyone seemed content to just get to the next clue and go from there. It's also grown glaringly obvious where our issues are, so maybe the others are finally catching on.

"Okay, everyone fan out. Let's pace in a line with 8-foot spacing," Chief Miller directs once we reach the edge of the flats. This is the first direction the Chief has given us, so I wonder if it's mostly to prevent another hissy fit about Parker or I taking the lead.

Sandy beach leads into the mountain rock. Vegetation grows in abundance here and so many little bushes of bright yellow and orange cover the whole flat. It was once a part of the lake but, over the years, the water receded enough that this part now remains above water. Still, hundreds of small and large pools are scattered across the valley from one side to the other. We all make a line and start walking slowly, scanning around our feet as we walk along the pools.

I take care to walk around the larger pools to avoid getting my feet wet and make sure to check them thoroughly as we walk. I'm yet to think about what the clue is trying to tell us or what we should even be looking for—all I know is that this is the best place in the area to catch a reflection. The rest of the lake would be too choppy as fall winds race across the top of its surface to create tiny waves, whereas this part of the valley is protected from most of the wind, causing the water to be calm.

As I scan the ground, a flash of light catches my eye. I kneel at the edge of a medium-sized pool, probably four feet across, and look closely under the water's surface. Now that I'm bent down, the flash has disappeared, but I could've sworn I saw a glare right here—like when the sun reflects off a piece of glass or a mirror and sends a beam of light back.

Just then, the sun peeks out from behind the clouds and I see it once again. Just at the edge of the water is a tiny glass bottle that's been shoved between two rocks. I reach down and gingerly pull the bottle above the surface. It's sealed tight, but a few drops of water have made it inside.

I twist the cap and pull a small piece of beige paper out of the bottle. It's not unusual to find trash here or there around the park but, for the most part, it tends to be some sort of plastic. It's strange for a glass bottle to be in such a place and even stranger for one to have a handwritten note inside.

Looks like I've found our third clue. I unfold the slip of paper, turning it over in my hands. The few drops of water that made it into the bottle have smeared some of the writing, but there's enough left for me to read it clearly.

"Hey, I found the clue!" I yell to the group. I don't wait for them to ask and read the message aloud, "It's all up to you now." I look up at Jack and then Bill. "That's it. That's all it says."

"See, I told you guys looking for these clues was a waste of time!" Landon growls. Unfortunately, it seems like he might be right; the clue leads us nowhere. The whole point of looking for the clues in the first place was to get a hint at the location of Janice, our injured dummy.

Everyone around me begins arguing, particularly Jack and Landon, but I drown them all out. This can't be it. We must be missing something. Whoever put these clues together wouldn't have told us they were there to help us and then not actually have them help in any way.

I look at the piece of paper again. In the bottom right corner, there is a smudge of ink—so smeared I can't tell what it was supposed to be beyond maybe an S and an L. That doesn't make sense; I don't know anyone with those letters in their name, so I doubt it's a signature.

I think back over the other clues we've found and that's when it comes to me. If this clue had a mark there, surely the others would, too. Perhaps I could use them to figure out what it means.

"Hey, Chief, can I see that first clue again?" I ask him.

He steps forward, digs the paper slip out of his pocket, and hands it to me. He doesn't say anything to me, nor does he participate in the argument that's still going on between Jack and Landon. Everyone else turns their attention to me.

I search the slip for writing in the corners, but there is none. Confused, I read it over in my head.

It makes no sense. Clearly, the smudged mark was supposed to help somehow but, now that it's gone, I'm at a loss for what it could be. I examined the two clues in my hand, analyzing them for even the smallest detail.

I can't contain my laugh once I figure it out. It's a freaking puzzle! I thought the clues sounded strange when the others read them out loud, but it wasn't until I saw them that they came to me. Specific numbers were written in numeral form, which had to have been done on purpose.

"What is it, Val?" Parker asks.

I smile wide, "It's a puzzle! Each clue has numbers in the phrase that I imagine will help us figure out Janice's location. I didn't figure it out until I saw the numbers on the Chiefs clue."

I didn't have the clue Landon found to confirm there were numbers on his, but I could get it from him later. His face sours as I explain, fists clenched at his sides. I look at him a little more closely, trying to understand where such severe animosity came from. We were never friends, sure, but this seems a little extra—even for him.

A cool breeze shifts through the group, sending a shiver down my back. Landon turns away, stepping behind Bill. Hoping to move past the strangeness, I suggest lunch to the others, who all soundly agree. Everyone breaks away and tries to find a dry place to sit among the rocks. This part of the lake is all flat bedrock—so, not as comfortable as the beach—but it would take too long to hike back just to eat. Waves ripple across the lake and the sound of them softly lapping against the shore adds a peaceful ambiance to the scene. It's the warmest part of the day but the breeze brings in plenty of chill. I'm grateful for my fleece jacket and snuggle even further into it as I pick a spot to sit and unload my supplies.

Once everyone is settled with their protein snacks, jet boils, and dehydrated meals, I explain my idea. "Okay, if we look at the flier and the first clue, three numbers are written out: five, four, and one. Landon, are there any numbers written out on your slip?" I ask him. He doesn't move immediately to look, just stares me down before finally reaching into his pocket.

"Three and four," Jake says, putting his jet boil together to heat his lunch. "I remember the clue; it said *three geese walk on four feet*. I'd be surprised if they weren't in number form."

I look at Landon, who nods his head with an eye roll and glares at Jake. *Mad someone else is stealing your thunder?*

"Okay, so that's what? Five, four, one, three, four?" Parker asks.

"Yeah, I think so," Jack mumbles around a piece of jerky he's just taken a bite of.

"That's too short to be a coordinate; longitude and latitude are both 6-digit numbers." Bill is our most experienced tracker, so I'm not surprised he's the first to mention that.

At first, I assumed it might be one or the other, but I've spent a lot of time hiking this specific area, and I know the coordinates for Sugarloaf Mountain started with either a 45 or a 70—not 54, which were the first two numbers in the clue.

"The flier says, *somewhere within a 5-mile range of the lake, starting at its center,*' so couldn't that be the first clue? Don't look past five miles?" Jake says before diving into his warmed lunch. It's Chili Mac, so his enthusiasm is understandable.

"And start from the center," It's the first time Landon has joined the conversation since we all sat down for lunch.

"Good thinking!" I tell him. See, I can play nice when it benefits the group. "So, start at the center of the lake and don't look past 5 miles. That leaves four, one, three, four."

"Is that like 4,134, or do you think it's the numbers individually?" Jack asks before shoving another large piece of jerky into his mouth as he restarts the jet boil now that Jake is done with it.

"Still not enough numbers to be an exact location." That comes from Bill, who has demolished one PB&J sandwich and is now starting on his second.

"Yeah, I think it's individual numbers," I say. "Let's think broadly for a second. First, we know we don't have to look past five miles. So, what's another broad way to determine a location?" I ask.

There are a few seconds of silence as everyone contemplates my question. Chief Miller smiles broadly at me over his bag of chips, so I know I'm heading in the right direction.

"A compass?" Tucker guesses before repeating himself with more confidence. "A compass! North, south, east, and west." It's the first time he's spoken since we all sat down for lunch. I beam at him, proud that he spoke up in front of the entire group. "Which direction is the fourth?" Tucker asks, smiling back at me.

"West," Bill and I both say at the same time.

"So, no more than 5 miles west? Basically, around Call Mountain?" Landon looks between Bill and I and, for the first time since this whole exercise started, there's no irritation or annoyance in his voice. Maybe this really is all we needed to come together as a group again.

"Yes, exactly," I say back. "I think we're onto something, guys. I say we pack lunch and search the mountain's base for the last few hours of daylight. If we're unable to locate Janice during that time, we'll head back and set up camp, then start again tomorrow."

Everyone nods in agreement and packs up their trash and gear wordlessly.

Parker divides us into groups of two or three so no one is alone and each group can take a section. Even though this is just an exercise, it's vital that we still practice safe search procedures.

My group consists of Bill and Tucker, who I'm happy with. Parker sets off with Landon and Chief Miller, leaving the twins alone. They don't comment on the grouping, and I'm sure they prefer it that way, anyway.

Since the only way to easily reach the top of Call Mountain is by hiking to the peak of Sugarloaf and then across the ridge between the two, all three groups focus on searching around the base of Call Mountain and the lake, itself.

When everyone finally reaches camp, there's just a little daylight left and no one has seen any sign of our stranded hiker.

We all make a start on setting up our tents and get a fire going in preparation for the big search in the morning. We start at first light, so I'll have to set an alarm pretty early to ensure I'm up, packed, and ready to go by then. Finally, after some light chatting about the plans for the next day and eating a wonderful meal of dehydrated spaghetti and electrolyte gummies, I head into my tent to crash for the night.

I'm slightly saddened that Corvus hasn't made his presence known through-out the day. I'm sure he was busy, off doing whatever he was doing, so I've tried to not look too hard into why I've missed his presence so much. I hadn't noticed any other signs of the crow, but I was happy he was at least there when I needed him. Though, I'm pretty sure I could've handled anything Landon tried.

The sounds of zippers crackling and tents rustling surround me as everyone else finally heads to bed. We each decided to put a little distance between our tents to offer a slight sense of privacy.

The fire's soft glow is starting to dwindle; it'd surely be out by morning. It was mostly for light around the campsite, anyway, as our personal gear had a temperature rating for far colder than a fall evening.

I try to force my eyes closed and demand sleep come to me, but unanswered questions plague my mind and the chill of being alone prevents my body from resting.

Chapter 28
Valencia

I'm finally about to fall asleep when a large, shadowed silhouette creeps into my tent.

"What the fuck?" I jerk up, but my zipped sleeping bag prevents me from going far.

"What?" Corvus asks as he crawls into the cramped tent. He folds down into a seated position with his long legs sprawled out in front of him after zipping the tent flap closed again. He's wearing his normal, all-black attire but I notice he doesn't have a jacket on. It's cold enough outside that I not only went to sleep in a subzero sleeping bag, but I also put on a warm hoodie before I went to sleep. Corvus seems completely comfortable in his dark cargo pants and black long-sleeve top.

As Corvus settles himself against the far end of the tent, his feet touch the opposite side. *With* a bend in his knees. My tent is rated for two people, but they must not consider one of those people to be a literal giant.

Note to self, I'm gonna need a bigger tent.

"You scared me. I wasn't expecting anyone to come into my tent," I say quietly. At this point, there's no noise in the camp, so I imagine everyone else is fast asleep, but I don't want to risk anyone other than Parker, knowing he's here.

Corvus picks up my legs and drapes them over his lap. They're still trapped inside the bottom of the sleeping bag. When he barged in and made himself comfortable, my legs were shoved to the side to make room. The rustling of the slick fabric sounds far louder than usual in the otherwise silent night.

"Did you think I'd sleep outside?" Corvus says just as softly.

"Isn't that where birds normally sleep?" I ask as I unzip myself from my sleeping bag. Now that I'm free of the warm cocoon, the cool air nips at my exposed skin and I shiver against the cold.

"Ha. Ha." He deadpans, though I can see the gleam of his white teeth as he smiles. "So, how did your day go?"

"It was mostly uneventful. We spent the morning looking for clues and then spent the afternoon looking for Janice. Since no one found her, we'll hopefully find her tomorrow. We have until five, *'or else'*." I air quote. Corvus just looks at me with a cocked brow and a blank expression.

"Who's Janice?" he asks.

"You mean you weren't following me around all day like a little feathered stalker?"

"I was there for the important parts." He smirks.

"Thanks for dealing with Landon, I appreciated your enthusiasm." It truly was a highlight of my day. The look on Landon's face as the crow attacked him was priceless.

"Trust me, it was my pleasure." He pats my legs, which are still lying across his lap. "Who is Janice and why do you have to find her tomorrow."

Right, he must've missed at least that part. I go over the day's events, from the whole purpose of the exercise to the details in the clues. "That's as far as we got before we started our search. We'll hopefully figure out the rest of the clue during breakfast tomorrow and then hike to the top of Call Mountain since that's our best guess where she might be hidden."

"Well, talk me through what you've figured out so far—maybe I can help you. I *am* a lord of Hell, which means my strategizing skills are at least slightly above average," he says with a laugh.

I review what we've figured out and what remains to be deciphered before handing him the clues, which he promptly reads out loud.

"You can see in the dark?" I ask incredulously. Sure, it's probably at the far end of his list of abilities yet, the more I learn about him, the crazier it gets.

"Yes, it's as clear as day. The only darkness I can't see through is in the Stygian lands in Hell," he murmurs. I want to ask what that is, but I don't want to distract him. I'm also not sure I even care to know about some random place in Hell—I don't plan on ever going there if I don't have to.

As Corvus quietly pours over the clues, questions start to circulate in my head. Questions about Heaven and Hell. The war between them and how I fit into all of it.

What all of this has to do with my family's deaths.

"I think you're on the right track about the first few numbers. The last set could be distance or something similar. Without knowing more about this area I'm not sure what the last few numbers could be. I'm sorry." He returns the clues to me.

"I appreciate any help we can get, though I think Chief Miller has mostly realized that the main problem is Landon," I say, staring into space as I force myself to not yawn.

"Well, good," Corvus murmurs. I can feel him looking at me but I don't turn his way. For the most part, I can see his features but, if what he said is true, he can see me in great detail.

"You're tired. Why don't you get some rest and start fresh tomorrow?" Without waiting for me to answer, he shifts his big body around.

It's awkward at first and pretty noisy as he rubs against the slick material of the tent. I don't think to argue as he gets us situated side by side, wrapping me up in his long arms and pulling us both down to our sides. He opens my sleeping bag most of the way, giving himself just enough room to pull me back against his chest.

Because of his height, he's forced to curve his upper body around me while his legs bend at the knee. We touch from the bottom of my neck to where my calves press against his shins.

In an instant, I can feel the heat radiating off of him and into my back. He's like a living furnace, burning the cool air away from me entirely. Now that I've felt the heat coming from him, I doubt he'll grow cold through the night.

"Are you always so hot?" I ask in a hushed whisper.

"Most of the time, yes. I'll tell you more about it later," he responds. I can feel him shift around me slightly, but he doesn't say anything else.

"But,"

"Rest, Valencia," he whispers, interrupting me, lips pressed against my neck in a soft-spoken kiss. A burst of hot air rolls down my neck, blowing the little hairs around my nape and causing goose bumps to erupt down my arms.

"Corvus," I groan. I don't know if it's a question or a statement.

"Be quiet," he growls, and the sharpness of his words turns me on even more.

I can't contain the soft moan that escapes. My mind has lost its hold on anything other than the feeling of his body pressed against mine. When I'm with him like this, the stress of the world just washes away. I push my hips back farther, into his body. The pressure of his growing erection is unmistakable. When his cock firmly presses into the dip of my back, I can't help but moan again, a little louder and a whole lot needier.

"You think it's smart to defy me, Kitten?" Corvus growls at me. He places one hot hand on my stomach, sliding it underneath my shirt to rest against the bare skin that's there, and presses my body tighter against his front.

I wish he'd drag that hand down lower, but sadly he doesn't. His other hand snakes under my neck and wraps around me to land directly on my mouth, which he covers unashamedly.

He starts actively pressing wet kisses up my neck, and I feel the sharp sting of his teeth scrape against my ear lobe. I try to withhold another moan, but it rushes out of my mouth in a wave of hot air. Thankfully, with his palm pressed firmly over my mouth, the sound is trapped.

He starts rubbing slow circles on my stomach, drifting closer and closer to where I really want him. He growls low in my ear, "You want me to touch you?"

Since his palm prevents me from speaking, I nod my head rapidly. His hand still makes slow circles on my stomach but, as my thighs squeeze tightly together, it's obvious I'm craving his touch somewhere else.

The hand on my stomach makes a few more laps around my stomach before slowly, blissfully dragging lower. I can feel the rough bumps of his calloused palm slide across my heated skin as he slides his hand inside the waist of my leggings. His rough fingers are met with bare, feverish skin.

Because his hand is so large, the tip of his longest finger nudges my clit, causing my hips to jerk back against him. A rush of air puffs out of my nose in an almost wheezing fashion. His palm prevents any sound from coming out, but my throat vibrates with a hummed moan.

He presses his hips forward, pushing his cock firmly into the dip of my back as his hand slides lower. I have no time to mentally prepare before he slides two fingers in between my thighs, dowsing them in my arousal. He swirls them around, causing my thighs to separate slightly before finally dipping one inside.

A shudder rolls through my entire body at the sensation. There's a slight stretch, enough that I know it's there, but I'm so turned on that I want to beg for more. It's a good thing he hasn't moved his hand from my mouth, otherwise this entire camp would know how needy I am to be filled by him.

He slowly slides one finger in and out a few times, coating it in arousal but not really giving me any relief. It's a cruelly sweet type of torture. He switches fingers and repeats the same process, slicking the new finger with my arousal. He then does it again, but switches between the two now-damp fingers, never putting more than one inside me at a time.

My pussy clamps with each withdrawal and I start to squirm as the teasing sensation becomes unbearable. Corvus swirls his fingers around my clit a few times before pressing down firmly against the needy bud. My body jerks as shocks of pain and arousal flow through me. I'm so turned on and frustrated that I'm about to demand he get on with it or let me finish myself.

But, I learned my lesson last time about suggesting letting someone else do it. Though, the thought of his growled claim makes my clit pulse. It's an odd sensation, how the blood flows so powerfully through my body. I can feel my heartbeat pound through my clit and into the fingers he has pressed there. I wonder if he can feel it because he presses his hips forward in almost perfect rhythm with the beat.

I nearly moan in relief when he finally drags his fingers away from my clit and dips them straight inside, stretching me further than he has yet. I can't contain the groan that rumbles out of my chest and throat and his palm does a poor job of suppressing the loud sound. At this point, I'm beyond caring. My only thought is of reaching the orgasm he's offering.

Corvus begins furiously working his fingers inside me, going from a rapid flutter to a sharp, thrusting motion and then back. It's an endless back and forth between the two that my brain seriously attempts to short-circuit as the orgasm quickly approaches.

He must notice that I'm close because all of a sudden, he shoves his fingers as far inside as they will go and then proceeds to curl them forward with his palm pressed firmly against my clit. I nearly come at that alone but then he clamps down even tighter and starts moving his whole hand in a jerking motion. This causes the fingers he has shoved inside me to rub against my inner walls in a spot no man has ever reached. His palm rubs furiously against my clit. My whole body shakes with his intensely controlled hold on me.

My legs start shaking uncontrollably, and the orgasm starts building in my lower stomach, sending fire through my blood. The air is ripped from my lungs as the wave finally crests and crashes and tremors are sent throughout my body.

Sharp stings of pain bite into my skin as Corvus clamps his teeth into the base of my neck as he groans loudly, the sound just barely muffled against my skin. He rides the wave of my orgasm like that. His hand is no longer moving. Instead, he just holds my center in the tight clamp of his palm, his large fingers still pressed deeply inside my pussy.

He hums against my neck, releasing his teeth to press light kisses to soothe the slight ache. "You're so beautiful when you come," he whispers.

He removes his fingers from inside me, bringing his hand up past my view. A low groaning hum rattles through his chest into my back, and I can only assume at what he's done with the fingers that were covered in the evidence of what he just did to me. He places that hand back on my stomach, holding us close together.

"You taste like the most delicious sin, Valencia." The sound of my name coming from him causes flutters to race from my center.

The sharp edge of my arousal has finally come down but, based on the bulge still pressed against my back, his hasn't. Not only that—but between the dirty words and his kinky actions, I think he could convince me to go all night.

I start to roll over, but he holds me firmly by the hand on my stomach and removes the hand over my mouth to drag his fingertips lazily across my chest. "Just rest."

I ignore his statement and instead shove my hand between our bodies in an attempt to touch him like he just touched me. I feel crazed with the intense desire to feel him under my skin. To bring him to his knees like he's done to me twice already. Make him hunger for more. I want to ignite a fire within him that burns with such fierce intensity, he is consumed by the flames and all that remains in the ashes is *me*.

"Valencia," he mumbles, using a hand to grab my arm and pull it away from him, "We can't."

Honestly, it must be another superpower of his, his ability to piss me off so soon after getting me off. I rip my hand from his grasp and move as far away as the cramped tent will allow. I sit up and face him. Twice now, I've put myself out there, and twice he's rejected me. I feel weirdly used in a way. I know he's been giving me insane pleasure but the way he continually denies my touch stings sharper than you'd think.

"Why the hell not?" I whisper though it's definitely not a quiet sound. I can't really see his expression, but I can see his chest rising and falling rapidly as he breathes.

Not so unaffected now, are we? I sneer in my head.

"Don't get me wrong; I want you. Badly," he starts, and I can't help but roll my eyes at him.

"Clearly, or your dick wouldn't have been hard enough to poke a hole in my back. I'm asking *why*. Twice—you've rejected me *twice,* now. I'm beginning to get complex about it." I snap, unable to keep the emotion out of my voice.

He leans on one elbow and places a large hand on my cheek. I resist the urge to lean into the touch, but it's difficult. This pisses me off even more, so I pull away from his touch entirely and just stare him down.

He sighs softly, tipping his head back with a deep breath. "There's something I need to tell you."

"If you tell me you're with someone else, I will literally rip your dick off and beat you with it," I growl.

He laughs softly, but I can see his forehead crease in a wince. "No, no. It's nothing like that."

I'm at a loss for what could possibly cause him to be okay with continually giving me pleasure but refusing to get any for himself.

"I. . . I have," he stammers, voice more subdued than usual. He pauses, his fingers fidgeting with some threads that hang loose from my sleeping bag. His limbs, once relaxed, now seem tense.

"Do you have an STD?" I blurt. It seems unlikely that he would, since he can heal himself from anything, but it's the only other thing that comes to mind. My brows pinch and my stomach turns at the thought of him with someone else.

He laughs, though it sounds like a cough as well. "Definitely not that."

I just sit quietly and wait for him to explain because I don't have the slightest idea what it could be, and constantly asking him isn't getting us anywhere.

"I have this thing with the Devil," he finally says.

"What kind of thing?" I question, confused since we established I'd be going for his dick if he were currently with someone else. Well, I didn't believe I'd actually be able to rip his dick off but, hey, what was the phrase for if not to invoke a little fear?

"I bargained with the Devil to be able to come to Earth in this form," he states plainly.

"Why would you have to do that?"

"Because, when I was much younger, I made a stupid mistake. The Devil was, let's just say, more than pissed when it all went down. He banned me from returning to Earth in this form and exiled me to the Barren lands for six years to be chased by his Hellhounds."

"Must've been some mistake," I say, not sure what else to offer as I mull over what he's told me.

"Yeah, it wasn't my finest moment," he murmurs.

"You said this happened when you were much younger but I wouldn't guess you to be much older than 35. How old are you?"

"Time moves differently in Hell than it does on Earth. Technically, I'm around 34 years old by Hell's standard."

"And by Earth's standards?" I'm not sure why it matters, but I'm curious now that it's been brought up.

"It doesn't really translate well. If you want to get technical, biologically, I've been alive for 34-ish Hell years."

Again, this felt like one of those weird conversations where he wasn't necessarily withholding information or being purposely deceitful, but none of his responses actually answered the question.

"When was the last time you were on Earth?" Maybe it was about asking the right question.

"Around 200 Earth years ago."

"The fucking 1800s?" I snap a little too loudly.

"Hush," he warns. "There was a lot to gain from the depravity of the once Wild West," he says it in an almost mocking tone.

I try to understand how he's been around that long. "If you fucking remember the Wild West enough to be a smartass about it, then you're not 34 years old. Tell the truth," I demand.

"Fine. My body may be biologically close to 34, but my mind is much, much older. I can heal myself from anything life-threatening and, as soon as my body matured, I basically became immortal. We can be killed, especially in a place as dangerous as Hell, but not by time alone."

Being intimate with a 200-year-old man just gives me shivers—and not the good kind. I don't even know what to say at this point.

"Aging is a disease, Valencia. As soon as humans figure that out, they'll live longer than they ever have. You're not only human, there's a part of you capable of living hundreds of years, too."

The thought terrifies me. "I don't want to be dealing with this shit for eternity. Mortality seems kinder."

"Humans really have wildly romanticized immortality," he murmurs quietly.

Speaking of, "So, how does you being old as fuck have anything to do with you not wanting me to touch you?"

"It's not a matter of what I want, Valencia. I *can't* let you," he says.

"Because of the bargain?" He nods. "So, what were the terms of this bargain? Help me understand, because you're not touching me again until I know exactly what's happening here."

That must finally get his attention, because he sits up a little straighter now. His head brushes the top of the tent as he settles across from me. "The Devil loves playing games," he begins. "He's been trapped in Hell for far longer than either of us can comprehend. Therefore, he sources his entertainment through his Hellspawn. The Devil sent me on a mission but I quickly realized I wasn't going to be able to complete it while stuck in my crow form. I vowed to the Devil that I would complete my task but I'd need the use of my body—this body—to do so. I offered to serve 100 years in the Death Pit as a gladiator slave if I fail. I thought that would be enough to appease him, but unfortunately not. He accepted my terms on one condition; under no circumstances am I allowed to get pleasure from you. Not until the mission is complete."

Wow, there is so much to unpack with that one simple statement. Questions instantly start swirling around in my head, so I focus on the most obvious.

"What's your mission?" I ask quietly.

"You," he states plainly.

Chapter 29
Corvus

"What about me, Corvus? Why did you come into my life?" She draws her knees into her chest and wraps her arms around her legs.

"It's complicated. And I'm not saying that as a copout. I truly mean this whole situation is extremely complicated." I watch as Valencia curls into an even tighter ball, clearly blocking her body off in defense.

I take a second to quickly think about how I want to handle this. It's the first time she's truly asked me why I'm here. It's not that I didn't know it would come up eventually but I'd hoped it would happen after everything had settled down so I could sit her down and explain everything in a way she could easily understand. I didn't want her to make this kind of decision under duress—it was her fucking soul at stake. The least I could do was wait until she fully understood what giving it up meant.

Sure, it wouldn't change her life all that much right now, but that didn't mean she didn't deserve the opportunity to decide for herself. Dumah had already tried to take that choice away from her and I imagine whoever was responsible for her family's death had tried then, too. I wouldn't be like them.

There wasn't exactly a time limit on when I had to do it, so we could deal with Dumah and then I'd explain. She'd be angry at first that I hid it all from her, but hopefully not forever.

Valencia stares at me silently—well, she mostly just looks in my direction. While I assume she can't see me all too clearly in the dark, I can see her as if the sun were shining overhead. Her dark brows are dipped down in a pinch, and an almost worried scowl covers her face.

"Listen, I can't tell you much because I don't know all the details myself. But I will tell you everything I know, if that's what you want." She nods her head, but I haven't started explaining just yet. She doesn't know what's really at stake. "But you have to understand something, with knowing comes more danger. Things may seem dangerous now, but this is nothing compared to what else is out there. I just want you to be safe; to be alive. Fuck everything else."

The constant battle between completing my mission *no matter what,* as the Devil had said, and not wanting to take the choice away from her feud within me. I can't deny that something about this woman has drawn me in. With everything I've learned in the last couple of weeks, I wonder more and more why the Devil sent me in the first place.

Many other higher demons in Hell could've come to Earth and gotten her to join Hell that first day. She would've died, most likely, but the mission would've been complete. The more I think about it, the more I realize death never even crossed my mind. I could've killed her that first day. Death dealt by my hand—or wings—would've been enough to send her soul to Hell as the Devil demanded. It would've been difficult, stuck as a crow, but I could've managed it. I didn't have to save her, either—but then the Scale would've decided which side her power went to.

It all reminds me of the conversation with the Devil. He didn't seem surprised when I asked him for permission to use my middle form on Earth, almost like he was expecting it.

The truth sits like an oppressive weight on my chest. I've been fighting it ever since the cabin but I can't deny it any longer. I want her—and not just for her body. I'm starting to fall for the very person I shouldn't want. She's more than forbidden, she's from a different world entirely.

"I want to know," she says, snapping me out of my thoughts. Damn me for being proud of her strength while also fearing how this could change everything. The words are like shards of glass in my mouth, but I spit them out anyway.

"The Devil called on me two days before I saw you for the first time. He told me I was being given a task and that I'd have to go to Earth to complete it." I take a deep breath and steel my spine before continuing. "I was to find you and claim your soul, by any means necessary."

There's a long, silent pause. The faint noises from the surrounding forest drift into the silence. She takes a deep breath before asking, "And have you?"

"To claim a soul is either done by death or offering. Since you haven't offered it to me, and I've tried very hard to make sure you don't die, your soul is still very much yours." I lean towards her, placing my hand on one leg.

"How would I even offer it? Why would I?" she questions with a more confident edge to her voice, though I still sense her doubt.

"I can't tell you why. It's your soul and only you know what you're willing to give it up for. Truthfully, a soul offering is pretty straightforward. In Hell, words have meaning, so you can offer it away with just a statement. A verbal contract, if that makes more sense. But, I promise I'm trying my hardest to ensure you never have to." I explain in the most general way that I can, trying not to throw too much more at her.

"No special ceremony?" She asks, her eyebrows scrunched so tightly it creates creases in the middle of her forehead.

"No," I respond, shaking my head.

"I still don't understand why everyone wants *my* soul," she implores.

"Truthfully, I'm not sure either. It's common knowledge that Hell's in trouble. The Scale has been tipped in Heaven's favor for far too long and I'd assumed the Devil sent me to get your soul because he was getting desperate. No offense, but I thought you were just another random human in the beginning but, with everything that's happened, there's got to be more to it. Between your angel heritage and the fact that Dumah is after you as well, something about your soul has to hold strategic importance in the war."

"I'm just one person. It's just one soul. How much change could it actually make?" Valencia asks, sounding more confused than ever.

"It's a guess, but if you're as powerful as everything that's happened is suggesting, your soul could very well shift the balance of power that's been offset between the realms for hundreds of years. A beacon in the darkness Hell has been suffering. But that doesn't mean you shouldn't get a choice, and I'll do anything to ensure that you do."

Her soul truly is unlike any other I've encountered. It resonates with her goodness, a vibrant energy that radiates out to everyone she touches. There's also a depth to her, an untamed veil that's encased in shadows, a darkness that refuses to be extinguished. I recognize the value of her rarity, but even if she's the catalyst to save the entirety of Hell, I'll fight to ensure that the choice isn't taken away from her. No matter the benefit, I can't force her. The part of me that wants to protect her grows more everyday and this is the only way I know how.

"I'm just a pawn in a twisted game," she huffs in defeat.

She's not entirely wrong. The realms *are* treating her as a pawn. They think her powerless since she's from the mortal realm but they'll have to fight harder because her soul is woven into the fabric of her being, and not even Death has been successful in making her a victim of fate.

"I get that you're mad, and I'm truly sorry you're being dragged into all of this but know this—you are not a pawn. You are a key that the realms think they can use to manipulate their own agendas, but *you* hold the power. You are a prize, a maxim of determination and perseverance. You may be in the midst of a twisted game but there are many pieces on a chessboard. Be a Queen, a harbinger of chaos. Show them they chose the wrong woman to mess with."

She pauses for a moment, lips rolling while deep in thought, then says, "Thank you, that was. . . really kind and oddly motivating, but there's so much going on and I'm not sure I can handle adding more to my plate. I appreciate you telling me about my soul, I just don't know where that leaves us. You've saved my life at every opportunity, and I want to believe you would never betray me, I just don't know what to think right now," she pauses, unfolding herself, but there's still a tense edge to her features. "And I can't deny that I'm attracted to you or that I want you, but I'm pretty pissed you didn't tell me about the bargain until now. I also don't understand how your bargain works; you can't have sex with me, right? But, you've gotten me off twice now."

"I'm sorry I didn't tell you sooner, I just couldn't find the right time. The bargain prevents me from getting pleasure *from* you. The Devil never said anything about giving pleasure *to* you. That's the tricky thing about bargains; there's always a loophole or a way out. The Devil is known for making bargains you can work your way around if you're clever enough." *I'm sure he knew all along that I would want you and just wanted to torture me a little beforehand.* I don't say the last part out loud.

"So, you don't enjoy it? What we did?" she snaps. She doesn't curl around herself but I can hear the vulnerability in her tone.

"Oh, Kitten, I've enjoyed every second of it. I just can't get off from it. For now." I say the last part softly, but she needs to understand that even though I may not get to have her body right now, I fully intend on having all of her later, no matter how long it takes.

She nods her head slightly but doesn't respond.

"You don't have to worry about all of this right now, dealing with Dumah is our priority. Once that's taken care of, I swear we will figure out everything else," I say, softly patting her sleeping pad beside me.

I can tell she considers staying up and arguing to demand more answers and, if she did, I'd tell her everything I could. I won't lie to her for personal gain, though the danger that comes with the truth doesn't bring me much comfort, either.

I offer quietly, "If you need space, I can leave."

"No, stay. I appreciate the thought but I'd rather you be here, even if I don't understand why." The last part is whispered so quietly that I don't think she meant for me to hear it, so I don't comment. The tent fabric rustles loudly as she crawls back over to me but quiets down when she snuggles back into our spooned position. Despite her doubt, it's more than I could ever ask of her.

Valencia falls asleep quickly, but sleep evades me. It's not something I particularly need, but I can enjoy it. The jump between Hell and Earth was particularly rough this time, draining my energy from having recently healed a near-fatal wound.

Over the last few days, I've been going nonstop trying to piece together how we'll fix the Dumah problem. The talk with Danti in Hell comes to mind, though I couldn't make sense of her meaning about the Devil, she did mention something weird going on with the other Lords.

Us lords of Hell have never been known for sunny dispositions or for getting along. Nightmare wasn't so bad, but he and I rarely speak and all I know about him is that he's the second lord and controls the Dreamscape as well as its nasty creatures. Definitely not someone whose bad side you ever want to end up on.

I've never interacted with the first lord, nor have I seen him in the flesh. He's been a lord since nearly the beginning, though, and if the gossip is to be believed, he despises both Nightmare and me equally because we took power from him when we became lords.

As if being a lord of Hell was ever a choice. It doesn't matter that he was the *only* lord for hundreds of years, we all do what the Devil demands.

My intel produced nothing of value about Dumah's plan or where he could be hiding but I know he's not far. I can almost feel it in the air, like tiny sparks dancing across my skin. Dumah is extremely task-driven and power-hungry, so I know he won't give up on Valencia easily.

Which makes me question why he left the bar so suddenly that day. He had us beat. I swear my heart plummeted out of my fucking ass when Valencia charged him. I tried to stop her, but she was so unnaturally fast that she slipped through my fingers.

Parker was down and out from the beginning of the fight, but I don't think that surprised anyone. A handsome face and nice teeth weren't exactly useful weapons in battle.

Usually, Dumah and I were so evenly matched that it would be a vicious fight before one of us came out on top. With Valencia in the middle, he had a great advantage. He knew I'd want to protect her above attacking him.

The agony of the wound from his holy blade made me drop to my knees. It consumed every cell in my body, burning them from the inside out. It took everything I had in me not to pass out right there—which was to be expected from holy fire, any lesser demon would've combusted on the spot.

Though I survived, the memory of the pain will be imprinted on my brain forever. Not to mention the scar will act as a lasting reminder.

I stretch my side slightly, feeling the skin pull tight around the scar. His sword nearly cut me in half, yet she was unscratched. I never asked the Devil why she was so important, not when he first sent me for her nor when I met him for the bargain. It didn't occur to me to wonder why in the beginning. Now, I think I'm starting to understand. She's part angel; a far more powerful being than a human, even in halves. She has to be significant for both sides of a long-lasting celestial war to be volleying for her power.

If her supernatural speed hadn't given her heritage away, her ability to withstand holy fire was a clear indicator. Not only that, but she exhibited signs of super healing without even trying.

Her ankle was clearly broken on that mountain, but it healed in no time. The cut on her arm had gone from a gushing gash clear across her arm to a seeping slice and she had no adverse symptoms following being knocked out. Healing was a known angelic power, so between that and the holy fire, it was unquestionable that one of her parents was an angel. And more than likely, a very powerful one. I just hadn't put the pieces together until the whole picture was available for me to see.

I wanted to ask what she knew about her family, but I didn't want to bring up an old wound. She was so young when they died that I doubted she'd remember much, anyway.

The best thing for us to do right now is deal with Dumah. We'll hunt down the answers to all of her questions together afterwards.

No being in this universe will be able to keep her from the truth if I have anything to do with it.

CHAPTER 30
VALENCIA

I WAKE WITH A shudder, the chill from the early morning air nipping at my nose and cheeks. The rest of my body, however, is consumed by a scorching heat. It feels like I fell asleep with my back to a raging fire and sweat gathers at the base of my neck, my body sticky from the heat.

I blink away the last remains of my sleepy haze. There is, without doubt, a grizzly bear hibernating at my back. It has to be, considering the heat radiating off of it, not to mention the rattling, growl-like snores that blow baby hairs across my face and send vibrations through my back. Although, the human-shaped arm that is currently wrapped around my waist is an odd limb for a grizzly to have.

As Corvus slumbers, spooning me tightly, he snores so loudly that a lumberjack would be jealous of the sawing sounds. Somehow, though, the sound is soothing. I never thought I'd enjoy the sound of someone sleeping but there's comfort in such a dangerous man sleeping around me like a teddy bear.

Now that I think about it, though, I can only *assume* he's dangerous. He has the kind of body type to be wary of but, sometimes, the biggest trees fall the easiest. In the only fight I've seen him a part of, he was severely injured. But, despite knowing this, I can't deny that there's an underlying darkness to him, which must come from his being a demon.

And, anyway, his being injured was my fault. Corvus got hurt simply because he was saving my ass, so it's not fair of me to doubt his ability to be a badass when necessary. Things might've been different if I hadn't gotten in his way. My thoughts start drifting to him fighting Dumah the old Roman way, all oiled up, muscles bulged, with nothing on but a tiny loincloth.

This train of thought is as enjoyable as it is disturbing. Just because Dumah's beautifully attractive doesn't mean I want to envision him mostly naked and covered in oil. Why do the villains get to be hot? There should be a universal bad guy ugly gene.

But boy, does the thought of an oil-soaked, naked version of Corvus make up for it.

"What are you thinking about?" a deep voice whispers, blowing more tiny hairs across my face.

Thank goodness he's behind me, so he can't see how my cheeks flame at his question. That is *not* something I will be discussing with him, now or ever. I choose the much safer option, and lie. "Wondering how you plan to sneak out of my tent unnoticed."

"*Mhmm,*" he hums. Shivers shoot down my spine as I feel him drag his nose slowly down my neck. "Why don't I believe you?"

That deep, whispered question must have my pussy on speed dial because she responds instantly.

I tense my muscles against the urge to push my ass back against him. The last thing I need is another round of his oddly satisfying one-sided mating ritual. There's so much going on right now that I've got to seriously start thinking with my brain and not my heart. And, when I say heart, I mean clit—since it pulses just like the other beating organ in my body.

I tamper down the urges my heart whispers to me as I'm surrounded by wisps of temptation. I try steeling myself against the building emotion, but it continues to simmer beneath the surface. It's like a stubborn shadow that refuses to leave my side, constantly telling me that my heart wants what it wants, even if it defies all reason.

Even if resisting is a battle I can never truly win.

"You said you wouldn't shift near me in case Dumah is looking for that, so how do you plan on sneaking away?" I ask him, trying to get away from the thoughts of how badly I want to go another round with him. Lying to him is much easier when I lie to myself, too.

"No one else is awake yet," he responds.

I wonder how he knows that. I can't hear any noises around the camp beyond the sounds of the forest in the early morning. The tent is still nearly pitch black, the sun hasn't had a chance to rise above the horizon yet. That doesn't mean much, since most of us are naturally early risers. It won't be long before they all start to wake.

A pit begins to form in my stomach. There's literally been no time to plan or even discuss what the next step will be. I know the first priority will be to just get through this damn exercise so we can make it back to the station and regroup. There's been so much going on that I feel like I haven't consumed a drop of knowledge in all the shit I've learned over the last couple of days.

I thought your life wasn't supposed to start falling apart until after 30.

"I know you're worried about, well—about everything," Corvus mumbles, his arm briefly pulling me in a tight, weird sort of hug before slowly pulling away to sit up. I don't focus on the way I mourn his touch almost instantly. "Just get through today and we'll figure out a plan from there. I'm going to take a hike further out before shifting. I'm going to look for Dumah, but I will stay close. Don't forget that I'll have eyes on you, so don't stress too much about everything and just do what you need to do for your team."

Before I can argue or demand he tell me where he's going, Corvus leans down and plants a heated kiss on my lips. Instantly, the temperature of his body warms my skin and chases away the chill. He grips one side of my face in a large hand, using the other to hold his body over mine.

Our tongues dance together in a slow and sinful motion. Just as I'm about to beg him to stay and put his mouth to better use, he crawls over me and promptly leaves the tent. Oddly, I don't hear any footsteps as he leaves. He said he wouldn't shift, so it's scary how a man of his size can vanish silently.

Definitely another marker of his dangerous qualities.

I ignore the pounding of blood as it courses through my body and decide to start the day. Getting dressed doesn't take long—my clothes are packed perfectly for convenience. I exit my tent as quietly as possible, leaves crunching under my feet as I make my way over to an already-started fire.

The warm blaze emits a comfortable heat that chases away the morning chill. Bill, who sits on a small stump, turns at the sound of my approach. "Morning,

Val. Coffee'll be done soon." He turns to the fire and fiddles with the embers with a long stick.

I panic for a second, wondering if he noticed Corvus leaving my tent. He doesn't mention it, so neither do I, figuring it's better to feign ignorance than accidentally tattle on myself. You'd be amazed at how many people give themselves away by not shutting their mouths.

A soft, bubbling sound emits from the fire and my heart races excitedly. There isn't much that's better than a hot cup of cowboy coffee. I'm not sure why it's called that, as you don't have to be a cowboy to make coffee on a fire, but who am I to question the coffee gods and their weird phrases?

Bill hands me a steaming cup, and I inhale as the steam wafts from the top. I close my eyes and sigh deeply. As Corvus requested, I release as much stress as possible and focus on the day. Bill and I sit in a comfortable silence while waiting for everyone else to come around and I cook our breakfast as we wait, so the fire will be free for the others when they're ready.

It's not long before the soft rays of the morning sun glows through the trees, and the others are all awake and surrounding the fire in various states of morning prep. I look out across Lake Agnes and think of the day's task. Finding Janice is our number one priority

Regardless of a pass or fail, our team has never been the type to sit idle and not follow through, it's one of the things I love most about this group of misfits. And, though Landon has pissed me off more than once over the years, I don't wish for the guy to lose his job just for being an asshole.

It's like I'm Dominic Toretto but with boobs and considerably more hair. However, I'm no less loyal to those I care about.

Thinking back on our tasks for the day, I struggle with the fact that I haven't figured out the rest of the clue. I know Janice is somewhere near the peak of Call Mountain but, though the clue said 5 miles from the center of the lake, there are no actual trails out there, so a typical hiker wouldn't make it that far.

I watch small waves lap at the shore as I think. Just on the other side of Call Mountain is a road that sits at the base. Well, maybe 'road' isn't the right word—but it's a dirt trail that people have driven over enough that it's essentially become a road now. After checking the map and making some minor calculations, we've determined that the end of that road is two and a half miles from the center of the lake.

They would've wanted this search to be challenging but achievable, hence the clues. The hike to the top of Sugarloaf would be straightforward, as the trail is mostly clear, but the rest of the way to the peak of Call would be more difficult. Most of that part of the trail is wooded and rugged terrain, we'd have to get started early to reach the peak with enough time to conduct the search and then 'rescue' Janice.

"Today can kiss my ass." I hear as a hand thumps down on my shoulder and squeezes, jerking me from my thoughts.

"Good morning, Parks. Cheerful as always," I chuckle. He's never been a morning person, so his grumpy demeanor doesn't surprise me. I'm sure he only gets up early with me so he doesn't have to work out alone. He also always talks me into sharing my morning smoothies with him, so that's probably part of it, too.

He clinks his full coffee cup against my mostly empty one, smiling. "There's absolutely no chance we're actually completing the exercise today."

"Nope," I emphasize the 'p'. I've come to the same conclusion that he has. Not only do we need more information to pinpoint where Janice is hidden, but we have yet to completely figure out the clue, so there's no help there, either. "Chief just wanted to see where our holes were as a team, which I think was glaringly obvious yesterday."

"He's about as fun to be around as a dumpster fire," Parker sneers. Based on his tone, I imagine he's talking about Landon, not Chief Miller.

Excellent, just what we need. As if Landon's shitty attitude wasn't enough yesterday. However, the more he acts out, the more likely the Chief realizes he's the problem. I thought we were making progress with his attitude yesterday afternoon but if what Parks says is true, it sounds like our good luck has run out.

I don't realize how much, though, until an hour later as we all group together to figure out the plan for the day. Everyone packs their stuff quickly, making sure all trash and human traces are cleaned up. Someone put the fire out with water from the lake, so a gray plume of smoke wafts toward the sky and the air smells slightly burnt.

"Today's the day, I know we can do it, team," Chief Miller calls out and promptly steps to the back of the group. He's got his favorite coffee cup in one hand and the other hand stuffed in his front pocket.

The group descends in a brief moment of silence, so I start detailing the plan for the day. "The trail to the ridgeline will take about two hours, so that already puts us at mid-morning. To Call peak is another two, which puts us around noon. That only leaves 5 hours to find and rescue Janice. That's not a lot of time, so it's important we work as a team today. Efficiency will ensure we succeed."

I won't comment on the fact that this is literally impossible without figuring out the final clue. This is precisely how missing hikers turn into missing person cases that are never solved. It's a huge reason why we encourage the visitors of the park to stick near known markers, or provide park rangers with trackers, because a lost hiker with no known location is a nightmare to figure out.

"We still have a couple of clues that we haven't figured out, so does anyone have any other ideas before we take off? Even the littlest thing can make a difference," Parker continues when I stop talking.

"We've got a four-hour hike ahead, and y'all are still wasting our time on these fucking clues!" Landon snaps, but I'm unsure if he's talking to Parker, me, or the group as a whole.

"Having a better idea of the location will only help us, Landon," I say. I try to keep the irritation out of my voice, but it's drier than it usually is when talking with a team member.

"I'll ask once again; who put you in charge? *Hmm*?" he asks, hands on his hips as he stares me down. It's clear he's attempting to intimidate me but it's an unsuccessful attempt.

He's nothing compared to the Archangel who has tried to kill me multiple times already.

"I'd say she's done far more in this exercise than most of us have," Parker responds, his arms hanging loosely at his sides. I don't miss that his hands are clenched into fists.

"Nobody wants either of you to lead us. Don't think we don't all know that you two fuck. That you give *special* treatment to each other," Landon exclaims, and I can't help but laugh at the idiocy of his statement.

Everyone here knows Parker and I have never, nor will we ever, be anything other than platonic towards each other. Parker has not once hidden his conquests from the group. Landon just refuses to believe that Parker is more successful in that area than he is. Men and women flock to Parker like he's honey and they're bees. He's never been one to hide that.

On the other hand, I have hidden my random hookups quite well. I don't appreciate anyone in my business when I don't want them to be, nor do I care to delve into my personal life with my team. I always make sure anyone I meet is far away from the station and outside of our small town. Not that I've tried meeting anyone since a certain demon barged his way into my life.

Landon, apparently, has been blind to both of those things. I want to snap at him, put him in his place as he so deserves, but I also don't care to put up with his childish bullshit.

"Landon," I try to stay calm, "Parker and I's relationship has nothing to do with this exercise. Please, can we get back to the task?"

"No, we can't. Everyone says this is all about coming together as a team. Well, let's get it all out in the open, shall we!" Landon yells. A vein in his forehead starts to bulge slightly and his cheeks tint the slightest pink.

Before either Parker or I can put Landon in his place—or even the Chief—Tucker speaks up. "Parker and Val are the best leaders we have in this group. Your eyes are just so full of shit that you can't see it!"

Oh. Fuck.

Instantly, Landon looks at Tucker with a glare so full of malice that I wonder how Tucker hasn't combusted from the heat of his gaze. Tucker, who stands on the opposite side of the group to Landon, looks back unflinchingly. This is quickly heading in a direction none of us want to go in.

"Hey, let's just calm—" Chief Miller starts to say, but he's quickly drowned out by yelling.

"Fuck you, you ass-sucking wannabe," Landon snarls at Tucker, stepping in his direction.

"Back off," Jack steps in front of Landon, forcing the man to stop.

Bill grabs Tucker's arm, holding him back from advancing on Landon, but his face is as red as a tomato, so I doubt he's putting much effort into it. I imagine his hand on Tucker's arms is more to hold himself back.

"Careful," Jake growls, stepping up to Jack's side. The twins are quite the force when they come together like this. They move so similarly and fluidly that they'd definitely make a formidable fighting pair if it ever came to that. But, for everyone involved, I want to avoid that outcome at all costs.

"Guys, let's all calm down. Take some time. Chill out," I say, but not a single person is listening to me.

"As always, the whore opens her mouth when no one wants her to." Landon snarls, looking between the twins to glare at me.

Okay, so one person heard me, at least.

It appears that was the absolute wrong thing for Landon to say.

I'm not sure about the physics of how this happens, but Jack literally picks Landon up off his feet by the straps of his bag and slams him down on the ground. The air whooshes out of Landon's lungs with a pained groan. I go to step into the fray, but a hand on my elbow holds me back. I look behind me to see Chief Miller tugging me to his side. He silently watches as everything unfolds.

Jack pulls his arm back as if preparing to land a vicious punch to Landon's face, but at the last second, Jake wraps his arms around Jack's chest, trapping his striking arm, and drags him away.

Landon rolls over, crawling on his knees a couple of feet before struggling to a stand. He laughs, almost manically, and then points a shaky finger at me. "You're dead, bitch."

Wow. I did not think this morning would consist of a hot make-out session *and* a death threat. As Parker mentioned earlier, today can kiss my ass.

Landon starts stomping in my direction, angry steps thumping through the sand.

Before anyone can react, loud cawing echoes across the beach and a murder of crows descend on the surrounding trees. There's got to be over 50 of them, the trees rattle with their landing. So many black wings flutter wildly I can almost hear the normally silent action. Landon flinches, freezing in place, shoulders hunching over himself. His wild eyes scan the trees as if looking for the first attack.

I'm shocked there are so many. He's only ever appeared as the one crow, so I didn't think he could control more than that. Perhaps a few, but not this many.

Landon barely managed one crow; he'd be obliterated by a whole murder of them. Which is really weird to think about, because that's exactly what it would be. If they go for his eyes, he could be finished in seconds. It might take a while to actually kill him, but I imagine the mental trauma would if the physical didn't. The last thing I want on my conscience is his death. Even though he just threatened me and has been an asshole to the entire team, the man doesn't deserve to die for it. If all the people in the world died for being an asshole, we'd have never made it past the Stone Age.

I hold my hand up in the air and shake my head viciously. I'm sure I look ridiculous, but no one pays me any attention because they're all too focused on the crows. Hopefully, Corvus at least notices.

They all caw angrily in response. It's so loud that all other sounds are drowned out.

Chief Miller lets go of my arm and stomps toward Landon, gripping him tightly. Still scrunched like a terrified turtle, Landon doesn't fight against it. Was that first encounter with the crow enough to create a phobia? Or has he had other visits from Corvus that I don't know about? It would serve him right either way.

"The exercise is over. Everyone, please head to the trailhead; I've seen enough," Chief Miller starts pulling Landon along with him, heading off in the direction of the trailhead. We all follow along, and no one comments on the unfinished exercise, Janice, or the ungodly amount of crows and their timely descent. Everyone ignores the crows, who watch as we go, no longer angrily cawing. I can feel their beady eyes watching me as we head back.

Being surrounded by so many is unnerving but I'm ultimately thankful for their presence, as they probably prevented something terrible from happening. Between the threats, name-calling, and body slam, we were one step away from actually needing a rescue team. I'm not sure Landon realized it, but he didn't have a single ounce of support and, had he followed through with his attack, he would've been on the receiving end of more than one angry fist.

The hike back is blissfully uneventful. Landon, who finally snapped out of his phobia-ridden state, ripped his arm from the Chief and stomped off in the direction of our vehicles but the rest of us hike back slowly as a group. Parker walks determinedly in front of me, his steps sure and confident. Bill hikes behind me, following closely but not close enough to get in my way. I appreciate their presence more than they know.

I can feel their protectiveness surrounding me like unwavering pillars of support. It's a lifeline, a beacon in the darkness that tries to consume me. Their presence reminds me that I'm no longer alone, no longer forced to face the bullshit by myself. They relieve the weight of the grief that I feel daily. I'm not sure they know how often they've kept me from drowning myself at the bottom of a bottle of whiskey. With this team by my side—especially Parker—I've been able to reclaim a part of my life I thought I lost. Landon tried to take that away from me at every turn. He tried to rip us apart at the seams, but I'm forever grateful that we were able to overcome his idiocy.

I breathe a sigh of relief that he's no longer a dark cloud looming over us and just bask in the comfort of having my team whole again.

One step at a time, we all hike back down the mountain. No one is concerned with Landon taking off ahead and, as soon as he was out of earshot, Chief Miller told us that he was placing Landon on immediate leave until the board could officially present his termination from the group.

To ensure Landon, in his tempered state, didn't mess with anyone's vehicles, Chief Miller called in a Park Ranger to wait at the trailhead for our group to arrive. No charges were being pressed, so she was there to ensure that Landon left peacefully. He also told us that, though we weren't supposed to know this, he knew Landon was causing the issues in our group but the board had insisted on this exercise as a last-ditch effort. Basically, their way of avoiding any unnecessary red tape if Landon decided to argue about the reasoning for his being fired.

As we return to our vehicles, Landon is gone, no trace of him left behind. A tall woman exits the Park Ranger truck and walks to our group. She's nearly as tall as most of the men and her long, dark hair hangs in a braid down her chest. She's decked out in the regular Ranger outfit; her badge and gun clasped to her belt. She's tan, and her skin has a beautiful copper tone that I envy. She and Chief Miller have a short conversation before she nods her head and takes off back to her cruiser, smiling to all of us as she goes.

I don't miss the lingering look she gives Parker, her eyes drooping briefly before she gives him her back and continues. Parker shoots me an evil grin before tossing his bag in the back of his truck and then hopping into the driver's seat.

How the fuck Landon ever thought that we were a thing is beyond me.

Chapter 31
Valencia

It's been a really nice couple of days off. The board had to offer us time off after the exercise because we were technically on the clock the whole time. Anytime we were required to work 24 hours straight, for any number of days, they had to give us that time off in equal amounts.

A few of the crew spent the break traveling, enjoying the last few days of warm weather a Montana fall could offer. A few stayed at the station, like Parker and me, just basking in our time to rest and taking advantage of modern advancements.

I spent a gross amount of my time reading, drinking wine, and wondering where the fuck Corvus was. I didn't want to be needy, but I was starting to get worried. Sure, I'd seen a crow or two quite a few times over the last couple of days but there was no way for me to tell if they were Corvus or just a regular fucking bird. I was starting to go crazy at all the second-guessing.

He said he had one more thing to check but what if he got caught up, or if he found Dumah, or Dumah found him? He didn't fare so well during their last meeting, but maybe he'd do better without having to protect me at the same time.

Thoughts and what-ifs plague me so much that my rest days weren't as relaxing as they usually were. I caught myself checking my phone like a magical *'I'm okay'* text would pop up from him. Which is impossible, considering we'd never even exchanged numbers. Come to think of it, I don't even know that he has a phone. I doubt that kind of technology works in a place like Hell, but how would I know? He spends enough time on Earth to use one. Except, a crow can't carry an iPhone around without someone asking some questions.

Okay, so maybe we won't exchange phone numbers but I will demand that he tell me how to contact him next time he does this.

I voiced my concerns to Parker after that first day. All he had to say was—*"Corvus is a big boy. I mean that literally. He's a fucking giant. Nothing is touching that guy and surviving it, so I wouldn't worry too much. I'm sure he just got busy."*

I grab a glass of wine—generously poured, if I'm being honest—and make my way to my bathroom. I turn the water to nearly scorching and start filling the tub. It's small and, were I any taller, it'd be impossible to comfortably fit for a full soak. But baths are a guilty pleasure of mine, so I make the tight space work.

I mindlessly scroll through my phone as I soak in the too-hot water. Parker once said I like my shower water as hot as the Devil likes morning tea, which I later learned, according to Parker, is too hot for any normal person to handle. This is the same man who once complained the ocean was too warm, though, so I don't overthink his opinion of water temperature.

Everyone made it back to the station earlier today. Our official start back at work to relieve the other stations is midnight tonight.

Over the years, we've had recruits complain about the schedule, saying it didn't offer them enough freedom. They never stuck around long. It's why having a good group dynamic mattered so much, one bad apple wasn't the worst thing until it started stinking up everything around it as it rotted from the inside out.

This morning, Chief Miller sent out a station-wide notification informing us that Landon's contract had officially been terminated and that he would be by later this week to pack his things. I really hoped I wasn't here for that. At first, the argument had been such a shock that I hadn't had time to fully register the severity of his threat or behavior but, after having some time to reflect, I think it's for the best that I didn't catch on sooner.

Lately, the fuse on my temper has been getting shorter and shorter. The rage that consumed me when dealing with Dumah at the bar had been as powerful as it was scary. I didn't like that feeling, the slimy, toxic anger—but I was also too weak to fight it once it started.

Because, as much as I hated the feeling of it after, part of me loved the feeling of power that coursed throughout my body during the rage. How it burned away the rough edges of feelings like sadness, and grief, until all that remained was the sickening fuel to hurt, maim, and *kill*.

A ping sounds, distracting me from my thoughts. My phone rests in my hand, nearly touching the tepid water. I've been here long enough that the water is getting closer to that weirdly warm temperature that's cold when you move too much.

A series of pings and vibrations draw my attention back to my phone.

Fools On Ladders Group Chat

Today at 6:55 PM

Bill Hatton

> Val, someone's here for you. He's waiting in the family room.

Parker Rand

> You just let some rando into the station!? What if they're a serial killer???

Jack Howell

> It's very unlikely that there's two serial killers in the same place at the same time.

Parker Rand

> Who's the other serial killer??

Jack Howell

> *finger point emoji*

Jake Howell

> *finger point emoji*

Parker Rand

> *finger point emoji*

Chief Miller

> *finger point emoji*

Parker Rand

> *Ohmigod! It's one of us!!*

Chief Miller

> *Sorry team, Nessa had my phone.*

Chief Miller left Fools On Ladders Group Chat
Parker Rand invited Chief Miller to Fools On Ladders Group Chat

Me

> Thanks Bill, be out shortly!

I hurry out of the bath, dry off, and dress in the clothes I laid out on my bathroom counter. I slip on the black shorts first before throwing my large gray shirt on. My wet hair slaps against my back, the towel not doing much to dry it.

The shirt has *West Montana Community College* scrawled across the chest. It's a small college in a nearby town and though I never attended classes there, I enjoyed attending the sports games occasionally with Parker. It had a beautiful campus and a good student program. We've been fans of their rodeo teams for years and haven't missed an annual banquet yet.

I think I would've liked to go to college there in another life but higher education just wasn't in the picture for me at 18. Quite frankly, I'm lucky I made it through high school as is. After my family died, I spent a lot of years in a grief-filled haze. I bounced around foster families until I turned 18, then, I promptly started fire training and never looked back. None of the families ever stuck; I imagine that's mostly my fault. Looking back, none of them were memorable enough to vividly remember that time in my life. Knowing some of the sick stories of others who grew up in the foster system, I was lucky how it all turned out.

Once decent, I head to the common room where we all mostly gather in the evenings if we're not in our rooms. It was a popular hangout space between the comfy couches and giant TV. This meant that my guest would most likely be surrounded by every member of my team. Bill's text surely sent them that way if they weren't there already.

Corvus sits on one of the couches with a beer in one hand. He's leaned back comfortably, talking with Parker. Bill and Greg are in the kitchen messing around, but they keep shooting looks at the back of Corvus' head. The rest of the team are seated around Corvus on the other couches and I get a quick flash of deja vu. It wasn't long ago that I walked into a similar scene, with a different man at its center.

The twins listen to Corvus and Parker's conversation with rapt attention, Jake intensely staring Corvus down. Jake's always been a good judge of character, so I wonder if he can feel the enigmatic energy rolling off Corvus. When Jake catches my eye, the first to notice my presence, he nods at me and then hops up, heading back towards our rooms.

"Hey Val," Bill calls out, rounding the kitchen island and heading my way. "Your friend here was just telling us y'all met at the open house. I must've missed that," he finishes cheerfully. Too cheery. It's his way of saying he knows Corvus is lying but doesn't want to call the man out to his face. He's trying to give me an out in case Corvus isn't who he says he is and I don't want him here.

"Yeah, he saw her whip Landon's ass in the equipment race and has been her smitten little puppy dog ever since," says Parker, shooting Corvus a cheeky grin in the process.

Corvus rolls his eyes, taking a drink of his beer, but I don't miss the smirk he tries to hide with the bottle.

Bill still looks at me, waiting for my answer. I give the man a broad smile and pat him on the shoulder. "I mean, who could resist such skill, am I right?" I say. The wrinkles around his eyes crease with his smile and he nods, backing away to the kitchen to help Greg with whatever they're doing in there.

"Well, as much as I love to entertain—oh, wait, I don't. You guys can fuck off." I smile at them all while flipping a two-handed bird to the whole group. "Nosey Nellies," I say with a wink.

Corvus stands with a grace most would envy, nodding to the group before approaching me. I don't wait to see if he's following; I just head to my room.

I hear Parker yell, "Door open two inches, young lady!" I roll my eyes and continue on without comment. I will absolutely be shutting *and* locking my door. The last thing I want is a member of this team making an attempt at some stupid prank and Corvus ripping their head off—literally.

That seems like a thing demons could do.

His steps are so quiet I jump slightly when I turn to check he's still behind me, having followed closely the whole way.

"Damn! Wear a bell," I mutter to him as I shut and lock the door.

"I would think you'd prefer me wearing less, not more," he says as he stalks around my room, taking in the details of my most personal space—or the lack thereof.

"Do you ever think of anything other than sex?" I ask, deflecting to ignore my embarrassment while he investigates my room. It's clean and tidy, but there's nothing else to it. No personality or added personal touches. Just the same blank space it was when I first moved in. Four years ago.

"Most of the time, actually. There's always so much going on in my head, but sex seems to be the most prominent when you're around."

"That's. . . thank you." I say. It's a statement, but even to my ears it sounds like a question.

"It was a compliment," he responds with a smirk. He makes it to my bed and sits down on the edge. It's small, just like the one at the cabin, so he takes up nearly the entire surface as he leans back on his palms and focuses his attention on me. The view is so enticing that I curl my toes into the carpet as if that'll keep me from jumping onto his lap and riding him like a rodeo star.

There are too many things to figure out, too many unanswered questions, to just jump right to sex. Plus, I'm still pretty irritated about the whole bargain thing. I've gotten off multiple times by this man, not being able to touch him back—not having access to his body—has been the worst kind of edging I've experienced in my life.

"So, you should probably come sit down, I have something I need to tell you." Corvus pats the bed beside him. I walk over and sit on the end, leaving a comfortable space between us. I stare into deep chocolate eyes that hold a sadness I've yet to have seen on him.

"What, what is it?" I start to panic, wondering if whatever he's about to tell me has to do with his absence. Maybe he met someone else? Or he could just be tired of protecting me. Maybe both. Perhaps he's tired of wanting someone he can't have, so he decided to move on.

As always, anger starts to creep into my bones, trying to protect me from the hurt I'm actually feeling. I know I'm spiraling—that he hasn't even had a chance to explain—but his unexpected absence did things to me that I wasn't expecting. So many *what ifs* swirl in my mind, each crazier than the last. I feel that strange heat at the tips of my fingers.

Corvus grabs my hands, cradling them in his large ones as if he could sense my inner turmoil building but the heat in my fingers continues to burn and the worry remains.

"Remember I went to Hell while you were on the hike?"

I nod my head, unsure but curious. He hasn't really mentioned his time in Hell, but I assumed that was because he didn't find anything out.

"I talked with a demon there who is good at knowing secrets."

"Okay?" Anticipation starts to build inside my chest.

"I didn't find out anything about Dumah, but she did tell me something else. It's about your family," he states.

My heart plummets. Of all the things I thought it could be, I was *not* expecting that.

Chapter 32
Dumah

Sat in a cafe in downtown Seattle, I patiently continue to wait. Just like I've been doing for the last four hours. The kind lady behind the counter refilled my coffee without question, never once asking me to leave or questioning why I'm here in the first place. I don't have a computer, nor do I have a phone, so I pretend to read one of the books I noticed on a cart when I first entered. Gabriel never told me a time to meet; just a day and a place.

It's been four hours, and he has yet to arrive.

God's messenger isn't known for his timely manner. I suppose, to him, everyone but God is on his time. It's why I prefer to work with Uriel; he never wastes someone's time, nor does he believe himself to be above others, no matter the fact that he is at the top.

I scan the words on the page slowly to simulate the reading motion, turning pages when expected, but I don't focus on a single word. Instead, I scan my surroundings, constantly checking for a sign of attack or Gabriel's presence.

Despite it being an urgent matter here I sit, four hours later and no sign of the other angel. It's what's expected of me, to be a faithfully *patient* disciple. Waiting, no matter how long it takes, because patience is the truest test of faith. Patience is a virtue—a heavenly approved one. It was also one I've struggled with throughout my years. I manage it well, but at times like this when everything weighs heavily on my shoulders, I struggle.

Struggle was such a human feeling. As angels, we were supposed to be beyond that. Humans think our purpose is to guard and protect them and, in a sense, we do, but not so directly—not really at all, if you think about it. We protect God and Heaven. Nothing else matters—not our lives, the lives of our brethren, and definitely not the humans. We protect them because it serves us. When it doesn't, they're on their own.

"Dumah," a man says as he sits down across from me. It is not a face I recognize, nor would it be overly memorable.

Grey hair, wrinkles, blemishes—human. The man sitting across from me looks human, but it's a glamor, though I'm not sure why it's necessary.

"Gabriel," I acknowledge quietly, so as not to alert any other customers to his presence.

"You can speak freely, child. I have silenced their ears to our conversation," he says with a wave of his hand. He snaps his fingers, and a hot cup of coffee appears on the table before him.

I inhale sharply but don't comment. Right before angels are allowed to come to Earth, we are told, with great force, that we would be severely punished if we were to ever reveal our presence to the humans. Punished for the rest of eternity.

At the time, punishment seemed a harsh response to me. A Hellish response. But who was I to question the ways of the almighty? The fact that Gabriel blatantly exposes his powers is shocking.

We are also strictly forbidden from manipulating humans in any way. He committed both sins in less than three minutes of being here, scrambling my brain and leaving my thoughts in a jumbled mess. I have never had to deal with other angels outside of Heaven who so obviously skirt our rules.

Though his behavior concerns me, I don't let it show. I have a strong faith and know that if God didn't trust Gabriel, the angel wouldn't have been in his position as long as he had.

"Do you plan to speak or waste my time?" Gabriel snaps, shocking me out of my stupor.

"I'm sorry, there has been much that has happened," I begin.

"Father," he states plainly.

"Excuse me?"

"I'm sorry, *Father*, you mean." Grayish blue eyes stare into me as if looking at my soul.

A pit forms in my stomach. He is not my father. Angels are created, not born, so I have no paternal lineage. He can only mean one thing by asking me to call him that. It goes against everything I believe to give him such a name and to refer to him with such respect. Though he is my superior, it is not a title he has earned. Only one being deserves such a title.

I repeat what he says, though softly. "I'm sorry, Father." Hoping that if I whisper the words, God won't hear me call another by his name. It leaves a nauseated bubble in my stomach, but refusing would be even worse.

I push through the sick feeling and tell him about the woman, my thoughts on her lack of faith, how I left her on the side of the mountain to determine God's will, and how, against all odds, she survived. I also tell him about her dangerous companion.

"She is powerful. Far more powerful than I expected. There is something about her, something different. She was not injured by holy fire, a feat only achievable by angels. That means she's part angel but she is also something else. There is no way to tell if her power will grow or what side she will end up on. I think—"

"You are not to think. You are to listen and you are to obey. Your orders are to kill the woman, so that is what you shall do. She is an emotionless parasite who will murder you at first chance. We do not have room for the likes of her in Heaven." He says, cutting me off. It irks me that he refuses to listen. He says we do not have room for her in Heaven, but all who believe are welcome into the embrace of God's love. Or so we've been told. By saying that there is not room for her, he goes against everything we're supposed to embody. Not only that, but he's saying that she may not be good enough for Heaven, but her power is? If that's all angels are good for, then when will my name end up on the chopping block?

"Angels do not kill their own, unprovoked. This changes things. We do not kill angels," I argue. Had I known she was an angel before I left her to die, I would've tried harder to get her to join our side, instead of left her fate to chance. She's a fighter, otherwise she wouldn't have survived. I admired that kind of strength.

"You will do as I say, boy," Gabriel sneers at me, stepping out of his chair and heading toward the exit, clearly done with this conversation.

"What does God say?" I ask as I stand as well. The chair scrapes across the ground, but no one notices the noise. My eye tries to twitch at the condescending reference he's made about my age, but I hold the muscle still. I am not a child by any standard, least of all Heaven's. I've been around long enough, at least, to see a lie when I'm told one and there are things about Valencia that Gabriel is keeping from me. I can't figure out why, yet.

Gabriel freezes at the edge of the door. No part of him moves. For a second, I wonder if I need to brace for an attack. To attack me so blatantly in front of the humans would invoke a challenge, which he's pointedly avoided in the past, always managing to instead find his way out of them. Challenges are one of the ways angels move up the hierarchy ladder. One of the more deplorable ways, but it's still done, all the same.

He won't invoke one now. I know this and, more importantly, Gabriel knows this.

"I am the Messenger God, Dumah. You do what I say," he says before sweeping through the door, leaving me alone in the café.

Doubt churns in my chest, making me sick to my stomach all over again. There is so much going on here that goes against everything I have ever believed in, and my faith has never been more tested.

"Can I help you, Sir?" The woman behind the counter now stands at my side, a smile on her face. She has a warm presence, and I don't miss the cross that sits just at the base of her neck. I see it as a sign—a sign from God that I am on the righteous path, that he sees the good I am doing. I shake my head at the woman but thank her anyway.

As I leave the café, already planning my trip back to Montana, I realize that Gabriel called himself the Messenger God. Not a messenger *of* God.

CHAPTER 33
VALENCIA

"WHAT DO YOU MEAN this has to do with my family?" I demand, hopping up off the bed to stare Corvus down. My standing height doesn't give me much advantage over his sitting height, but it brings me a slight sense of comfort, anyway.

"I told you, I had to speak with a contact. I wanted information on Dumah but I found something else. Danti, the secret teller, heard some rumors going around Hell. She said I'm not the only lord involved and that you have more ties to Hell than we can imagine. That the Devil—" he pauses briefly.

"What is it?" I pant impatiently. I can't handle the anticipation—not when it comes to my family.

"Your family, they—"

BEEP! BEEP! BEEP!
"Dispatch. Station 20. Dispatch."
BEEP! BEEP! BEEP!
"Station 20. Code 9. Fire in Progress. Station 20. Code 9. Fire in Progress."

"Fuck!" I give a frustrated yell as I hurry into my closet, stripping down to my underwear before throwing on my fire-protective under layers. It's muscle memory at this point, so even though my mind is racing full of trauma, my body does what it knows.

"Valencia, what are you doing?" Corvus asks, standing from the bed.

"I'm getting ready. There's a fire."

As soon as I'm dressed, I race towards the garage. Corvus runs behind me; for once, his steps make noise as he follows.

"No. You can't go out there; this is Dumah. It's not safe," he pleads.

BEEP! BEEP! BEEP!
"Dispatch. Station 20. Dispatch."
BEEP! BEEP! BEEP!
"Station 20. Code 9. Fire in Progress. Station 20. Code 9. Fire in Progress."

The loud, automated announcement cuts off anything else he might've said. I make it to the garage quickly, sliding into my station. For once, I'm nearly the last to make it here. Corvus stands behind me, chest heaving as he watches me dress.

"You don't know that," I snap.

"Seriously, Valencia, there's so much going on you don't know. It's not safe. Just—just hold on a second."

Pulling on the last of my gear, I see the others getting the trucks ready to go. Tucker is already at our tanker, preparing the equipment and ensuring that everything is in good condition. I trust him to clear the truck, so I take a few seconds to explain to Corvus.

"It's a *Code 9.* That means a wildfire is in progress and a fire team is trapped. We're supposed to be off until midnight, so it's bad if they've had to call us in early. I know a lot is going on and that it's dangerous but I refuse to sit back while another team is out there possibly dying!" I yell at him over the loud alarm. I plead with my eyes for him to understand. For him to realize that I will always run toward the fire no matter the danger.

Reluctantly, he finally nods and steps to the side, eyes closing as though it's hard to watch me leave. "I'm going to regret this," he breathes.

I blurt out a quick *'thank you'* before taking off towards my tanker. As we peel away from the station and head towards the park, I swear I see a dark blot in the sky following us along the way.

***

I drive the tanker as fast as it will go, following behind the others as we make our way to the center of the park. It's about an hour's drive to where we've been told to meet the other teams. Four different stations have been called in to fight this fire and it's already consumed over 2,000 acres in the short time it's been burning.

They're calling it the Ruby Valley Fire.

Since we're the augment station, we got the call last which means we're the last to arrive. As we're also the farthest station away from this part of the park, we broke quite a few speed limits on the way here. Thankfully, there's only one road that goes through the mountain to the spot we're supposed to meet, so it was a pretty straightforward drive.

As we pull up, the meeting spot is doused in flashing lights of all colors that would make any nightclub jealous. There are so many people here that it takes a second for our group to get parked and situated enough to assist the other teams. Chief Miller will take point with the other station leaders and tell us where to go. Our ultimate goal is to rescue the team currently trapped at Torrey Lake.

On the drive over, Chief Miller explained the situation to us. They think the wildfire started at the base of Torrey Mountain, just north of Torrey Lake. From there, the fire likely traveled through the valley, burning up both mountainsides.

Without looking, I'd bet the ridge between Tweedy Mountain and Mount Alverson have gotten the worst of it. Ruby Valley is a significant spot in the park. For one, our town was named after the valley. Secondly, it was one of the most beautiful hikes in the park, having earned its name from how the evening sun shines onto the southwest-facing slopes, turning them a beautiful ruby-orange color in the evenings. Sitting at the edge of Torrey Lake and looking down the valley at sunset was one of the most beautiful sights I've seen in my entire lifetime. Sadly, that's likely gone now, probably for many years to come.

Because the sun hits the southwest-facing ridge the longest and during the warmest part of the day, it will burn the quickest. The vegetation there is drier than anywhere else in the valley and, unfortunately, that makes for great wildfire fuel. Not to mention that a fire will race up the side of a slope nearly 10 miles an hour faster than flat land simply because heat rises.

The western side of the valley won't burn at such a fast rate since there's not as much wind or slope. Instead, the fire will move with an almost languid pace, making it easier for the fire suppression teams to manage containment on the western side and prevent the fire from moving further into the park.

Our team will be on a rescue mission as two teams have already been assigned to suppression and containment.

A Polaris City fire crew hiked to Torrey Lake yesterday to rescue an injured backpacker. Because they were already out there when the fire started, they're now all trapped. Torrey Lake is surrounded by sharp mountain slopes on three sides, so there's no escaping that way. The only way out is through Ruby Valley, which is currently engulfed in flames.

We've been told they attempted to start a drop fire to help prevent the main wildfire from reaching them, which is where we purposely set a fire to burn all of the fuel in an area. This helps to contain the fire and prevent it from spreading. But, starting a drop fire is sometimes a risk and, unfortunately for the Polaris City crew, today was not their lucky day.

We've been informed that, as they started the drop fire, a large gust of fiery wind engulfed a patch of shrubs. Before the crew could contain it, the fire jumped, splitting the team in half. One team is currently on the far side of Torrey Lake, away from Ruby Valley, and were able to contain the fire from their side. However, the other team remain trapped with a fire raging from both sides. It's up to us to get to the Polaris City crew and help them rescue their trapped members.

"Okay team, everyone pay attention," Chief Miller says as he returns from meeting with the other fire Chiefs. "Here's our plan. We've named the teams Polaris 1 and 2 and this will be how we communicate over comms, to avoid confusion. Polaris 2 is trapped just past Torrey Lake and Polaris 1 is still working on the far side to protect the injured. Polaris 2 is nearly surrounded, so we will have to work quickly."

Everyone nods their heads in understanding. The support from the Air Fire team would make a huge difference, they could offer us enough time to get to Polaris 2 and get them to safety.

Chief Miller pulls out a map of the area and shows us the route we're to take to get to Polaris 2. "Air Fire is arriving in five from the south and has been instructed to escort us to Torrey lake so we are able to assist the trapped team as they get the injured out safely."

Because the fire has engulfed the entire valley, our team will have to hitch a ride on the Air Fire helicopter to Torrey Lake. It's not something we regularly practice but we all know what we need to do once we're on the ground, so getting there is of no consequence.

As we all quickly check our gear, Chief Miller tells the others we're heading out. I walk to the edge of the road, looking across the wetland. The sun set hours ago, shrouding everything in view in the dark shadows of night. I take a second to look out at the world around me.

Lights flicker and dance off the surrounding pines, but most trucks are behind me, so I only catch flashes that bounce off the tree limbs overhead. Without the fire, the wetlands that sit at the base of the valley would be nearly as beautiful at this time of night as they are during the day. I've spent many occasions camping in this very area; fishing in David's Creek, hiking to the different peaks, and photographing all of the various wildlife.

There's a full moon tonight and it shines a pearly white, casting a soft glow on us while we raced here. Now, you'd think that giant storm clouds filled the sky as the smoke billows high into the air, creating creepy waves of dust and ash. The ash isn't falling too badly where we are now, only a few pieces are floating around here and there, but I know that the ash will fall like autumn snow once we reach Torrey Lake.

There's a burnt taste to the air like a peppery toxin that floats around us. Some say a forest fire can smell sweet, while others think it smells more like plastic. For me, all I ever smell is the sharp scent of destruction. When I first started fighting fires—each time I came up to a burn in progress—I'd lose the last thing I ate as soon as I stepped out of the truck.

The same thing happened with the sound. The pops and crackles of fire would send me into a panic, and my muscles would shake uncontrollably as my brain begged to flee. It was a big reason I decided to join a wildfire crew over a regular city crew. The sound of a house fire was just too familiar, causing bile to rise in my throat every time I heard it.

There's nothing quite like the sound of a forest fire, however. Most of the time, the raging sound is nearly identical to a jet engine. The roaring is so loud as it consumes everything in its path that you can't hear the individual snaps and cracks like you would with a smaller fire.

A piece of ash floats in front of my face, slowly descending before landing on my thigh. This part of the wetland, where everyone is currently gathered, is pretty clear for the most part. Across the wetland at the start of Ruby Valley, however, it's a much different story.

A vicious orange haze covers the entire valley. Smoke billows from the mountainsides, forming angry clouds that race to the sky. At night, you can barely see the mountains in the distance. Now, they're covered with bright orange spots as burning flames expand across the slope. Pine trees stand tall as burnt silhouettes of what they used to be, their pine needles now gone, leaving just the trunks and scorched limbs.

It's an intimidating sight, knowing we're about to head in that direction, knowing we're risking our lives facing one of the world's worst natural disasters.

Everyone's speculated about what started this fire, but I think Corvus was right. This fire got too big in such a short period to be a typical wildfire. No, this was started on purpose. Normally, a fire starts in one area before traveling in a specific direction—whatever way the fuel and wind determine it to go. Not only that, but there's always something specific that starts the fire—a lightning strike, a poorly timed fireworks display, a campfire, for example. But the weather has been great the past two days, and those who camped out here wouldn't have set a fire that they couldn't control.

Once our team is cleared for action, we take off across the wetland and board the Air Fire helicopter. We load into the aircraft, tossing our bags under our seats and buckling ourselves in. My helmet clanks against the metal wall behind me as I get settled and a loud whirring sound engulfs us as the blades start spinning for lift-off.

The last time I was in a helicopter, Parker and I were being given a tour of the park during our first week of joining the team. We'd see Air Fire often throughout the years, racing through the sky, dropping water on some of the more vicious fires. We just never had the need to be escorted by them, until now.

We lift off, the copter tilting at such an angle that my stomach rolls with nerves. We rise quickly as it flies toward the south and swings around Torrey Mountain.

The adrenaline starts to kick in. I look to the side, out of the small window, and glimpse the destruction of Ruby Valley.

Fire blazes on both sides, licking up each slope as if crawling on infernal fingers painted bright orange. The roaring of the fire echoes off the walls of the mountains so loudly that we can barely hear anything else and it all becomes one constant droning sound that makes my eardrums rattle.

"I can't see shit outta this fuckin' thing," Parker jokes beside me. It's an inside joke that we've shared for years, a quote from one of our favorite movies. I just laugh and shake my head at him. But he's not wrong; the sky is so filled with the burning orange haze that I can barely see anything besides the raging spots of fire.

The flight to Torrey Lake takes 15 minutes. The pilots had to fly south of Torrey Mountain to avoid the cloud of dust and ash which made visibility an issue around the mountain peaks. They've only recently been able to fly in these conditions at night and I'm unsure how they're able to navigate where they're going when they can barely see anything beyond 100 feet in front of them. Aviation technology has come a long way, much like everything else, though and I trust them to get us there if they believe they can make it.

In no time, the helicopter rounds Torrey Mountain and lands at its base, just at the edge of the lake. We scramble to grab our gear, and a mixture of gravel and moss crunches under my boots as I jump out of the aircraft. My knees burn as I run, crouched down to avoid the whirling blades, and gather with the rest of the team. Hair that's escaped the cover of my helmet whips across my face, causing stinging bites of pain on my cheeks.

I see a group of people rushing our way, a stretcher held between two. "Y'all don't know how happy I am to see your faces!" a large man yells at us, his voice barely carrying over the sound of the helicopter still running behind us.

"We're here to help! What's the plan?" Chief Miller yells back.

Few in his position would be willing to give up the leadership role and defer to another, especially not someone of a lower rank, but he knows what needs to be done, and he'll do it, no matter what it takes.

The two people carrying the stretcher rush by our group, heading for the waiting helicopter. A tall, lanky man in a fleece hoodie and cargo pants follows, holding a medium-sized child. I can't see who is on the stretcher, but I imagine it's another hiker. I didn't realize that a whole family was out here but, seeing the child being carried away despite seemingly being unhurt, confirms that I was right to come out here despite all the risks. This wasn't a call I could miss, anyway, or my job would be on the line. I had no idea what my life would look like in the coming future, but uncertainty didn't mean I could abandon the one I've made for myself. No matter how stressful, my job and my team matter to me.

"Two of my team will head back with the civilians! That leaves four of us on this side! Six are trapped between Torrey and David Creek!" the man hollers, pointing across the lake and towards the valley. The view from here is just as sickening as seeing it from the other side.

Ugly spots of orange and red twirl in a deadly dance across the slopes and down the middle of the valley. Where there aren't bright spots of fire, the blackened husk of what this valley used to be is all that remains. It'll be years before it regains its former glory. All we can hope for is that it bounces back better than it was before.

Once the civilians are loaded into the helicopter, it takes off, following the same route we took here. I imagine they're headed straight for the nearest hospital, so we might have to wait a while before they can return to assist us. We're fortunate to have the resource in the first place, but there's only one—so we'll have to hold off long enough for it to get back.

"We've got everything covered on this side of the lake! Our best chance at rescuing Polaris 2 is to clear the fire on the eastern side and make our way to them from that direction! The fire in the valley is close to reaching them, but they're containing it the best they can as they wait for us!" he yells at Chief Miller over the roaring fire in the valley. Now that the copter has left, we can all hear him a little better, but there's still too much noise to speak normally.

Chief Miller nods, and we all follow the man to meet up with the rest of the Polaris 1 team. They're waiting on the opposite end of the lake, clearing a route out as we speak. The last thing we need is two different stations getting trapped here.

With the civilians transported away, a lot is taken off our shoulders and we can focus on doing all we can to ensure our trapped fire family makes it off this mountain, too. Losing a firefighter today is not an option any of us will accept.

As we follow the unknown man, I glimpse what I assume to be his last name printed on the back of his helmet. *Lawrie.* He's tall and probably bulky with muscle, but his gear hides any signifying details of his size beyond his height.

We all hustle around the lake, putting out small fires as we go. Ash falls so heavily here that a winter snowstorm would be jealous. The rest of Polaris 1 huddles on a small rocky beach. Between drop fires and water, they've managed to create a small area that's entirely fire-free. Thankfully, this will keep the fire from reaching the end the helicopter landed on, giving us a clear path out of here when we're ready.

"Okay, everyone!" Lawrie yells. "We've got 6 trapped just north of here! Last I heard, they had two injured but I couldn't tell how bad. We'll have to assume it's bad and that we're going to need to possibly wait there for evac!"

The rest of his team joins us, but I don't catch their names. They're all wearing the typical protective gear—a yellow fire-resistant coat and thick green pants, hard hat and either a backpack or chest bag. It makes them blend in with our group, creating just a large crowd of firefighters huddled together.

One man stands out amongst the rest, tall like the western pines. It's like he could reach the sky if he raised his arm in the air and I almost wonder if he's taller than Corvus. He doesn't have Corvus' muscular bulk, though. Even with his gear, I can tell he's more of a wiry athletic type than a bulky, strong one. He has a graceful way about him as he moves, though, as though he floats instead of walks.

"Lawrie, we're yours to direct! Tell us where you want us!" Chief Miller responds.

"Listen up! Polaris 2 is less than a mile from here, but they're in the mouth of the valley! Our best chance of getting there without issues is cutting a line following David Creek! It's important we all stick together so we know everyone is safe!" Lawrie swoops his hand in a circular motion, signifying that this part of Polaris 1 and our team are now working as a joint unit. This brings me immense comfort; it will be harder for Dumah to attack if I'm in a large group.

Without anything else from Lawrie, he directs his members in front of him and they set off. Our team follows closely behind, cutting down vegetation and spreading debris as we open a path for when we return with the rescued firefight-ers. It's always good to have multiple action plans in the event of a fire.

It's rigorous work as we make our way towards the stranded fire team. There isn't too much slope here, which helps protect our knees as we make our way down, but I still slip a few times. A few others do as well but, thankfully, no one gets hurt.

When we reach the opening Lawrie mentioned, my palms ache from gripping my shovel so tightly. A dull ache pulses in my forearms, and small beads of sweat gather at the back of my neck. I'm almost shocked at how easy it was to make it. Sure, it was hard work but, still, I expected. . . *more*.

There's no active fire here but, with the ash and smoke in the air, we can't see very far in front of us. We follow along as Polaris 1 cross the field towards where Polaris 2 supposedly waits for rescue. We got here with minimal difficulty, barring the hard work it took to clear the way, and I start to question why they needed us in the first place. We were told they were facing fire on two sides, but there's no active fire here.

The ground crunches loudly beneath our feet and when I look down, I notice that the grass is already burnt. We were told this team was trapped on all sides by fire but, if the ground beneath me is to be believed, the fire has already come and gone.

If we've made it this far without issue, what were they waiting for?

Chapter 34
Corvus

I'VE BEEN SEARCHING ALL over this fucking valley for Dumah and he's nowhere to be found. It's taking much longer than I was hoping. The fire rages through the valley so fast that ash and smoke fill what feels like the entire sky. Because the crows I shift into are still beings of Earth, they die quickly from the exposure. I've already shifted into 20 different crows in the two hours I've been here, and though it pains me to kill so many, I know it's necessary.

If I don't find Dumah before he finds Valencia, a few dead crows will be the least of my worries.

I stuck close to Valencia as her team made it to their meeting spot and were directed to rescue another crew stuck on the other side of the burning valley. Once they'd loaded into the helicopter, I followed as best I could—taking shortcuts to make up time—and, when I reached where they were dropped off, the aircraft was already leaving.

Valencia and her team were all huddled together, talking with a group of people I hadn't seen before. They all wear the same protective gear, so I imagine it's part of the team they were supposed to rescue. I missed most of the details but, based on the pit of dread that's been settling in my stomach, none of it can be good.

This situation has all been a fabrication and we're falling right into the trap that's been set. Regardless of my doubts, I couldn't convince her not to come out here, so now it's up to me to make sure that whatever Dumah has planned doesn't come true but he's managed to evade me at every chance. His ability to fly in these conditions is far greater than my own. If I were to shift into my true demon form, no angel could beat me, but I don't have the time to beg the Devil to let me shift into that form nor do I want to kill every human I come in contact with from just the sheer fear of seeing me.

I growl out a frustrated sigh but what comes out is just a loud caw. He has to be close. I can feel his sickly sweet presence like a slimy coating that's wrapped around my senses. I highly doubt that he plans to let the fire do his dirty work, so he'll be close by to finish her off himself.

The woman is as stubborn as she is selfless, and no amount of begging would've kept her from being out here. It frustrates me as much as it makes me proud. Dumah now knows she's a weakness. He knows I will put her life above my own and he'll exploit that at the first opportunity. All I can hope is that I find him before it's too late.

With two more dead crows and not a single sign of him, I fly back to where I last saw Valencia. I catch a glimpse of her and the others heading through the trees, following a small creek. It's slow work as they clear a path through the burnt forest and she swings a small shovel around, clearing the debris on the ground. An older man I recognize works with a group of two others just behind her, cutting down trees as they go.

They all work seamlessly and it's impressive, considering four new people are working with them. Valencia and her team have always worked as a well-oiled machine in every situation I've seen them in, but watching them take on new members and work just as smoothly is something else. I guess it really does pay to be good at your job and be able to work in any environment.

Despite trusting her safety to those around her, there will be no true peace until Dumah has been dealt with. I can't kill him outright, as that would cause more trouble than good, but I can encourage him to never come after her again. I plan for it to be a vicious lesson.

A gust of hot wind rushes under my wings, burning the edges of my feathers. My body starts to shake as heat exhaustion takes hold. I level back out, floating over the top of the trees to watch the crew working below me as the tiny heart in this body races, trying its hardest to keep up with my demands.

Just a little longer, I plead—though it won't make any difference. These crows can't withstand the heat at this height. It's so hot that I feel like my blood is boiling. My heart flutters and I involuntarily drop a few feet before catching myself on tired wings. My vision becomes a haze of blurred bright orange and black mesh. It was hard to see in all the smoke and ash; now it's nearly impossible. My wings beat one, two, three times before failing completely. I plummet, air rustling through lifeless feathers. I'm out of this body and into another one before it hits the ground.

Because I can't make crows out of thin air, I have to possess the body of one already alive. As soon as I realized they could not last long in these poor air conditions, I called many of them to this area. They wait a few miles away, safe from air pollution, so they're fresh and ready to go. It's morbid how I make them wait for slaughter, but they are ultimately servants of Hell, and though their bodies perish one after another, they serve a greater purpose just as they were created to.

I return to the fire crew in a fresh body. Swooping down to the lower limbs of the trees above them, I hop from tree to tree as they continue to work hard. Since I've had no luck finding Dumah, my best bet is to stick with Valencia and wait for the angel to show up. As much as I'd prefer to face him alone, I put her in more danger by leaving her to search for him.

Honestly, I'm surprised he hasn't showed up yet. From what I know of Dumah, he's as power-hungry as they come, always willing to do whatever it takes. I told Valencia he wasn't always that way, which is mostly true, and there was a time when I would've never thought he would be an enemy. We weren't necessarily allies but avoided direct confrontation out of respect. It's bad form to be allies or friends with the enemy but hate is a learned trait—and we didn't learn to hate each other until much later in life.

Something changed in Dumah. I never heard exactly what happened, as I was stuck in Hell for a considerable number of years, but I heard the rumors of the vicious battle between some of the higher angels. Dumah got his position, I was told, by taking out the angel above him.

It's also rumored that God hasn't been seen since. Some speculate He abandoned his winged children, leaving them to deal with their problems, themselves. If it's true—*how human*. I'm sure they loved that.

Others, however, state that God has left his highest archangel, Gabriel, in charge. Now, who would ever leave that psycho in charge is beyond me. There's something slimy about The Messenger. I'd never met him in person but, from what I've heard, there's something not quite right about him. Gabriel reminds me of the first lord of Hell; willing to do whatever it takes, to whomever, to gain ultimate power.

I would've never guessed Dumah to be a blind follower of a nefarious leader but, whatever changed him, it changed him for the worse. In a different universe, we could've been allies—maybe even friends—before all of this history came between us. But a line was drawn in the sand before we even knew we walked upon it.

Finally, the fire crew manage to break through the tree line and onto the field. The ground is scorched black, so the fire must've already come and gone. Little puffs of smoke roll up, scattered across the field, and the creek they were following winds in a jagged snake-like fashion through the field. It flows quickly, steam rising off it in parts. I fly overhead to see if I can glimpse the other group, but I can't see much beyond Valencia's group due to the poor air conditions.

The heat at this height instantly starts to affect my body. My heart races as the crow's internal temperature soars. I ignore the discomfort, push through the pain, and continue to scout the area from above. The worst part of being able to shift into a familiar form and taking over a body in this way is that you feel everything it feels. I've felt the death of each crow I've inhabited since I've been out here, and each is worse than the last. Each death adds a toll to my already waning energy and, eventually, the strain of dealing with the pain of it will be too much.

Ignoring the signs of another failing body, I look back at the group. Three men stride across the field, their steps sure. I recognize all the faces in the middle of the group as members of Valencia's team. Now that they're out of work mode, they travel in a clear pack, just a couple steps separated from the others. A straggler trails behind the group, a couple of paces away from the last person in Valencia's crew. He walks with a fluid grace that not many humans possess. He's tall—taller than any of the other human men. He's probably close to my height but, even with all the gear, I can tell he lacks the amount of muscle I have.

Everyone is a threat until proven otherwise. I trust the people on Valencia's team—Parker, more than any other—and I know they would all have her back if necessary. However, I'm slow to trust these other humans. I can't sense any supernatural markers on them but my senses are currently clouded by Dumah's angelic presence.

From above, I watch as Valencia scans the field, as if suspicious of the situation like I am. Nothing feels right about this. Based on how a layer of dread buzzes around my mind, I'd have thought Dumah would close enough for me to see him but I've yet to see even a speck of the damn angel since the night he ran from the bar.

Scanning the field again, I see a flash of white out of the corner of my eye but, when I turn my attention in that direction, there's nothing there. I fly overhead, coasting along, and scan the tree line. There are no more flashes of white, just charred pines and dots of burning embers. I start to question if the white was just a sign of impending death for this crow, its vision going out as its body slowly fails.

I turn, about to head back towards the group of humans, when something else catches my eye just beyond the tree line, where a burning flame races through the trees. It moves at blinding speed, weaving through the charred remains of the pines. Everything is already burnt here, the only things still alight is the trees' bases and random spots of debris.

I tuck my wings and dive, chasing the fire like a moth to a flame. It draws me away from Valencia, but I don't mind. I know this is Dumah; I can feel it in my very being. She is safest as far away from the fight as possible.

About a mile into the valley, the racing spot of fire suddenly stops. Pausing just at the edge of where the wildfire burns. I swoop my wings to slow down and shift into my middle form—a seamless transition from crow to man. As my being is ripped from the crow and put into my middle form, the crow falls to the ground with a dull thud. Dead. I was at least spared the pain of its heart stopping but it's an added notch to my mental toll, to be responsible for another innocent death.

I stalk towards the fire line, black boots crunching ash beneath every step. Floating embers burn tiny holes into my clothes, but I feel nothing against my skin. A perk of being Hellspawn is being impervious to natural fire. I could bathe in this and not receive a single injury.

"I can see your exhaustion from here, demon," Dumah calls to me. I stop before I get too close, leaving plenty of space between us. His flaming sword rests at his hip, hanging from a belted holster. That must've been what I saw racing through the woods; his blade of holy fire is probably what started this wildfire in the first place. I want to be angry at his recklessness, and demand he explain why he's doing this—what he plans to achieve by taking an innocent soul.

"The woman is clearly part angel. Do you have no loyalty to your own kind anymore?" I respond, my voice calm and stoic. He's already noticed my exhaustion but I refuse to confirm his suspicions.

"Oh, so she's just a woman now? Was I wrong to think she's more to you?" Dumah paces slowly. I can't tell if he's stalking me or wasting anxious energy with movement. Is that doubt I hear in his voice? I have so many questions, and I'm smart enough to know that the longer I keep him here talking, the longer he's away from her. I just hope he doesn't catch on.

"Regardless of what she means to me, she's an innocent woman. An *angel*, Dumah. Am I wrong to think that meant more to *you*?" I press, my voice unwavering, though it takes a lot of will to not let my emotions bleed into my tone.

"We both know that hasn't mattered in a long time," he whispers. I know he means for me to hear and I do, thanks to my elevated hearing abilities.

He speaks softly for a different reason; there *is* doubt in him for this whole situation—or for certain parts of it, at least. Either way, this is the first good sign I've seen since this all started. Dumah may be a righteous asshole most of the time, but I've always known him to be fair, even in his own, extreme way. He truly believes in his God—in the path God has for the angels. If I can get him to focus on that, I can hopefully buy enough time to get Valencia off this mountain. I'll deal with him another day.

"Why would He have you turn on your own kind, Dumah?" I question loudly, keeping his attention on me. I really would enjoy kicking his ass for all he's done in the past few weeks, between almost severing me in half with his stupid sword and nearly killing Valencia multiple times, I have more than enough reason to want to end him but I hold my anger back and focus on avoiding confrontation for as long as possible.

"She's your kind, too," he responds with a scoff.

"She is not mine. I have not claimed her soul, nor do I plan to. Her soul is hers to decide," I say determinedly. I realize how serious I am. I hadn't really thought much about the fact that the Devil sent me here to claim her soul. I've been so busy trying to make sure she doesn't die that I haven't once thought about what it will mean when I have to tell the Devil that I won't steal her soul—I can't bring myself to extinguish the brightness of her soul's flame by clouding it with the darkness of Hell.

"You don't know," he scoffs.

"Don't know what?"

He shakes his head at me, grimacing. "This is so much bigger than we were ever aware of. It saddens me to face you this way, but I must do my duty."

"This can't be what God really expects of you! To take an innocent life!" I yell at him, the anger starting to bleed into my voice.

"I imagine I know about as much of what God expects as you do of the Devil. Corvus, truly, I am sorry for having to take her from you; I see that she means more to you than just a soul to reap but I must think of everyone else. Of every life that gets put in danger every day she remains alive. No single life is worth more than all; not even if you love them." He starts to walk away, as if I'm not a vicious predator he just turned his back to. That would've set me off if I wasn't mad already.

"You don't know what the fuck you're talking about!" I try to deflect, drawing his attention back to me. Though I don't want to admit it, he sees too much. I've given too much away and he sees what she means to me, even though I've tried to hide it.

I've placed the value of her life above my own, and Dumah knows it. He's right to think that I don't really know what the Devil expects. Yes, we made a bargain, but that part was more of a game than anything else. And, yes, he did tell me to reap Valencia's soul by any means necessary—but he never once said it had to be through death, nor did he mention a timeline.

Dumah pauses but doesn't turn to face me. I see his shoulders rise and fall with a deep breath. "I know more than you," he says before taking off and disappearing in a blur of white.

I take a second to figure out what he could mean by that. What could he know that I don't? He's an impossible puzzle to figure out, all hidden lies and half-truths. I could spend an eternity trying to decipher his every action. Why would he draw me out here to rub it in my face that he knows more than me?

My eyes widen.

No.

No. No. *No!*

I take off at a sprint, running as fast as my legs will carry me. It's faster than any human can run, but I'm disadvantaged, considering the fallen debris and a steep incline. I don't have time to shift into a crow to fly as they're all too far away. Despite running as fast as I can, the mile between us will still take minutes to travel.

Dread pools in my body as my legs pound a steady beat into the ground. Embers fly all around as I run right through patches of still-burning fire.

Dumah didn't draw me away for a fight. He drew me away for a distraction and, because I'm a fucking idiot, I fell for it. I was so blinded by the need to pull the danger away from her that I didn't realize the threat was already there.

That's why I could sense the danger so close to her without finding Dumah.

It was never him. It was another angel right under my nose the whole time.

Chapter 35

Valencia

"This doesn't feel right," I murmur to Parker, who walks closely beside me. He's close enough that our shoulders brush every now and then but I speak quietly, regardless.

"Why are they waiting around if the drop fire was successful?" he responds, seemingly just as confused as I am.

There's too much about this situation that puts me on edge. As far as we were told, Polaris 2 faced a fire on both sides yet, from where I stand now, there doesn't appear to be a fire on either side. The drop fire they started was successful. Only little pockets of embers burn, with small puffs of smoke here and there. All the brush is gone and there's no raging fire in this area and no bright orange flames eating away every chance the team had of escaping.

I hate to think it but, Lawrie, could've gotten confused about the situation in the craziness of rescuing the civilians.

Or, there's also the chance that we could be walking into a more morbid scene. Maybe, in the chaos, Polaris 2 was trapped by the fire and unfortunately lost the battle. But—then why would they have told us they were in contact with Polaris 2 not too long ago? Somehow, they've been radioing back and forth this whole time. Or so we're to believe.

We continue walking across the field, closely following David Creek. Lawrie and two members of his crew walk ahead of us, leading the way. He's been communicating with Polaris 2, so it makes sense that he's navigating.

I haven't been paying much attention to who was working around me or what they were doing, we all have a job to do here. We all put our heads down and got to work. Working so hard for so long is mind-numbing and exhausting, but it does help time to go by fast. Now that we're all just walking across the field, I've had time to question the dynamics of those around me.

Since clearing the trees, the tall man from Polaris 1 has been missing or, at the least, not working alongside his group. I'm walking in the middle of our crew, my friends on both sides of me, but I still turn to look behind us.

The tall firefighter stalks behind us in that graceful way of his, floating above the grass more than he seems to walk upon it. I can't make out his face from this distance, but it's like I can feel him looking at me as the hair rises at the back of my neck. I see a flash of white, with what I assume is a smile, then turn back around. Unsurprisingly, his reaction is not exactly comforting. My anxieties crank up even higher.

Something is not right here and it's only a matter of time before the other shoe drops.

I really hope that Corvus wasn't right and that I didn't come out here just to die and, not only that, but I hope that I didn't doom my entire team at the same time.

I haven't caught a single sign of Corvus' being here the entire time we've worked clearing a line. I thought I caught a glimpse of a crow on the drive but it's hard to see a black bird flying in the night sky. Once we got here, everything's been so hectic that I haven't had the chance to focus on anything other than my job. Now that we had a few minutes' downtime, I'm able to notice his absence more.

I'm not ignorant to the fact that I'm starting to fall for him. It could be a bit of a savior complex—being that he's saved my life multiple times now—but I like to think there's more to it; some deeper emotion that I can't explain. I don't really know what love is anymore.

I love my work and team, but that doesn't seem to help me navigate romantic relationships. I love Parker most of all, he's all I have left of what a family would be, but he's like a sibling, so it's still different.

I remember moments of my parents' love for each other. How they were both adorably in love. They're connection was easy to see, even at eleven. I remember they loved me, and I remember the love of my little brother and how fiercely protective that love felt while also being annoying at times. How I wish he were still here to annoy me.

This doesn't feel like any of that.

This feels like being on a roller coaster; blindfolded and without a safety strap. My heart races from excitement, but also worry. This is pure frustration. Somehow, he knows how to push every single one of my buttons whilst making me crave the thrill of it all. It's a chaotic whirlwind that is as intoxicating as it is maddening.

But, how can I fall in love with Corvus if I don't know what it feels like? What if I'm wrong, and it's not love at all? What if I don't remember enough about love to know for sure?

I was eleven years old when my family died. Compiled with time and trauma, even the clearest of memories can become distorted. Even the strongest of loves can fade away. Either way, whether I understand my feelings or not, I know there's something there. Something deeper and different from all the ways I've experienced love before.

I've had enough hookups over the years, I can definitely tell what lust is, but that's never really helped in the emotions department. We haven't even had sex yet, but if Corvus had control of his sexual freedoms, I think those condoms would've come in handy in the cabin.

"Heads up, I think I see them," Jack calls from behind us, snapping me out of my thoughts.

We make it to others, surrounding them in a half circle as everyone moves around to get a view. Huddled together are two bodies crouched close to the ground. One person wraps their arms around the other as they both rock slowly. I don't need to question what's going on; one, or both, are clearly in shock.

Two more figures, both men—based on their sizes—huddle close to Lawrie, talking animatedly.

I look around, searching the field for more crew members. Supposedly, there were six total out here, and we've only seen four so far. As I gaze around, a gasp escapes me. Just at the edge of my sight, I see what's happened.

Two bodies lie on the ground, huddled together, almost embracing. I missed them initially because they blend in with the scorched ground around them. Bile crawls up my throat, burning as it comes. I can hold it in, breathing to keep it down, but someone else isn't so lucky. The sound of retching draws my attention away from the burned bodies and I see Tucker bend over and begin heaving, though nothing comes out.

In this job, we're never too far from death. Though we may face it daily, it's not made any easier, and it's so much worse when it's a fellow firefighter. We all see ourselves in those burnt bodies. Guilt consumes me so sharply that I'm now the one bent over, hands on my knees, attempting to purge my stomach.

Lawrie approaches our group for the first time and includes us in what has happened. "They got caught in a gust. They were, they—" he pauses, unable to finish his sentence without choking up. My heart breaks at his pain because I understand how he feels. I'd feel it for any member of my own crew.

"They were partners. Newly m-married. It's how they would've wanted to go. Harrison tried—" The words get caught in his throat again and he looks at the pair crouched on the ground, still shaking and swaying. I realize now, that it's not shock but grief as Lawrie points to one of the men on the ground. "It was William's brother and brother-in-law. It happened too fast. Nothing c-could be d-done." He chokes up at the end, turning away from us so we don't witness the worst of his own grief.

Pain slices through my chest. I feel as if a fiery hand has plunged into my chest and is squeezing the life out of my heart. I don't know how much more of this I can take.

Corvus assumed Dumah started this fire—a fire of this magnitude is extremely rare this late in October. No matter how much I don't want it to be true, once again, innocent lives have been taken when this pain was meant for me. How many more people have to die before the guilt is what finally finishes me off?

One of the men I haven't met comes to our group, patting Lawrie on the back before facing us. "You can't know how thankful we are that you're here. We couldn't have made it out by ourselves."

Now that he's mentioned it, I look over their group again, wondering why they stayed instead of meeting us at Torrey Lake once the fire was out. I understand not wanting to leave the bodies of their fallen members behind, but there had to have been something else keeping them here. Looking closely at this man, I notice he holds himself stiffly and that his pants are ripped and charred. He walked fine, which ruled out any serious leg injuries, but, as I scan his body, I see the issue.

Both of his hands and lower arms are blistered and bleeding. Parts of his shirt sleeves are gone, but most of the damage was done to his hands. They're clearly badly burned; he must've tried to save his friends. My heart aches even more for him. He hasn't been properly treated yet, so the pain must be intense. I notice, then, that none of the trapped team members have bags, so maybe they lost them elsewhere and didn't have the medical supplies to treat their injuries.

The other man is now crouched down by the two sitting on the ground, and though I can't see any signs of injury on him, I imagine he's not unscathed. I'm sure their injuries forced them to stay here and wait—and that's not even taking into account the two on the ground who are clearly lost to their grief.

I, perhaps, understand what William's going through more than most. To lose a brother in a fire you're facing is sure to cause years' worth of trauma.

I want to express my condolences but, coming from experience, I know a stranger coming up to him is the last thing he'll want. I'll have to wait until the funeral and express my sympathy there. Everyone wants to say sorry to those who are left behind, but sorry hasn't made the death of our loved ones hurt any less. Unfortunately, however, it's the only word we can come up with and it's what I feel now. So unbelievably sorry.

I can't let myself drown in the despair though, so I start envisioning how we will get everyone off this mountain safely.

Getting this entire team to where we landed for extraction will be difficult, given all the injuries and the two still trapped in their shock. Air Fire will have to pick us up from here. The field is mostly sloped, but there's a flat enough spot for it to land. Since there are so many of us, they will have to take us back in groups—the injured first and the rest of us second.

Chief Miller sends the call to Air Fire to notify them of the change of pick-up location. Surprisingly, they've been back for a while and have been waiting for word from us, so they'll be here for the first group soon. While waiting for them, Chief Miller directs our team to help the injured and ensure a cleared space for the aircraft to land.

Parker grabs medical supplies out of his bag and starts treating the man's burnt hands. There's not much he'll be able to do, as burns are always the trickiest injuries to treat, but he can at least patch them, so the man is less susceptible to infection. The true killer of burn victims is not the fire, the burns or blisters; it's the infection that catches up to them after.

The rest of us start to work on clearing the area. It doesn't take long with so many of us, so we start assembling those who will be on the first flight out.

There are now 17 of us; four of whom are injured. That leaves room for 6 more people to fly out on this first flight. Surprisingly, this sparks a bit of an argument over who will go first.

"I'm not leaving first!" Tucker demands, his hands resting on his hips and his feet spread in a stance that oozes, *I'm tougher than I look.'*

"You'll leave when I tell you to!" Chief Miller snaps. The kid is brave for going against the Chief's demands.

"I'll take the kids' place. You know how JeanAnne gets when I'm gone too long," Greg offers to Chief Miller. Since his wedding, he's been slowly distancing himself from this lifestyle. He's a great friend and a greater firefighter, but he's starting a family and this career isn't good for that. It won't be long before he's settling down and joining one of the city departments.

"Fine," Chief Miller responds, not wanting to focus too much on who does or doesn't fly out on this round. We'll all get off this mountain one way or another, and arguing about it won't get us there any faster.

When Air Fire arrives, Lawrie enters the aircraft, assisting the man with the burned hands. Greg helps another from Polaris 2, who limps as he goes.

Gathering the other two members is a little more complicated. The man comforting William slowly untangles himself when Air Fire lands. He attempts to stand, pulling William up as he goes. William sobs, tears pouring from his eyes even as they're clamped shut tight. At first, I think he will go peacefully—but then all hell breaks loose.

Once William realizes they're trying to take him away, he breaks away from his crew member, dashing toward the set of remains. Jack jumps into his path, nearly tackling William to the ground before he can make it there. They struggle briefly on the ground before Jack is able to overpower him. With his arms around

William's chest, he traps the other mans arms to his sides, preventing him from attacking. Jake, seeing his brother struggling, jumps in to help and, between the two of them, they pull William up to his feet and drag him to the plane. The man who had been initially helping William follows closely behind.

Now that I can get a good look at him, I see that the front of his gear is burnt to a crisp. I can't tell if he's burnt underneath but, since he's already on his way out of here, I don't stop to ask.

William wails loudly as the twins drag him to the plane and my stomach turns. There's not much that any of us can do for him now beyond getting him out of here so that he can live to see another day. The helicopter lacks room for the remains and we don't have enough time to properly retrieve them. However, I'm sure—as soon as the fire has been contained—arrangements will be made for a safe recovery of those lost.

Chief Miller looks at Parker and me, letting us know we're in charge when he leaves. It was always in the plan that he'd be leaving on the first flight; he has to ensure that everything goes smoothly on the other side and direct the injured to where they need to go while reporting the incident to officials. Since the fire is contained on this part of the mountain, it's just a waiting game for those who stay for the second flight.

As the helicopter lifts off, we duck and wait for the craft to clear us and it quickly ascends high in the sky, beyond the top of Torrey Mountain. As it flies into the distance, it takes all the sound with it and the field is plunged into an uncomfortable silence.

Three members of the Polaris City team are all that remain. The tall man, another with a large beard and a kind smile and, finally, a shorter man who looks as muscular as his other teammates. It's the look on this man's face that sets him apart—a mix between a smile and grimace, as if he can't decide which one he wants to show. It's far less comforting a look than the other smiley man—far too many teeth are visible to be normal.

Parker, Tucker, Bill, and I are all that remain on our team.

I selfishly wish that my entire team had left on the first flight and can't help but worry that something big is about to happen. It's like a live current flows over my skin. I keep a sharp eye on the Polaris City crew members and find myself constantly scanning the surrounding trees. It's so dark that I can't see very far in front of us, but I keep watch none the less.

We gather together in a tight group a couple of paces away from where the fallen lay. I have my back to them, so I don't have to focus on the fact they're there. Still, it's like a physical burn on my mind, plaguing my thoughts.

I catch a glimpse of movement from the corner of my eye that draws my attention to the three members of Polaris 1. The creepy smiler, who shows too many teeth, suddenly slumps over—upper body folding over as his knees give out. He hits the ground in a heap, causing ash to billow up around his body. The bearded man lunges to catch him but is too slow. I jerk forward to help but, instead, the bearded man's bright eyes look at me with terror before rolling into the back of his head and he slumps over his teammate's body in the same fashion. The rest of us jump into action, pulling the men apart and checking their vitals. They both have steady heartbeats pulsing in their necks but are completely unconscious.

I can't think of any reason they would just pass out, so I look to Parker, who doesn't offer me any comfort. "I don't know what the fuck is going on, Val," he says without me having to ask.

"Maybe it's the smoke," I mutter, confused.

I look around at my team to make sure none of them are suddenly passed out. Everyone is panicked but otherwise awake. I throw my bag down on the ground and open the left side pocket, yanking the particulate monitor out of the bag and frantically starting to press the buttons. I can't see any smoke, but that doesn't mean there isn't a toxic level of it in the air. I wait impatiently for the monitor to power on and test the air and, after a couple of agonizing seconds, the monitor comes back with the all clear. The air isn't *clean*, but it's breathable. Which means, whatever the two Polaris City team members passed out from, it wasn't the smoke.

I look around the group once again to see if I can determine a cause. Parker focuses on trying to help the bearded guy while Tucker and Bill help the other. Tucker's sitting across from Bill, their bodies leaned over the guy with the weird smile who passed out first. A shadow moves in the night behind Bill, drawing my focus away from my team members. The tall man is suddenly standing just behind

Bill who is crouched down, unaware of the presence behind him. An instinctive feeling takes over, so I look closer at him, watching as a dark look passes through his face before he breaks eye contact to look down at Bill.

Just as I'm about to tell Bill to move, the man grabs Bill by his shoulder and he slumps forward—now unconscious, too.

"Shit!" Tucker startles, jerking from the weight of Bill's body slumping against him.

Tucker lays Bills body down and starts checking him over. I'm already heading towards them, loud stomps thumping against crispy grass. I think I know what the problem is.

The tall man isn't a man at all, but something else. Something dangerous.

"Don't let him touch you!" I yell to Tucker. Three people are already knocked out, and I can't deal with one more.

Parker and Tucker jerk their heads up at my yell, finally noticing that there's only three of us still awake.

"What did you do?" I demand as I put my body between Tucker and the strange creature in front of me. I don't know what he is—angel or demon—but it doesn't matter, because we're in a fuck load of trouble either way.

"Go to Parker," I say to Tucker over my shoulder. He doesn't argue but steps closer to me instead. Parker frantically looks between us and then back to the three unconscious bodies on the ground.

"Val," Parker hisses at me, but I ignore him.

All of my attention is on the *man* in front of me. I don't know how he's done it or really even what he's done, but he's clearly responsible for what's going on. It's like he's put them under a sleeping spell with the simplest touch.

"They don't have to be involved," he tells me. He doesn't move any closer now that I've faced him directly, but his intention is clear; he intends to put all of them to sleep until only the two of us remain. It's honestly a tempting thought—and would help me to get them out of the way, so they don't get hurt during whatever this man has planned.

I thought I got a weird vibe from him but, with everything going on, I ignored it. I naively thought I'd know when danger was coming because it'd be coming from a face I recognized. Corvus told me Dumah wasn't the only one likely to come after me. I should've listened.

Chapter 36

Valencia

It's too late to think about everything I could've done differently. Fear pools in my belly at the thought of my friends getting hurt; I refuse to let this man touch them. I don't know what his touch does and I have no idea if my angel side is likely to make things better or worse. Is it just a little nap they're taking, where they'll wake up in a few hours drowsy but alive? Or are they in a coma, never to wake again?

It's too risky to touch him and potentially add myself to list of helpless individuals. He's already put three people asleep with his spooky gift, I can't allow any more.

"I don't trust you," I say back. No point in giving more away than I intend by being a nervous, chatty Cathy. My body fills with sharp little tingles as I face the man down.

"But you trust the demon?" he asks, tone light, calm, and almost airy before he growls out *'demon'* as if it's a dirty word. He might as well spit on the ground and curse Corvus' name with how much hatred rolls off of him.

He must be an angel like Dumah if his weird animosity is to be believed, but I don't know how to confirm that.

"The demon hasn't tried to kill me. In fact, he's continually done the opposite. Not something I can say for your kind." The words snap out of my mouth like a whip, trying to lash against the force of his hostile aura. I clench my hands into fists as my fingertips start to burn with the anger filling in my blood.

"The Messenger was right; you are beyond saving," he's staring me down as if he's decided I'm prey.

Parker and Tucker remain quiet but I can feel them standing close and hear their clothes rustling as they shift nervously. They don't know what they've fallen into, even if they can tell it's a dangerous situation that we've found ourselves in. Not that I know much more, but I know enough to understand that what's about to happen will change all of our lives. Fear is a heavy weight to carry and it tries to choke the fight out of me; whispering words of doubt into my ear.

As sad as the thought is—and, thankfully, Parker and Tucker are the only ones awake to witness it—I think I'm about to die. There's no way I can defeat an angel by myself. Corvus assumes I'm part angel but what good does that do if I don't know how to utilize it to my benefit? Having some special power but having no idea how to use it is useless, leaving me in the same situation as everyone else here besides the angel in front of me.

A basic-ass human.

When I fought Dumah, I took him by surprise. I don't think I'll get such a benefit with this angel, not with how he looks at me, cataloging every micro move I make. He probably also has some holy relic weapon like Dumah, which puts me at an even greater disadvantage. I can't survive a sword fight with just my fists.

Fire burns in my palms as I clench my knuckles, my nails digging into the soft flesh. How dare fate put me in this position? Dangling a gift of power in front of my face, then hiding it away before I can ever learn to use it.

This *gift* feels more like a curse, a sick twist of fate as if the shadows of my past aren't haunting enough. Memories of all I've been through ignite red within me as anger builds in my chest, burning away most of the agitation and doubt.

I may not be able to use my angelic side, but what I can use is my anger. I can use it to fuel me, to stoke the fire of my rage at everything that's happened in the last week—the rage at everything that's happened to me since I was 11, when my family was taken away from me, and everything horrible that happened after that. Because I now realize that they really *were* taken from me, and that makes my anger worse. I look at this angel and my blood boils, jaw aching from clamping my teeth together. When I look at this being in front of me, all I see is someone trying to take my family away from me again. And, maybe he was there the first time, too. Maybe he took my first family from me and now he's back to do it again.

But I'm not 11 anymore, and I won't stand frozen while watching it happen.

No. This time, *I'll fight back.*

"Valencia," Parker yells at me but I ignore him.

An inferno has consumed my body. Rage has taken control. It is hot and painful, but it is glorious. It burns away all my doubts and reservations about doing what is necessary to protect those I care about.

I couldn't do it before, fear had control of me.

I much prefer it this way, anger is far more fun an emotion to play with. I smile viciously, with far too many teeth showing to be considered friendly.

Then, the burning soars as pain slices through my fingers like someone is trying to cut them off. The pain distracts me for a moment and I lift my hands up to inspect them. It is a weird mix of agony that simultaneously feels like a thousand knives and being boiled all at once.

As I bring my hands closer to my face, fear slams back into me.

My hands are covered in blood. They shake from the pain but still look like my hands. Sort of. Where my blunt, pale nails used to be are now sharp, inch-long points. They remind me of those sharp nails that fashionable women pay a lot of money for, but these are much more gruesome. The skin around my nails is now ripped and jagged, and each finger bleeds profusely.

I have claws. Literal fucking claws. They're dark with blood, but I can see a black-tinged color underneath the gore. My knuckles protrude in a near grotesque way and the skin at my fingertips visible through the blood is black as night, fading up my fingers before blurring into tan skin. The nails curve slightly, reminding me of the claws I've seen birds of prey have, and there's a slight ridge to them that runs down the center of each before coming to a sickening looking point.

I slide the pad of my thumb across a claw on my left hand and feel the sting of my skin being sliced. They're *sharp*.

The pain starts to dampen the rage. I notice it more now that I'm focused on my hands. I don't know if it's shock, fear, or something else. This can't be real. Corvus told me I wasn't fully human, but I never expected something like this to happen. When he said I was part angel, I thought that meant I'd maybe sprout wings one day, not grow vicious Lady Wolverine claws. This doesn't seem like something an angel would have.

"Demon," the angel gasps, taking a step away from me.

The crunching of his step against the ashy ground draws my attention back to him and a red haze fills my vision until all I see is the angel before me, cowering under my stare.

Ah, there it is. My sweet anger.

I don't know what he's getting on about, nor do I care. He no longer has that overconfident air about him he did before. Instead, his brows pinch down in doubt, and I can see that he now fears me more than before. He stills and braces himself as if readying for an attack. My eyes narrow, tracking his movements as any predator would. His frightened behavior feeds a part of me that hungers for destruction—that hungers for blood.

He started this fight, who am I to deny him what he so clearly wants?

I attack without further thought, feet carrying me faster than ever before. I'm on him within only a few strides. He's braced for the fight but, surprisingly, he's no match for the force with which we collide. I hear my friend's cries, but I ignore it. There's nothing more important here than taking this weakling down.

We both slam down into the ash and soot. Clouds of it ripple up around us, causing the angel to choke and cough as he inhales it. Somehow, it doesn't affect me. It's impossible not to breathe it in as it coats my nostrils and throat with its gritty texture but I relish in its smoky flavor. A hunger for chaos stirs inside me at the scent.

I clamp my hand down on his throat and squeeze, my claws digging into the sides of his neck, slicing through what delicate skin is there. He freezes, fear clouding his eyes as pain causes him to grit his teeth in a grimace.

I breathe deeply, drawing the ash into my lungs, before blowing air out of my nose directly into the man's face. In my head, it's how I imagine a dragon would blow steam into the face of its prey.

The man shivers in fear with a small whimper. He closes his eyes and flinches as if the air from my lungs could burn him. He's weak. I wonder if the bravery and confidence I saw in him before was only because he thought there was no way I could beat him. He underestimated the level of my rage. He underestimated me because he thought I was a weak little human, but I am no longer human, angel, or even a being of body, blood, and brain. All that remains is a frenzy of fury that clouds all thought until only one remains. *Kill.*

My rage purrs inside of me, feeding on the dark shadows of my soul that beg for the destruction of this being beneath me. It is like a whole other side of me rattles at cage door, begging for release. He is no match for me now. He must lie still and pray for my mercy. If he moves the slightest inch, he could accidentally cut his own throat.

What a shame that would be.

My fingers start to clench tighter, the smell of iron fueling the darkness even more.

"Valencia, let him go," a voice calls to me.

A voice I *recognize.* It's melodic and calm and sends ice through my body.

I slowly turn my head around to look at the scene behind me. Dumah stands over a group of four slumped bodies, with Tucker kneeling at his feet. I search the bodies and realize that Parker lies limply on the ground.

I grit my teeth, forcing my mind to thrash through the shadows of anger until I can see clearly again. The world starts to come back to me, the red haze bleeding away into shadows, leaving just the darkness of the night.

I swallow hard, my throat dry and tight. I feel muscles flex beneath my palm. I look down to see a youthful face full of fear and despair. Red dots tinge his neck beneath my claws. This wasn't how this was supposed to be. I wasn't supposed to be the monster in this fight.

I slowly release my hold on the man's neck, making sure to not cause any more damage with my claws. He's okay for the most part, just a little cut up. I stand over him but he doesn't move, as if afraid any movement will cause me to strike again.

Now that I get a closer look at him, I realize how young he looks. Whereas before, I saw a middle-aged man; now I see is a youthful face covered in fear. It's like the glamor of age has dropped away and his true face is being revealed. The way he looks at me in fear makes my stomach turn slightly. Who would send an inexperienced youth to a battle they had no idea how to win? Evil people, that's who.

Despite his youth, he was sent here to kill me. How innocent is he, really? Dumah wants me to let the angel go but, how do I know that he will do the same for Tucker if I do?

I realize I don't—but Tucker's life is more important than needlessly ending an angel's. *I'm not a killer.*

I repeat it a hundred times in my head and finally convince my rage to turn away from the angelic youth. There's a bigger target now in sight.

"I never wanted to hurt you, but I will do anything to protect my family," I murmur to him as I slowly step away, giving him room to get up. He just lies on the ground, though, staring up at me with big, round eyes. There's still fear, but now there's also confusion. He's surprised I've let him go. "Get away from here, and don't come back," I say quietly.

He scrambles up and takes off in a flash of gray. It's so fast I can't tell how he's disappeared, but a cloud of ash engulfs me entirely at his exit. Once the air settles, a light gray feather floats to the ground and everything becomes clear again. I turn my attention back to Dumah.

He still has Tucker kneeling at his feet. I now notice he has a hand on Tucker's neck. Based on the pained look on Tucker's face, it's probably an uncomfortable grip. "Val, what's going on?" Tucker asks with a slight shake in his voice. I want to console him but can't bring myself to do it. I can't promise he will be okay when I don't know if that's true. I can't bring back the rage, even if I wanted to. Rage isn't not for comfort, it's for destruction. Now all I'm left with is chilling emptiness.

"You let him go," Dumah softly states, talking over Tucker.

My brows furrow. "There was no reason to hurt him further. Not when you're the real danger," is all I can manage in response. My eyes bounce between Dumah's face and his hand that's still wrapped around Tuckers neck. A thousand scenarios play in my mind, none of them good.

"So are you, it seems," he says, nodding to my bloodied clawed hands.

He's right. I am dangerous. We no longer battle on an uneven playing field.

The other angel only knocked a few people out—he didn't hurt anyone, as far as I'm aware, and he didn't keep any hostages. Dumah now has a hostage, and he's tried to kill me multiple times. Being angry with him comes easy.

"Let him go—let them *all* go—and face me alone. No one else needs to be involved," I tell him. It's similar to what the angel said to me earlier and I now realize how easy it was for Dumah to beat Corvus. He was at a great disadvantage trying to protect me.

Now I'm the one sacrificing myself to save those I care about.

"You care for them that much? To give yourself in their place?" he questions, head tilting slightly.

"I would do anything for them," I say truthfully. There's no reason to lie or pretend that I don't care when it's clear I do.

"Even hand over your own life?" he almost scoffs.

"If that's what it took," I snap in agitation.

Dumah stares at me in shock, his mouth dropping open slightly. His eyes go from round globes to pinched slices.

"He said you were a mindless beast. At least part of that is true," he contemplates, staring at my wrecked fingers. I don't let it get to me; I don't have time to worry about what the state of my hands means.

"I let your friend go. You let mine go," I push.

"You released a child! He should've never been out here!" he yells back, snarled words that make his voice sharp and choppy. It's the most uncontrolled I've seen him. He cares for the other angel—and it's clear that I was right about his being young. While, he wasn't a child in human terms, he was in angel terms.

"Then maybe your Messenger shouldn't have sent him out here in the first place!" I snarl right back, my hands clenched into fists. The jagged claws bite into my palms but I relish the pain and let it fuel me. I deserve it, anyway. I was almost responsible for another innocent death—and I didn't even know it. I nearly killed a *child*. It doesn't matter that he was the size of a grown man. If he was young, then killing him would've made me no better than whoever sent him here in the first place.

"You lie. Gabriel would never," Dumah stammers though, again, I see the confusion and doubt bleed into his features. He still holds Tucker, but I don't know how focused he is on keeping him. I catch Tucker's attention and shift my eyes to the side, away from Dumah to the group of bodies. I hope he understands but he just blinks in response.

"I never asked for this—none of this!" I shout, keeping Dumah's attention to me. "I didn't know any of this shit existed until *you* tried to kill me! My family died in a fire when I was 11. No one told me they were different—that *I* was different. The only family I had was ripped away from me once already. How can you expect me to not viciously protect the only people I have left?"

Dumah focuses so hard on my speech, on the pain it causes me to give it, that he doesn't notice Tucker gearing up to escape. I can sense it, but I don't look at him to confirm, afraid to draw the deadly angel's attention to what's happening. It rips me in two to expose my painful past so callously but when I said I'd do *anything* to save my friends, I meant it.

Tucker chooses that moment to dive to the side, his body slamming to the ground with a grunt as he slips from Dumah's hold. Shocked, Dumah simply stares down at him.

Tucker instantly starts scrambling towards the bag still strapped to Parker's back. There's a SAT phone in there I'm sure he's going for to call for help and, though the thought of more humans joining this fiasco worries me, I can't think of anything beyond watching Dane's every move.

Dumah looks back at me as if not sure how to move forward.

"*Mayday. Mayday. Mayday.* Come in! Anyone!" Tucker yells into the phone. It's a big, blocky thing, but I can see from here that it's somehow damaged. "Fuck!" Tucker snaps, slamming the phone into his palm as if that will make it work. There's none of the standard static there usually is when it's turned on.

Dumah and I both stand frozen, watching as it all unfolds. I keep an eye on him to ensure he doesn't move toward Tucker, while he surveys us both equally. Confusion is practically written across his face, as though invisible chains hold him frozen with inaction. I see a calculating glint in his eyes but doubt and uncertainty seem to be more in control of him.

"*Ugh*!" Tucker growls. His heated gaze lands back on Dumah and he grips the phone tightly before chucking it as hard as he can at Dumah.

Because the angel's focus was split between us, he barely dodges the phone flying at his him but the corner clips his forehead, creating a split in the skin. He touches his eyebrow and pulls his red-tipped fingers away. He stares widely, as if surprised at the injury.

"Wake them up right now!" Tucker demands, finally drawing himself to his feet. He starts pacing backwards, towards me. Somehow, in his search to get the SAT phone, he found a pickaxe which he now steadily holds.

Dumah should be very worried. Tucker holds the record for most home runs in our Ruby Valley Softball League.

"Tucker, let me handle this," I plead, trying to get him to back down.

Just as he sucks in a breath to argue, a groaning sound startles all three of us. I can't tell who it's coming from—but someone is waking up. Dumah frantically starts to scan the huddle of unconscious bodies with concern.

Before I can question his fear, a thundering crash sounds from our other side and we all jump, looking in the opposite direction. A pounding echoes through the valley and I struggle to see anything in the dark—however, I notice a blur of movement too fast to focus on.

The next second, Dumah is swept off his feet and tackled by a blur of black. At first, I think it's a bear, but I instantly disregard that thought. Any animals living in this area would be long gone due to the fire. Nonetheless, a deep bear-like growl reaches me as the crunches of crispy grass and thrashing bodies reach my ears.

"Check on the others!" I snap at Tucker, charging over to where Dumah struggles against that dark mass that tackled him.

It's no bear or any other animal that attacked him. No, it's a vicious barbarian demon who seems *very* pissed off.

CHAPTER 37
CORVUS

MY FEET THUNDER ACROSS the ground—loud stomps that crush the ground beneath me. My blood sings in my veins as my true demon form begs for release from the cage of this body. I don't however, but how badly do I wish I could.

"Wake them up right now!" A man screams the words into the night, fear and anger bleeding together.

I push myself harder. I can hear other voices but, from this distance, I can't quite make out what they're saying. *Almost there.*

I thunder into the clearing in a blur of black shadow and ash. All around me, bodies are slumped on the ground and, based on their bright yellow jackets, they're all firefighters. Two others remain standing, facing off with the asshole Archangel, himself.

A growl rises in my throat, alerting Dumah to my presence a second before I reach him. The others were too distracted staring the angel down—Valencia and her younger teammate, who holds a pickaxe in one hand and an empty fist in the other.

Dumah tries to turn toward me but he's not fast enough; no being would be while the true demon sends euphoric power through my body. He's just as eager to demolish the wretched, winged bastard as I am.

We collide with the force of a thousand realms, and the battle begins. *Got you now, Motherfucker.*

We hit the ground with an audible thump as we grapple, arms flailing as we fight for dominance. I've got both height and weight over him and manage to get on top, straddling his waist, but he catches my jaw with a powerful hook. My head jerks with the force of the hit but I continue fighting, powering through the pain. We can't kill each other in a fistfight, but it still fucking hurts.

He hooks an arm around one of my arms, trying to throw me off balance and prevent me from raining blows upon his face. I grip the hair at the top of Dumah's head before slamming it down onto the ground. He groans in pain and loosens his grip, and I'm finally able to bring one fist up high. I'm preparing to slam my fist back down onto Dumah's face, when I notice a flash of white and feel a sharp pain stabbing into my side.

A pained yell rips through my throat as blinding hot fire sears into my side. Memories of how my skin burned and tore the last time Dumah's angelic fire blade ripped through my side cause my muscles to spasm. This pain isn't as bad as it was then, but it sure doesn't feel good.

Dumah thrashes under my hold before finally bucking me off and my shoulder jars against the ground before I'm can catch myself. He scrambles away from me before I'm able to grab him and an angry snarl wrenches itself from my throat. I take a moment to rip something out of my side. Flesh tears a second time as a blasted white angel feather slips from between my ribs, its serrated edge having created a jagged cut that is surely unlikely to leave a pretty scar. Fucking angels and their stupid fucking feathers.

I throw the feather to the side, not taking my eyes away from Dumah. "Big fucking mistake."

My shirt is now ripped, much like my skin, and there's blood covering my side, but my black clothes conceal it.

"Corvus, what can I do?" Valencia's panicked voice calls out, her tone sharp and shrill.

"Just stay out of the way!" I snap, stalking towards Dumah.

"You don't want to battle me, King of Crows, not in front of her," Dumah sneers, his top lip curling up to show shiny white teeth that are tinged with blood.

Yes, the demon within purrs in excitement.

Dane flinches, fear clouding his face. Shit, the demon must be closer to the surface than I realized if Dumah's able to recognize his presence.

We both attack at the same time, trading blows.

Dumah's face is bleeding in multiple spots, and redness and swelling surround one of his eyes. Judging on the warmth that tracks down the side of my face, however, I don't imagine that I look much better right now. Rage hums in my veins, feeding the demon. It begs me to let it get involved, and I'm slowly losing the grip on my control. If the fight goes on any longer, I'm not sure I'll be able to hold him back.

In a blur of movement, Dumah rushes me—trying to catch me of guard. With the demon so close to the surface, however, time seems to slow and I can see his movements clearly. Just as he's about to kick me, I grip his ankle and twist.

A vicious snarl of pain leaves his throat but he's able to rip his foot from my grasp. I reach out again, trying to grab him, but he flutters away before I'm able.

My side burns with a vengeance. If I could just grab him, I'd be able to snap his neck and give us a fucking break for a second. It wouldn't kill him, but it'd at least give me some time to heal and get Valencia and her crew off this mountain. Then, Dumah and I would be having words. Vicious, deadly ones.

I gear up to lunge, amping my muscles to jump the great distance, but a flash of absolute despair crosses Dumah's face, throwing me off guard. He's not even paying attention to me, completely focused on something happening behind me. Panic seeps in, my heart racing. Valencia is back there.

"What has the Devil done," Dumah curses, my maker's name a curse on his tongue.

Fear floods my system, washing everything else away. I no longer care what the bastard angel is doing, or even acknowledge his presence, as I turn to face Valencia and the rest of her crew.

My world nearly ends as I hear the blood curdling scream.

What a huge fucking mistake I've made. I've been so worried about the angels, I never thought that there would be another *demon*.

Chapter 38

Valencia

I want to jump in and help Corvus, but I know how hard it is to focus on fighting while worrying about protecting the people you care about. I thought of turning and helping Tucker with whoever was waking up, but the rage still has a grip on me, keeping me locked in place. Anxiety sinks into my bones like a toxic poison, rooting my feet to the ground as I watch Corvus fight.

My body shakes uncontrollably. For a split second, I was so happy to see Corvus—to know that he was okay and that he hadn't abandoned me. Quickly, however, my happiness was drowned in the worry that yet another person I care for will face danger meant for me.

The motion of the fight blurs before me, both figures moving too fast to make out individual forms, but I watch with rapt attention.

Then, a gurgling sound steals my attention from the fight and I turn. Tucker stands facing me, his expression pained. He's wobbling on weak knees, and his hands hang loosely at his sides. Slowly, he looks down at his chest. I follow his gaze.

Something white sticks out of the center of Tucker's chest, the tip covered in red. It's ripped backward, causing Tucker's body to jerk with the force. He chokes, blood splattering out of his mouth and covering his chin. Thick, deep red liquid starts to pour down the front of his body and he looks back at me, a single tear falling down his cheek as he slumps to his knees and falls over.

Behind him stands the man who smiles with too many teeth, still wearing his yellow firefighting gear. He looks down at Tucker's body with a sort of sick satisfaction.

It never registered in my brain to worry about any of the other Polaris City crew members. He had been knocked out by the angel first, falling unconscious like all the others had, but the man that looks at me now doesn't resemble a man at all. It's the same face—but something other has taken over his body, the dark aura instantly permeating the air.

Confusion and fear war inside me, turning all of the cells in my body to ice instead of fire. My legs feel like lead and my heart pounds so hard that I think it's going to beat out of my chest.

The man steps over Tucker's body as if it's simply an obstacle and starts in my direction. The knife-like object is still gripped in his hand, covered in Tucker's blood. It looks different, not like any knife I've ever seen before. He blocks my way so I'm unable to get to Tucker and start treating him and I pant as I try to think of anything that will help. A stab wound to the chest isn't always instantly fatal—but it won't take long for the blood loss to kill him if the wound hasn't already. I can't stand here and let him die but I don't know what else to do.

Flashes of my family home on fire blur my vision, bouncing me back and forth between one tragedy and another. I keeping seeing Tucker's face and the single tear as it slid down his cheek. My family's faces plague my mind, each happy and smiling before turning into a melted and charred mess. A loud screeching stings my ears. I beg for it to stop, but it just gets louder when I cover my ears.

I realize it's me. I'm the one screaming.

The man begins to stride towards me.

Pain roils in my heart and trauma squeezes its horrible fist around my lungs. Tucker has so much to live for, and there's nothing I can do to make sure he survives such a horrible fate. Once again, I misjudged the danger right in front of me, and someone I care for paid the price.

All I can do now is make sure this piece of shit never steps foot off this mountain.

The pain inside me is blinding, but the rage can light the way. It's like flipping a switch. I'm no longer weighted down by anxiety as it hinders my ability to breathe. In fact, there's no need to breathe at all. This darkness inside me takes over my body, possessing me, turning me into something else. The killer instinct comes flaring back, begging for release. This time I don't hold her back.

I become an embodiment of fury—a harbinger of chaos.

I charge, no longer helpless or afraid. My vision sharpens, the red haze descending on the world once again. Time seems to slow as I stalk forward, allowing me time to prepare for my first attack. The man smiles viciously before lifting his arm and launching the knife at me. His throw flies wide, so I'm able to avoid it easily. I don't see where it lands, too overtaken with bloodlust to care. The rage has taken over and all it cares about is *attacking*. We collide with a booming force, but the man doesn't fall to the ground like I expected him to.

He's more muscular than the two I've fought before him, so he can maintain his stance following the impact. He lands a heavy-fisted blow to my face, knocking me off balance. It makes my jaw ache and spots dance across my vision, but it doesn't stop me completely. I've never been in an actual fight like this. Even with the rage in control, I don't know how much more of his vicious hits I can take.

I regain my composure and attack with a vengeance, using my claws to slice and rip any part of him I can touch. I swear chunks fly out of the man but he still fights back as if he can't feel a thing. Blood splatters all over me as the sharp tang of iron fills my nose. It smells rotten. Toxic. I don't let it stop me, honing in with a blind fury and shred skin and muscle like it's paper.

He lands a hard punch to my side. I heave, the agony instant. No matter how many times I slice into him, he continues to rain blows with ease with a vicious smile on his face. They come so fast I barely manage to dodge them. Misery blooms across my face once again, flaring through my cheek and making my brain rattle in my skull. Dots dance across my vision.

I stumble back a couple steps, losing my balance as the agony reaches heights I've never experienced before. Rage starts to mesh with shame; I'm not as strong as I thought I was.

With a primal scream, I fling my gnarled claws around wildly, no longer caring to aim—just to shred and destroy. Hoping to tear into his flesh and bone. With each slash, I hope I've done enough to hit something fatal and save me from this brutal agony. I feel grief surge inside me, a relentless force that tries to tear me apart from the inside while this man breaks me down from the out.

More hits come in quick succession, causing a hurricane of pain. The fire inside me starts to wane as my injuries overtake the rage. A cacophony of noise echoes around me and it takes a second for me to realize that it's coming from me. Though, no matter how much I scream, the pain doesn't lessen. Even as I unleash my fury upon him, he inflicts pain and suffering like it's second nature.

"You're an animal—just like she was!" he laughs in my face, continuing to viciously attack my battered body.

I have no idea what he's talking about; I can't focus on anything other than the agony. My body being beaten and battered by a being clearly far stronger than me. The ache from my heart being ripped out by grief. The torment as I realize it was all my fault in the first place.

The pain of not being able to save another person I care about.

I nearly drop to my knees as it consumes me and the desire to just give up and let this man end me as he so wishes washes over me. That way, no more people have to die because of me.

He sees my anguish; sees it eating me away from the inside out. My arms shake with exhaustion, stars dancing before my eyes.

He takes advantage of my suffering, dodging my swinging arms and grabbing both sides of my head. Fingers dig into my hair and nails scrape across my scalp painfully.

"You're weak. You must've gotten that from her, too," he laughs again as if the thought of my pain amuses him. I don't know who he's talking about or what woman I remind him of. But I'm thankful for the break between hits as he mocks me.

Did he kill her? Was she just trying to protect the ones she cared about, and did he see her love and devotion as a sign of weakness? Did he take someone away from her, with sick glee, as she was forced to watch it all happen? Did she give in to the pain, or did she fight till the very end?

I'm not sure what the answer to any of those questions is but the thought renews my anger tenfold and sends fire racing through my veins once again. My hands still shake, but now from a mix of pain and vengeance. I'm reminded of the vow I made to fight back, even if it's the last thing I do.

"You have too many teeth," I whisper, offering him my own creepy smile. Based on the coopery iron taste on my tongue, I'm sure my pearly white teeth are now covered in blood, making the smile even more unhinged.

He doesn't let my head go, but he does pause for a second, confused. "What?"

Before he can stop me, I plunge my clawed fingers into each side of his face, at the back of each cheek. He freezes, jaw popping open with a pained gasp as blood drops spatter across my hands and my fingers easily slide into his soft skin. I can feel the backs of his molar teeth press against the smooth side of my fingers. His hands drop from my head as he grabs my wrists to try to pull them away.

He waited too long, though, and let his mind believe he won and that I was already defeated. Now, thanks to his oversized ego, he's at my mercy. My fingers curl, the edges of my claws slicing the inside of his mouth, causing a pooling, bloody mess to drip from his open lips.

He really starts to thrash and panic then, but my grip on his face is too tight. I feel the bones in my wrist crunch under his tight grip, but I still don't let go.

"May your smile forever shine as ugly as you are," I growl, not recognizing my own voice.

His eyes widen in fear as his grip clamps down on my wrists. I scream through the pain as I rip my hands forward, slicing the inside of his mouth to shreds while I rip his bottom teeth out of his mouth.

The lower half of his face tears off, and the gruesome sight of it turns my stomach. What's left of his face is just mangled skin and muscle. I must've torn his tongue because it hangs onto the mess of tattered shreds. Most of his top teeth are gone as well and there's so much blood that it covers the entire front of his body, puddling at his feet.

I did that.

I ripped his jaw off, as if it were as easy as pulling out a single tooth. I drop the offending piece of bone and muscle to the ground and watch as the man takes a few, tumbling steps back before crumbling to the ground in a lifeless heap.

I can't be sure he's dead, since I doubt he's human, but the sight of his body ripped to ugly shreds consoles me, if only slightly.

I turn to Tucker, ready to check his vitals and see if he's truly gone. It makes me sick to see his body lying there, face down in the charred grass. There has to be something I can do. It can't end this way.

I'm just about to kneel next to Tucker's body, I hear Dane call out to me. "Valencia," he snaps, and I jerk my eyes up, afraid of an oncoming attack. I can't take any more beatings.

Corvus kneels, hands on his chest. The blinding white blade that killed Tucker protrudes from his chest, right over his heart. He's covered in blood. It darkens his entire stomach and thighs.

"No!" I scream. I race to his side, slamming to my knees. Sobs start to escape my lips, ugly wailing sounds I can't control. My knees scream in pain but I can't focus on anything but the blood covering the front of Corvus' body.

"Why! Why would you do this?" I shriek at Dane. I don't look away from Corvus, who kneels before me.

"I didn't, it was the demon," Dane responds, pointing somewhere behind me. Now that I can get a close look at the knife, I realize it's not a knife at all but a white feather. It's the same deadly weapon that's been passed around the group—*an angel's feather*, I think with a pang.

I realize then that the feather was never meant to hit me. It hit its intended target with deadly accuracy.

"What do I do?" I beg Corvus. Pleading. Begging.

"You're viciously beautiful, Kitten. Now you have real claws," Corvus coughs out, blood pouring from the wound that's clasped between his pale fingers. His body shakes with violent tremors and, looking into his eyes, I watch his pupils expand and contract as his breath stutters.

"No, no, no. Please, not you, too. I can't lose you, too," I beg, but I already see the light starting to leave his eyes.

His pupils expand to nearly his entire iris before he slowly slumps over. I catch his big body in my arms, resting his head in the crook of my neck. My damaged muscles strain with the effort it takes to hold him up, the weight of his large body pushing me down. He's deathly still as he leans against me. The only sign he's still alive is the tiny movement of his back with each small breath he takes.

"Please," I beg, looking up at Dane, who is watching the scene with an emotion I can't decipher on his face.

"He doesn't have much longer; the feather pierced his heart. Deadly to demons," he says bluntly as if I can't tell that the man in my arms is quickly on his way to dying.

"I'll do anything. Just, please—help me," I plead with Dane, hoping he sees the truth in my face. I'm not sure when Corvus worked his way onto the list of people I would give my life for, but it's glaringly obvious he's there now.

"I see that, but begging me to save him won't work. I don't have that kind of power."

Tears start streaming harder down my face. I can feel the time between each breath Corvus takes is beginning to grow longer. Too long. He has minutes, maybe seconds, before he's gone forever. I look up into the blue eyes of the angel before me and, for the first time in my life, I pray. I pray that a miracle happens, and that he isn't stolen from me.

God, I will give anything for him to live.

As if Dane can hear my thoughts, his eyes widen in shock. "You will give *everything*. Stupid girl." Dane paces away, turning back and forth before finally returning and crouching down at my side.

"I can't heal him but the Devil can. Offer your soul to the Devil in exchange for Corvus' life; he's the only one who can save him now," Dane says softly.

"I thought you wanted my soul," I murmur, tears streaming down my face, unable to understand why he would give up everything he's fought for. What do all these deaths mean if he so easily gives up on the very thing that got us all here in the first place?

"I don't know what I want anymore," he mumbles, then disappears in a flash of white.

I'm left alone in the quiet of the night. There's no sound beyond the sporadic wheezing of Coruvs' final breaths. His back rising in a great heaving breath before deflating completely.

I've run out of time.

CHAPTER 39
VALENCIA

A SOB ESCAPES MY lips and I scream at the top of my lungs. It echoes off the slopes, gliding up the mountains before bouncing back to me.

"Devil! I offer you my soul! I offer you my soul," I beg through choked sobs and strangled tears. Corvus doesn't move or make another sound in my arms. I drop my forehead onto his shoulder, leaning into his body. He's somehow still warm, almost hot to the touch, but I know that won't last long as the blood in his body cools.

I sob, the pain and grief finally consuming me enough to wipe out the remnants of my rage. I grip the back of his shirt, holding him tightly as though I can squeeze the life back into him.

My claws slice through his shirt and into my palms once again. I deserve it. I couldn't save him. I couldn't save Tucker. Both of their lives are in my hands.

So much blood on my hands. For a split second, I'm grateful the others were knocked out through it all—that I still have Parker—but it's gone in an instant. Guilt is a relentless beast that is gnawing at my resolve. In the chaos of everything, I never checked on Parker. Nor Bill or the other Polaris City firefighter who was knocked out, too. Tucker's body lies motionless, dead to the world. It's a hard pill to swallow, the truth that my inaction could have meant the deaths of everyone on this mountain, leaving me the only one to survive. Again.

I nearly beg for death instead.

I don't think I'll ever be the same after tonight. I don't know how I'll ever move on from this loss, from the guilt that will always be a constant reminder of my failures. A new shadow I'll never be able to escape.

"Devil, please, take me instead," I plead with a whisper, my throat too raw to yell anymore. I choke out a gasping sob, knowing it's too late.

Dumah was wrong. The Devil isn't coming to save the day. Nor is he coming to answer my prayers and release me from this agony.

Crunching thuds sound behind me. I don't have the energy to look up and see who it is. If it's someone here to kill me, I'll happily take the blow; I have no more fight to give. And, if it's miraculously one of the others, woken up finally and here to check on me, there's too much grief to feel joy at the fact that they're awake.

"C'mon dear, he doesn't have much time," a woman's soft voice whispers. I slowly lift my head to see who it is.

An older woman stands over me, wearing an all-black dress that is more modest than warm as she stares down at the pair of us. She looks nothing like what I expected the Devil to, but it's rude of me to assume. There's no other explanation for why she's suddenly out here. "Devil?"

She chuckles. "No, dear. I'm Greta, the Devil's assistant. We must hurry if we're to save him," she insists, pointing down at Corvus' slumped body.

"He's already gone," I whisper. He hasn't taken a breath in a while. There's no way he can be saved now.

"Not yet—but he's very close. We must hurry. The Devil awaits you for the exchange." She steps forward and places a small, wrinkled hand on Corvus' back before reaching toward me with the other.

I growl at her, mostly because she touches him without permission—though, there's not much she can do to an already dead body. I don't know how she thinks she can save him now, but I told Dumah I would give anything. Maybe trusting this woman is a part of that.

"I have to touch you to ensure we all make it to Hell in one piece," she uses her light voice to soothe my anxious nerves, not offering any other details.

I look back over to where four bodies still lie motionless—three unconscious, one probably dead. How can I leave them behind? What if something happens to them while I'm gone? Who will explain what happened to Tucker?

"Your friends will be fine. The helicopter is already on its way back. We must go now," she says urgently and I hear the emotion in her voice for the first time.

I don't know what will happen to me if I agree but I'm beyond caring. If there's even a chance that he can be saved, I'll take it. I nod my head at Greta and brace for her touch.

Everything is so painfully sensitive that I expect to feel more of it when she places her hand on me. Instead, I feel a soft caress at the back of my head, and then the world blinks out of existence in a swirl of blinding light and infinite darkness.

***

The first thing I notice is the pain that envelopes my stomach as I heave. My hands shake as they grip my knees. I don't puke, but that's probably because there's nothing to come out. My body aches all over, the motion causing stitch to flare from head to toe.

"Realm travel is never easy, I'm afraid," a smooth, ambiguous voice rolls across the room.

I jerk into a standing position and take in the room around me. It's small and homey, with warm red walls that are filled with loaded bookshelves. There are no windows, so I'm unable to see anything beyond this room, and the only door is shut. Between the books, desk in the far corner, and the fire which roars in the hearth.

There's a couch in front of me where Corvus now lies. His chest rises and falls slowly, evenly, as if he's sleeping and wasn't dead in my arms what feels like a moment ago.

I gasp and fall to my knees at the edge of the couch, reaching out my hands to touch him before remembering myself and jerking sharply away, afraid to hurt him with my claws. However, relief floods through me as I see normal, blunt fingernails instead of the vicious talons I wore on Earth. They're dirty, though—covered in mud, blood, and other things I don't want to focus on.

Tenderly, I slowly trace Corvus' relaxed face with my fingers, not quite making contact with his skin. I can feel the warm brush of his breath against my palm as he exhales and his eyes shift back and forth behind closed lids, as though deep in a dream. His face is now completely unblemished. There's no sign of his fight earlier with Dane.

"How," I whisper, too afraid to believe what I'm seeing.

"Did you not offer your soul in exchange for his life?" That same, calm voice asks, gliding over to me again.

The voice comes from a figure just off to my right—a man, I think. He's neither beautiful nor ugly. He wears an expensive three-piece suit, but that's the only feature I can focus on that doesn't become blurry. I squint but, each time I try to focus on any aspect of his face, my eyes cross and I have to shake my head to clear them. I can't tell if it's the pain in my head that causes him to distort or if he's doing it on purpose. I try to focus harder, but with more effort comes more pain.

"Oh, right. Stupid glamour. How's this?" The voice blurs from masculine to feminine as it crawls over my body, urging me to look again despite the pain.

Oh! I see then that this is not a man at all but a woman. A strikingly beautiful woman, in fact. She still wears a suit but this one is burgundy and shows far more skin than the one she wore as a man. Her caramel-colored hair hangs high in a slicked-back ponytail and she has a timeless youth to her face but what shocks me most of all is the strange amber eyes that seem to stare directly into my soul, even from across the room. They're so bright that they appear illuminated within. They remind me of a wolf's eyes, and there's no doubt that a predator stares back at me.

I hear an audible gasp, and I almost wonder if it came from me but looking toward where it came from, I realize the older woman from on the mountain stands just off to the side of this new room, her mouth clasped over her mouth in shock.

"Hush, Greta," the young woman demands, though not unkindly.

Greta looks between the two of us, panic in her eyes. Is she scared for the woman or for me?

"Who are you?" I ask the woman closest to me. I already know who Greta is—well, sort of.

The woman smiles with perfect white teeth and berry-colored lips. "I'm the Devil." It's the most beautifully alarming smile I've seen. "But you can call me Lifera."

She exudes boss bitch energy.

This is *not* what I was expecting.

"I thought the Devil was a man? And isn't Lilith the mother of all demons?" I say dumbly.

"That's what they all think," she scoffs, flipping her hand around, "but they only think that because they're under the misconception that a woman can't be in charge. I never cared to correct them. It's easier to give them exactly what they want, and glamour as a man. It's come in handy over the years, being able to hide in plain sight," she explains animatedly.

"Why show me, then?" I can't keep the thought inside. I mean, who am I to question the Devil?

"I like you. You don't trust easily. That's good, it will help you around here more than you know." She walks away, heading for the bar cart that's tucked off to the side. After she makes her drink, she stalks back to where I kneel beside Corvus' sleeping body.

"What did you do to my eyes? Why couldn't I see you clearly before?" I stutter through the words, fear pooling in my stomach.

"I had wondered if that would happen. Must be a family trait," the Devil smirks, not even remotely answering my question.

Panic like I've not felt before builds in my chest. The fucking Devil is in the room with me—and she's showing me her true self.

"So, shall we get on with the exchange? As you can see, I've already healed your lover," she points to where Corvus lies unmoving. His color has returned to normal and his breathing is even. He looks so peaceful lying here. His shirt still has a tear, but the skin underneath is closed and healed. Only a small white scar remains.

Thinking of Corvus is an instant distraction from my other, crazy thoughts. I lean into it, focusing on him instead of the blinding fear.

"How?" I ask again, amazed that he's alive when, not that long ago, I was sure he was dead.

"He is my creation. I created all demons. I brought him into this universe once, I simply did it again," she takes a sip of her drink, smiling behind the glass.

"It doesn't sound that simple," I say, looking back at him. I hold my hand over his body and feel the heat as it radiates off of his skin. I never learned if that's a demon thing or not.

"Clever girl," she purrs at me, a smile growing as she says it. It's a seductive sound, one that sends chills down my back. It's the sound of a predator luring its prey into a trap. "It is only simple when something of equal value is offered in exchange, like, say, a *soul*."

My soul is what she means. I now realize where she's going with this. She was only willing to offer him his life back in exchange for my soul. I meant it when I offered, though now that I'm faced with the actual Devil, I fear what it truly means to give my soul away.

She's already healed him, though, so I have no choice in taking it back. Not that I'd want to. It was an easy trade, saving him over keeping my soul. It was a wrecked soul anyway, so consumed by grief it had ripped in half. It's still not whole; there is too much grief to have been put back together completely. But, with every rise and fall of Corvus' chest, it doesn't disintegrate entirely.

"So you have it already? My soul?" I ask her.

"I do," she nods.

For some reason, I thought I would've felt different, being a body without a soul. But I still feel like me. It doesn't feel like anything has changed.

"Does that mean you have control over me? Like, do I have to stay here?" I wonder aloud. Does offering my soul directly to the Devil mean she's now got some power over me? Corvus never explained what happens after you offer up your soul. There are so many things I wish we would've spoken about sooner but it's too late for all that now.

"You wish to leave so soon?" she asks, looking at Corvus on the couch as she says it, clearly asking why I wish to leave him.

I shake my head. "I don't want to leave him, but there are others I need to see more. Someone I need to say goodbye to, who didn't have Lilith to save them." I whisper the last part to myself. I realized how lucky Corvus was at this moment—that he had someone willing to offer their soul in exchange for his life.

Tucker didn't have that. I wonder if that makes me a horrible person, that I chose to exchange my soul for a demon who's probably committed some pretty lousy acts in his lifetime, over an innocent man who was just in the wrong place at the wrong time. The grief starts to turn to shame. How can I continue living with myself with that kind of choice?

Is that also why I wish to leave so soon? The pain of losing Tucker is starting to take away the joy of seeing Corvus alive yet I can't help but drop my forehead to rest against his warm, muscular arm.

What have I done?

Every breath starts to feel like an ember of betrayal that burns inside me.

Parker's face fills my mind. *'Why did you leave me?'* he asks.

Now Tucker's. *'Why him, and not me?'*

My family. *'Why us?'*

They all blur together. Voices yelling on top of each other, demanding answers—demanding justice for themselves. Demanding I answer for why I'm here and they're not.

What have I done?

It's a mantra of self-hatred that repeats endlessly in my mind. Will each moment spent with Corvus be a constant reminder of what I've lost? Will his survival be a testament to my betrayal? Will the price I finally pay for the choice I made be to lose him, too?

Reality is a bitch with a violent bite.

Greif and shame intermingle so tightly that there's no solace. No peace. No moving forward from such an inescapable shadow.

I am not human, nor angel—nor any other being. I am a *monster*.

"I can taste your despair. It is as sweet as it is painful. You'd do well to mask your emotions better when you return to Hell. And, if it helps, I would not have saved your human friend had you begged for his life, instead. He is not one of mine to save," she states plainly but it only dampens my grief, not taking it away.

I try to nod, feeling how the hot skin of Corvus' arm rubs against mine. Tears prick my eyes, but I force them back. There are still too many questions and too much to do. As much as I wish to stay and wait until Corvus wakes up, I know I need to get back to the others. Greta said the helicopter was already on its way back. Corvus never explained exactly how time works differently between Hell and Earth, so I have no idea how much time has passed.

I just hope I haven't missed Tucker's funeral.

I just hope that Corvus doesn't hate me when he's realized I've left him.

"Still wish to leave, pet?" she asks, eying me from head to toe.

"You'll let me go back, just like that?" I ask her, standing to my full height. Even with my work boots on, she's still inches taller than me.

"Just like that," she repeats, snapping her fingers for effect. "It was never about trapping you in Hell if you wanted to stay on Earth. I just needed your soul, by any means necessary. Sending the King of Crows seemed like the easiest option. You're free to go back to Earth but know, we'll be seeing a lot of each other in the future. I'll send my crow as soon as he's ready to fly." She pauses, cocking her head to the side. "And, now that he's fulfilled his part of the bargain, you'll be free to enjoy him fully."

All I can do is nod, figuring she's speaking about the bargain. Corvus told me the details of it but, so much has happened since, I can't remember the specifics.

They say to never trust the Devil, but what else do I have to lose?

I want to question her on why she sent Corvus. What was it about him that made getting my soul the easiest option? What does she know that she's not telling me? But, too many questions are wiggling in the back of my mind for me to focus on just one and I need to get back.

I step up to her outstretched hand, wondering if Lilith plans on transporting me back herself.

She grabs my hand, gripping me tightly. My eyes jerk to hers. As if hearing my thoughts, she warns, "I'm Lifera, not Lilith. Lilith is a human construct to help men feel righteous despite their greedy ways. I'm much worse than Lucifer, Lilith, or any demon your humans have tried to come up with."

It seems an odd time to make such a distinction. I've never been religious, so I wouldn't have caught my mistake if she hadn't corrected me. I feel bad calling her by the wrong name, but it's not like I have a lot of knowledge when it comes to the history of Hell. She'll have to forgive my lack of care.

I nod, stamping a reminder in my brain to remember the next time I see her. Whenever that will be. First step is getting back to Earth and taking care of my current problems, the Devil can wait her turn. She seems to recognize my silence as an answer.

"I'll see you very soon," is the last thing I hear before the world turns upside down again in a white and black blur.

CHAPTER 40
VALENCIA

THIS TIME, I MANAGE not to puke but my stomach still rapidly turns. It's not that I thought traveling like that would be easy, but I didn't realize it would make me sick. Corvus never seemed unwell when he popped in and out of existence—but maybe it's a tolerance thing and I'm just new to all this. Thankfully, the Devil must've healed me along the way, because my body doesn't hurt nearly as bad as it did.

I shake the haziness from my head and try to focus on my surroundings, realizing I'm in a bedroom back at the station though, based on the mess, it's definitely not *my* bedroom. I take a few more seconds to look around but it's so dark here that I can barely see anything besides some clothes piled up and some bedroom furniture.

I've been to Hell. I just met the Devil. *Lady* Devil. I did not have that on my bingo card.

Corvus never mentioned the Devil was a woman, which makes me wonder whether he even knows. She made a point to say that she doesn't tell anyone she's a woman and she appeared to me as a man at first. When she changed her form and dropped whatever illusion she was maintaining, even Greta seemed shocked or concerned. Maybe Lady Devil didn't share that with any others. It's just another thing to add to my *'why me'* list.

I can't tell what time it is since there are no clocks in here, and I have no idea where my cell phone is. I don't know if it's even the same day as when I left. It's clearly nighttime, but I suppose that doesn't mean it's the same night.

I was only in Hell for a short time. I have no idea how much time has passed here. Is it more or less? Thinking of Corvus makes my stomach's already heavy pit of stress sink even further. Will he be angry that I left him in Hell? Will he even care?

Flashes of him taking his last breath plague my mind. It's such a strange feeling, but the grief I felt when he stopped breathing literally shattered me. I was already drowning in grief and guilt by that point that my heart couldn't take it anymore. It broke into so many pieces that I knew I'd never get them all back together.

Then, I saw him lying on the Devil's couch, breathing normally as if just resting. I could barely believe it. Giving my soul for his life was an easy decision. He had earned my trust time and time again. And I'd be lying if I didn't think part of it was because of my feelings for him, even if I can't explain them. The joy of seeing him alive glued some of the shattered pieces of my heart back together but there will always be a part of me that's ashamed I chose him over Tucker. Even though the Devil said she wouldn't have been able to save Tucker, I didn't even try.

I would've never recovered, if I'd lost Parker. But, that doesn't make it fair to Tucker. He was so young—too young to be taken from this world.

Dumah said the creepy man was a demon. I'm not sure whether he meant just a demon in general or something else but, what I do know is that if ripping half of his face off didn't kill him, I will hunt him down to finish the job and make sure he knows exactly how it feels to have an angel's feather rip his heart in half.

I want to go out into the hall, but I'm afraid of what I'll walk into. If I just disappeared off the mountain, I can't magically show back up; everyone would freak the fuck out. *I'm* freaking the fuck out. I was only in Hell for a short time, 20 minutes max, but I have no idea what's happened here while I was gone.

I panic even more as I hear the soft thud of footsteps walking this way. The door handle jiggles before swinging open and blinding me with the light in the hall. I cover my eyes briefly and then drop my hand to see who just walked in.

"Val?" he says, eyes huge and round.

"Parks," I sob, throwing my arms around his shoulders and squeezing tight. He whispers something too quiet for me to hear but wraps me in an equally tight embrace.

Parker quickly lets me go to look out in the hall. He shuts the door behind him, locking it. "Where the fuck have you been?" he whisper yells.

Tears stream down my face. "Hell. I've been through Hell." I mean it literally and emotionally.

"It's been days, Val, basically a week! Four of you went missing. You, Tucker, and two from Polaris City. Where did you go? And, why are you in my room?" Now that he faces me and tears no longer cloud my vision, I get a chance to look at him properly.

He looks like shit. His usual, lightly tanned complexion is pale and he has dark rings around his eyes. He looks haggard, like he's battling a severe hangover. His clothes are a rumpled mess, much like his room. His typically styled hair is long and shaggy and he's sporting more facial hair than I've ever seen on him.

If they'd deemed all of us missing, they would've been out there searching nonstop. Parker has probably been running himself ragged every day trying to find us. Four people don't go missing without somebody noticing.

Wait.

"What do you mean *four* people went missing?" I knew one of them would be gone because I watched him leave but Parker had been knocked out by then, so he would've missed me telling the young angel to go.

I expected the creepy, smiling demon to be gone. I can't understand why he would go after Corvus, but it's not shocking that he was gone. I'm sure having his face ripped off wasn't pleasant, but demons can supposedly heal from any-thing—perhaps barring angelic feathers.

So where the fuck was Tucker's body? He wasn't anything other than human, as far as I was aware, so why would anyone want to mess with his corpse? What purpose did it serve, taking him away? Grief and guilt battle each other in my mind as the replay of his death begins in my head.

He died. I know he did. Who the fuck took him?

I start to get angry, and I welcome it. It's a much more comfortable emotion than the pain and grief, not to mention the shame.

"Val, where's Tucker? And those other two guys? What happened?" Parker demands. I know he's not angry with me, just the situation.

"He's—" I don't know if I can bring myself to say it.

"They did something, didn't they? I remember that guy knocking the others out," Parker asks quietly. I can see the strain in his body as he stands. His shoulders slump, and he's lost all the confident vibe he usually gives. I guess he noticed more than I thought.

I slump down on the edge of Parker's bed and pat the spot beside me. He comes over without question, sitting down close and grabbing my hand, giving it a squeeze. "I'm so happy you're here. I thought you were gone forever. I've been losing my mind," he says, holding my hand in his, and pressing it against his forehead.

I rub big circles around his back, but I'm not sure if it helps. "Parker, I made a mistake," I murmur, unable to keep the despair from bleeding into my voice.

"Whatever happened, we'll fix it. We will figure it out. All that matters is you're back," he squeezes my hand tightly, looking into my eyes. Tears fill his own, making them shiny and golden.

"He's gone. I can't fix that," I choke out, another sob climbing up my throat. My eyes feel puffy and sore from all the crying I've done but, somehow, there are still more to come.

"Who is?" Parker asks softly.

As much as it hurts, I tell Parker everything.

I tell him how I attacked the angel, pinning him to the ground. Digging my claws into his neck. Parker doesn't interrupt but we both silently look at my clawless hands. All I see are the same fingertips I've always had. There's no more jagged, ripped skin or sharp, spiky nails. They're even clean as if I washed the blood away. I don't remember doing that. They were dirty in Hell but they seem to have been cleaned at some point, I just don't have the energy to wonder when.

I rush through the rest of it, choking back sobs as I tell him every single detail. Even the ones I'm most ashamed of.

"I don't know how I can live with myself, Parker. I chose a demon over him," I bury my face in my hands and cry as my chest feels like it's being torn open all over again. Lilith said she wouldn't have been able to save Tucker, he wasn't one of her creations. Begging for his life wouldn't have gotten me anywhere. But, I still chose Corvus in that moment and it's killing me.

"Fuck," is all he says back, wrapping me in a hug I don't deserve but will gladly accept.

We spend a long time just holding each other, sharing our grief. I'm not sure how much time has passed but I start to see the sky outside his window brighten ever so slightly with the coming sun.

A new day has begun, and we're nowhere near figuring out what to do.

"I don't know what to do, Parker. Where do I go?" I plead, panic starting to set in. The last 24 hours have been a roller coaster of dread, panic, and grief—then rinse and repeat.

"Don't you have to go back to Hell?"

"I think so? I don't know. The Devil didn't really give me any details on that part," I say, standing up to start pacing around his messy room.

"Is it weird not having a soul? You don't seem any different," he says, mimicking my pacing with one hand.

"I don't feel any different," I say, turning on my heel. "I didn't even know it was taken. Corvus was alive and I didn't want to ask too many questions. You know how my attitude can get. I didn't want to make the Devil mad by seeming ungrateful—or, whatever. Plus, I was more concerned about getting back here."

He pauses for a moment. "So, now that Corvus is your literal soulmate, do I get to say I told you so?" he smirks at me, though it lacks its usual luster.

"Parker, now is not the time for jokes. He's not my soulmate, so no. Just stick to the real problem," I shake my head at him, scraping my hand over my face as if to wash away the dread that begs to seep in.

"Dude, he's literally your soulmate. You gave up your soul for him. That's, like, Soulmate 101."

I pinch the bridge of my nose in frustration. "Parker, seriously, what the fuck am I supposed to do? Tucker's body is missing, Corvus is in Hell, probably pissed I left him behind, and The Devil has my soul. Oh—and I'm currently a missing person and can't be seen by anyone but you."

He stands and grips my shoulders in his big hands, halting my pacing. "You don't have to do this alone. I'm here for you. You and I both know that Corvus isn't going to be happy you left him behind but he'll get over it. We'll figure out the rest one step at a time. If you want to find out what happened to Tucker, we'll do that. If you want to disappear and start over again, we'll do that, too. Just—just, please don't leave me behind. Let me come with you."

"What happens when I have to go back to Hell?" No part of me will ever be okay with leaving Parker behind, but I can't know what dangers he may face by just being in my life now that so much has changed.

"Easy. I'll come with you," he says, as if it were truly that simple.

"Parker, I don't know anything about Hell. I don't know how dangerous it is. I don't know if you can even survive there. What if it's like space and you can't breathe?" That feels like a stretch, even to me, but it's just a drop in the ocean of the endless worries I have.

"First off, clearly Earth is dangerous, too. So what if Hell is just a little spicier? And, if a squirrel can live at the bottom of the ocean, then I can live in Hell."

"I can't believe you just used a *cartoon* as proof you could live in Hell," I somehow manage to laugh. This is why Parker is so important. He has to be protected at all costs. No matter the situation, he finds a way to bring light back into a world surrounded by darkness.

"If you can give me one factual reason why I shouldn't follow you to Hell, I'll never bring it up again."

He knows I can't. I've barely been to Hell. I can't even confirm that I was ever there, either, or that the woman I met is actually the Devil. I never left the room, and I never met anyone other than Lilith and Greta.

Although. . . that is concerning in itself. How did she know I'd want to see Parker? How did she know how to get me to the *exact place* he'd be when she sent me back?

"You can't," Parker says, reading my expression. "So, it's settled."

"Parker, you can't want to live in Hell," I urge, trying to get him to see sense.

"Valencia, yes I can. Because if you leave me behind, I'll already be in Hell anyway." Parker's eyes burn into mine, their light blue depths rivalling my own. I've never seen him look so rough. His eyes are dull and bloodshot. His clothes are a rumpled mess and his shoulders slump unnaturally and the hollow edges to his face make me think he's probably lost some weight.

I grab his hand, squeezing it for comfort, "I understand." Just like me, Parker is unwilling to lose the only family he has left.

"So, if you're going with me, how are we going to explain another missing person?"

"If we're in Hell, I don't think we will need to worry about explaining anything."

"What about the team?" The thought of leaving my friends behind makes me sick to my stomach once again. I have a feeling it's for the best, though; being close to them will only put them in more danger. I just don't know how I'm going to cope with leaving them behind.

"What about them?"

"We—we need to tell them what happened—tell them about Tucker. His family needs to be able to say goodbye." Acid burns in my throat, making it difficult to talk.

"No, we don't," he snaps, jerking my attention to him. "We don't actually *know* that Tucker's dead, Val. You saw him get stabbed, once and, yes, it was in the chest, but with proper care, there's absolutely a chance he's alive."

"I—I can't hope like that, Parker. I can't have hope that he lived only to find out he truly did die. I can't grieve his death twice. I don't know how I can survive any more people dying because of me."

"None of this is because of you, so get that thought out of your head right now. This shit sucks, but it's happening. We just have to deal with it. I can't tell you how to feel, but I can tell you that hope will lead us to the truth much sooner than grief will, and it'll be a lot less painful."

I hate to admit that he's right, but he usually is. I do want to know the truth of what happened. If that means finding out Tucker really did die, then I'll make sure to release all of the pain it causes me onto whoever is responsible.

"That still doesn't solve the fact that I'm a missing person and can't just go walking around. And I have a feeling it won't be long before Corvus shows up. We don't need an angry demon around here." I sit back down on his bed. The sun has already started to turn the sky a light blue. We're running out of time.

"We're going to sneak you into my truck," Parker says, startling me and turning my attention back on him. "And, then, I'll drop you off at Heath Cabin. It's the slow season, and no one is scheduled to stay there until the spring. Then I will come back here and pretend like nothing has changed until you're ready." Parker is already up, mind made. He fiddles with the clothes that lie around his room, finally starting to clean up a bit.

"Why come back here? Why not just stay in the cabin with me?"

"Because I do not want to witness what Corvus does to you once he's figured out what you've done."

Chapter 41
Corvus

My chest burns. I try to rub away the ache but my body feels like it weighs a thousand pounds, so I can barely lift my arm up by an inch. I feel cradled, like I'm lying on a warm pillow. I sink into it a little further.

"Are you. . . wake him up?" a voice murmurs from somewhere near my pillow. I can't understand it fully, my ears don't work. Do I even have ears anymore? All I feel is pain—burning, then stabbing, then burning again.

I try to turn my head to hear better, but it feels like my head has turned into a bowling ball. It weighs a ton and pounds as though continually slamming into rattling pins. I take a deep breath, taking in the smells around me, but so much fire shoots through my chest that I can't distinguish a single scent. I can only focus on the inferno within that burns every cell it touches.

A garbled groan vibrates in my chest. More pain. Only pain. A bowling ball head doesn't seem so bad when it feels like a thousand hot pokers are stabbing me.

"I don't. . . should wake him. . . not ready," the voice says again, closer this time but still out of reach.

"Well, that's too bad," another voice responds, much closer than the first. "Wake up." Too close. I recognize this voice. It's the Devil's. The Devil could seduce a lion to love a mouse with just the sound of his deep timbre. Normally, even I'm able to notice the bewitching edge to it, but now all I hear is ridged sharpness.

I try to open my eyes, but they refuse to work.

Smack!

I instantly feel a sting against the side of my face, causing the burning in my chest to travel upwards. The bowling pins in my head rattle around some more before it all starts pounding again. Hard enough that I can't tell which hurts worse, my head or chest. Burning. Stabbing. Burning.

"I think he's opening his eyes!" the first voice calls out. Did they move closer or did I grow new ears?

Am I opening my eyes? I can't really tell; I forgot I had them. I forgot everything besides the pain. I feel each cell burn to nothing.

The muscles in my face still twitch from where the Devil just slapped me. More burning, just a little less this time. It's more warm than painful now.

I focus on the feeling and use it as a tether to pull myself out of my daze.

I try, and I try, but there's something holding me back from waking. There's too much pain in my chest and head. I can't fight against it. It's putting me back together just to tear me apart again. It's like swimming against an ocean tide in a hurricane. Maybe if I rest just a little longer, it won't be so painful to wake up next time.

"Don't stand too close. He might attack."

I'm jerked back out of the dark. Back into the blinding pain. Stabbing and burning. That voice—I have to know it. If the other is the Devil, then this should be Greta. Though I've never heard her speak so freely, she talks confidently and warmly, not fearfully. Did the constant pain scramble my brain, too?

"Oh, he's going to freak out either way," the Devil says in his cool timber. He slapped me earlier. I don't know if it was a way to wake me up or just a fun way for him to punish me. Does he not think burning alive is punishment enough?

"Just wait till he finds out you sent his woman back to Earth!" Greta hisses. *What. The. Fuck.*

A new fire consumes me but this one doesn't eat away at my body; it rebuilds it. Like a shot of the best drug in the world. Adrenalin flows through me, eating away the worst of the agony. There's still an ache in my head and fire in my chest, but it's nothing compared to the fear that boils the rest of me.

I'm finally able to open my eyes and get a look at the world around me. I don't have the time to focus on where I am because all I can see is the Devil's evil grin smiling down at me. He's so close he takes up nearly my entire field of vision with his smug grin and clean-shaven face—all bright eyes and dark brown hair.

My hand finally decides to work, flying off the couch to snatch the Devil by the throat. "Where is she?" I growl in his face.

He just laughs at me—that crazy, maniacal laugh that always forms a pit in the bottom of my stomach. I ignore it and just squeeze harder. I can't kill him, but I can sure ruin his day if he doesn't start talking.

I hear Greta gasp, but she doesn't come any closer. She seems to know what's going on. Maybe I should've grabbed her throat instead.

"Careful, Corvus. Let's not be too rash," he says, though it sounds creaky since I've got a death grip on his throat. I don't think he can read minds but he definitely must've understood where my thoughts were going when I looked over at his assistant.

"Where is Valencia?" I ground out slowly, drawing my attention back to him. I think, in all the burning, my soul has been replaced with that of a feral animal who scratches at my insides to get free. It yearns to rip apart the universe until we find her.

The Devil points to the hand I still have wrapped around his windpipe. I release my grip, enjoying the red marks left behind. As he steps away, I push myself into a seated position and see that I'm on an enormous leather couch, not a pillow.

I scan the room once more. We're in a cozy, office-style room with red walls, shelves of books, and comfy furniture surrounding a fireplace. This is far too homey of a space to belong to the Devil.

Is that a *plant*?

"Do you like my library? Get a good look because you won't be coming back here, ever," he snaps, drawing my attention from the room and back to him. Now, he's lounging on a couch across from me, holding a tumbler of liquid that looks far too light to be whiskey in one hand and twirling a knife in the other. I never saw him move an inch.

"Where's Valencia?" I ask once again.

"You're not as clever as she is," he smirks at me.

"What does that have to do with anything?" I look over my shoulder at Greta, who stands just behind the couch I'm on. Maybe she knows more than the Devil.

Perhaps I should be asking her.

"I just wonder if you're perhaps unworthy of her," his snipped comment draws my attention away from the older woman.

I try not to let it show on my face how much that hurts. "You're... probably right."

"*Hmm.*" He narrows his eyes at me as if he can see if I'm telling the truth. "Let's skip all the posturing. You want her alive. I want her alive. That is your only priority now: keeping her alive. Is that something you think you can handle?"

"Of course," I don't hesitate to answer. If the Devil wants me to be Valencia's personal bodyguard, I'll do whatever it takes to make sure she stays alive. I've already been doing that; it doesn't really matter that the Devil thinks it's his idea now. It's probably better that way, actually.

That does bring one thing to mind. "You said you don't want her to die—that you want me to protect her. If that's the case, then who sent Davgus?"

"Who?" he asks, taking a sip from his tumbler. He looks down at his nails as though bored.

"Davgus. He's a mid-level demon. He possessed one of the humans and then tried to kill me. Apparently, he has poor aim." Everything's a blur, but it's hard to forget how Davgus threw that angelic feather at me.

"I think his aim was pretty good, actually," the Devil says, looking down at my chest.

I can still feel a slight burn there, but it's low enough that I can think through the pain. I rub my chest, my palm meeting warm skin where the feather ripped through my shirt. I can't understand why he'd say Davgus had good aim. Clearly, he missed, or I wouldn't be here.

"Regardless, you say you want me to protect her. Why now? Why send Davgus to kill me and then turn around and tell me to protect her?"

"And where is this Davgus now?" The temperature in the room starts to plummet, and even though there's a fire in the fireplace, I start to see my breath puffing in the air in front of me. The devil's anger manifests in many ways, and this happens to be my least favorite. It gets so cold, so fast, that I can feel my fingers and toes become numb as frostbite starts to set in.

The question throws me off. If the Devil sent Davgus, why would he be angry about me asking about it? Why would he ask where Davgus was in the first place?

Did someone *else* send Davgus?

I replay the memory of it all in my head, trying to piece everything together.

The other angel had taken off before I got there, so I never saw his face. There were a few people who had been knocked out, lying in a pile on the ground while another guy stood over them. I didn't pay them any attention; an angel's sedation wasn't harmful in any way, even for humans. I only saw the immediate danger. Dumah.

I was so distracted by my fight with Dumah that I completely missed Davgus being there. He must've possessed the man at some point during the fight. I hadn't noticed that he wasn't a man at all. I didn't see him grab Dumah's feather, that I had so carelessly tossed to the side and, by the time I did, Valencia's friend was already dead at her feet.

I'll never forget the sound of her despair. Before I could beg her to stop, she charged Davgus.

He smiled that ugly smile as she rushed him. Even in a human body, Davgus couldn't hide his fucked-up smile.

When he readied his arm with the feather in his hand, I thought she was done for but, instead of her, I watched the feather launch from his hand and fly wide. Too wide. I was looking at the back of her head when it struck me. A flash of white was my only warning before pain engulfed my entire chest, crippling me to my knees. The pain was blinding, but there was also relief. Relief that it was me and not her.

In my mind, I begged her to fight back—to not let him win.

"She ripped his face in half," I whisper quietly, more to myself than anything. "He had her by the hair, and she ripped his jaw clean off his face."

I remember the way her clawed hands were covered in blood as she cradled me in her arms. Angels shouldn't have claws. They *couldn't* have claws. The ability to shift like that was a Hellspawn trait, not a trait of Heaven. She's not only part angel but also part something else—something *more*—which puts her in so much more danger.

"Not dead, then. But it will still take him a while to recover," The Devil's sharp tone pulls me out of my thoughts. "I can't wait to meet this Davgus."

I don't mention the claws to him or my thoughts on what it might mean. I'm not sure what he knows, and I don't want to give too much away. He says he wants her alive, but I still don't trust what he means by that—there's too much hidden behind everything he says and does for him to ever truly be trusted. And he still hasn't mentioned our bargain or her soul.

Getting back to her is my number one priority. I have no idea how long I've been knocked out, so who knows what's happened to her in that time. I think through our conversation, picking apart any details I might've missed before.

"When I was waking up, Greta said you sent Valencia *back* to Earth. She was here?" I ask him, standing to my full height. I feel a burning sting in my chest as I stretch, but I ignore it.

"She was."

"Why was she here?" I demand, uncomfortable with her having been so close to the Devil without me there to protect her.

"She had to be. For the exchange," he responds matter-of-factly. His tone is snarky, as if I'm the idiot here.

"What exchange?" I press, confusion and fear warring inside me.

He also stands up, setting his tumbler on the small table beside the couch. He steps closer to me, lifting his hand to hover a finger over the rip in my shirt. His finger doesn't touch my skin, but it's close—too close. I don't know what his intentions are. He could cure me a thousand times over with one touch or send me to a thousand different locations—different realms, if he wished. Regardless, I hold still.

"Did you know an angel feather to the heart is fatal for a demon? Some would even say, *deadly*." The Devil smirks at me.

"I don't know—" I start, but he interrupts me.

"Ask her what price she paid in return for your life," he smiles viciously before slamming his finger against my chest and catapulting me from his room, then from Hell entirely.

CHAPTER 42
CORVUS

I HATE WHEN THE Devil forces realm travel on me like that. It's always more disorienting than when I do it myself. It's a sick game he loves to play, he can send someone anywhere, but he can't leave Hell himself.

It only takes me a couple of seconds to realize he's sent me to the same little cabin Valencia and I stayed in before. It's dark here, the night sky offering little light through the front windows. A small fire burns in the fireplace, but it's just about puttered out. A brown jacket is flung over the back of the couch and a pair of jeans lie crumpled on the floor.

I silently approach the bed. A lump lays under the covers, cuddled down as far as it can go. She must have gotten cold as the fire slowly went out. My fingers itch to rip the covers off her body, to prove to my eyes that she's really there but, instead, I step away, focusing on rebuilding the fire. I need time to cool the anger pulsing through my veins. Since I've been awake, my blood has done nothing but burn.

Burn with pain, burn with fear, and, now, burn with anger.

The Devil's ominous words keep echoing around in my brain. *'Price she paid for your life,'* he said. I can't even focus on being happy that I'm alive because all I can think about is what she had to do to achieve it. Nothing with the Devil comes free.

After I've thoroughly stoked the fire and made sure the door and both windows are locked, I walk back to the bed, taking a moment to just look at the lump that lies there. I run through scenarios of how I want this to play out in my head and hope some patience will let the anger burn itself away so I can confront her with a less. . . vicious emotion.

The angry side of me, the true demon, wants to rip the covers away, bare her ass, and spank her so many times her ass cheeks burn as hot as my chest does. It's a lingering pain that's a constant reminder of what happened, and the worst part is I don't even know what happened.

The other side of me just wants to crawl into the bed, drag her into my arms, bury my nose in her neck, and be grateful that we're here. Be thankful that she's *alive*. If the Devil is telling the truth, and I died on that mountain, then she was alone with Dumah, who could've easily killed her. Then she was alone with the Devil—who could've also easily killed her. And though he says he doesn't want her dead I can't tell how much of that is actual truth because it's undeniable that one of the Devil's minions was sent after us.

The lump of covers starts rustling until I see a single, bare foot stick out before settling again. It's starting to get warm in here, and she sheds some of the quilted layers she hides under. Another foot pops out; now both her legs are uncovered from the calf down. Didn't anyone tell her not to stick her foot off the bed or the demon lurking underneath would eat it?

With a growl I can't contain, I grip one ankle tightly while throwing the covers off of her completely. All she's wearing is a loose shirt and a pair of panties, but I don't let the sight distract me. She squeals, pulling at her ankle, but my grip is too tight for her to take it from me. She starts scrambling back across the bed but I follow her, kneeling on the mattress and trapping one of her legs between my own.

I can see a sleepy haze tinging her eyes, so she doesn't notice it's me yet. The leg that's stuck between my thighs jerks a couple of times and a sharp sting radiates from my hip.

"Your claws can't hurt me," I snarl at her. It's a lie, it hurts like a bitch, but it's nothing I can't handle. I have more pressing matters to attend to, like spanking her for whatever she's done.

She instantly freezes, no longer thrashing against me. She leaves her little claws in my leg but uses her other hand to wipe the sleep from her eyes. "Corvus?"

"Were you expecting someone else?" I purr, the angry gravel in my veins leaving me as soon as she whispers my name.

"You're here?" She jerks upright, patting her hands down my chest and sides. When she notices the small tears in my shirt, she gasps. "Oh fuck, I hurt you."

"It's nothing," and I mean it. The scratches will heal in no time, and there's too much on my mind to focus on the little bit of pain it caused me.

She starts to squirm around again, pulling at her ankle and jerking her thigh around between my legs. I'm sure she can't tell, but her thigh brushes the crotch of my pants multiple times in her attempt to escape. The rough denim of my jeans drags across the sensitive skin each time, instantly causing my dick to swell. How weak I am that I get hard at the brush of her *thigh*. It doesn't help that she isn't wearing a bra, so her boobs have been rolling around in her shirt, nipples pressed against the soft fabric. Still, I've got to get control of my cock, because I need my brain to have a conversation with her.

"I'm glad you fought back when you didn't know it was me, but now that you do, I need you to hold still."

"I just want to make sure you're okay," she snaps, wiggling her thigh even harder to try to slip away from me. It's almost cute how her attitude always finds a way to come out, no matter the situation. For some reason, that snarky mouth of hers makes my dick even harder. If I don't get control of her soon, we'll never get to the conversation part of tonight.

I use my free hand to press down on her chest, right at the center. The sides of my hand brush against each boob, forcing me to grit my teeth against the groan that wants to escape. She allows me to firmly push her down onto the mattress, not hard enough that she can't breathe, but with enough pressure that she can't wiggle around anymore.

"What did you give the Devil in exchange for my life?"

"My soul," she says without the barest hint of hesitation, as if it's no big deal. As if she didn't literally sign her life—her entire existence—away to Hell.

That is exactly what I didn't want to happen. She was supposed to be able to *choose*. I've spent all this time and effort making sure the choice didn't get taken away from her and then I had to go and die.

I let this happen. The beautiful brightness of her soul is now forever tied to the darkness that is Hell.

"Why the fuck would you do that?" I growl at her.

"Because I was trying to save your ungrateful ass! You died in my arms! I had to do something. Dumah wouldn't help. He told me the only way to save you was to beg the Devil for your life, so I did. Tucker was already gone; I couldn't lose you, too." She's growling, her blunt words as sharp as knives.

The way she chokes the words out at the end, tears evident in her voice, guts me. I do sound ungrateful, demanding that she explain why she did what she did without thinking of what else she experienced.

I saw her friend die. I heard the anguish in her scream as she ran to his body. Davgus had already hit me with the feather but I remember the pain that radiated from her, even as she tore his jaw off. From there, everything became blurry. I didn't know she held me as I died. I didn't know, so I ripped the truth from her instead of being there to support her and comfort her in her grief. Even though I'm back, her friend is still gone.

The Devil's right. I don't deserve her. "I'm so fucking sorry," is all I can say as I let her go and start pulling away.

"Fuck you!"

I don't see her foot flying toward my chest but she hits me dead center, just to the side of my still-healing heart. It's like being burned by a thousand suns, but I don't let it knock me back. I deserve anything and everything she throws my way. I lean back on my knees and finally allow her to scramble out from under me. She also rises to her knees, pointing an angry finger at me.

"You don't get to do that. You don't get to make me feel bad for the choices I make. News flash, I already feel shitty enough! But you know what, it was *my* soul to give. Who are you to make me feel bad for that? Can you honestly say you wouldn't have saved me if the roles were reversed?" She's flinging her hands around in big movements and poking me in the chest again. Thankfully, her claws are gone, so it's just the blunt, human tip.

"I never wanted you to have to give it away—not unless it was your choice. I wanted to prevent your soul being taken from you before you knew the consequences," I plead, my voice soft now.

She stares at me down in that way of hers. Drowning me in the blue of her eyes. "I may not have known the consequence, Corvus, but you dying wasn't something I could live with."

"There's just so much you still don't know," I murmur, all the fight leaving my body.

"Then you'll just have to explain along the way. You promised to help me find the truth about all this. I'm still holding you to that," she asserts, the demand evident in her tone. If she had her way, she'd demand every truth out of me and I'd rip my chest open to spill every secret for her.

Just—maybe not yet. She's been through an immense amount of trauma, and the last thing I want to do is dump more onto her plate. There's already so much to deal with. Everything else can wait, at least until she figures out what giving up her soul really means.

"I will personally hunt down every mystery myself." *I would do anything for you.*

Chapter 43

Valencia

We kneel on the bed, facing each other as though in a Mexican standoff. He slumps too much to look confident, and I'm too short to be intimidating, I stare into his dark chocolate eyes as they stare back just as intensely. His eyes are alive, full of a multitude of emotions—some I can recognize and others I can't. His full lips are pursed into a serious expression, like he's afraid if he lets go of his stress, this moment will disappear.

All I can think about is how I just want to strangle him. Wrap my fingers around his neck and shake some fucking sense into him. How dare he die. How dare he put my heart through something like that.

Even if it wasn't his fault, being angry at him is easier than focusing on how it all made me feel. How the thought of him dying ripped my soul out, so giving it away to the Devil hadn't seemed like anything of consequence.

I also want to strangle him with my thighs. Grab a fist full of the wild hair at the top of his forehead and force his mouth straight to my clit. Make him beg *her* for forgiveness, too. I don't think I've ever craved his touch more than I do right now; my body burns. From every fiber of hair, to every muscle, to every drop of blood that pounds through my veins. I want him. I *need* him, and that need ignites a primal hunger inside me that blazes with relentless fury.

I want to suffocate him between my thighs so he can't do anything but beg my pussy for forgiveness. With his mouth, and teeth, and tongue. God, the things he can do with his tongue. Just the memory of what he did to me with his mouth on this very bed starts driving me closer and closer to insanity. If something doesn't release this fire, I won't be held liable for burning the whole place down.

I see his nostrils flare wide, chest rising. "Valencia," he growls in warning, top lip twitching with discomfort. The hair around his mouth is dark and wiry and I want nothing more than to feel the burn it will leave behind on the soft parts of my thighs.

I start moving around, about to stand. I don't know if this bed can actually handle that, but I don't give a fuck and do it anyway. Corvus still kneels, ass pressed against his heels, and his shoulders still slumped in defeat, though there's a new tension in him now. I wobble slightly as I rise, the springs below me wiggling as I shift my weight, but large hands instantly grip my hips and squeeze lightly to steady me. He doesn't move them any further.

That's okay. It's my turn to be in control. All the times we've been intimate, he's been leading the charge, calling the shots—all give and no take. Well, I'm done. I'm in a taking mood and I plan to take exactly what I want. I realize now that this is what the Devil meant when she sent me back to Earth.

Once settled, I look down at him. I sort of tower over him now, his head right at the junction of my thighs. He looks up at me with such longing in his eyes that I almost change my mind, take the sweet approach, and bask in his arms. I cup the side of his face with one hand, needing to touch him. He leans into my palm, beard pressing against the soft skin there, his cheek hot to the touch. His eyelids flutter like they might close, but he manages to keep them open.

The thought of cuddling into his arms and curling into his heat makes my knees weak. I want him badly, it's true, but this is really what I *needed*—this connection. This is proof that he's real, that he's here, and that he's alive. He licks his lips as he looks at me but doesn't say a word, just leans further into my touch, nuzzling his nose into the inside of my wrist and inhaling deeply.

Each breath he takes brings me immense joy, but it also stokes my anger. Reminds me that there was a point not so long ago when I held him, and he didn't take a breath. Couldn't.

I slide my fingers through his hair, slowly pushing through small tangles in his curls. At the gentle touch, his eyes finally flutter closed and, as soon as he takes his eyes off me, I grip his hair tightly and pull the strands through my fingers hard enough that I know they pull painfully at his scalp.

He growls through the pain, eyes flashing open at the sting. Long fingers bite into my hips in warning. He still doesn't speak but narrows his eyes as we look at each other.

"I want you to understand something. If you ever try to die on me again, I will hunt you down, bring you back to life, and kill you myself." It's a cliché threat—unoriginal and not something I thought I'd ever be saying—but I cannot live through him dying a second time. I refuse.

He nods, but it's a slight movement since my fingers are still buried in his hair. "And your mouth has a lot of making up to do for all the seconds I had to watch it not breathe," I snap, tugging just a little harder.

He licks his lower lip, the muscles in his neck flexing and releasing. I'm tempted to lean down and kiss him but I hold back. I feel like the sweet kiss I'm envisioning in my head would ruin the boss bitch energy I'm trying to throw around right now. I need him to know how serious I am.

"My life is only yours to take from now on," he proclaims reverently and it's enough to satisfy the fearfully angry beast that recoils at the thought of his death. His soft, open smile slowly becomes a scowl as his eyes darken. "And there's something you should understand, too."

"What?" I pant at the gravel that's returned. I can hear the vibrations coming from his throat.

"Enjoy this control you have over me while you can because it won't last long." Now he's full-on growling and, though he agreed to let me be in control, just the thought of what that means for later floods my panties. I want to moan at the way his voice crawls over me but I have to remain stoically in control or I'll lose all the power I have.

I don't question him and demand what I want. "Undress me."

He smirks but listens. Soft cotton glides over my shoulders as he pulls my sleep shirt from my body, tossing it to the side. His hands instantly cover my waist and my skin pebbles from the chill in the air. It's beginning to heat up, but it's nothing compared to the heat his skin can provide.

He slides his hands up an inch. Then another. He doesn't take his eyes off me as he slowly glides his rough palms up my sides and cups the side of each boob, swiping his thumbs across my nipples, once, twice. He goes for a third, his eyes finally drifting down to my chest, but I smack one of his forearms lightly. The loud snap echoes in the room and he jerks his attention back up to me. His brows scrunch down tightly but his pupils are blown, so I know he's not unaffected. Anger isn't the only thing he's feeling. He said I should enjoy having control, which I intend to do.

"I said your mouth," I ordered.

He takes a deep breath, shoulders rising with tension. I realize then how hard it is for him to relinquish control. *Well, too bad.* Maybe he'll think about this before nearly getting himself killed again.

Just when I think he's going to refuse, he leans forward and swallows my right nipple, sucking instantly. The wet heat of his tongue, as it rubs against the bud quickly, makes my knees grow weak. I start to straighten back up but he clamps my nipple tightly between his teeth until blood rushes into it, causing it to swell. Then he flicks his tongue back and forth across the swollen, sensitive button.

I can't keep the moan from escaping me. It feels so good, so sinful. Corvus devours my nipple, abusing it with pain to the point of pleasure. While he worships my right nipple with his mouth, he uses his other hand to squeeze and pinch my left into a similarly swollen state. His eyes don't leave mine once, nor does he stop to breathe or do anything other than worship my body.

An especially painful pinch buckles my knees but he lets go of my nipple and catches me before I'm able to fall. I wobble a little, relying on his strength to hold me while I regain my balance. I never thought I'd be someone who enjoyed nipple play that much but there's something about his eagerness to please me sends that burning fire in my blood to collect at my center. My clit pulses with each brush and sting of pain.

My nipple pops out of his mouth in my stumble so, now that I'm standing again, he's dragging his lips across my stomach, kissing as he goes. He's no longer looking at me, but I don't punish him for it this time. He clamps down on the skin under my right boob and sucks viciously.

I groan. I know he's leaving a mark, teeth drawing my blood to the surface of my skin. There will undoubtedly be a hickey there now but I don't mind. I'm so consumed by lust that I think I'd let him mark me anywhere.

He starts dragging his mouth down further, switching between painfully sweet kisses and burying his nose into me and taking deep breaths. I never thought of my stomach as being an erogenous zone but, somehow, it's driving me just as crazy as when his mouth was wrecking my nipple.

Corvus pulls his mouth away from my body after placing a light kiss right at the hem of my panties. They're nothing special—plain, light blue, and honestly a little too big.

Parker refused to grab anything from my underwear drawer when he packed me a small bag of clothes and said it was crossing some weird line a little too much for him. I told him it was all clean, but he said it was too much—so he ran into the store on our way here and bought me new stuff. One of those assorted designs packs. They're all plain colors and have more coverage than I'd typically wear, no lace or frills or anything that could be deemed sexy.

So, he basically got me granny panties. Too big ones at that, but I didn't really care. I was just happy to have something clean to put on after the scorching shower I took earlier.

They're ruined now, of course. My arousal soaked the gusset to a point where I could feel the cool dampness press against my feverish skin. And, who cares if they're not sexy if they're just going to be taken off, anyway? Corvus doesn't seem to mind as he looks at the light blue material and then back up at me. His face is right there, mere inches away. It's close enough that I swear I can feel each exhale drift across my skin. He stares at me, squeezing his hands a little tighter. My knees start to shake again, so I lock them and hope it's enough to keep me standing through whatever he has planned.

He sticks out his tongue, not taking his eyes off me once, pressing it flat and leaning forward slowly. So achingly slow that the tremor in my knees travels through my whole leg. He presses his flat tongue right on my clit and then slowly starts to turn his head from side to side. His hands pull my body even tighter against his face, the pressure is so intense that I can't control my legs from starting to shake even more.

I place my hand on the back of his head to steady myself and try to stay standing as long as possible. It's almost turned into a challenge. How long can I last? How soon can he bring me to my knees?

His tongue against my cotton-covered pussy is more torture than pleasure. I can barely feel the heat of his mouth, but it's too muted to enjoy fully. And, though the pressure feels excellent, I want more. So much more.

"Take them off," I command. I had hoped it would sound strong and stern but what comes out of my mouth is little more than a breathy plea. I'm already giving in; it's only a matter of time now. The muscle under his left eye twitches and he pulls his face away, causing me to whimper at the loss. He smirks briefly, but it goes so fast I know he's making an effort to hide it.

He slips his finger through the front of my panties, in one leg hole and out the other. Then he grips the fabric tightly and lifts his hand toward my stomach, pulling the fabric into a small, thin line that rubs right across my clit. The damp gusset presses against the sensitive nerves, causing it to pulse.

There's a defiant look in his eyes as he tortures me with my own panties and I have to press a hand onto his shoulder so I don't collapse. The fabric rubs up and down with each pulse. My pussy weeps; I can feel the cool dampness rub between my thighs. I moan out a plea for relief.

He finally yanks the fabric away, ripping it from my body. The waistband burns against my back as the fabric tears apart from the front. Somehow, the waistband doesn't rip off, so it just hangs low around my hips.

I stumble at the sharp tug but use my hands to steady myself. He growls, baring his teeth as the hand buried in his hair tugs his head back. I don't feel bad; my back burns where the hem rubbed fiercely, so I'm sure I'll have a mark there, too.

He drops my torn panties and reaches up to pull my fingers from his hair. Once free, he sweeps his other arm behind my knees and I drop down onto my back. He still has my legs and my knees are hooked over his forearm as his hand wraps around to grip my shin.

On his knees, he rises to his full height, pulling my legs up a little higher so the lower part of my back lifts off the bed. Then, he releases one leg, hooking it around his waist. I jerk as the motion spreads me completely open. Cool air rushes between my legs, causing the wetness around my pussy to chill. I try to pull my other leg from his arm but he's got such a tight grip on it that it barely moves. I want to squeeze my legs together, but they're being firmly spread wide between his hip and arm.

A sharp sting flares through my clit as he slaps his fingertips right onto the swollen nub. It's debasing and erotic at the same time. I also think it means I've finally lost control.

"Fuck," I moan out loud.

"Don't move," he grumbles.

Now that I'm not trying to pull away, his fingers rub slow, hard circles around my clit. My eyes roll into the back of my head and darkness engulfs me. My head tips back onto the mattress as my hands clamp around the soft, quilted covers.

The way his fingers work around my clit, so steady and consistent, I might get off from them alone. Men always give up too quickly when it comes to getting a woman off with clit stimulation, it's like their fingers have ADHD and refuse to stay in one spot. *Right there* never means move elsewhere or change pace—but they haven't figured that out yet. Part of me wishes he'd move his fingers and plunge them inside me, but what he's doing now is also causing that burning heat to build; if he just kept it up a little longer, I know I could come just by this alone.

My pussy flutters, begging to be filled. "Inside me," I groan the demand.

He lifts his fingers to land another sharp smack against my clit and my whole body jackknifes off the bed at the sharp sting. The whimper that leaves my mouth would make a pornstar horny.

He smiles viciously at the sound, knowing exactly how much he's torturing me. "You're not in charge anymore."

"Please," I beg, moaning loudly.

"That's better," he purrs.

He finally drags his fingers away from my sensitive clit to rub circles around my wet entrance. His fingers glide through the folds, rubbing and pressing but never entering. How he continues to find new ways to give me what I want while still torturing me is as frustrating as it is pleasing.

"Corvus, please, inside me." My voice is now just a mix of breathy moans and vibrating groans. I look back into his dark gaze, pleading with my eyes.

He smirks, giving me a dark look. Finally, the tip of one finger slides inside; a single inch. Swirling around briefly before pulling back out.

"No," I groan. The way he denies me is becoming borderline painful.

More gliding, and then two fingertips slip through the wetness to slide inside me. Two inches. He swirls them around, then curls them forward, pressing against the front while sliding them slowly back out.

"No. More. Oh go—*agh*!" I moan at the withdrawal, but then he slams them fully inside, cutting my words off and turning them into a garbled mess. It feels so good to finally be filled but the intrusive stretch burns slightly. The last time he touched me this way, he was much more gentle. I haven't had more than two fingers inside me for so long that my pussy burns at the forceful intrusion. Not that I don't enjoy the rough treatment. My body wants it. Clearly, the dripping wetness is trying to prepare me for much more.

"Do *not* call to God. He can't save you from me," Corvus snaps, plunging his fingers back in and my inner walls clamp around his fingers.

"Corvus, please, I need more."

I'm so close. Between the stretching punishment and the clit abuse, I'm right on the edge. Just *one more finger*, and I'll tip right over.

"Good girl," he hums, groaning as my pussy walls anchor down even more. "So fucking tight."

I thought I needed another finger but it seems I just needed a little praise. The tidal wave of pleasure that's been building starts to crest, just barely tipping me over into bliss.

I gasp. "Fuck," I breathe, stretching the vowel out as I groan. "I'm—" I'm right there, so close I can feel my clit pulsing in preparation.

He rips his fingers out of me so fast I barely feel them slip out. My walls clamp down, but there was nothing to hold.

"No, please, I was right there. Please, Corvus, I need to come!" I beg him in earnest now. It's the worst torture he's given and I feel more than edged; I feel ripped in half. My body shakes at the pressure, sitting on the cusp of release.

He grips my thigh tightly, the one hitched in the crook of his arm and smacks a hand down on the other, just under my ass cheek. I gasp at the sting.

"You're not coming until your pussy is wrapped around my cock," he growls as the hand he just smacked me with goes flying to the zipper of his pants. He drags it down and then hooks his fingers around the waistband and pushes both his pants and boxers down his thighs. The edge of his shirt covers him from my view, making me growl. I want to see him, too. In my haste to feel his mouth on me, I got distracted from having him undress and I'm paying for it now.

"Your shirt, too." I plead. He looks at me sharply but obeys, dragging one hand behind his head to rip the dark material up and off.

I suck in gasp. He is fucking beautiful—all corded muscle and tan skin and dark, swirling, tattooed masterpieces that are cut apart with bright white scars. His chest is dusted in dark hair that covers rippling muscles. I follow the hair down his chest to the dips at his hip. He's not too lean, and there is a thick bulkiness about him that makes my mouth water. Right there in the middle of his sexy Adonis belt is the biggest cock I've ever seen. It points up, freed from the confinement of his jeans. The skin is the same tan as the rest of him but the tip is slightly red, as if swollen and angry. It pulses as I stare, the vein on the underside flexing.

It looks thick—far thicker than two fingers—and I wonder how it will ever fit inside me. I may be wetter than a swimming pool but that looks dangerous. It will rip me in half. It's long, but not too long. He can stretch me wide, but I can't magically get deeper.

This is the kind of dick that I know will ruin me from all others in the future. My pussy starts fluttering all over again, begging to be filled.

He wraps a large hand around the thick base, forearm flexing as he squeezes tight. He groans, sliding his fist up the shaft to the tip, which makes it even redder as precum leaks out. I moan again at the sight. Seeing him weeping for me makes all my lady bits ravenous for more.

"I need you," I whimper softly, which causes him to groan.

"Fuck," He spits through gritted teeth. The hand that's wrapped around my thigh drags me even closer and he starts sliding the tip through my folds. It feels so good, yet it's nowhere near enough.

He rubs the tip around my clit a few times before tapping it twice. The little taps cause my hips to spasm each time, and he slowly starts dragging it down towards my entrance.

"W-wait," I stumble through the words. He pauses instantly, but I can feel the hand around my thigh shaking.

"If you don't want this, I swear I will stop right now," he chokes out. He doesn't move or continue to rub his swollen tip against me, though I can tell the restraint causes him pain. It's comforting to know he'd stop if I wanted. I think about prolonging the torture to get back at him for edging me earlier.

"I have an IUD, but what if. . ." I huff, trying to force the awkward words out. It's never a conversation anyone wants to have but I have to bring it up before we continue. "What if your demon sperm gets me pregnant? I do *not* want a demon child right now." With everything going on, it's just not something I want to have to worry about. Not anytime soon, at least. Maybe one day in the far, *far* distant future.

"Honey, an IUD is good enough or we can use condoms," he responds seriously. He doesn't look away from my eyes. I can tell he doesn't want to stop but I'm glad he's willing to take this at my pace.

"I want you to fuck me. Bare," I tell him, hoping he can hear the severity in my tone. Knowing there's no risk. "I don't want anything else between us."

"I can't wait to watch your pretty pink pussy weep with my cum," he growls in that animalistic way of his before pulling our bodies flush together. Using one hand on the crook of my hip, he drags my pelvis up and down his length and his hard shaft slides through my wet folds. He pulls back slightly to wrap a hand around himself once again. As much as I enjoy watching him touch himself, I need him too badly right now to watch. Just as I'm about to beg him to get on with it, he leans his head down, rolling his lips.

He spits onto his cock, rubbing the moisture in with his hand. I know he was already wet from sliding around in my arousal but somehow the usually degrading action makes me burn hotter. My pussy squeezes tightly in anticipation.

"Are you ready, Honey?" he asks softly, dragging his tip back to my entrance and pausing to look at me.

"Please," I nod my head vigorously.

He slowly pushes his hips forward, and I feel the intrusion instantly. I stretch open with just the tip and moan at the feeling. It's too much and not enough all at the same time. He slowly pulls out completely before shoving back in a little farther.

"You're so fucking tight," he enunciates each word with every thrust of his hips, continuing the soft drag and rough plunge, slipping further inside me each time.

It's the best kind of torture.

My hips and legs shake with each thrust and he slides in again, rougher this time, forcing my pussy to stretch around the thickest part of him.

He pulls out again, stopping with just the tip inside me, before sliding all the way in until our hips meet. Absolute rapture.

"Fuck," he groans, his hands shaking as he holds us tightly together.

It takes a second for me to get used to his size but, finally, the burn of the tight stretch transforms to warmth. Heat builds in my lower stomach, climbing back until I'm where I was before. I'm not going to last long, he feels too good. He's thick, hitting spots inside me I didn't know could be reached.

"I'm going to move, okay?" he warns, voice a gravely mess.

I nod my head in response, my own moan slipping out.

"Take a deep breath for me, Baby," he murmurs.

I do, filling my lungs with as much air as they can. He slowly pulls out as I start to exhale, then thrusts back in at the same speed—just a constant back and forth. There's no more burning from adjusting to his size; now it's just heat that gathers in my stomach and makes my clit pulse.

Without me having to ask, he starts speeding up, pushing in harder with each thrust. The bed frame rattles with the force. My back pressed into the mattress firmly. The rough denim of his jeans hangs loosely around his thick thighs, rubbing against the underside of my legs each time we come together.

He uses the hand on my hip to pull my body into each thrust and the tip rubs through the most sensitive parts inside me at this angle. I'm getting close, that intense feeling building all over again.

I watch his body flex each time he pushes himself inside me, and his abs roll with the motion, shoulders rounded as his muscles strain. The slight dampness to his skin shines in the ambient light from the fire. It's hot now, the heat of our bodies mingling with the warm air around us and each place our skin touches burns with such intensity that I wonder if we will both be permanently marked by it.

He keeps thrusting with a steady roughness, ramping my body up higher and higher. He tilts my hips up a little more, tightening his grip.

"*Hmm.* Oh. Oh, my G—*agh*!" I squeal out as a sharp sting radiates from my clit.

"Don't fucking say it," he doesn't elaborate. We both know what he means.

It's not like I'm actually trying to call out to the real God. It's just a word that's tumbling out of my mouth, so I can't help the snark that slips out. "Fuck you."

He pounds into me a little harder, punishing me for the almost slip and for the attitude. I'm not mad; it all feels so good. My clit aches something fierce, pulsing nearly as hard. I need to come soon, or I'm going to explode.

"You have such a pretty pussy, all pink and wet," he slams in a few more times as if to emphasize his statement. "But such a nasty little mouth, I can't wait to fuck it."

His growled words, and the thought of him stretching my jaw wide as he slips into my mouth pushes me right to the edge. I moan loudly—a mix between a gasp and a whimper—and start to beg. My pussy clamps down, forcing him to fuck me harder.

"Fuck. Fuck. Fuck," he groans in a dark whimper of his own. He grits his teeth into a snarl, looking down at our joined bodies. It feels like he's gotten larger, but I think it's because my body squeezes so tightly. A flood of new arousal rushes out of me, making his thrust clap against my skin each time he slams forward. The burning sensation builds so high that every cell in my body catches fire. I tense, my stomach flexing and my back arching more off the bed.

It only takes three more thrusts before I implode. The tidal wave tips over, and I come so hard I see stars dancing in my eyes. Pain scores through the arches of my feet as my toes curl. He slowly thrusts through it, praising me with each one though he can barely move through the tight channel that's wrapped around him. I jerk a few more times, coming down from the blissful high and feel him pulse and flex inside me. Each movement causes my body to jerk. I'm so much more sensitive now that I swear I can feel the vein on the underside of his rubbing against me.

"You did so good, Baby. You're so fucking sexy when you come," he praises me in a soft purr, not stopping his slow thrust once. I whimper at the slight pain. I'm thoroughly stretched to his size but I am so sensitive that every movement sends shocks through my body.

I start to loosen back up so he's able to slide further in and out. I shudder. I've never come so hard in my life. I am completely ruined. I look down to where our bodies meet to see that he's still sliding in and out languidly. He's not as rough or forceful as he was earlier but he's still as hard as a brick, forcing his thick shaft in with little effort.

It's so wet down there that my slickness glistens against our skin and I shiver at the sight, lust creeping back in as the tidal wave builds anew.

"Come here," he murmurs, letting go of my hip and leg to wrap both arms around me, lifting me easily. He's inside me the whole time, so the shifting presses his hardness into new places, causing another moan to be ripped out of me. I wrap my legs around his waist, pulling us even closer.

"I'm not done with you yet," he purrs as if hearing my thoughts.

CHAPTER 44

CORVUS

IT TOOK EVERYTHING IN me not to come—not to blow my entire load inside her on the first thrust. She was so hot and slick. And, then, watching her fall apart—how her head tipped back in ecstasy—really tested my restraint. I've never felt something so life-changing. Sex has never felt like anything other than a quick release but this was euphoria. Pushing through her folds as she came around my cock was otherworldly.

I wrap my hands beneath her ass, dragging her onto me. This angle somehow feels deeper. She clamps around me again, causing my hips to jerk. I'm so fucking close. I want to make her come again but I don't know if I'll last. I've been harder than a fucking rock for so long, I'm afraid that any movement will make me blow.

Her legs wrap themselves tighter around my waist, heels digging into my ass. She's a greedy little thing, that's for sure, clamping down on my cock every time I pull out.

I sit back on my heels, letting gravity help push her down on me. I put one hand on the back of her head and drag her lips to mine. Her lips part with a sigh, granting me access to slowly fuck her mouth with my tongue. I roll my own against hers, feeling the warm wetness of her mouth, so similar to her pussy. So greedy and eager to please.

She moans into my mouth, holding me tightly to her body as she kisses me just as fiercely. Her pussy flexes, tightening its hold on me and reminding me that, even though I fill her, it's not enough. My dick flexes, twitching up into that spongey sensitive spot at the front and she squirms, trying to find her own relief without breaking our kiss. I lower my hand back down to her ass and lift her up till just the tips remain inside of her, then slowly let her fall back down. It's provocative and drives me absolutely insane.

She starts to kiss me with frantic urgency like she knows she won't be able to for much longer. She bites down on my bottom lip hard and pain shoots through me, making my cock jump. I growl, forcing her hips to slam down on me hard. She is so wet that our skin claps together with a loud snap.

She tips her head back, moaning loudly to the ceiling as her legs start to shake. She's already close again. Her insides tremor as fiercely as she does on the outside. I lean down and suck on her skin at the base of her neck, continuing to pull her against me with hard thrusts. It draws a whimpering moan out of her and I feel it vibrate through her neck against my lips.

Fuck, I want to feel that around my cock but I can't—not right now. I can't do anything other than slam her body down onto me. I'm *right there*. Every time she clamps down onto me, my balls tighten up and beg for release.

"Fuck, Corvus, I'm right there," she groans, the words patchy from her heightened desire. I bite down on the muscle at the crook of her neck and slam her down onto me one, two, three times before her pussy wraps my dick in a vice and she comes all over me for a second time. She's so tight it's hard to thrust, so I pull her hips closer against me and roll her body up and down.

She screams through her release, her entire body shaking, and I can't hold back any longer. I release the bite I have on her so I don't accidentally tear her skin and bring our lips together once again—and then I bust so fucking hard my body curls around her, jerking multiple times with each spurt. She instantly becomes a sloppy mess, our combined arousal slipping between us to drip down onto my thighs.

We slowly kiss through it until we rest our foreheads together, sharing each inhale and exhale.

She twitches around me, legs flexing against my side. I'm still hard, just not as much as before, so I slip around inside her. More cum gets pushed out, now cool as it drops on my skin and I groan low in my throat. I'm still sensitive, so every move she makes is like a tiny bit of torture.

When I can't take it any longer, I slowly lift her off me. We both groan in unison as our skin glides together one last time. My cock slips out of her, slapping against my thigh and I jerk slightly at the impact.

I then wrap my arms around her and slip off the bed, rising to my feet. My knees wobble, but I force my legs to move anyway.

"What are you doing?" she murmurs into the side of my neck. She's still wrapped around me and her arms hold on tightly while her ankles barely remain locked in the middle of my back. Now that I'm standing, she's higher up on my chest, so her short legs just about reach around my waist. It doesn't matter, though, I've got a good hold on her and I don't plan on letting her go anytime soon.

I make my way to the back of the cabin, stepping into the pristine bathroom. Shifting her weight into one arm, I start the shower, turning it hot. Steam instantly fills the room, so I shut the door to stop it escaping and, once the water reaches a warm enough temperature, I step into the shower. It beats against our sides, slipping between us before dripping down the rest of my legs. She moans softly and warm air is exhaled against my neck. My cock starts to get hard again at the sound.

I ignore it, focusing on holding her under the warm spray. She wiggles around before kissing me softly on the lips, then asks to be put down. Once on her feet, she steps back into the warm spray, closing her eyes as it pours over her head. I can't help but look at her body, so tan against all the white, dark hair hanging down her body. It's so long it hangs well past the peaks of her breasts. Her nipples are still hard, the deep wine color contrasting the cool tile of the bathroom. A light dusting of dark hair grows at the juncture of her legs, as if she trimmed recently.

I wish my body didn't instantly react to the sight of her naked. She was so tight at first, even with my fingers, that I know she's probably sore right now. My brain knows she needs a break, but my dick begs for another round.

She quickly finishes washing her hair, the soap running down her body in the same way I wish my fingers could all over again. She starts to step out of the water to let me under, but I grab her hip and hold her there.

"What?" she asks, looking up at me with those crystalline eyes.

"Let me take care of you," I murmur, cupping my hand so the water pools in my palm. She gives me a confused look, unsure of what I mean. Once there's enough water in my palm, I slowly lift it to her thighs, washing away the evidence of our combined arousal. I repeat this several times, brushing through her folds lightly. She tenses but doesn't comment; definitely too sore for round two. I mean, I didn't really go easy on her. "I was too rough."

I start to pull my hand away, afraid I'm causing more discomfort, when she catches my wrist with her own. "You were rough, but I liked it. Don't stop," she guides my hand back to her center.

"We can't," I lay my hand flat against her pussy and she starts to scowl, probably misinterpreting my meaning as the little she-devil inside of her claws to come out. I continue before I find her little kitten claws shoved into my side. "I don't want to hurt you."

She looks between my eyes, her scowl holding firm. I can see the gears working in her head, thinking too hard so I bring my lips to hers, kissing her deeply before stepping back. I grab one of her hands and use my fingers to wrap it around my dick. It twitches, hardening even further. "I want you. I think I'll want you every second I'm not inside of you, but there's a difference between pleasurable pain and actual pain. So, for now, we're going to finish cleaning up, and then we're going to go to bed."

She rolls her eyes at me and mutters a sassy *'fine'* before stepping around me so I can wash myself off. I hurry through the motions, not wanting her to stand in the cold for too long. She tries to hide her yawn, but I see it.

I flip the water off, wrapping a towel around my waist before grabbing another and drying her off before I do the same to myself. We both use the spare toothbrushes before finally heading out into the room. It's nice and toasty, but I add another log to the fire so it stays burning through the night.

When I reach the bed, she's already curled underneath the covers. I slip in on the other side and pull her body close to mine.

She moves around before finally laying her head down on my chest. "Any bright ideas on how to get us out of this mess?" she asks softly.

I don't answer right away. There's a ton we've yet to figure out, more mysteries to be solved. We still don't know why Dumah urged her to ask the Devil to save me, instead of taking her soul for himself. We have no idea if the Devil will want her back in Hell anytime soon. I don't even know what day it is on Earth. Time moves so differently in Hell. It could've been an hour or months could have passed. I haven't had time to check. Well, I could have—but I had more important things on my mind.

"None at the moment," I say. It's the most honest answer I can give.

"Me neither," she murmurs, sleep heavy in her voice. "We can figure it out tomorrow."

"Thank you."

"For what?" She still sounds sleepy, but awake enough to hear what I say.

I lean up on my elbow. "For saving my life. For giving your soul to the Devil. For being who you are. For trusting me, for a thousand other things—for everything," I ramble, forcing my mouth shut before blurting out too much more. I'm not used to feeling this way.

"Corvus, I would do it all over again." She places her palm against my cheek, and her thumb softly rubs along the edge of my jaw.

"Why?" I mumble into her wrist. I stare at the base of her neck, afraid to look into her eyes. Doubt tries to work its way into my mind, telling me there's no way I'm worthy of her.

"Corvus, I'm sorry, I—"

"I'm falling in love with you," I blurt.

Fuck. What kind of idiot just blurts something like that out? I just couldn't stand to hear her apology or hear her tell me she felt nothing and that what she did for me meant nothing.

There's a pause, and I wait. She's been silent for so long that I almost wonder if she's fallen asleep. Maybe she didn't even hear what I said. I look back to her face to find that her mouth has dropped open—almost like you see in cartoons—and her eyes are wide, the whites pearly even in the dark.

"I'm sorry, I shouldn't have said anything." I start to pull away, sick at the look of panic on her face. I lay back down, putting some distance between us.

"Wait, why?" She leans up on one arm, mirroring the position we were just in.

"I didn't mean to scare you. It's okay that you don't feel the same. I won't pressure you into anything, I swear." I stare up at the ceiling, avoiding her sharp gaze.

"Pressure me? Corvus, I want you," she snaps, trying to draw my attention back to her. I refuse, unable to stand the look in her eyes.

It's not a question of whether she wants me. Her coming on my dick twice was proof enough for that. But sex, albeit really good sex, doesn't always mean that feelings are involved. And we've never talked about it.

I didn't want to pressure her, but how can she not feel so? By forcing my feelings onto her, I'm making her confess how she feels, whether she's ready to or not. It's selfish of me to assume she's even in the right headspace for anything like that.

"Listen, I really am sorry. I didn't mean to just push my feelings onto you. I don't want you to feel like you have to feel the same way if you don't, we can be friends if that's what you want. This doesn't have to change anything." I finally look into her eyes, hoping to make her believe I'm telling the truth, hoping I didn't just ruin everything.

"Nothing is changing," she smiles down at me.

Okay. That's good. I also don't know what the fuck that means, but it's not like I'm going to ask and potentially ruin the moment again. I'm going to shut the fuck up and be happy with what she's given me.

I start to pull her back into my arms so she can go to sleep, but she tenses against the attempt. I freeze, looking into her eyes.

"Corvus, I want you," she repeats. For a second, I thought she meant round two, so I opened my mouth to remind her it was too early. "Not just for sex," she continues, practically reading my mind. She smiles, though I'm unsure if it's comforting or scary.

My mouth snaps shut. "What does that mean?" I question softly, too afraid to assume for myself and needing to hear it directly from her.

"It means I have feelings for you too. I—I'm not sure what kind of feelings. I haven't had the best life or the best examples of love, so I'm struggling to figure out what I'm feeling, myself. It's why I didn't say anything to you about it, I thought we had more time. But, then, you died, and I realized that if you hadn't come back, you would've died never knowing how I feel. I don't want to be just a friend. I want more; I want all of you. I want your love and I want to give you mine. All I ask is that you be patient with me. This feeling—this is all new to me and I'm probably going to mess up; but I'm willing to try and figure this all out if it's with you."

If I thought the burning in my chest was bad before, it was nothing compared to how it feels right now.

I'm at a loss for words. My throat constricts so tightly with emotion that I wouldn't be able to speak even if I knew what I wanted to say.

I drag her lips to mine, kissing her deeply, driving my tongue into her mouth. She moans into my mouth, shifting closer. We're both naked already, so it takes little effort to roll over on top of her. My cock is hard already, pressing firmly into the mattress. She wraps her legs around me, dragging my hips closer.

"Fuck, I need you," I groan into her mouth, reaching down to gently play with her clit. The last thing I want to do is hurt her but my brain is scrambled. I feel her hand slide overtop of mine before she pushes my fingers down until they're sliding through the all-new wetness that's gathering between her legs. Despite wrecking her once already, her body still begs for more.

"Please," she whimpers against my lips. "I swear I am fine. I need you, too."

Sweeter words have never been said. With a groan, I grip the tip of my dick and slide inside her to the hilt. She's even tighter than before, her soft body swollen from earlier.

I'm already right on the edge. I grab her hand and push her wet fingers against her clit, circling them around a few times before pulling my hand away to grab her hip.

"I'm close," I say as I start to gently thrust into her, holding her hip still so I don't go too hard.

I kiss her slowly, drawing another moan from her mouth. I can still feel her hand rubbing circles on her clit, her knuckles brushing across my lower abdomen.

We move together in unison, a mix of tangled limbs and joined breaths. I've never felt closer to someone in my life. I've been around a long time, but not once have I felt this kind of connection in the past. I feel like she's turned me into someone else. Every dark part of my soul now feels the warmth of the sun.

"Corvus," she moans my name. Her eyes roll back as she finally gives into the feeling—this time, soft and leisurely.

Her moan is a sweet purr against my lips and it's the best sound I've heard in my life. I can't hold back any longer, so I tip over the edge again. My hips jerk and my cock pulses out cum with each small thrust. It feels like my entire being has been ripped out of me. I've never experienced pleasure so consuming.

I roll to the side, pulling her with me to avoid breaking our connection. My muscles instantly start to relax as all the stress and tension leave my body, all the worry and doubt going with it. Valencia snuggles into my body, wrapping an arm around my waist.

I can feel cum slipping between us again, but I don't have the energy for another shower and neither does she. Plus, I hate to admit it, but the thought of her being covered in my cum all night pleases me. It's primal and messy, but it soothes a chaotic part of me who wants to claim her in such a dominant way.

It's not long before she falls asleep, curled into my side, my heart beating under her ear.

There's so much to do, yet I can't bring myself to care about any of it right now. She's in my arms, sleeping peacefully, warm, safe, and naked—things I've wanted from the beginning but didn't think I'd ever have. I don't know how we move forward from here; all I care about is that we do it together.

The Devil may have gained a soul but I got so much more.

I slowly drift off to the sound of her light breathing, basking in the warmth and comfort her body provides.

"King Crow," a voice whispers in the quiet cabin. Soft as a breeze but endlessly full of shadow, it slithers through my mind, alerting all of my warning systems.

I jerk out of my sleepy daze and open my eyes—or at least try to, but it's so dark that I can't tell if my eyes are actually open. I try to turn my head but I'm frozen in place, unable to move.

My heart starts pounding double time and I swear a light flickers across the ceiling occasionally, but it's not enough to confirm I'm still in the cabin—that could just be spots in my vision. My chest starts to heave.

Valencia still sleeps soundly in my arms, undisturbed by the voice or my panic. I try squeezing her closer, but I can't move. It's like a weight sits upon my chest—no, it's more than that. It's like I've been glued to the bed and am now unable to move any part of my body. It reminds me of how I felt when I woke on the couch in the Devil's library. There was a lot more pain, then, however. Now, it's painless. I can feel the soft weight of Valencia's body against mine, but that's it.

If my hands could move, they would be shaking. My heart thunders so hard I fear my ribs might break. I stare hard above me, trying to see something through the swirling darkness, anything, but there's nothing. It's like the cabin is full of onyx smoke.

My throat constricts, and I struggle to breathe through the panic. This can't be a dream; I was barely asleep. It has to be the cabin. I'm still in bed and she's still tucked into my arms. I chant it repeatedly but it doesn't help.

The onyx smoke starts rolling around, swirling rapidly and roiling angrily before disappearing in a poof, leaving nothing but flat blackness again.

"King Crow, you look panicked," the voice now says aloud. It's neither soft nor loud, but low and deep, yet not gravelly. I don't recognize the voice, but it's definitely male and almost certainly belongs to a demon.

Only a demon would call me King Crow; but which demon? That's the question.

I try to respond, but all that comes out is a garbled mumble of sounds. No words.

"You don't need to speak. Just listen." His voice lacks inflection and emotion—it's dark and blank, much like the room.

From the corner of my eye, I'm able to make out the slightest hint of movement but I can't move to look closer. Agonizing seconds pass before the speaker finally comes into view, standing over me at the edge of the bed. Valencia lies, tucked in my arms, between us. The panic renews; I still don't have control of my body. I can't protect her against him like this.

I try to growl out his name, demanding he explain why he's here but my voice still won't work. He stares down at me, watching as I struggle through the paralysis he's put me in.

Lord Nightmare, the second Lord of Hell. He's decked out in an all-black suit ensemble, looking far too sharp with a serious look on his clean-cut face. There's no hair to hide the angular lines of his face. His cheekbones stick out, making his cheeks look almost hollow. His black hair is well-groomed and swoops perfectly into place. There's not a single part of him out of place. The only thing out of place is the slight haziness to him.

I realize, now, that he's not actually here at all but using his mind control to appear in my thoughts as though he were. This only serves to piss me off more as it means he can do whatever he wants to us, but we wouldn't be able to hurt him in return.

He looks between me and the woman snuggled into my chest, his ice-blue eyes so penetrating that they look white against all the black. I try to growl and warn him to look away from her, but all that comes out is more of the same garbled mess.

Valencia must hear it this time because she moans softly in her sleep, pressing closer to me. She mumbles something but it's not anything I can understand.

"Hmm," Nightmare looks at her closely, his face is like a blank piece of ice.

Since I can't talk, I can't exactly ask why he's here and why he's fucking trapped me in paralysis. It's rude and we both know I'll be paying him back for it later. He doesn't seem to care, though, because he doesn't release me despite knowing how I struggle against it.

Finally, he takes his eyes off her and looks back at me. It only brings me a small amount of comfort. I'd rather his dead, emotionless eyes focus on me, but it doesn't mean she's out of danger yet.

"She's not susceptible to my power. That's strange. Strange is not good," he says to me, his hands hanging loosely at his sides.

So, he's tried to put her under, too, but failed. As much as I appreciate her not being able to be controlled by him, he's not wrong; it is strange that she is not under his mind spell. Strange is not good when it comes to greedy, power-hungry demons who will do anything to get ahead. If this is an ability of hers, many will hunt her down to try and steal it.

I want to pull her closer to me and shield her from everything bad in the universe. The true demon scratches at my skin, begging for release to protect the woman in our arms. He wants blood, but he's trapped, too. We're shackled by invisible chains.

This is why Nightmare paralyzed me. He knows I would've killed first and asked questions second. He put me in his mind spell for *his* safety, not hers. He may be older than me and more powerful when it comes to mind control, but he would not be able to beat me if I thought he was a danger to her.

Why are you really here, Nightmare? I project into his mind.

He must hear me, or at least have an idea of what's running through my mind.

His calm voice doesn't give anything away as he warns, "Keep her close, King Crow. He's coming for her."

THE END

OR IS IT?

Afterword

Holy Moly.. that wasn't so bad right? Everything's good, we're all happy with how things ended? Well... mostly ended.

This is just the beginning, Corvus and Valencia have a lot more story left. They're still learning about themselves *cough* (*looking at you Valencia*) but have no fear, I have some big moments planned for their future, full of self discovery and plenty of sparks. Also expect a lot more of the best friend everyone loves, Parker Rand. He was an unexpected knockout character and I know without him, there'd be a little less sun in all of our lives.

Writing is a deeply personal journey, and sharing these characters, who feel like family to me, has been both exhilarating and nerve-wracking. I hope you have come to love them as much as I do. These characters have become a part of my soul, and to bring them to you is a dream come true. Thank you for joining me on this journey and for embracing these characters with open arms and open hearts.

If you want to keep up with me, you can join my newsletter, The Emerald Readers Society, for all things Kissing Fire, sneak peeks, giveaways, and more. You can also find me on Instagram and Tiktok.

As a thanks, keep reading for a sneak peek at the next installment

<3 Samantha

Chapter I
Parker

I think I'm about to be arrested.

The cop berates me, crowding in my personal space. I'm pretty sure he just spit part of his lunch on me. Ruben sandwich, maybe. His breath smells atrocious, but I'm forced to stand here and take it. I try to glimpse his badge, but his arms are flailing so much that I'm not able to catch the name on his chest.

His really large, *rounded* chest. I mean, the man is as rotund as a ball. I bet if I pushed hard enough, he'd just roll away. Then, I wouldn't have to deal with the lunch currently being sprayed into my face or his stupid questions.

"Are you even fucking listening to me?" he snarls.

I'm not. I can't recall a single thing he's said in the last 15 minutes while he's stood, yelling a thousand questions at me that I can't answer.

No, I don't know how four people went missing.

Yes, I really was passed out the entire time.

No, I don't know where the fuck my best friend is.

Well—that last one is a lie, but he doesn't need to know that. It's not like I've known for very long, either. Val snuck into my room like a shadow in the night, scaring the absolute shit out of me. The minor heart attack I'd received after seeing her appear, as if from nowhere, didn't dampen the joy I'd felt at that moment. She'd hid in the darkness of my room like she hadn't been missing for almost a week.

I'm still exhausted from all the hours I've worked searching the entire Beaverhead National Forest for four bodies I know will never be found. The days before

Val showed up had been full of struggle and exhaustion, but adrenaline had fueled me through the long hours. Pure terror was the only thing keeping me going through the long days and nights, searching for the last person I call family. I wouldn't lose her, too.

Now, pretending that I don't know what's going on is its own kind of torture. I have to lie to the people closest to me—pretend I didn't smuggle my best friend to the Heath Cabin last night.

I mean, there's still so much I don't know. I have no idea about the two members of the Polaris Fire Team who somehow managed to disappear. Nor do I have any idea what happened to Tucker.

My chest squeezes at the thought of the young firefighter—his tall, lanky awkwardness, willingness to learn, bright green eyes and messy brown hair that flash in my mind like a bright memory. He radiated happiness. People always considered me the happy-go-lucky one, but that's a learned skill. It's easy to bring joy into a room with a good joke. Tucker was truly happy, no front or jokes were needed.

It fucking *burns*, losing him. He had so much life left to live.

I grit my teeth against the thought, forcing my mind to focus on Officer Whatever. As I told Valencia last night, there's no reason to dwell on the unknown.

"I swear to God, if you don't fucking answer me," Officer Whatever spits, and a drop lands on my clenched cheek.

I force myself to relax, my jaw muscles slowly loosening enough so I can answer. "I'm sorry. Would you like me to listen or answer?"

"You little shit, I'll—"

"Do we have a problem here?" A voice barks from my left.

Saved by Chief Miller.

I look at the Chief, a pleading look in my eyes. He doesn't react in any way, simply looks between me and the officer before focusing on Officer Whatever. "Is there a reason you're interrogating one of my team members on our station lawn?" Chief Miller asks.

"This Mother—" the officer blurts, barely stopping himself before the curse leaves his lips. "He knows something." He points that big meaty finger my way again. "It's in your best interest that he confesses what he knows before the entire police force gets brought into *your* mess."

"Officer... Paral, this is a very emotional situation, and handling it with compassion and professionalism is the only way we can figure out how four firefighters are still missing. We have conducted searches nonstop over the last week. My team is distraught, exhausted, and beyond confused. I can assure you that no one here knows what's going on. Targeting Lieutenant Rand, just as he's coming in from an 18-hour search, is a little cruel considering finding missing persons is your problem, correct?"

I have to clamp my teeth together to keep from laughing. In a handful of seconds, the Chief delivered the politest burn I've heard in a long time.

Officer Paral's face has turned a shiny shade of red and I swear, a vein on his forehead dances with each beat of his overinflated heart. Chief Miller has him in a vise, and we all know it. The entire station has been running ragged, myself included, for the last week. Conducting searches over hundreds of miles in the park. If we were guilty, why would we all be working so hard?

That fun little team building exercise we went on seemed like a walk in the park compared to what we've been going through. If only they had left clues behind. It's getting harder to not spill that Valencia made it back. What could I even say, though? *Hey, Valencia made it! She came and saw me last night. Oh, where has she been? Well, she said she was stuck in Hell for a bit, but she swears she doesn't know what happened to the other guys.*

Yeah, that's not going to happen. The Polaris City Fire Department has been radio-silent over the last couple of days. The day after the fire, they sent a team to retrieve the ashes of their two fallen firefighters. We assisted in the retrieval—but they didn't mention their two missing team members . I thought it odd then, but now I know nothing in this situation is as it seems.

I can't wrap my brain around the fact that Heaven and Hell are not only real—they're battling in a celestial war. They've brought the fight to Earth, and my best friend has become involved in a very dangerous way. According to Val, it had been a literal angel who'd knocked my ass out before holding Tucker hostage. My chest clenches at the thought of what Tucker went through.

"Look at him! He's been staring at the wall for the last twenty minutes I've been talking to him. He knows something, and you are all hiding it. I'm coming back with a fucking warrant and you better pray your shit is squeaky clean, Chief Miller," Officer Paral spits out. He stomps off back to his cruiser, slamming the door and peeling out with a squeal of his tires.

"If you hadn't just come in from a shift, I would seriously suspend you. Parker, what the hell? We are all trying to figure out what's going on. The last thing we need is to piss off the police department." Chief Miller tries to chastise me, but it's clear his heart isn't in it. I imagine he's only saying this because he feels obligated to say something after that shit show. Either way, I'm over it.

"None of you understand what this does to me. Valencia is the only family I have left. I have been searching nonstop, day after day, spending hours out in the field, hoping that I'll find her because I *refuse* to lose another family member. So, I'm sorry that Officer Dipshit is angry, but *so am I*." All of the fear and anger I've been holding in over the last week bleeds into the statement, and I ignore the ache in my chest that follows. My shoulders sag. "I'm really fucking tired."

Chief Miller just nods his head, patting me on the shoulder. "Get some rest, Parker; we'll find them... I just hope whatever we find doesn't tear this team apart."

My steps echo off the concrete floor as I trek into the station. Normally, a hundred different things create an ambient 'lived-in' sound that fills the area. Now, it's silent. Everyone has passed out, trying to catch a few hours of rest before we head back out for another round of searching. I would've been in here an hour ago, but it was my turn to check the equipment back in—and then Officer Paral caught me on the lawn. I would've loved to avoid him, but we've been instructed that doing so would reflect poorly on us . We're not guilty, but it's also important that we don't look guilty—Bill and I especially, given that we were the only two on the mountain when the rescue team returned to collect us.

We had both barely started to wake, but we were out enough that we'd had to be carried into the helicopter. After some testing, they determined we had passed out due to a lack of oxygen from having inhaled some of the smoke from the forest fire. Neither of us had our masks on, but there wasn't much smoke in that area by then. Either way, it gave us an alibi. A reason to be knocked on our asses with no answers as to what had happened to the rest of our team.

Still, Officer Paral has an issue with our story for some reason. He's been coming round since day one but hasn't caught Bill or me alone—until today.

I get to my room and undress, not bothering with a shower. The sheets are beyond disgusting anyway, and what's one more day of sleeping on ash and soot? I roll around in an attempt to get comfortable, but the blankets scratch against my skin and my stomach continues to roll uneasily even though I'm lying down. It's been doing this since the first night back. They wouldn't let us begin searching until we were cleared by the paramedics—which had taken almost twelve hours—but getting back onto the field and searching had given me purpose. It gave my mind something to focus on other than reality.

Trying to sleep offered no peace from my damaged thoughts. The panic I'd felt as I woke in the helicopter, drugged, woozy, and disoriented, still haunts me. There was nothing but terror left when I realized Valencia wasn't in the helicopter with me—it was simply as though she and Tucker had vanished, like ash in the wind—and there was nothing I could do but search every inch of Beaverhead National Forest until I found them.

When she showed up in my room, roughed up but alive, joy had washed away the fear. As she told her story, my heart broke, but nothing could over-shadow the fact that she was back. After I dropped her off at the Heath cabin with Corvus—who apparently is a literal demon, but I have purposefully not given that much thought—I went directly to the park to help with search and rescue efforts. There were still missing people out there, if only technically.

A few small fires had sparked up over the week, but the other teams had been able to manage them. Thankfully, no one asked our team to do anything other than search for our colleagues. Chief Miller had even remained by our side the entire time, only taking a small break to clear us with the police department on that first day.

I have no idea what we're going to do about Officer Paral. He knows something, or at least thinks he does, and I have no idea how. I haven't told a single person about seeing Val or taking her to Heath Cabin. Sure, I took her there in my truck and made a few stops along the way, but she'd remained hidden the entire time.

Officer Paral just has a gut feeling; unfortunately for me, he's right. I just have to get Val out of Montana before he finally catches on.

***

My eyes flutter open as my racing heart beings to slow. Another nightmare. At this point, my sleep schedule is so off that I don't know when I last slept through the night. The bright light from my phone blinds me briefly and I squint to see the time. Nearly 9 PM. I only got a few hours of sleep.

Clangs and bangs echo down the hall through my open door, and the smell of coffee wafts into my room—the aroma helping wake my tired bones. I can't help but groan as I get up. My muscles scream in refusal, but I push on.

I throw on a pair of jeans, not bothering to check they're clean. I forgo a shirt and head to the kitchen, where Bill ambles around, pulling random things out of the cabinets as he gets stuff ready. It smells like cooked food, but I can't see any.

"Bill, you okay?" I ask, leaning against the counter. He simply huffs in response and continues working without a word. I get it. He's in the same position as I am, unsure of how we had been spared while two of our other teammates had disappeared. They cleared both of us eventually, but Bill had taken the events pretty hard. He's older—has no kids—and looks down on us younger members as family. He and Tucker have always been close. I wish I could tell him what I know, but I can't. I can't put everyone in danger like that, so the secrets sit on the tip of my tongue like acid.

A beep comes from the oven, breaking the silence. Bill turns sharply and yanks a pan out, setting it on the island counter. A steaming breakfast quiche fills the room with the delicious smell of sausage, eggs, and peppers. Silently, I grab a couple of plates and silverware, serving us each a portion, and sit on one of the bar stools.

We eat in silence, and though it burns me, I offer him the only thing I can: company.

Footsteps fill the room as more of the team walk in. The smell of fresh food and coffee must've woken them all. Jake loads two plates, and Jack fills two glasses with chocolate milk before they sit down. They're like clockwork, an extension of each other, and need no words to communicate their needs. I envy their closeness—how they always have someone by their side, no matter what.

Greg grabs a plate, sitting beside me. He told us during our first break from searching that he's put his notice in and won't be coming back next fire season. Sadly, I don't think any of us will be.

Bill can retire at any time, and I imagine he probably will after all of this. The twins have no connections here; they could go anywhere in the world, and they'd still have each other.

Chief Miller's family is here, so he's stuck, but a hundred of other fire teams would love to take him. He would have no issue finding a new team.

That just leaves me. The quiche turns to ash in my mouth as I realize that if I want to stay with Val, the only family I have left, it might just mean leaving Earth entirely. So many questions swirl in my brain, but I don't give them a second thought. I don't care what dangers I may face or what lies ahead in the parts of the universe that I know nothing about.

I won't hide from the potential dangers, not this time.

Chief Miller clears his throat, drawing everyone's attention. "So, I know everyone is exhausted. We'll head to the main camp and then drive along Elkhorn Creek to the old, abandoned lumber yard. It's a while from where they went missing but it would be a good place to get away from the elements. We can't go far; the police department will be here in the morning to question us, so we have to be back by sunrise."

"Why are they questioning us?" Jack asks, looking around the group before refocusing on Chief Miller.

"They just want to get everyone's stories and make sure every detail has been covered." I can tell by the look on the Chief's face that he's not happy about it.

"We've already been questioned twice—Bill and Parker three times! What do they want from us?" Jack seethes, his fist clenched around his fork. Jake looks equally angry but seems fine to let Jack ask the questions.

I guess no one knows that Officer Paral was here again earlier this evening. I've been asked to explain what happened four times now, and my story has not changed.

"Another officer was here this afternoon and cornered Parker when we got back. I called their Chief, and we worked it out. They'll come and ask their questions one more time in the morning, and then leave us alone. It's just a precaution. Everyone here has been cleared, and Parker and Bill will be fine. We just need to jump through their hoops one more time, and then we can move on with our lives."

No one comments on the fact that *moving on with our lives* might just mean having to move on from losing two team members in one night.

I don't have the heart to tell them it might be three. I refuse to be left behind, so if Val goes to Hell, I'm going with her. Considering I've now gotten my ass kicked by an angel twice, Heaven doesn't seem that much fun anyway.

Acknowledgments

Wow, what a journey this has been! As I sit here, reflecting on the path that led to the completion of this novel, I am overwhelmed with gratitude for the incredible support and encouragement I've received along the way.

First and foremost, I want to thank my family. To my Granny, who has always believed in me, even when I doubted myself, your unwavering support has been my anchor. You believed in me on that very first poem. I remember standing together in the kitchen to write it, as well as months later opening it in that exact same spot. You've always had my back no matter what and I cannot thank you enough.

To my husband, thank you for being my sounding board and for your endless patience as I rambled about plot twists and character arcs. For letting me highjack every trip, project, and basically any free moment to ramble on about these characters. They've lived with us for almost three years now, and I fear they're not going anywhere anytime soon. Tyrel and Jay, thank you for believing in me and my story. Your guidance and advocacy have been instrumental in bringing this novel to life. Without you, the opportunity to print my own novel wouldn't be possible. I have learned so much from you in this process and I am so grateful to have you both in my corner.

To my friends, who cheered me on from the sidelines and celebrated every milestone with me, your encouragement kept me going on the toughest days. Thank you for listening to my fears, sharing in my excitement, and always being there with a comforting word or a well-timed distraction.

Mandy, you were there for me from DAY ONE! I sent the book out to over 15 people, and each new chapter, a few friends would drop off here and there, but you stuck with me through it all and I cannot thank you enough for that support.

Lenora and Lesley, your insights, feedback, and honest critiques were invaluable. You both helped shape this story into what it is today, and I am eternally grateful for your time, effort, and belief in this project. Also a huge shoutout to Lenora who gave me the drive to start writing again after my long break, I can't thank you enough for that imperative motivation.

To my editor, thank you for your keen eye, your gentle guidance, and your unwavering support. You helped me see the potential in my work and pushed me to make it the best it could be. I am incredibly grateful for your expertise and dedication.

Katrina Mohr, thank you for your service as a wildland firefighter as well as being an amazing human and letting me ask you a ton of questions right in the middle of the fire season.

Finally, to my readers, thank you for taking a chance on a debut author. Your enthusiasm and support mean the world to me. I hope this story has brought you as much joy and excitement as it brought me while writing it!

This novel would not exist without the love, support, and encouragement of so many incredible people. From the bottom of my heart, thank you.

MEET SAMANTHA

Hello and welcome! Meet Samantha, a devoted enthusiast of all things Romantic Literature.

Samantha Treat is a debut author who writes stories that are witty, romantic, and steamy. A life long dreamer of writing, she is conquering her goals by sharing the many stories in her head with the world.

Born in central Missouri, she grew up in various places, even changing schools 13 times. As a hopeless romantic, Leo, and all around introverted-extrovert, she enjoys writing characters we can all relate to. She can found reading in her library, traveling with her husband, playing with her dogs, or partaking in some crazy adventure.

Samantha still resides in Missouri, though she's settled in the northwest corner of the state with her two doggos and husband. Finding her very own Happy Ever After, made it all the more easy to write.

HEY THERE, AWESOME READER!

If you enjoyed diving into this wild ride of a book, I'd love to hear your thoughts! Think of it as leaving a tip, but instead of cash, it's all about those sweet, sweet words. Your reviews keep the magic alive.

If you fancy leaving a review, may your coffee always be the perfect temperature!